MW01128939

Ramjet Warriors
of the
High Command

SOUND OFF!

What did you love?
What did you hate?

Author Email: whgwrought@gmail.com

Earth's Atmosphere

-------------------------------------- Sea Level --------------------------------------

Troposphere   Clouds

---------------------------10 km-------------6 miles-------------31,680 feet-------

Stratosphere   Airliners

---------------------------50 km------------30 miles-----------158,400 feet-------

Mesosphere   Meteors

---------------------------80 km------------50 miles-----------264,000 feet-------

Thermosphere	100 km	62 miles	Karman Boundary[1]
	120 km	75 miles	Re-entry Effects[2]
	160 km	100 miles	Low Earth Orbit[3]
	260 km	160 miles	Ionosphere F Layer

------------------------- 700 km----------434 miles------------------------------

Exosphere   2,000 km   1,243 miles   Medium Earth Orbit

-------------------------9,920 km--------6,200 miles------------------------------

Interplanetary   35,786 km   22,236 miles   Geosynchronous Orbit[4]
Medium   High Earth Orbit
                   384,400 km   238,900 miles   Moon

--------------------14.8 billion km -----9.3 billion miles --------- Heliopause[5]-------

Interstellar
Medium

1) Here outer space is said to begin, and pilots are called astronauts.
2) Atmospheric effects on re-entry are significant below this altitude.
3) Rapid orbital decay from atmospheric drag occurs below this altitude.
4) GSO has a period of 1 day. Satellites hover over a point on Earth's surface.
5) Here the interstellar wind becomes stronger than the solar wind.

Chapter 1   - High Wire

"Boy, that was a real fireball."

John Glenn

Jimmy hung above the impossible sky-filling bulk of Earth, its brilliant blue-white glowing through the thick sapphire of the cockpit canopy, his velocity the invisible wire suspending him above the thin planetary sea of air. To his rear the sun was occulting behind the limb of the planet. A kilometer ahead the solar panels of the station glinted gold in its last rays.

Hundreds of miles ahead, Katia was a swath of white fire lighting the evening sky over the whole of India. In the huge streak of incandescent plasma, no two atoms remained bonded, their electrons stripped away, ionized to their innermost shells. Hers had been the death of an orbital warrior, hyperenergetic nearly instant disassembly down to the subatomic level in the blowtorch of a too-steep reentry.

Still farther ahead, a thousand miles farther than he could see, past the dark rim of the planet, huge boosters burned, laboring to ascend from Iranian launch pads to bring kinetic kill vehicles to the station. Katia was gone and it was on him to drop into atmosphere and light off the ramjet, to speed ahead on a cone of fire to kill the antisatellite missiles in boost phase, unless he too broke up into infinitesimal bits of fire, another cloud of incandescent ions smeared across the sky.

Jimmy swallowed. He said, "Rock 5 ignited fuselage."

Polya's truncated grammar grated in his earpiece, the English slurred into deep Russian tones.

"You are hot Rock, Jimmy."

Polya had the worst of it, floating in an orbiting aluminum can, a few sheets of Kevlar his only armor against three kill vehicles closing at twice orbital velocity. The International Space Station had no capacity for quick maneuver.

Dirtside, the ground controller, cut in. It was Tom Broadhead.

3

"Drop the Rock. Boost phase lasts three minutes. They launched a minute ago."

The station could not evade, but it could shoot back, and Jimmy was the brain guiding its bullet. It was on him, to hit the switch that would drop him into a high-hypersonic reentry. A simple task, but for the cold stinging fluid which seemed to fill his belly. The icy burn seeped up his chest and into his arms. It was passing odd, how here in microgee with no weight at all to his body, he didn't know if he could lift his hand.

Chapter 2   - Slim to None

> "Survivability of the space platform is crucially dependent on a capability to destroy the ASAT booster before it can deploy its miniature kill vehicles."
>
> IDA, Institute for Defense Analysis

Though floating in zero gee, Polya slumped at his workstation on the wall of the habitat module. He wore dark blue shorts and a white tee shirt stretched over a thickening middle. Though his dark curls showed but a hint of gray, he seemed sunk into himself and prematurely aged, especially under the eyes.

He waited for Jimmy's radio call, the acknowledgement that a second Smart Rock interceptor was dropping toward atmosphere. Unaware, he placed a hand on the locket hung inside his thin shirt, a gift from his parents when he left for the army. It held a tiny image of St. Michael.

Three ASATs this time, more antisatellite missiles than the Iranians had launch pads. Something new was up. He shifted his feet in the loops that held him steady at his workstation, looking for a moment at his light brown woolen slipper socks with their soft leather soles, one of his favorite things about living on the station.

He heaved a sigh and toggled the switches to open the private link to Dirtside. He was a middle-sized man, and his voice was deeper than it had a right to be.

"We have lost Katia," he said.

"Yes. The staring infrared array in geosynch orbit saw it. Most of South Asia saw it," said Tom. They spoke English, the only other language they had in common being the dialect of Pushtu spoken in northern Afghanistan.

Polya rumbled back at him, "She was best of us. She is gone. Vlad's Rock needs valve. I must remain to run mission. You must send girl, if Navy pilot cannot drop."

Tom winced. Polya was not sensitive to the American hypervigilance on language. Of the women's platoon, two switches remained, both former Marine Corps attack pilots. They had adapted well to the Smart Rock spacefighter and had several combat drops to their credit. He didn't want to lose another experienced switch. Jimmy had to come through.

Tom leaned an elbow on his desk, rested his balding head in his hand. He had spoken to Jimmy, had looked into Jimmy's face. He said, "Jimmy will drop. He may not take out all three boosters. He may not live. But he will drop."

Chapter 3   - The Absolute

*"Islam says: Kill all the unbelievers just as they would kill you all....
Hundreds of Hadiths urge Muslims to value war and to fight. Does all
this mean that Islam is a religion that prevents men from waging war? I
spit upon those foolish souls who make such a claim!"*
                                                        Ruhollah Khomeini

Half a world away from Tom, but a scant two hundred miles below Polya, a white-bearded Persian in clerical black studied a flatscreen. As he bent his head to scowl at the video display, the black ball of his turban canted forward and his full white beard spread across his chest.

Onscreen, swords of fire in the night sky marked ascending boosters, rockets as large as ICBMs. The first had cleared the densest part of the atmosphere and had pitched over from the vertical. Two more climbed after it.

The Supreme Leader of the Islamic Republic of Iran, onetime student of Khomeini, was more politician than religious scholar, despite his cleric's turban. He had won the job when Khomeini's expected successor objected to mass killings of political prisoners. He wielded the absolute religious authority and secular power of a medieval warrior Pope.

He was an old man. He remembered the Revolution. And he remembered the years before it, the uncovered women moving about, talking and working with men, painting their faces. As was written in the Book, they needed his protection. It could not be otherwise.

There were many pictures of this man, in nearly all of which he scowled, a furrow between his lowered brows, above a Groucho nose and thick glasses and tiny dark eyes glittering behind. In a few pictures he smiled, but always the crease appeared between his brows.

Only in the earliest images, taken when his beard shone black and before a bomb splintered his right arm, did he appear happy. The bomb had nearly killed him. The bomb had explained things, had shown him what was necessary.

Chapter 4   - The Brink

"Get a bicycle. You will certainly not regret it, if you live."
Mark Twain

The orbital deployment became fated for Jimmy just eighteen months before, as he lay sprawled awkwardly with his face pressed into a spicy layer of crushed dry oak leaves. He moaned as feeling returned and a dull ache awakened throughout his chest and then stabbed sharp into his right shoulder. He tried to roll onto his back, but he was lying head down on a steep rocky slope with the mountain bike on top of him. Another over-the-bars crash. He hadn't unclipped from the pedals in time. Damnit.

"You doin' alright?" a voice floated down from upslope.

Jimmy grunted out, "Just a second."

He struggled to move the bike off him and crabbed around in dirt and leaf litter to sit up with his legs down the slope. The shoulder was calming down to a dull ache, so was not separated in the impact. He sat for a few more seconds, then pushed himself unsteadily to his feet, leaning on a knee-high blade of cold stone.

He took off the helmet and looked it over. Smeared with dirt. Not cracked. Upslope, a guy in a yellow jersey straddled a Stumpjumper. The guy liked retro or just hadn't bought a new bike for quite some time. Kind of thick-bodied for a mountain biker, with faded sandy hair. His forehead ended at the crown of his head.

Jimmy lifted his bike by the top tube, resting it across his shoulder as he climbed upslope, grabbing with his free hand at the fangs of dark gray stone which jutted up everywhere and which made for such a tricky descent.

The guy spoke again. "You gonna try that again?" He stood beside the red warning flags at the top of the rocky drop-off.

"Haven't failed 'til you stop trying." Jimmy said. He wasn't feeling chatty.

The guy nodded, looking at Jimmy's bloody shins and the abrasions on his arms, taking in the whipcord physique, finally lingering curiously on Jimmy's face as he spoke. "I'm not much for downhill obstacles, myself. The difficulty I don't mind. The risk is kind of gratuitous, though."

"Guess you're more of a trail rider than a mountain biker, huh? This is probably not the hill you want to be on." Jimmy said.

"I'm actually out here looking for you." The guy unzipped a pocket on his bright yellow jersey. He withdrew a card and offered it to Jimmy. "I'm needing pilots with military experience. If you make it to the foot of the mountain, I'll buy coffee at that shop next to the trailhead."

Jimmy shot a fast look at him, wondering who knew where he was and when. He reached out for the card without hurry, not wanting the guy to see how the thought of flying again was releasing the band from across his chest.

The card listed Dr. Tom Broadhead, Ph.D., as staffing officer for a company called Concepts in Innovative Aviation, with the three initial letters in red, white, and blue. Spooky. This wasn't going to be a vacation charter gig.

Within himself, Jimmy leapt at it, could not keep himself from blinking away sudden moisture in his eyes. He nodded, but said only, "OK, let's talk."

The guy nodded back at him. When Jimmy said nothing more, the probable spook walked his bike downslope, passing to the right of the nearly vertical rock garden that had crashed Jimmy three times. He saddled up below the obstacle and drifted on through the dense shade of the oak canopy, downtrail.

Chapter 5 - Origins

"Love. It is as strong as death, and as hard as Hell."

Meister Eckhart

In a previous life, Tom Broadhead studied applied mathematics at little Brown University in Providence. That life ended one summer evening after he wandered into the RISD[1] Museum.

He had chosen an art museum because the student hangouts on Thayer Street were either upscale bars or had too much of a headshop vibe. He had only his scholarship stipend and he didn't like the easy certainties of the folkies who sang in the bistros. And the Astronomy Club had nothing on.

His steps echoed from a gleaming herringbone pattern of amber-colored hardwood. In a gallery of classical statuary and friezes, a young woman moved lissome as a willow among figures frozen for millennia in pure white dead stone. Her headcloth told him at once that she was a Muslim. She turned on him large eyes of rich dark brown, soft and shining, liquid eyes.

"Are you here for the statues?" Her voice too was liquid, and musical.

He had not stopped staring. "I'm seeking beauty of any sort," he said.

She laughed, yet more beauty in the delicate chimes of silver ringing in her breath. They turned and walked on to other galleries, nothing being said until his nerves played up and he ranted for several minutes about a painting, a gray abstract thing evoking solitude and stillness, the mood of a cloudy winter day seen above water, bare uninterpreted awareness, and was struck dumb when she laughed again. He could ever after hear that laugh, and was still grateful that she had cut short his blather.

---

[1] Rhode Island School of Design, said "ris'-duh".

He sought her company. She studied mathematics, the pure, hard stuff, at the graduate level. Tom had barely the wit to see the power of her work. She crafted huge logical sequences, all to infer a result contradictory to an assumption made pages before and so proving its negation. She tried to explain Gödel's Incompleteness Theorem[2] to him, how it had ripped the axioms out of Whitehead's elaborate *Principia* like a submerged fang of rock breaking the keel of a meticulously crafted caravel.

Other times she played her piano for him. She somehow found the hours to master the slowest crescendo in the Emperor Concerto and the subtlest arrhythmic in the *Gnossiennes*. Tom was no musician, but he perceived musical structure, and, rarely for him, felt the works as she played them and knew what she was feeling, and was sure that Beethoven or Satie felt just so when the melody coalesced under his hand.

He learned, after more months, of her origins. That she had been found wandering in Afghanistan, mutilated and abandoned. Afghans had never practiced the female mutilation endemic to some of the African countries. It was abhorrent to them and to Islam, but demanded by the more extreme of the mullahs newly arrived from other lands and other wars.

When she spoke of what they had done it was as if a shock front flashed out from his very center over the whole world, searing everything and leaving a clear thin layer of scar tissue over it all. He thought he would never directly touch or see anything or anyone again, that what he now knew forever separated him from everything and especially from everyone.

It took more time to realize that what was taken from her was also taken from him. She would not marry. He begged and she refused, again and again. He offered to convert. She threatened to refuse to see him.

She wore the hijab. Her forehead bore the mark of one who bent five times a day to pray. She forbade him to speak of revenge. And he spoke no more of it, while his brain swam in a broth of rage. It cooled with time, but never left him. Daydreams bubbled up at odd times, of a man viewed through a rifle's optic, of exit wounds. For a time he stopped noticing the constant calculations that underlay his thoughts.

---

[2] Google this anytime you think you have a firm grip on things.

And then, on a day when she had waved him gently away, when he had returned to his own small room, its brown laminate desk and bed and single window, a thunderclap in his mind struck all doubt from him and he knew what his life and work would be.

It was the CIA which armed and trained the likes of Gulbuddin Hekmatyar in the 1970s, even back then famous for mutilating women with acid for failing to cover themselves. He would use the CIA to destroy the monsters they had helped create.

Chapter 6   - Nascent Nemesis

"Their system of ethics, which regards treachery and violence as virtues rather than vices, has produced a code of honour so strange and inconsistent that it is incomprehensible to a logical mind."
Winston Churchill

The careful management of his young career and the support of his agents had brought Tom to the chamber in which he now stood, a jarring admixture of dungeon, medieval forge, and 19th century operating theater. Small barred windows placed high up lit rough stone walls in soft grey. To his left was a finely made but much-scarred wooden apparatus, an old-style gynecological examination table. In the corner to the right stood a few of his people in their traditional somber full-length robes, faces lit ruddy at intervals by a charcoal fire as one of them worked an ancient bellows to bring it to its highest heat.

Tom Broadhead had set out on a path through cryptography and information theory, data mining and statistical analysis, which brought his work to the attention of the CIA, and to that other Agency, the NSA. He had done analyses on a number of countries, but he bent his course always toward central Asia, studying languages, religions, and customs.

When the Soviets came in '89, Afghanistan presented opportunities to the Agency to build networks within the opposition to a communist puppet. To draw blood and especially money from the USSR. Men, only men, for such was the way with the Afghans, were sought to bring weapons, money, and tactics to the resistance.

Recruitment for the CIA Special Activities Division drew heavily on hard-bitten and smart career irregulars like Marine Force Recon and the Green Berets. It was only the depth of his immersion in the language and culture of the Pashtuns which had gotten Tom his chance.

Tom had an affinity for insurgency, liked working at high speed, low altitude, and on short notice. He liked weapons and warriors. As a paramilitary operations officer, he became a recruiter of agents and typically an agent is a man who betrays his country, seduced by the intelligence officer. To bring down the man he stood over now, Tom had found no need to seek traitors among the Pashtuns. Their primary allegiance was to their clans, clans already at war with the Taliban. And one such clan took an intense interest in prosecuting an atrocity now more than a decade old. A crime against one of their women was an existential threat to them.

The mullah's hair had fallen loose from his turban. It was long and dark, touched everywhere with gray, as was his full beard. Heavily robed, he sat with hands bound behind the back of a straight wooden chair. Tom bent to look closely. He held the man's black gaze for a moment, then said, "Hamdiya Durrani".

The face furrowed with fear for just an instant and he looked away. And Tom knew that this was the man. The long-sought. He felt heat in all his limbs and body, a terrible pressure in his head. He straightened and looked about the room. Each of the stones of the walls leapt into his vision all at once, their rough gray surfaces stained orange by the fire. It seemed he could see the heat-tinged air in the room.

Tom watched all this as if it were a movie, wondering what came next. He nodded, then heard himself rap out a command in the hard northern Pushtu dialect

"Cook his shit."

Still burning inside, he strode to the door. In the hallway, he leaned his back and neck against rough cool stonework. He began to think again. He had dreamed of, not just wanted, but literally had dreams about, what was to happen in that chamber of stone. That plenty of the Pashtuns in this valley were blood-feud ready to listen to his dream had at first surprised him. These were men who would give a ten year old daughter in marriage to an enemy to end a clan feud. But they placed a heavy price upon dishonor.

He would have considered them primitives had he known them early in his life. He had despised his father's feuding Kentucky relatives, dwellers in ancient grimy single-wides, always scheming over old injuries. Now he felt kinship with them. They had the mountain tribesmen's recognition of deep evil walking in the world, and the unblinking willingness to do any violence in service of its destruction.

The Afghan tribes recognized neither ethnicity nor nation. Tom spoke Pushtu. He respected their homes, the privacy of their women, their honor. A Pashtun would devote a century to take revenge and call it quick work.

He closed his eyes and thought he heard her laugh, then, and she was in his mind, hand waving in gentle insistence that he stop prattling on about art, or music, or life, and to calm himself. He pushed off the wall and hurried back over stone cobbles toward the chamber.

As he pushed open the heavy wooden door bright red iron was withdrawn from the fire. Leather straps at waist, chest, ankles, and wrists bound the naked mullah to the antique medical apparatus. Stripped of his flowing robes and thick turban, the man was scrawny, his belly pendulous. His thin legs splayed open, knees elevated, feet strapped into stirrups.

Tom bent over the man's head. He looked into the face. The grain of the wooden table, the rough leather straps, the hellish red glare of the fire shining in the wide eyes of the helpless creature whimpering in pure animal fear all snapped into clear focus, a scene in the film playing out again before him. The pressure he had felt in his head and the heat within him were gone now. There was a new cold within him, yet the terrible clarity remained.

He straightened to pull the nine millimeter from his hip. His people looked up, puzzled, lit in red by the naked hot iron, ready to carry out the thing he had asked. He waved them away and stepped up to the dark wood of the table. He bent again to bring his lips near the man's ear, and pressed the gun through the thick tangled mane against his head.

He spoke, again in Pushtu, "I have not the strength to give you your life. I give you this quick death."

Their faces inches apart, the nine-millimeter blasted a crimson jet from the man's head. Deafened, Tom walked away.

Chapter 7 - Well Met

"No one ever wants to go to war. It's always fun to drop bombs ... if you know there's no one around and no one shoots back at you. But no one wants to get shot at. "

Lt. Timothy J. Naughton,
A-7 attack pilot

The gunner looked at Tom through the bubble canopy at the nose of the attack craft, peering around the starred section where the armor glass had spiderwebbed around shrapnel impacts. He had grey eyes over a long nose and a deep crease on each side of a wide lipless mouth. He didn't release his flight harness or remove his helmet. He had to know that the helicopter would burn. The engines were hot. Fuel bladders were ruptured.

Tom climbed the slope toward the smoking wreck of the Hind. The dull green helicopter looked like a huge grasshopper crushed onto the rock outcrop, rotor blades shattered to jagged stumps. The twin inline canopies which made it look so bulbous and insectile were both cracked, half the upper one blown away.

A tri-barreled chaingun hung below the chin of the helicopter, the bore of each barrel large enough to fit a thumb in. It did not track with the gunner's helmet as he turned to watch Tom pass round to the port side. Power and controls must be gone. The gunner hinged up the side of his canopy. He slid his helmet up and back over a scalp of black curls.

Tom called up, "Are you hit?"

"I am not yet hit." The words grated out, sour with Slavic vowels. It sounded as though he expected unpleasantness.

"Can you get out?"

"Yes."

"I suggest you get out."

"Shall I? You are American. I know you are CIA. You will give me to Pashtuns."

"I'm not here to kill Russians. I and my men are here to kill Soviets. The missile that hit you was a Stinger, a gift to my men from the United States. Your helicopter was Soviet. They have killed it. Are you Soviet?"

Tom left his nine millimeter on his hip. The gunner surely could feel the men looking across their sights at him.

"Some say soon there will be no Soviets, if Mikhail Sergeyevich has his way. I think I am no longer Soviet. But I am Russian."

"My men will want to kill you. But this is not my war, to war on Russians. I have my duty to war against Soviets, but I fight another war as well. One you can help me with. Shall I tell my men that you will help me?"

"You put this private war above your country?" asked the gunner. He seemed indifferent to the growing tang of kerosene vaporizing on the hot fairings of the engines.

"I fight this war beside the war my country fights. I am at the command of my country, but I answer to another chain of command, not higher than my country's, but a command as high."

The gunner considered. In a few moments he set a square black Makarov automatic on the control panel. He had been holding the pistol in his lap. The harness release opened with a *click*.

He said, "You must tell of High Command. Perhaps I help."

As he stepped onto the ladder beside the cockpit, he said, "I am Polya."

The Russian wore no insignia of rank, but the wings of a black bat spread across the patch at his shoulder. He was *Spetsnaz* GRU, one of the special forces units within the Soviet foreign intelligence agency, the counterpart of SAD, the Special Activities Division of the CIA. No simple trigger-puller wore such a patch.

14

It would require releasing him to return to Soviet lines, setting up clandestine communication. But this man flew Hinds, and the Mi-24 Hind could suddenly and precisely deposit a metric ton of high explosive, a thing Tom craved. If a mullah in a rocky hideaway needed to die, this man could kill him.

His Pashtuns would not like it, providing targets for the Russians to blot out, yet their particular clan liked even less the militants coming up from Pakistan. If a mullah needed to die, they would be willing that this man should kill him.

The gunner climbed down, crossed in front of the muzzles of the chaingun and went back along the starboard side and up another set of rungs to where the rear cockpit canopy had shattered, where the Stinger had exploded, blowing away as well the impeller section of one of the turbines.

He said, "I must get Grigori."

Perched there, he fumbled with the flight harness, grabbed a handhold on the fuselage, and twisted his free hand into the fabric of the pilot's flight suit. He curled his fist up to his shoulder and straightened, pressing the entire body upward, one-handed, letting it fall over his shoulder. Blood cascaded down his back. Tom realized why he had not seen the pilot earlier. Grigori had lost his head.

Chapter 8   - The Day the World Began Anew

"You exploit women like consumer products."

Usama bin Laden

"Tom, you need to see this."

One of the new analysts in his Central Asia group was peering around the office door, a weedy fellow in ill-fitting black slacks and a white dress shirt loose around his skinny neck. It was a weekday morning, a decade distant from his Pashtuns.

He rose from his desk to follow the man to the cafeteria. On the television, black smoke plumed away from the South Tower.

Tom knew what it meant. Hostages, bombs, bombs on airliners, and now airliners as bombs. Innocents taken, imprisoned, beheaded, dismembered, blown apart, burned to death, because women went about in a world which spiritual throwbacks would reserve to men.

The Soviets, including Polya, had gone back to being Russian and had left Afghanistan. Tom left to take up his old trade, spying from behind a desk, cloistered with bookish types who boiled down field reports, reconnaissance photos, and electronic intercepts.

Tom maintained his connections on the ground, and grew his own network of intelligence and military officers across national boundaries. Men and women who recognized the enemy.

Central Asia had grown no more peaceable with the departure of the Russians. Saudis, Pakistanis, and Americans had supported the Taliban against the Soviet Union. Twenty years on they had been displaced by Iranian money and weapons. As Iran had turned from the West, al Qaida turned on the West, as did the Taliban. The mullahs said it must be so.

No one was asking for analysis today. The target was clear. The CIA and the Army Special Operations Command had planned their response before the sun set on the smoldering ruins.

The West could not be other than what they had become. The need to educate offspring limited families to one or two children, and required the incomes of both parents. Women were liberated by economic necessity, not by the force of any moral imperative. Traditional religions called for large families and traditional roles for women. They sought to cloak their virtues as moral necessity. Feminists sought to cloak necessity as moral virtue.

The mullahs could not be other that what they had become. Now they had killed thousands of Americans, all in one go. The only way to top that involved a mushroom-shaped cloud.

Chapter 9   - Head of the Serpent

"I could have killed him."

Bill Clinton

Bill Clinton had a shot at bin Laden in '98. Slick Willie let him slip away, more concerned with harm to his image from Afghan collateral damage than with possible American deaths.

By late September of 2001 Tom was once again in northern Afghanistan, on the ground with Task Force Dagger, the fist of the Special Activities Division. He was too heavy and too bald, but he spoke Pushtu and he knew the clans, and this time the CIA had the American military machine at its back.

The mullahs were slow to understand. A Taliban main force convoy of soldiers and weaponry riding unarmored cars and trucks approached a Northern Alliance position, one with artillery support organized by American special forces. The column motored ahead, bright sun glinting from windshields. Soon, flaming shattered trucks blocked retreat. After, ragged pieces of sheet steel, blackened skeletons of trucks and corpses littered the roadway.

Frightened, the clerics dug into the hills and posted tanks and armored personnel carriers. The Air Force responded with B-52s, and the huge flying explosive trucks with bomb bays like shipping containers gathered above in a great aluminum overcast.

Within weeks the Northern Alliance took the cities and drove the Taliban high into the mountains. The mullahs learned to avoid combat or be hunted down. Those who could slipped away into Pakistan.

Then it was all up to the Pakistanis. Pakistan never allowed Special Forces teams to move around in their north, to establish networks on the ground. Bin Laden hung on for another decade. Al Qaida grew tendrils into Iraq.

America could not pre-empt the strikes of a few suicidal fanatics. Presidents quailed, slow to get boots on the ground, hesitant to fly strike aircraft over hostile political borders.

Those with the easy answers claimed to know the prime mover. Al Qaida was the villain, was said to be a nonstate actor, though they had operated with the Taliban government and with Pakistan's connivance. By the time bin Laden died with an American bullet in his forehead, dead Iranian commandos were being found in Afghanistan and CIA/SAD began crossing from Iraq and Afghanistan into Iran for paramilitary operations.

The Iranians set up centrifuges, began concentrating fissile isotopes. All the while al Qaida sought chunks of beryllium machined to reflect neutrons, precision electronic timers, enriched uranium, and their holy grail, suitcase nukes thought to be missing from Soviet labs.

Even in the face of this, the Americans tired of it. Tired of funding civic projects which were no more than bribes for headmen who could not see past the nearest mountain. Tired of carrying the entire fight, they left the Afghans to throw off the Taliban if they would. Urban Afghans expressed grave concern about whether their young women would be able to play soccer, but few picked up rifles when the extremists came down from the hills.

Only the High Command stood against the followers of the new angry god. They were in the beginning Americans and Russians in the military and intelligence agencies. They grew to be many more. When the mullahs gathered their poison together, the High Command would know of it and Tom would call down a blinding actinic light to cleanse it. He would ready a pre-emptive strike. And he would keep his finger on the trigger.

Chapter 10 - Davis-Monthan

"When they hear or see A-10s, they know the business end of combat is overhead..."
Hog pilot, speaking on condition of anonymity

Jimmy's career with the High Command began joyously. It had puzzled him at first why and how the CIA would train a pilot, until he remembered his history. The U-2 program. The Blackbird. Both aircraft born of the CIA. Now the CIA had a space fighter, and there were to be no hidebound Air Force procedures, no 'red light specialists' arguing with 'blue light specialists'.

His employment contract bore the name James Smith. They put him on an Air Mobility Command flight to Davis-Monthan AFB where he stepped down a set of metal rollup stairs into Tucson sun that hit him like a physical blow. Two instructors showed him to a van, trucked him to his quarters, and put him into the A-10 simulator the next morning. It would be his office for the next few days.

The first time he walked up to the nose of a Warthog, he could not take his eyes from the ring of muzzles where the seven barrels of the Gatling protruded, slightly off center, from the Warthog's nose. A deer rifle was .30 caliber. The autocannon's 30 millimeter diameter translated to 1.20 caliber, a bore over an inch across.

The wings stuck out straight, obviously subsonic, but each carried five hardpoints for mounting missiles or bombs. The plane bristled. An A-10 bristled with armament. This was a plane you flew at people, and even those in APCs or tanks, if they looked up in time, were prone to think "Oh my God, that thing is pointed at me." Where it went, it promised catastrophe.

He looked up at big twin vertical tails. A tight turner. To get off target as quickly as it got on. He climbed in and they closed the thick canopy. He could see all around, except for the heavy framing around the forward windscreen. The briefings explained that the armorglass windscreen would stop a high-caliber autocannon round, the titanium tub wrapped around the cockpit to armor the pilot, the redundant controls, the overbuilt structure of the airframe. In a Warthog, you expected to take some of what you gave. You were expected to go in harm's way.

There were A-10s available. The Air Force had never much cared for close air support. The Army, forbidden to fly fixed-wing, instead flew Apache attack helicopters to do what they could. But the ground pounders reverenced the Warthog, their deliverer from evil, built to fly low and slow, to linger long in overwatch, to tote a big heavy weapon, to get close up like the grunts did to deliver death. Someone wanted Jimmy to kill something big.

It was no trouble flying the slow, stable but maneuverable Warthog. It did not compare to his much loved F-14 for speed, but was not at all finicky as long as he did not let his airspeed drop too low. He did nothing with the plane's capability to launch missiles. He was tasked to learn 'The Gun', the big Gatling, to accustom himself to the sound like an extended explosion, the recoil like putting on a thrust reverser, the vibration like being shaken by an enormous beast.

After a few gun runs, Jimmy understood why a wad of chewing gum was stuck on the headsup display. Each aircraft reacted to recoil with its own combination of pitch and yaw. Pilots marked the direction of push with the gum.

Jimmy perforated rusty armor and raised great splashes of sand. Nobody shot back at him.

Chapter 11 - Old Friends

"Better a wise enemy than a foolish friend."

Pashtun Proverb

Tom stood up from the desk. He put a heel on the desktop, leg straight, and stretched a hamstring. He said, "Hey Siri, find me a date."

Siri suggested Match, and he took a few moments to download the app. He switched to stretch the other leg. He swiped and poked around, then punched a microphone icon to dictate a profile. "Professional serial killer specializing in destroying religious extremists seeks open-minded companion. Hobbies include cryptanalysis, small arms training, and Judo."

It was hopeless. Lara Croft wouldn't hang out on Match.

Siri interrupted, "Hamdiya calling."

Tom dictated, "Ahhh, shit." then deleted the profile and shut down the app.

He suspected that it was for Hamdiyah that he had become an aging bachelor, practicing a strenuous form of serial monogamy that chained together involvements either comic or tragic, but always somehow ill-advised. Through two deployments to Afghanistan she was out of reach but never far from his mind. Now he had again been stateside for a few years and they spoke and visited one another. She remained out of reach.

Tom poked the speaker icon on the screen of his iPhone and said, "The fraction 1/7 annoys me. It is beautiful for its repeated pattern, 0.142857142857…. It would be very beautiful if its repeated digits were twice seven, 14, then four times seven, 28, then eight times seven, 56. But the pattern ends with 57, which is thrice nineteen. How does nineteen get into it?"

She laughed, her voice slightly flattened by the iPhone speaker, but still flowing and clear. She said, "This number pleases me. It has presented this delicious mystery to us. You might try to work out the rules for obtaining its integer multiples by permuting the digits of its pattern."

He thought about the numbers, and was surprised to see that permutations were indeed equivalent to taking multiples. He was not surprised that she had surprised him, nor that she had contradicted him. Ever since he had met her at Brown they had spoken so. Of mathematics, music, and more rarely of her early years.

She had taught him the Pashtun tongue and to know the language in depth he had to know the traditions and legends. He had said nothing of his aims or his career. She had tried to teach him her creed, but he could not bear to hear from her the words that had been bent to her harm.

He told himself that he wanted to tell her that he was dating yet again, but Siri interrupted, "NASA Admin calling."

That would be Jerry calling about his trip to the Skunk Works. He said, "Another abrupt end to a budding number theoretic adventure."

He added in Pashtun, "May you be as you are now, always."

Chapter 12 - Ways and Means

"That damned Swede can actually see air."

Hal Hibbard,
speaking of Kelly Johnson

The fastest jet aircraft to ever carry a pilot came from the mind of a man named Kelly Johnson, who worked for the Lockheed company in the 1950s. Johnson was said to be able to see in his mind the airflow around a supersonic aircraft. His SR-71 Blackbird reached Mach 3.1, some say Mach 4, there and gone before Cold War SAMs could intercept. Blackbird skin had to be made of titanium. Aluminum sheeting would have been cooked, degraded by the heat of its passage through the atmosphere.

The history ran through his mind as Tom walked beside his friend Jerry, a big man in an engineer's dark slacks and a white dress shirt bulging with too much deskchair time. Jerry was an early High Command contact who had grown more useful as he rose within NASA executive ranks.

LED floodlights on a metal ceiling far above diffused bluish light down onto aircraft scattered over a seemingly limitless expanse of smooth white-painted concrete. The hangar was the showplace for the latest incarnation of the Lockheed Skunk Works, Kelly Johnson's old advanced development outfit, whose very name had been hidden away for the first decades of its life. They stood before a Blackbird.

They trudged until they came to a coal black daggerlike airframe a hundred feet long. Tom reached up and put his bare hand on the cold metal cusp that ran all along the black fuselage like the edge of a hollow-ground blade. The Blackbird knifed through air, driven by a pair of huge engines. The plane took off and accelerated with engines turning and burning as turbojets. At the upper limit of speed achievable by the turbos, their inlets were reconfigured and fuel was dumped directly into the airstream and the engines lit off as ramjets. The craft leapt to high-supersonic speeds.

Ramjets resembled turbojets as much as a top fuel dragster resembled a Ford Taurus. Turbos pulled air in, compressed it in a spinning cold turbine stage, burned it with fuel in a combustion chamber, spun a hot turbine stage with the stream of hot gas, and finally expelled it from the nozzle to create thrust. The hot turbine had to drive the cold compressor, and so the gas stream was sapped of power.

Ramjets shoved a craft through atmosphere so fast and hard that the air entering the engine throat was compressed by the sheer velocity of passage and rammed directly into the combustion chamber. Ramjets had to be accelerated to great speed to work at all. Keeping them burning was no more difficult than lighting a candle in a hurricane.

Jerry led him away to the back wall of the hangar, and then over to the left, near the building's corner. A bright orange needlenosed craft about the size of a fighter jet hunkered there. The long pointed nose and stubby thin wings said it was a high supersonic design. There was no cockpit, just a pair of canards far forward on the tapering nose. A round air intake as thick as the fuselage began halfway back on its belly and blended into what looked like an engine compartment just ahead of the large nozzle.

22

This was no follow-on to the Blackbird, no burner of torrents of kerosene. That massive intake fed a nuke. This was a disinterred Cold War nightmare. Tom said, "Sweet Jesus, that looks like something out of Project Pluto."

Jerry said, "Yeah, Project Pluto only went as far as testing an air-cooled nuclear reactor. NACA[3] shut it down after they proved it could heat a supersonic airstream. This is the follow-on CIA black project, the Pluto Missile."

Lockheed had built the Blackbird and the U-2 before it for the CIA. Tom said, "I'm in the godamned CIA and I never heard of a nuclear ramjet missile actually being built."

Jerry said, "Putin claimed to have one. He might. We do."

He went on, "You strap a couple boosters on it, crank it up to Mach 1 or so, and then gate the airstream through the reactor. The superheated air shoots out the nozzle and you have a ramjet."

Tom said, "So, this doesn't help me a lot. What I've got to defend is exatmospheric."

Jerry replied, "Yeah, your asset is orbital, but the threat will come at you from below."

He led Tom around the spike on the nose of the missile. Beyond, the corner of the hanger had been curtained off. Tom brushed by as Jerry held heavy white fabric aside.

The craft within was white-painted. Its rear section looked very much like the Pluto, including the big air intake. The nose, though, was rounded like that of an ICBM. It was a nose built for the hypersonic flight regime, a nose to bludgeon through the air, to shove the shockwave away from itself to keep its heat at bay, like the nose of the space shuttle which had to endure reentry to atmosphere at Mach 20 and above. The clear blister atop the tapering front section puzzled Tom at first, until he realized it was a cockpit.

Tom continued to stare at the craft, muttering each time it puzzled him anew. "It's manned? It's set up for reentry, but it's an air breather? Is this a

_____

[3] Before there was NASA, there was NACA. You could look it up.

spacecraft or an aircraft? How do you get it up to ramjet operational speed? How fast is it?"

Jerry said, "Meet the FS-2A Smart Rock. The space fighter that U.S. Space Command doesn't know it has. We just call it the Rock."

Tom decoded 'FS-2A' as Fighter, Spaceplane, Design Number 2, Series Letter A. Why was it a Smart Rock? Smart Rocks were conceived of in the 1980s as small autonomous rockets housed in orbiting satellite battle stations. The battle station would detect a ground-based missile launch and loose its rockets to self-guide to intercept. As an anti-ballistic-missile weapon, the system suffered from the need to have a battle station in position near each hostile launch site. This required too many battle stations, because each station was out of range of the ground-launched threat for much of its orbit.

Tom had an orbital asset to defend, and so the problem was inverted. When the station itself was to be defended from incoming missiles, carrying smart rockets along had lots of potential.

Jerry said, "The Rock drops from orbit into a re-entry trajectory. It's already moving at orbital velocity, so as soon as the air is thick enough it's gated through ceramic channels bored through the core of the reactor. You get a beautiful bright yellow exhaust cone that drives the Rock through the upper atmosphere."

Jerry pointed out the weapons bay where a thirty millimeter autocannon lurked behind the nose, and had much more to say about the Rock, but Tom already saw its beauty. This craft could descend upon and destroy ground-launched antisatellite missiles in boost phase, while still suborbital and within atmosphere, avoiding messy and lethal orbiting debris clouds.

He said, "Yes. Yes. I'll get the money. I want them deployed with the station. As many as we can dock."

Chapter 13 - Domestic Dispute

"With a lot of these guys, once you get involved with them, you don't really get out. Especially if you're a woman - you become sort of property."

Tom met Ceelya where she had suggested, at the elevated train station. Introduced himself. She looked at his Dockers and smirked. She wore tight brown leather pants that strained to compress her butt and saddlebags.

"Where're we going?" he asked.

"Place I know. C'mon, this train. You're from DC, right? I love those tiny art-house theaters in Georgetown, the live music bars. It's like that, but authentic."

The elevated train clattered and swayed along, and she rattled along with it. About her collection of feminist lit. Her lit/soc studies at U of I. Alternatives to patriarchal cultures. Busting out of confining gender roles. She had not discussed any of that on her Match profile.

It puzzled him that the train was headed south. She was from a northern Chicago suburb, a place like Georgetown where Tom couldn't have afforded an apartment, let alone bought a house. They got off the elevated in south Chicago.

He looked around. He looked at her. "This is not at all like Georgetown."

Too, she was not like her profile pic, in which she appeared a decade younger and a few kilos lighter. Her hair was different too; tonight she wore tightly coiled rich chestnut-brown dreadlocks that showed a hint of lighter roots. He couldn't really fault her though. He wasn't the engine technician with a passion for maritime diesel mechanics that his profile described. And he wasn't in Chicago to visit Great Lakes Naval Station, as he had told her.

She pressed her lips together, annoyed. "I'm very Earthy. I like nontraditional cultures. I like the anarchy, people being really free."

She spoke a couple beats per measure too fast. He wondered if she was drug-addled. They walked along trash-filled gutters under streetlights, a few of which worked. He kept to the street side of the walk.

Ceelya turned to glare at him and said, "Men are pigs."

Tom jumped, surprised. "Pigs are part of the natural order," he replied, not sure what he meant.

"Men aren't even as smart as pigs."

"If they were, they wouldn't get near women." Now Tom surprised himself.

She stopped in the middle of the walk. "Well, we're here. Just a neighborhood bar, but lively. Live music sometimes."

Had she forgotten that she had just started an argument? He looked at the bar. The brightest lights were a couple very old Miller and PBR signs glowing in red and yellow neon behind sooty front windows. Fat tires poked out from the alley beside the bar. He paced over. There looked to be a dozen Harleys parked there. No colors on the frames or tanks, unless you counted black.

He hurried back to Ceelya. "I don't like this place," he said.

"It's edgy," she said. She took his elbow and pulled him toward the door. "C'mon, it'll get you down on the street scene."

Inside, the stink matched the gloom. There were old posters for folk musicians, but the sound system was off or maybe broken. Spindly wooden chairs sat around half a dozen tilted round-topped tables. A couple tables held the clientele, standard-issue bikers, some big bellied and some lean like tweakers and all hunched over glasses, pitchers, and puddles of beer. They wore ponytails or unkempt long hair. There were full neck beards, ornate Fu Manchus, long muttonchops. Some were just unshaven for the past week.

Tom had never recruited any bikers, a criminal element so unreliable as to be useless to clandestine ops. Sleeveless black leather vests proclaimed this bunch, in lines of text curved above and below the back patch, to be the DAWGZ MC, Chicago, Illinois. The center of the patch was a slavering, snarling pit bull in heavy garish embroidery.

"Let's sit at the bar," he said. He walked over to the end of the bar near the door.

They sat on cracked leather. Ceelya leaned both forearms flat on the grubby bartop. She said, "A beer."

The barkeep was a leathery old guy with a big white-fringed bare head perched on a skinny neck, fingers stained yellow.

Tom nodded, and said to the old barkeep, "Her beer, and a coffee for me."

She said, "You can get some good coke here. E too. But the coke is especially good. One line keeps you going for hours."

He knew then that she knew the bikers, but not well. They were giving her meth.

"I didn't know bikers were patrons of the arts," he said.

"Check the cover of that first album by Big Brother and the Holding Company, endorsed by Hell's Angels Frisco. The bikers are cool. The Angels were there when Janis did Monterey Pop."

He said, "The Angels were there at Altamont as well."

She had to be some kind of trust-fund radical, to know that little about outlaw motorcycle clubs. She should discuss bikers with William, a High Command prospect whose south Houston neighborhood looked a lot like this one except for the Spanish running across the storefronts. But then he thought William was probably too soft-spoken to school a bigmouth Trustifarian like Ceelya.

The half-dozen bikers at the nearest table included two women. One was sloppy fat with a mean look, stringy once-blond hair, big breasts gone flaccid and heading south, thirty going on fifty. But also, a young brunette. She looked relatively unworn and fairly slim. Conservative top and jeans. Probably not a habitual drinker or drug abuser. But she was wobbly tonight, resting her chin unsteadily on her palm. Dawgs tipped up beer to her lips.

The barkeep brought their drinks and Ceelya slugged down half her beer.

She said, "What's with the coffee? You got a spreadsheet to fill out?" She said it smiling, but with an up-curled lip.

"I'm thinking I might need to stay alert," he said. He was winding up inside, sitting up straight. His neck felt stiff.

The young woman was giggling, trying to hold her head straight, and two Dawgs packed in tighter around her, hands stroking her arms, resting on her thighs.

Suddenly she straightened up, her eyes wide.

She slurred, loud, "Hayeee!"

He could hear the Dawgs soothing her, "Hey we're just having a good time here have a beer and chill."

The girl looked around the table, wrinkled her nose.

"Hayee I wanna go home now!"

And the Dawgs were just like, "Hey mama we just got here, we'll getcha home."

She attempted to stand but on each upper arm a Dawg had a grip.

"Hayeeee, lemme go!"

Ceelya turned to him, big-eyed, "Do something!"

Her bar, her crowd, his responsibility? Tom had a what-the-fuck moment.

He snapped, "Did you just say to me, 'Hey you're a man, do something'? Is that my gender role? You want something done? Something forceful? You got a phone? Call a cop."

She hit him. Not a slap. Closed fist to the mouth. More of a hard push, her punch unpracticed.

He stood away from her and ran his tongue over his teeth and lips. His upper lip felt fat on the left.

He said, "I'll find my own way home."

The Dawgs were not too drunk to track the fight. He walked toward the door through loud haw-haw from the tables, mockery punctuated with deliberately nasty laughter.

"Punch 'er fuggin' lights out bro!"

"Who's wearin' the balls tonight?"

Behind him Ceelya began a rant on toxic masculinity which would have done credit to an MSNBC talking head, her brand of anarchy still not extending to freeing the pigs. He looked back to see the frayed-looking biker mama getting up. She cracked a feral smile and Oh Jesus, the black meth-rotted roots of her teeth. Toxic humanity. Shit, this was trouble.

As he passed the register the old barkeep wrinkled his forehead and shook his head, looking over at the table. Tom said to him, "You got a light?"

The old fellow shrugged. Then he slid a scratched chrome Zippo out of his trouser pocket.

Perfect. Butane wouldn't work. Tom took the lighter and laid down two twenties on the bar. He waggled the lighter at the barkeep. "OK?"

The barkeep nodded, showing the top of his head to be as bare as the front. Tom struck the Zippo alight, then shut its lid.

As he walked to the door, he said, "Slip out the back in a minute. Two minutes will be too late."

Tom left the door ajar, and walked over to the alley, slipping the Zippo into his trouser pocket. His multitool had an awl and he hammered the point into the gas tank on the nearest bike. He pulled off the rubber fuel lines and smelled gas as he pushed the bike over into a row of Harleys, taking several down. He punctured another tank and kicked that bike over among rising fumes.

Ducking back around the corner of the alley onto the sidewalk, he dug out his smartphone and held down the two buttons on the case that called 911. Then the Zippo lit first strike, and he underhanded it around the corner.

As he ducked back, a yellow/blue jet as big as the alley was wide *whooshed* close beside him. With any luck more fuel tanks would cook off. Then he had to pass back across the front of the bar an inside near the window two shadowy figures struggled, and the Harpy's screech of the biker mama was not quite muffled by the glass.

"You ain't gonna call nobody, bitch!"

Apparently a very funny line. More haw-haw.

No sign appeared above the door of the bar, or anywhere on the front. Tom read the number and gave the address to the emergency dispatcher.

She said, "I know the place. I see that address quite a lot lately. What is your name?"

He said to her, "You have my number. There's an ongoing abduction of a young female and an assault on a second female and there's a fire. A bunch of bikers called Dawgz, with a 'z'."

"I know the Dawgz too," she said.

"Did you get that? It's a gang-bang, a beating, and a fire." Tom squelched the call and set off at an unhurried but steady walk.

The police would want him to hang around. He would have to go a couple blocks out of his way for misdirection. Ditch the SIMM card and battery from the phone. And then head back to the elevated. Any follow-up would dead end at the Master Sergeant Jack Kelly cover he had constructed. Dating was so complicated.

Chapter 14 - Security Concerns

"Beware that, when fighting monsters, you yourself do not become a monster"

Friedrich Nietzsche

"Juana, I have a long term prospect. He's still a high school kid. Would you like to get him set up with flying lessons?"

Admiral Juana Abreu said nothing for a few seconds. Then, "High school?"

"Yup," said Tom. "He will need scholarship money in a year or so. I'm suggesting Naval ROTC."

"Where?" she asked.

"Best cybernetics or robotics department in the country. With an aerospace engineering department as well. You can leave that to him to sort out. I want his brain driving drone design programs in five years. He should also spend some time in a trailer in Arizona, eyeballing targets for Predator-launched Hellfires. At some time he will tell us how he can do the most damage. If he wants to go in harm's way, we will give him a try at that too."

"Tom, I've wanted to suggest for some time that you are putting everyone in the network in a quite vulnerable position. There are well worked out procedures for expanding covert organizations by adding cells of new people, linked by a cutout. Otherwise, more people equals more risk of leaks. And the leaks eventually happen. If they get to you, they get to all of us. You connect everybody."

Everything was a risk, but this one was worth it. William did not like bikers. William liked drones and large caliber rifles. And Tom had just realized what a wonderful target a motorcycle club would make.

"I'm an intelligence officer, Juana. This is known to me. What if the organization does not remain covert? No problem."

For the second time in their talk, she said nothing for several seconds. As always, Tom's belly pained him when she expressed displeasure. She was the most powerful of his High Command contacts, a non-politicized, deeply embedded mover and shaker in what was arguably the most powerful of the military services. The Admiral was like a thundercloud on the horizon. Lightning might strike anywhere for miles around.

Before she could speak, Tom said, "His name is Guillermo Morales, of Houston, Texas. Goes by William. If you would like to have Navy Personnel Command contact my head of staff, Jenny will oversee the initial contact. He's expecting the call."

31

"You want to bring a high school kid into this. Is his family on board?" asked Juana.

Tom had thought about it. Was he running an anti-terrorist unit, or a bunch of serial killers? William had that thin layer of scar tissue leaving him forever detached from love or hate, but also from pity. Yes, he was running a gang of serial killers.

Was he like a drug lord gathering teenage *sicarios* to him to take his risks and get the splatter on them? No, beneath the scarring, William was an explosion waiting for a spark. Better to contain it in the chamber of a rifle than to let the shrapnel fly in a shopping mall. Weaponized, William would fight his own battles.

Juana would come to see it in time. She had her own reasons for signing on with the High Command, firmly locked behind that straight line of hard-pressed lips.

Tom said, "He's not a minor. He was out of school for a year so he's a year older than his grade. His parents won't object. Oh, and he had a sister, but best not mention her."

Chapter 15 - R & R

"In all, she was penetrated no less than fifty times, in various ways…"
Hunter S. Thompson

He had the ugly fucker in the scope's field of view now. Tom sat before a rough plank shelf running along the white inner wall of a cargo van. His phone, clipped into a stand beside an unpainted sheetmetal control console, displayed the sight picture on the ShotView app. With the dual joysticks on the console, he steadied the Fazer in its hover and then carefully yawed and pitched the subscale helicopter to center the crosshairs on the biker's widest section, a hairy belly hanging over greasy jeans and protruding past the wings of his black leather vest.

The Dawg leaned on one of a couple dozen chopped Harleys crowded onto a patch of bare dirt in front of a big sprawling unpainted shack. The club had learned to post a guard, and it was likely an unpatched probie who had caught the shit detail and now peered up into the sky but apparently could not make out the little heli-drone backlit by the bright afternoon sky. It was surprising that the Fazer was either audible or visible from five hundred yards. Time to execute.

He called to William, "Half-pull."

His protégé William was fast becoming a friend. He was up for hunting Dawgz because Dawgz closely resembled *Las Almas*, a Southwestern variant of subhuman motorcyclist. *Las Almas Muertas* had gotten to his sister in the course of an initiation ceremony for her boyfriend. He and Tom never spoke of this, but William was an easy recruit. Bright kid, nearly college age. He took well to developing cybernetic systems, was coming out of his depression, and was motivated to the most benthic depths of his ruined soul. But was he steady in action?

William hit a button on a second console. He sat on a metal folding chair at his console near the rear doors of the van, leaning on the same shelf. He looked up between two dark curtains of straight raven hair and called over to Tom, who sat just behind the passenger seat.

"Ten bucks says we hit him. Half-pull, check."

A green dot cursor appeared, jittering as it tracked the biker's belly through the tiny instabilities of the Fazer's hover. This was Tom's first action with the TrackingPoint hardware and ShotView app, a system for automating the operation of a long-range rifle. On a range it punched tiny groups onto paper, but while shooting from a helicopter at better than a quarter mile he wasn't terribly confident.

"He's tagged," Tom said. "Pull trigger. And that's a bet."

William hit the second button, a big rectangular red one labeled 'FIRE'.

He said, "Pull, check."

Tom concentrated on ShotView, bringing the crosshairs back onto the biker. The damping algorithm William had coded into the Fazer's real-time control software smoothed out his muscle tremors nicely. At the moment the crosshairs aligned on the dot, just above the deep funnel that led into the biker's navel, the .300 Winchester Magnum hung between the helicopter's skids let go 220 grains of match grade bullet at close to 2600 feet per second.

The image jumped to all sky, and by the time Tom recovered the view the biker was splayed on his back, vest agape, blood streaming down the hill of his belly. A thick bare arm twitched. Just beyond, a towel-sized swath of the dirt yard was stained crimson, mottled with gray scraps of what Tom realized was intestine.

"Best two and a quarter I ever spent," he said.

Large caliber match grade ammo was expensive but worth it for the consistency. There was something about gut-shooting a biker, blowing out that obscenely bloated belly.

"Cost you ten more for your lack of faith," said William.

Tom would have preferred the more exotic .338 Lapua Mag, but buying those rounds would have screamed sniper. Even he didn't know all the watchers and what they watched. A .300 Win Mag said elk hunter.

At the far upper edge of the field of view, the door to the ratty clubhouse opened. Tom sighed and pulled up the collective with one joystick and pushed the other forward. The Fazer pitched forward and dove below treetop level. He circled it behind the woodlot back toward their van.

The hunt had been relaxing and satisfying, and fairly safe, since bikers got sniped occasionally. Hunting Dawgz was also a public service. After the abortive date with Ceelya, he had gotten into FBI files, looking for women with motorcycle club history. He had talked to a few of them about how they had gotten free. Pulling a pistol out of a handbag had worked.

He would have to thank Jerry for giving him the RMAX idea. Yamaha had a fine subscale heli-drone in the RMAX, but this later model, the Fazer, could fly 90 kilometers, had satellite commo, and carried double the payload. His Army contact at Aberdeen Proving Ground had furnished the Fazer and the TrackingPoint sniping system from a couple of projects there. Not even black projects. Projects with budget lines open to Congressional review. Projects with slight inaccuracies in their equipment inventories, which were monitored by

Tom's contact, who was a decorated soldier, a respected scientist at the Army Research Laboratory, and a father.

The Proving Ground had been one of the cradles of computation. ENIAC, he thought it was ENIAC, had been installed there, brought into being to assist that classically mathematical artilleryman's art, the prediction of the paths of unpowered projectiles, ballistics. The Proving Ground was still a center for computation. Tom and his new contact had walked through a much newer supercomputer there, literally walked aisleways between racks of processors, when Tom had visited to present his proposition.

He had of course first thing expressed his sincere sorrow for the man's loss of his daughter. Tom's talent for languages and cryptanalysis suited him for intelligence work. A still greater talent allowed him to read a man's dossier, look into his face, and know what the man needed. A psychologist once said he could see microexpressions, the quarter-second when a man's thoughts molded his face, the person all unaware.

The scientist, pausing before a rack of circuit boards, had worn a plea across his face, plain to Tom's perception. The men spoke of things that he knew not to bring up with William, whose face remained closed, resolute.

At Aberdeen, they spoke of loss and the lesson it taught. How hatred was not the opposite of love. Indifference was the opposite of love. How this realization allowed putting aside hot anger, focusing energy into cold purpose. Tom offered his new contact a way out of his vacillation between rage and fear, a way to focus on the possible. Tom offered the opportunity to change the world, one sociopath at a time.

The man had reached out and gripped the inside of his forearm. Tom closed his own hand in the same grip, and they stood for a long moment. Then they talked possibilities, spoke of hardware.

Tom was still impressed with the automated sniper tech. William found the gun easy to integrate into the Fazer, everything tied together through satcomm, and the ShotView iPhone app was just funny. It allowed for all the atmospheric conditions, range, Coriolis forces from the rotation of the Earth, even drift from bullet spin.

He said, "Love that image stabilization. And the control dampers help a lot with aiming. We have to try out the night scope next. Death from the darkness."

William nodded, swaying his mane of straight black hair. "It will be my great pleasure."

He had built the custom control consoles that communicated with the Fazer and with the trigger actuator, which he had also built. Along with the mounting, that was all that was required to integrate the sniper rifle and optics to the helicopter. It was a great system, if you wanted to look through a soda straw and hit one target at a time. He wanted to target the entire swarm of maggots who called themselves Dawgz. He needed an area weapon.

"I have something in mind a little more lethal," he said.

Tom didn't hesitate. "Draw it up. And maybe you would like to start flight school. Learn to fly a Cessna or Piper or some such. Think about Navy ROTC. I can arrange a scholarship. You're planning a tech major, right?"

William said, solemn as always, "I'm planning to be a trigger-puller. The bigger the bang the better."

Chapter 16 - Declaration of War

"Galvanized people do careless things. ... Rage has its place, but actions must be taken with discipline and thought."

George Friedman
The Next 100 Years

"Tom, you will not be surprised to learn that you are being watched," Juana said.

Tom was in his favorite workwear, cotton polo and Dockers, trail runners propped up on the desk. "I'm the watcher. If anyone is looking, I'm looking back," said Tom.

"This is us, Tom. We know about Chicago. That bar burned, along with a dozen motorcycles. There were some smoke inhalation injuries," she said.

He said, "Thanks for the information. I don't have a contact in the People's Democratic Republic of Chicago. Their police operate under very close scrutiny, very heavy restraint. The journalists tell the city government whom to prosecute. Often it's a cop. There is selective enforcement of weapons laws. A lot of gang-bangers walk on weapons charges."

She said, "Well the bikers had to walk. Or wait, anyway, for their buddies to show up to give them rides. The Dawgz are of course under sporadic surveillance and occasional attempts at penetration of their membership."

She went on, "Perhaps you know about the member who got thoroughly penetrated more recently? Outside Morris, Illinois, at a shack on the Mazon River."

Tom's heart skipped. She had looked into that pit whose existence he denied even to himself. He did not look back to such things and so it was as if they had never happened. He took some time, head bent, palm to mouth. Then he said, "Juana, I won't keep anything from you that you need to know."

"This is more about what you need to know, Tom. Shootings and fires draw attention."

"So you would like to request a moratorium on shitbag cleanup? You're uncomfortable about the Posse Comitatus Act?"

He hoped she would be satisfied with that. Juana could do him in, in a number of ways. He could feel the sweat leap out of him, his breathing all at once quickened, his pulse filling his chest.

"No, I would like to request a hit," she said. "On the whole gang. Those bikers peddle hard drugs. I want to roll up their network. Scout them out, hunt them down, and end them."

It was not like Tom to fall silent with her. Their talks always ran along expected lines. Outrageous, highly irregular requests for the development, or reassignment, or straight-up theft of black-ops hardware, but always within the anti-terror objectives for which she had signed on.

The shock of her statement faded, having added only marginally to his stress level. She seemed to accept and even approve what he had done. It made sense that the High Command could deal with the Dawgz, men who advertised their criminality on their backs, as the DEA could not, with extrajudicial executions.

His shoulders dropped and he rolled his neck, relaxing muscles. "If it is in my power, it will be my pleasure. We'll talk."

Chapter 17 - Star City

"It's only fourteen big houses."

Sergey Volkov

There was a letdown after the high-caliber excitement of gunnery training. It seemed like Jimmy was always on the phone. The latest call was from a woman named Jenny who claimed to be a friend of Tom's.

She said, "You'll get a chance to work on your Russian in an immersive environment."

And then they had flown him to Star City. Most of Star City was the Gagarin Research and Test Cosmonaut Training Center. It lay by the military airport twenty miles northeast of Moscow. He went through no customs or immigration procedures. A forty-something Russian named Polya awaited him, with the thick-necked younger Vladislav in tow.

They drove by the comfortable duplexes built by NASA. As many Americans trained at Gagarin as Russians. About a hundred flew aboard the Russian Soyuz.

Polya told him, grating out the English, "At first we leased dormitory to American astronauts. And staff. Americans threatened to call SPCA if dogs were ever kept in dorms. Then NASA built own dorms."

Vlad said nothing.

The grounds were quiet, woods surrounding buildings of Soviet vintage, but security was more like NASA's. Clumps of teens strolled the hallways on field trips, clambering into *Mir* mockups.

Jimmy lived in the Russian quarters, and took his meals with Russians. He guessed that the arrangement had more to do with Polya being the local High

Command contact than with acclimating him to the language and customs. He picked up some street hustler chess, enough to keep from being blown off the board, but refused to join the drinking sessions, which seemed obligatory for the Russians.

The best training on offer was in a Soyuz simulator. It was not a mockup Rock, but its operation required all the orbital piloting arts, ascent, rendezvous, docking with the ISS, undocking, and de-orbiting.

He and Vlad endured twelve hour sessions, focusing on spacecraft systems, status monitoring, commo, and all the flight stages. Vlad reminded him of the cowboy in Lonesome Dove, wanting to avoid unnecessary conversation.

Jimmy sought to avoid unnecessary physics lectures, after a nice old fellow had nearly knocked him unconscious with, 'A Langmuir Probe is a small electrode immersed in plasma, connected to a large surface area conductor in contact with the plasma, from whose current-voltage characteristics are derived plasma parameters.'

Jimmy knew that he would see a plasma envelope around his craft when he dropped it into re-entry. If it went bright white he would not have time to admire a detector's current-voltage response.

The ISS simulator was just virtual reality models of the station interior. Jimmy needed scant knowledge of station operations, which were reserved to a crew of six astronauts sequestered in a module separate from the interceptor pilots, their mission highly classified.

No one had constructed a full-up trainer for the Smart Rock nuclear ramjet interceptor that he would fly. He made do with a mockup of the control interface, which consisted of the switch-laden armrests of an acceleration couch and a headsup display. Banks of switches were the way you ran a warplane, and with these he practiced compulsively, surprising Polya with off-hours access requests.

He and Polya would talk, except about the newly compartmentalized ISS main crew. He seemed to know a lot about the Rocks, even though they were CIA black-budget hardware. He certainly knew a lot more aeronautics than Jimmy.

Polya thought it important to play slideshows of the spacecraft they might run across in low Earth orbit. One day a menagerie of satellites scrolled across the screen. The next, it was all upper stages, the final boosters which did exatmospheric positioning. There were old U.S. Agena boosters with optical spysats attached, Iranian third stages which were nothing more than thinly disguised ICBMs, Japanese and even Chinese vehicles. All had similar configurations, the cylindrical upper stage ending in a larger bulb-like cargo fairing, as if parallel tracks of technological evolution had converged on a geometrically idealized penis as the optimal form for entering outer space.

It was a welcome diversion when with Vlad he boarded a big Ilyushin 76, which operated out of the neighboring airfield. The pilot flew parabolic trajectories inducing thirty second exposures to weightlessness. Jimmy bounced around and somersaulted in the brief zero gee, avoiding plumes of vomit from space tourists who had paid for the ride. Taxiing back home from the runway gave him a look at the Antonovs which also used the field. They dwarfed the Ilyushin.

Immersed in the hydro lab, he practiced EVA skills. They did not centrifuge him. He had pulled gees for his entire career in an F-14. Astronauts trained here for years before their missions, but Jimmy and Vlad spent just two months at Star City. The High Command was in a hurry.

Chapter 18 - Street Evangelist

"... and a lone farting Harley carrying a fat gray-haired jerk in leathers. Reacher was offended by the noise and gave the guy the finger. The bike slowed and for a delicious moment Reacher thought the guy was going to stop and make an issue out of it. But, no luck. The guy took one look and twisted the throttle and took off again, fast."

Lee Child
Bad Luck and Trouble, a Jack Reacher novel

Tom stepped from his car, a black late-model M2 from BMW, all the while watching where he put his shoe. A condom or syringe crushed beneath the sole would leave a nasty residue.

Juana had asked that he be here, at this address in this street that functioned for the city very like a lower intestine, leaching the last usefulness from those

40

who soon would be dropped into nothingness. Black trodden wads of chewing gum dotted the cracked sidewalk. The old-style dark red bricks of the buildings looked tired, their edges rounded by weather and time. This was a street for addicts and hookers, forced by need or just plain forced, trudging along, lingering, searching or waiting for someone who would prey upon them.

Tom was in tan L.L. Bean hiking pants, the nylon ones with the zippered cargo pocket. He wore a light blue overshirt left unbuttoned over a dark blue UnderArmor polo. Shutting the door of the gleaming low-slung sedan, he looked like a suburban dad in a credit union commercial.

Juana wanted him here to track the supply lines of local drug sales back to the Dawgz MC, Baltimore. She wasn't working with the DEA. She wanted the club located and its members done in. He had come at the first opportunity, because Juana was the best contact he had. And because her request sounded a harmony with his deepest desire. After his initial blank shock, sweet delight had flooded him when he realized what she wanted. And he had some time. The office had been calmer of late. No one was shooting at the ISS.

As he walked along the curb he absently patted his favorite pistol, a slab-sided nine millimeter autoloader built to the plan of John Browning's classic Model 1911, nestled at his right hipbone out of sight beneath the loose overshirt. Ahead a quartet of young whores gathered to block the sidewalk, their eyes wide with some chemical, a couple jawing at wads of gum. It hurt to see the young flesh gone slack, faces and breasts and buttocks sagging too soon, the faux thinness of wasted limbs.

It was mid-afternoon, before rush hour and not so late that the highly intoxicated would be thick on the ground. The street women, presumably they were women, were of course importunate, but three left when he asked if they could recommend a good storefront location for his planned Christian outreach mission. It would be for a local Baptist congregation. The last hooker lingered, hooking her thumbs into white leather hot pants just at her hipbones and easing them lower to expose more of her slack belly, thinking her lure stronger than his faith. She shook her head and smirked when he asked would she like some literature, or to hear the message of the Gospel.

A black pickup truck announced its approach several blocks away. Roaring up the street, it jerked to a stop straddling the centerline paint stripe, directly opposite where Tom stood at the curb. The young sloven turned and walked away, rapidly, head down, drawing his eye to the bare orbs peeking from her hot pants. He grimaced as the loose flesh creased and jiggled.

The huge diesel 4x4 was the kind usually having high ground clearance, but this one's glossy black body rode low, on low-profile tires and oversize wheels with spinning chrome rims. He stood wondering which culture was appropriating which. The driver glanced at him and curled her lip below a long nose. A hot pink 'Bitch I Know You Know' gimme cap sat just above her thin penciled brows.

A black Harley, with the familiar gray-ponytailed thickbellied biker hanging on the bars, thundered up from the opposite direction. A Dawg. World champion lawn dwarf. The biker stopped in the traffic lane directly between the truck and Tom, putting a foot down.

The biker-gnome reached up a package the size of a pair of bricks, wrapped in duct tape. The woman handed down a flat one, the size of a paperback book, in white paper. There was a twinge just below Tom's navel, then a wave of heat came up from his guts, clear up to his head, suddenly tight to bursting.

Tom said, to the surprise of a passing pair of women in leather lingerie, "Now, is that any way to do a dope deal?"

From somewhere outside himself, he watched as he strode across the asphalt over to the bike. He brushed back the overshirt from his right side and the nine millimeter flowed from his hip to his hand and into the low ready position just at his belt buckle, two handed grip, muzzle leveled and forward. As he approached the Harley, the biker raised his left hand, pointing at Tom. Tom said nothing. He raised the pistol in his right hand, brushed down the biker's pointing hand and arm with his left, and clubbed the Dawg across the bridge of the nose with the butt of the pistol. The biker fell back with his free hand on his face. Tom leaned over the front tire of the Harley and extended the nine through the window of the pickup. The driver turned her head away as she reached for the gearshift. Tom fired a contact shot, muzzle to temple, into her head.

The Dawg had regained his seat, and shoved him aside. He cranked the throttle and the Harley burst into raucous life and shot forward. Tom thrust both arms out to level the nine at the biker's thick back, front sight just at the center of the bright pitbull patch on the black vest, but the gun's slide had not

42

gone back into battery, had not locked up behind the fresh cartridge to seal the chamber after the contact shot. It didn't even click when he pulled the limp trigger.

Still watching himself, he was pleased that his left hand grasped the top of the pistol, thumb pointing back, and racked the slide. An unfired round ejected to the right, and the slide shot forward properly, chambering another round from the magazine. As he got his finger back on the trigger he had time to be pleased, as well, that the biker did not appear to be carrying, or had panicked and forgotten to pull. He had gone cold again. That was better.

The biker accelerated hard, the fat back tire fishtailing and the straight-through exhaust pipe bellowing its huge mechanical flatulence. It was this fishtailing which caused Tom's next round, fired from a two-handed grip and fully extended arms, to miss the spine and thoracic triangle as the Harley barreled away down the street. A fireball appeared and vanished at the muzzle of the nine, the spent casing spun lazily out to the right and a shockwave ran out over black leather from where the Dawg took the round through the right shoulder blade. The bike wobbled, then made a left at the corner, and Tom realized he would make another left at the next corner to get onto the busy one-way street which led out of the neighborhood to the freeway.

He holstered the semiauto and opened the door of the pickup. He hit the seat belt release and pulled out the woman's lanky corpse, stepping back as it fell to avoid the bloody ragged ruined head. The headband of the bloodstained pink cap had been blasted through, and it fell free as the woman's torso hit pavement.

Tom sat in a small pool of blood. White bone shards, blood, and gray brain matter spattered the passenger seat, side door, and window. He took just an extra couple instants to belt up, letting out slack in the seat belt where the slim-hipped driver had fit. The big diesel was still throbbing, and the resonator built into the exhaust system roared as Tom dropped it into gear and tromped it.

Tom kept the pedal down and thundered away down the street in the direction opposite that the biker had taken. The calm reflection came to him that this was a vehicle built to annoy, to sneer, to dare the world to object. He ran the light at the next intersection, ignored a stop sign at the next, and drifted around a right turn at the end of the third block, tense and half expecting the hard-heeling truck to roll. A second hard right put him on the big one-way, accelerating onto the busy street in the wrong direction.

The Harley came juking through cars and small trucks, all coming at Tom. He swerved the big truck hard across the horn-blaring, tire-screaming vehicles, and the Dawg had no time to slow as a massive silver grille appeared in his path. The bike's impact with the pickup threw Tom's face into the airbag suddenly there in front of him. Blinded, Tom hit the brake, then fell back into the seat after the truck skidded to a stop. Another weirdly analytical thought came, telling him the smoke clouding the cab came from the airbag propellant and he need not fear that the truck had taken fire. He opened the door, lunged against the belt, remembered to pop the buckle, and stepped out.

The bike had struck just left of center and crumpled rather than flipping up. The Dawg ended up on his back when he peeled off the hood and tumbled to the street. His limbs bent in too many places, making him look like a disorganized swastika on the hot black asphalt. Tom lifted the nine millimeter from his hip, holding it low along his leg, and walked over to stand beside the lopsided torso. He bent and clamped his left hand over the pulpy nose and ruined mouth.

A moment of hot anger shot through him. He had been so lucky, and helped by so many, yet had acted on impulse, had not stepped back to think. Then he accepted that he was committing a broad daylight double murder and felt the cold again within him. Each of the pebbles in the asphalt, their outlines softened by their coating of tar and all precisely leveled by the steamroller, rainbows cast from shards of glass from the Harley's headlight, shiny highlights on the bright red drops of blood on the biker's tangled beard and his flattened nose, the purple blood pooling beneath the skin under his eyes, the fat cheeks bulging out around his left hand, all came into sharp focus.

The Dawg's eyes popped open. He tried to pitch his head up, his gaze wide-eyed and unseeing in his ruined face. Suction pulled at Tom's palm as he strained to inhale through blocked air passages. Tom kept the pressure on, but the Dawg was suffering in pure animal panic and that wasn't good enough.

Tom shook the biker's head, leaning closer, pressing harder. When the biker looked at him he said in a hoarse whisper, "If you want to look into the face of Satan, I know where to find him."

The dying fat man met his gaze, a look rich in primal knowledge, a man falling into darkness to an unimaginable end. The Dawg's eyes remained locked on Tom's until they lost focus and the face went slack.

On the sidewalk thin, drab junkies mingled with gaudy near-nude whores, all gathered for a gape, Tom saying shit when some crowded forward into the street and raised phones.

Tom turned to conceal the movement as he holstered the nine. He had no conscious intent to keep the gawkers at bay or to distract them, only that odd sense of watching the action as he stepped to the crumpled Harley and bent as though he would right it, instead grabbing fuel lines and ripping them from underneath the shiny teardrop tank.

Circling back behind the truck, he slipped off his light blue overshirt. Tying its arms about his waist made a sort of skirt to hide his bloody backside and the nine, his upper body now dark blue. Cars continued to move by, slowing and some stopping for a good long look. The spreading puddle of gasoline from the crushed Harley had reached the pickup.

Tom drew an old-fashioned Zippo from his left pants pocket, thumbed it, and stepped quickly forward to toss it underhand. He turned away, hearing the same huge *whoosh* he had heard in the alley but not seeing the gasoline ignite. Waiting an instant for the first startled shouts from the crowd, he joined them as they pushed and elbowed one another fleeing for the sidewalk.

A couple dope or pussy merchants in designer sweats slunk away, wary of further gang violence and certain of the coming cop trouble. Tom walked steadily after them to the end of the block, back the way he had come in the pickup, wanting to swivel his head but looking forward, pausing only at the corner of a building to glance back. The gaggle of onlookers still stared into the flames licking up around the crashed vehicles.

Tom ducked past the building's corner, out of sight. He wanted to be gone before a gas tank blew. He wanted to change his bloody trousers, to clean his bloody hands. A clear idea came of the tub of sanitary wipes kept on the back seat of his car.

Chapter 19 - LEO Arrival

Two things are different than being on Earth.
One is that everything is floating.
The other is you can look out the window and see Earth.

Tom Akers

Before it docks, the Soyuz capsule flies a ballet, circling the International Space Station while pirouetting to point at it. A forward-looking periscope displayed the station on the gray control panel directly in front of Jimmy. The ISS looked fragile as a dragonfly, with gossamer brown wings of solar panels stretched out on either side of a lumpy line of cylindrical white habitation modules.

When the radar picture was right, with the Soyuz pointed at the brightly lit docking cone at the free end of a hab module, the autopilot began closing the distance to the station.

To Spaceside, three sleek white shark bodies nestled up to the fat white hab like piglets at a sow. Atop each, a single shallow transparent blister sealed a cockpit. Further back, nearly to the black bell of the nozzle, the stubby suggestion of a delta wing bulged out. A rounded nose made them look like rockets, like missiles, except that each had a large inlet duct, a ramscoop, running along its belly. It made the interceptor look like an ICBM carrying a stallion's wedding tackle, a phallic symbol with a phallus.

The Soyuz capsule had small portholes to port and starboard lying slightly behind the crew's heads. Crammed shoulder-to-shoulder into the capsule between two dour Russians, it wasn't easy to crane his neck far enough to get a view out the port, but Jimmy got a glimpse down the black throat of one of the ramjets, just before the bright white cylinder of the module occulted it.

The ramjet's fuselage looked grayish just aft of the ramscoop, the open end of the intake duct, shading into white further back. On closer approach, the gray area showed many score marks in the paint where long streamers of molten ceramic had trailed back. Ablation scars.

"The training didn't mention getting that deep into atmosphere." Jimmy muttered.

Vlad and Polya were silent.

46

"In fact, none of the sims included flight profiles that might severely ablate throat linings."

Polya, he was the older of the Russians, shrugged, jostling them. "And ISS images never show ramjets at all, yes?"

"Well, yeah, but that's for the public, and the Rocks are classified. But the training, hell the classified orientation videos, never mentioned that scoop temperatures could melt your ceramic off."

Polya wasn't done hazing him. "So you Americans operate on need to know, yes? Now you know. And you best keep in mind."

"Not that this is about countries, but I will. Here's a Russian question. So why do you have a feminine name?"

Polya shrugged again, jostling Jimmy again with muscular shoulders further thickened by a layer of suet. Jimmy was glad they wore the new Boeing-blue suits, less bulky than the orange ascent/re-entry suits traditional at NASA.

Polya rumbled like gravel tumbling down a steel chute. "My father was mathematics fan. You could look it up. Polya. You might even find in English-language source. And you can thank me later for ride on fifty year old Soviet rocket."

"You ready to dock?" Jimmy had the center seat with the periscope view and manual docking controls. "We don't wanna use that thirty year old Soviet automated docking system, right? I mean, you remember the supply capsule impacts on Mir?"

Polya turned to look directly at him. A few deep black curls poked into view near the top of his faceplate. Polya had what Jimmy had come to think of as Russian eyes, eyes of slate gray with the distressed flesh below which spoke of habitual, perhaps unconscious, sadness. Or maybe just of vodka.

"Dock, then," he grated.

Neither of them mentioned the long and honorable tradition of mangling and incinerating the astronauts and test pilots of both nations.

Jimmy had not been present at either the Gagarin center or at Baikonur in any official sense, but he had lived with the Russian cosmonauts training at the Gagarin center, and also at Baikonur where the rockets went up. He was not an astronaut, and his companions were not cosmonauts. Neither NASA nor Roscosmos carried them on a roster. None of them had the bright, all-systems-go photo-op positivity of the astronaut corps. They were not holders of advanced degrees in the sciences, nor highly decorated aces, nor test pilots with thousands of hours in experimental aircraft. They were skilled pilots. They were unattached, anonymous, deniable, and willing to accept risk.

Polya had shepherded Vlad and Jimmy through the Russian training, and seemed to have some prior connection with Vlad, who often looked to the older Russian for a nod or a *nyet*. Jimmy recognized them as ex-military pilots like himself, but more, as combat veterans, unconsciously fraternal and exclusionary. Where Polya was hard-bitten, stern in speech and gaze, Vlad was relaxed, and sometimes smiling, but seemed incurious, and rarely spoke. He followed Polya's suggestions without hesitation. Of the two, Vlad was scarier.

Jimmy had some Russian now, more than he used. And a very little of their culture. He had the idea that it was very Russian to die in large numbers. One hundred and fifty had died at a single launch at Baikonur, not long after Sputnik.

Jimmy jockeyed about with the two joysticks, watching the docking cameras. Propellant hissed from attitude thrusters, then translation thrusters. With a nudge and a *thud* a clamp retracted to lock the Soyuz onto a docking port of the International Space Station.

They had attached at the end of *Columbus*, a smaller habitat module lying at right angles to the main line of larger cylinders. The Soyuz clung like a bud at the tip of a twig, and the string of modules wobbled and they with it until the oscillation damped out over a few seconds.

The hatch undogged with a faint hiss and a popping of their ears, and they punched harness quick releases and floated off their acceleration couches, as far as they could float within the very tight capsule.

Polya smiled, eyes framed in crinkles. "Not bad. Maybe you are competent switch. But Soyuz is of course fine Russian spacecraft."

"Thanks, Mr. Chekov." Jimmy wondered if he would get the ancient Trekkie reference.

Polya had called him a "switch", not in insult but in sardonic recognition of a Rock pilot's function. The control panel of a military aircraft or spacecraft carried a number of dials and displays, but also a great number of switches. Even the walls and portions of the cockpit floor were covered with double- and single-throw toggles, detent buttons, sliders, and rotary dials. The pilot's first task in mission prep was to set switches that governed the behavior of additional switches, and so on. During a mission, his function, as man-in-the-control-loop, was that of the highest level logic junction, himself settable by orders through the commlink. He was a switch.

Polya had still said nothing. Jimmy said, "I just didn't wanna be the first bounce-off."

They had to slide feet first one by one into the orbital module, the portion of the Soyuz ahead of their capsule, and then through the narrow hatch into the ISS habitation cylinder.

The flat white fronts of refrigerator-sized payload racks made up the interior of the *Columbus* module so that the spaceside, Earthside, north, and south walls were white and flat and met at right angles. The space spanned perhaps ten feet in width and height and about twice that between the end bulkheads, like a long narrow living room.

Several raw-looking rectangular gaps where payload racks of science gear had been removed provided storage. Three gaps in the Earthside wall were curtained off with green fabric as sleeping spaces.

A curtained toilet interrupted the north wall near where their Soyuz had docked. The toilet did not bear thinking about yet. They were not expected to shower.

Jimmy pressed his fingertips against a wall. Slick. Hard. Not healthful if a collision with a Soyuz or a missile impact shook them about like dice in a cup.

Jimmy torqued off his helmet and got his first whiff of the thick pong of the ISS. He sniffed again and said, "God, primates are such filthy animals."

He had never felt seasick and wasn't squeamish. But you could cut this atmosphere with a knife, and spread it on bread if you really wanted to sick up. He imagined skin cells, dandruff, tiny urine droplets, and fecal flakes all riding his inhales. Nausea pierced his belly. His mind ran away a bit. Scrotal skin cells. Russian fecal flakes. Damn. And sweat. Sweat droplets float in microgee.

He said, "So the official maximum ISS crew is six. No chance of upgrading the filtration to handle the twelve of us? This is making me want to hurl."

"As much chance you put out press release on mission." This from Vlad, who had not spoken since before liftoff. "Maybe drink of water helps stomach."

Jimmy tried not to think about the fluid recycling system. Or about spending ninety days with Vlad and Polya for company, rarely seeing the other platoon of three switches, and never the ISS "civilian" crew, the silent six.

Jimmy also tried not to think about how space sickness, a sometimes persistent nausea, usually started on day two.

He blew out a deep breath. "So, when's dinner?"

Chapter 20 - Confessional

"The problem with quotes on the Internet is that it is hard to verify their authenticity."

Abraham Lincoln

Tom sat mousing, typing, scrolling text.

Jenny said, "You can ask for help." She had walked in again without knocking.

Tom looked up, said, "It's my screw-up. I'll scrub it. Me and the NSA."

He was searching NSA ELINT archives and setting up targets for disinformation on YouTube and FarceBook, diffusing software agents through the net like a campaign worker leafleting windshields at a mall parking lot. Contacts at Twitter had been onboard with the NSA for years, so nothing would see the light of day there. The more general daemons to scan for keywords and scrub sites were next. There would be unexpected server failures, impossible failures of redundant disk drives.

"Not my subject matter," Jenny said. "It's a relief you have the NSA folks at your back. At least some of them."

Then she said, "Have you called Juana? Would you like to let me sit in on that? This concerns all of us. Not just here, but the whole network."

Tom picked up his iPhone. "Hey Siri, call Juana Abreu." He hit the icon for the speaker and pointed at the guest chair to his left.

Juana picked up on ring three. "Ready to talk about it?"

Tom hit the iEncrypt icon, "Yeah, the covert role will not work for me anymore. You wanted a recce so you could plan a hit. What you got was an aborted recce and an unplanned hit."

"True, that wasn't the hit I wanted. I wanted to know where that Dawg was taking that package. That was the hit I wanted. And yes, I know I'm not DEA. I'm also not the type to run with drug smugglers. That's a CIA tactic," said Juana.

Tom winced, but said nothing. She was right.

"Tom, would you like to let William take over the scouting? He can be the cutout. You don't need to know who he recruits to locate the one-percenters."

"William can do it. He doesn't need me. He knows that," said Tom.

"I want to stay with this, Tom. I'll put William onto the Army guys at Aberdeen. They're good for the hardware, and I'm good for black budget lines."

"No argument here. Target them where they cluster. We want to avoid petty street fights," said Tom. He asked nothing about the ugliness she must have endured to drive her to such a pursuit of the bikers.

Jenny cut in, "I saw some of the uploaded vids from Baltimore. It would have made a pretty good rap video."

"OK, no more domestic field missions for me," said Tom.

Juana said, "I also think it's time to branch out into other gangs."

There was a pause, then Tom said, "It's good to move this into the professional realm. I enjoyed Dawg hunting, but it *is* getting to be a distraction."

Juana said, "It's in motion. I'm happy we have a source in the Baltimore police. You don't know her, which also makes me happy. William doesn't know her yet. Her information is that the woman in the truck, the one whose mind you opened, was management. She was two jumps up from the street-level dope runners. Most of the gangs have a very flat management structure so that's pretty close to the top."

"We can't stop the drugs or the whores. Too embedded with the locals," said Tom. "But she wasn't exactly collateral damage, more like a twofer."

Juana said, "We could target the street bangers' leadership, like you SpecOps SAD guys in Afghanistan, offing Taliban commanders."

"William's working on an approach that's more agricultural than surgical," he said.

Siri said, "NRO calling."

He said, "Be well, Juana. The big eyeballs are calling."

Chapter 21 - To Business

"In the Troopers, it's always Bowb Your Buddy Week."

Bill, the Galactic Hero

Jimmy awoke refreshed. Sleeping weightless was apparently no problem for him, despite the fluid swelling his face and filling his sinus cavities. A light net of black bungee cords kept his arms close and kept him snugged to a thin gray pad. A dull green curtain blocked the gap in the wall that led to his sleep space. He lay thinking and drowsing.

Dinner had not been so bad. A food cache and potable water tap lay near the suit storage at the hab's inboard end. The food cache was just dehydrated meal packets loosely held in a bungee net. The Russians served the same dehydrated fare sampled in training, plus NASA's famous freeze-dried ice cream, though he did not like having that much sugar.

The evening, that is to say the orbits apportioned to downtime, had passed without much further discussion. The three switches had stowed their gear and clothing, mostly shorts and tee shirts. In their sleep spaces they spread their pads, strung sleeping nets, and brought the lights down. Jimmy drew his curtain.

The Russians stayed up for some minutes longer while Polya murmured to Vlad, perhaps to avoid disturbing Jimmy, or perhaps so he would not overhear. Vlad still said next to nothing.

After Polya fell silent, there sounded an occasional high-pitched hiss. The ISS kept constant orientation with respect to the Earth by spinning the reaction wheels of large gyroscopes, which were noiseless, but as well as by bursts of propellant hissing from attitude thrusters.

Orientation control kept the ramjet interceptors behind the station and out of Earth view, justifying the propellant expenditure. A Rock looked like nothing but a weapon, its engine and ramscoop dwarfing the transparent blister tacked on at the cockpit.

The station was never entirely silent. Fans kept air moving through the oxygen regenerators with a constant susurration. Jimmy fell asleep to an intermittent rumble carried through the hull as the station's solar panels continually sought the light, grinding slowly around on bearings whose diameters spanned the entire width of the main truss.

Polya rapped on the wall beside the curtain. "Knock knock. Wakey!"

Too chipper for Jimmy. Probably deliberately so. He asked, "So is the Eggs Benedict ready?"

Neither spoke further, thinking of the slime that rehydrating Eggs Benedict would produce. Searching through the heap of packets produced curds and nuts, which were surprisingly good, though the two men argued about whether the curds were cottage cheese or the Russian *tvorog*. The instant coffee was dishwater with a hint of insecticide, but the Russians had a smoky fresh-brewed black tea with a pleasant bite.

The switches had the converted laboratory module to themselves. Firmly to themselves. The hatch at the inboard end, at the attachment to the main ISS hab cylinder *Destiny*, had tack welds spaced along the seal. The hatch window had a tack welded cover.

On the north wall, the panel at Jimmy's work area had an array of telltales glowing green, amber, or red, showing the status of the systems and components of his Rock. Camera images tiled a large flatscreen, giving views of Earth, of the posigrade and retrograde horizons, and of the Rocks guyed to the outer spaceside wall of their module. He had been assigned Number 3, an interceptor that showed, more than the other two, dull gray ablation stains trailing aft from the ram scoop inlet.

Jimmy keyed in requests for updates, and text scrolled up a window. Auxiliary propellant tank topped up, its air pressure nominal. Attitude thruster valves functional. Battery power, nav, engine control, and armament computers all nominal. Reactor shut down.

Polya looked over his shoulder. "Three has seen action. Throat lining is not what was."

Jimmy frowned. "Funny that it ended up at my station."

"Well, American Rocks have had maintenance and availability issues."

"So how's your Rock?"

"Number 1 is OK. Vlad has problem. He will EVA after lunch. Look at valve."

Lunch was borscht and potatoes. Jimmy liked the borscht, even though he could never hold a chunk of boiled beet in his mouth, much less chew or swallow it. He worried about the potatoes. Farts were flammable. Farts lingered. Farts on the ISS were a danger to international cooperation and even world peace.

Hardsuits took up most of a storage space across from the food cache, spooned one to the next like white plastic fat men. Vlad spent nearly an hour in

54

his suit, checking electronics, scrubber, oxygen tank, thrusters. Hardsuits were more single-man spaceship than suit, especially when the propulsion backpack was attached. They would use hardsuits for exterior maintenance on the Rocks.

The Boeing blue softsuits were less robust pressure suits and would be worn when piloting the cramped Rocks. Any serious problem after dropping a Rock would likely produce a plasma cloud, rendering suit selection irrelevant.

During their sleep period, the Soyuz had been undocked from their airlock module. Polya keyed the inner hatch button, undogged the mechanism, and swung it open. Vlad slid feet first into the lock tunnel. Polya swung the door shut, dogged it, keyed something into the electronic panel, and struck twice with the side of his fist. Two thumps answered. Soon a whistle vibrated through *Columbus's* walls as atmosphere streamed out of the lock.

Jimmy returned to his work panel and looked up the location of the propellant valve that Vlad would replace on his Rock, Number 2. Then he glanced up from the schematic when motion showed in the camview overlooking his own Rock, Number 3. A gauntleted hand held a power wrench to the fasteners of a fairing. It was the fairing over the propellant lines, where Vlad's Number 2 had malfed.

"Polya, your boy is opening up my Rock!"

"Oh? He is confused." Polya keyed his headset to the EVA freq. "Vlad, you are Number 2 Rock this mission."

Vlad keyed his mic twice to acknowledge. But the telltale for the Number 3 Rock's propellant system go red. Jimmy's Rock, his ride, showed red. It stayed red as Vlad buttoned up the fairing and moved over to Number 2.

Jimmy jumped down the module to the suits and began levering himself into the rigid plastic.

Polya said, "No. You do not need to do. We straighten out when Vlad is back."

Polya was the platoon leader. Jimmy torqued off the hardsuit gauntlets and squirmed out of the suit torso. His insides began to cook, but he said nothing, floating near that end of the cylinder. Polya continued to scroll through layers on his flatscreen. Surely they knew he was a Navy pilot, a carrier pilot. Jimmy thought it over.

His knowledge of the chain of command above Polya was limited to the spook who had recruited him, and Jimmy had not heard from that guy for months. The training and the Soyuz ride to the ISS had been as promised. It had also been promised that neither his death nor his survival would be noted by any government. There were no military regulations, and no personnel departments or inspector generals to take an interest. He was on his own here.

Neither of these guys was well known to him. They were helicopter guys, attack pilots, but they might also be special ops. Vlad was a hard looking guy, maybe had some *sambo* training. The Japanese had handed the Russians their bloody buttcheeks in 1905. The Russians had taken from the fight only a respect for Jiu Jitsu and Judo. Mix with wrestling and brawling and you have *sambo*. So it could get ugly.

But it was already ugly and Jimmy had an inop ride. Jimmy had flown F-14s off carriers over a long Navy career. Complex supersonic fighter jets suffered component failures, carriers operated far from parts depots, and it often happened that three jets were kept flying by cannibalizing a fourth, usually the ride of the squadron's most junior, or least liked, anyway least respected pilot. Jimmy had learned. Respect is given to avoid the consequences of withholding it. Hell, if he was unhappy everybody was gonna be unhappy.

After nearly an hour's EVA, Vlad locked in. The telltales on his Number 2 panel all showed green. Jimmy waited until Vlad crawled from the torso of his suit. Pushing off from the spaceside wall, he cocked his right fist near his chin, and Vlad raised his left arm to ward him off. Jimmy slid the blade of his left hand down the outside of Vlad's arm, deflecting the arm inward, and then delivered a right cross to Vlad's left cheekbone. As the two rebounded apart, Vlad grinned, a thin-lipped slash between Tartar cheekbones and thick neck.

Now Vlad pushed off and drifted near where Jimmy hung in the middle of the hab. He caught Jimmy's side kick, and then it was like a man-sized cat was scrambling up his body, taking powerful grips on clothes, limbs, and loose flesh. He got onto Jimmy's back, hooked a leg around his waist, and locked the other knee over his own ankle. The leg lock tightened until Jimmy struggled to take breath.

A forearm snaked under his chin but Jimmy peeled off the choke by gripping the little finger side of Vlad's hand and torqueing, hoping to snap a finger. Then his left ear detonated as Vlad slammed a palm over it. This time the forearm got under his jaw. Vlad locked the choke in, wrapping the crook of his opposite elbow around his wrist, and the pressure on Jimmy's jugular vein trapped blood in his brain, making his head feel like a pimple about to burst. Then the carotids, under equal pressure, shut down their blood supply, and darkness crept into the edges of Jimmy's vision and closed in. Goddamn *sambo*.

Chapter 22 - But I Insist

> ... *those principal traits that make up the strength of the Russian, simplicity and stubbornness.*
>
> *Leo Tolstoy*

Jimmy awoke for the second time on the ISS. He did not feel refreshed. His head pounded and his ribs ached.

Polya was at the curtain again. "Congratulations. You landed blow on *Spetsnaz*."

"What is he? Federal Security Service? Airborne?"

Polya sighed, "That would be telling."

"So the American availability issues are diagnosed. Vlad has my valve."

"You will get one through resupply. I want Vlad to fly first intercept."

Jimmy pushed him away, his hand over Polya's face. He did not have to look far to find Vlad's wide-cheeked grin.

This time Vlad caught the right cross before Jimmy could snap his arm back. Not before it landed, though, right on the fresh bruise on Vlad's cheek. Then Vlad was climbing up the arm. The grappling was unequal as before, and Jimmy slept again.

...

The Russians floated him over to the pad once again and secured the net. Polya asked, in Russian, "So that choke, do you think it does any real damage?"

Vlad shrugged. "As long as the carotid is not crushed he will recover. The initial blood pressure spike in the brain can be nasty, though."

"Can you convince him?"

"Not without injuring him."

"*Cyka blyat!*" Polya wasn't calling anyone in particular an effing bitch, but the situation was pinching intolerably.

He did things to keep his crew alive. It had appeared that thing would be to drop Vlad, whom he knew and trusted, for this first mission. It now appeared he could not do that unless he pushed Jimmy out the airlock, losing a switch. The men talked quietly for some time, and then Vlad resumed his hardsuit and Polya returned to his panel to write his first daily report, and then write another in Russian, which he encrypted. The reports went out over the digital data link that was their only commo with dirtside.

...

Coming out of the black again, pain stabbed from his eyeballs back into Jimmy's head. And his neck was cranked. A strange ticklish-sharp bite told him a rib had cracked under the pressure of Vlad's leg lock. He lay in the bungee net, trying not to move his head.

Then Polya was there, flicking water in his face and offering the bulb. He was silent, his gray-eyed heavy face unsmiling under lowered thick black brows. Jimmy drank from the bulb.

Then Jimmy said, "So the real question here is whether you can keep my fingers out of your eyes." The next fight would not be an athletic contest of gentlemanly close-fisted blows.

"You have shown ability. To get to my face. Vlad has something for you."

Vlad drifted over, holding a small hexagonal valve body with the light gray patina of titanium. Polya went on, "So you will have honor of flying first mission."

Vlad handed him the valve, his grin lopsided below the swollen deep purple flesh on his cheekbone. "We thought maybe you want to install yourself."

Chapter 23 - The Starlight Room

"... when something quite new and singular is presented... [and] memory cannot, from all its stores, cast up any image that nearly resembles this strange appearance"

Adam Smith

Jimmy slid feetfirst from the outer hatch. His helmet was locked to the hardsuit torso, and so he scanned space by turning his head within, in small movements made cautious by his tender neck. The view spaceside was unexpectedly mundane. Space appeared to be a chamber about thirty yards across, with pinlighted black velvet walls, the infinite throttled down through his Earthborn brain.

Nitrogen puffed from his backpack thrusters to move him past the end of the station, where he glanced Earthside. All of Earth was moving past all at once and it nearly stopped his heart. So much blue-white and beneath the white the ocean and each wave-patterned patch of it caught the light in its own way and the seas were one sea, and the seas and the stone waves of mountains bounded the continents, so much forest and plain and equatorial jungle and bands of desert with their own wave-patterned dune fields, and he laughed and looked and had to stop because the seeing and knowing were too much and he looked back to the row of three Rocks.

He jetted to the farthest one, Number 3. The valve replacement was routine, just like EVA practice ops in the water tank at Star City. Easier, because no air hoses or supports for the hardware were needed. Taking a hold with his off hand to brace against the torque, the fairing screwed off and on as simply as the valve cover on a Chevy. The power wrench eased the load on his ribs, and his neck. The valve went into the attitude propellant line with an unpowered wrench, which took longer.

Once again in the hab, all telltales shone green at his panel. Sliding from the plastic carapace, he said to Polya, "You knew what would happen when you touched my ride. Why did you do it?"

"How do I know you react so strong?" Polya spread his hands.

"This collection of tin cans is an aircraft carrier. I'm a carrier pilot. You let your ride get cannibalized once, you don't fly for the whole deployment. It's almost worse than losing the aircraft."

"Perhaps you will forgive ignorance of tradition. Soviet Union, and Russian Federation in turn, has no aircraft carriers. Some few helicopter carriers only."

Jimmy realized how much he hated Russian-accented English. Polya sounded like he was talking around a mouthful of mush.

"Yeah, well. At this point, if I don't fly, nobody flies."

Polya shrugged and turned away toward the hardsuit rack. "Vlad and I must go begging to other platoon. If Dirtside asks, we check throat linings. For report, we never left."

Chapter 24 - Otherworldly Visitation

"The curse of Russian men is vodka.
The curse of Russian women is Russian men."

Slavic apothegm

A thumping on the lock's inner hatch roused Jimmy from his nap. His head felt better for the rest. Someone had locked through the external hatch and wanted the internal one keyed open. An override could key it open from within the lock, but it was polite to ask and warn.

Jimmy pushed over to the hatch panel. Booted feet and the legs of a hardsuit appeared through the Plexiglas porthole. The boots looked oddly small, perhaps a lensing effect of the porthole. The lock atmosphere telltale showed green and he stabbed the glowing backlit latch button. He wondered why Vlad or Polya didn't just key in the code from the lock side.

The hardsuit slid feetfirst through the hatch. It was small, much smaller than what Polya or Vlad wore. The new arrival jumped off from the hatch cover, no small trick since it stood hinged open. The figure pivoted middrift, and did a bent-knee arrest on the inboard bulkhead next to the hardsuit storage. Jimmy gaped at the grace of it.

The nameplate on the left side of the hardsuit thorax read 'Kuznetsova'. A woman. A Russian woman.

He helped her out of the rigid helmet and torqued off the gloves. She squirmed unassisted out of the torso, fluid as an eel. An elfin, tiny woman, her hair a short blond bob, she wore the same soft blue cotton shorts that he and his habmates wore, but a ribbed tank top instead of a tee. The muscles of her thigh came into sharp relief when she pushed away from the inboard bulkhead, and her pectoral jumped, and her small breast with it, as her palm met the spaceside bulkhead and she cushioned the stop.

Jimmy pulled his glance away, to read again the nameplate on her hardsuit.

"Kuznetsova, huh. Pleased to meet you. I'm Smith." Expecting more Russian 'friendship', he was making a jape on her very common and quite unbelievable surname, which did in fact translate to Smith.

"You can call me Katia." She smiled, not looking at him.

"Yekaterina Kuznetsova? That's like calling me Jimmy Smith. Can I help you in any way, Ms. Smith?"

Jimmy wondered if he should call her Agent Smith. Had they shown *The Matrix* in Russian theaters? He pushed off to give her room and hooked a foot under one of the loops near his workstation.

She dead-centered a look at him, held his gaze a moment, and looked him over, face and torso.

She nodded her head a tiny bit. "Will you show me the switch sequence for the Gatling deployment and firing?"

He loved that voice. Her vowels were Slavic, but she didn't drop her 'a' or 'the' and her words were crisp as wind chimes.

And switch sequencing was his thing. He pushed off for the simulator, the mockup of the Rock control panels which he would use to drop and fight. In the Rocks, the panels were built into the flat upper surface of each armrest of the acceleration couch. The simulator was just a pair of armrests extending from the hab wall.

Each panel, where it extended past his hands, carried a multitude of glowing buttons of various sizes and colors and several kinds of switches. Some were to be thrown fore to aft, some in the opposite sense, and a few actuated left to right. Under hard acceleration, it was much easier to throw a switch fore to aft.

He pulled on softsuit gloves, the kind that were touchscreen capable, the gloves he would wear when he dropped. He looped his feet in, powered up, and ran through the switch sequence twice, ending each by nudging the big red FIRE oval with the heel of his hand.

She drifted over to rest against the hab wall beside him, and reached to lay her hand over his where it rested on the control panel. Her arm lay along his left arm. Her small breast spread against his triceps, impossibly firm and soft at once. She said, "I like the way you move your hands, smooth, no jerking about."

Her touch sent a spark shooting to the base of his belly, but another pang of disquiet locked Jimmy up like a statue. That was something you heard about over a game of darts at a pickup joint near a Naval Air Station. Here on deployment it made less sense.

His frozen mind asked "What?"

"Jimmy, the deployment is long and my platoon mates like one another rather more than they like me. My situation is complicated. It is not just that I am lonely. It is important that you are not Russian and therefore do not recognize me. I like the look of you. And we haven't much time."

She smiled. Jimmy smiled through a milder attack of nerves. Was this more slavic duplicity? Couldn't be worse than fighting Vlad. He liked the look of her, too.

"You come in peace, then."

"That's the idea, yes. The peace too. You do not know my true name. But I want someone to know me. To remember me."

A nimbus of gamine-short blond hair floated about her head. She continued to look directly at him with large pale gray eyes above a firm jaw and delicate pointed chin. Maybe she was a Russian spy, but what could he tell her that she did not know? He was a switch. She was a switch. She had taken the same clandestine training which had been given him at Star City. His doubt evaporated. This woman was interested.

"Permission to come aboard?" she asked. She smiled wider, her lean cheeks crinkling beneath bladelike cheekbones. God, she had dimples. He withdrew his feet from the loops of the simulator and turned to her.

She worked her way hand over hand up his body, reminding him of Vlad for just a disquieting moment. She rested her forehead on his and he said, "I hope someday we can go through the introductions."

They breathed together for a moment, bodies relaxing into contact, and then started in on each other's clothing. Shorts and shirts flew away to drift. Bare, she was magnificent, paper-thin skin over finely striated muscle, delicate bones, small and perfect at breast and hip.

She grabbed hard on his upper arm and pushed off for a sleeping space, towing him along until she pirouetted them both in mid-flight. Jimmy was not surprised when she pinned him to the pad, grabbing a pair of loops and pressing her mouth to his. He pulled the bungee net over them so it held them closer. She thrust her feet through a second set of loops, and light of touch in the zero gee, found him.

With a hand at either side of his jaw she raised his face to meet hers and then closed her eyes and pulled him close and then he was away in a place he hadn't known he sought.

When they had cooled a bit, Jimmy looked at her again and wanted to tell her how it had been like falling all the way from orbit into the warm ocean of a newfound planet somewhere very, very far away. He had never said such a thing, didn't know how to say it so it sounded right.

He felt OK. Everything was OK. He would not change anything, the hard-finished white walls of the hab cylinder, the killing vacuum outside, the homicidal mullahs gathering their isotopes and fueling their direct-ascent kill vehicles.

He said, "You OK?"

"Yes, I am feeling OK," she said.

He had to try to tell her something more. He said, "You're a specimen. You know this expression? You're definitely a specimen."

"I was a gymnast." She smiled even brighter than before.

It was important that she smile at him many more times. He lazily followed as she kicked away from the pad toward the suit locker. He wondered at her energy. He was warm all over with a weight behind his eyeballs, as if he had not napped just before her arrival.

"You still are," he said. Perhaps they could skip the explanations after all.

But then she said, "Each watch I stand, I expect to be cooked on a bad trajectory, or to end as a flash of plasma in collision. I will drop Rock 5 this mission. I was, of course, never here. Your NASA recoils in official horror from orbital sex."

So it was emergency sex, last-chance sex. She asked nothing about his service, how he lived, and had told him almost nothing of herself. This quieted Jimmy's suspicions, but it was a touch sad. In the space of minutes she had awed him and he wanted to live a while beside her. She began squirming into the hardsuit torso, abdominals leaping into relief where her shirt rode up. She said, "I must return to maintain Rock 5 before Vlad and Polya pass along the ratlines."

He planted a kiss at the base of her neck. As he held her helmet, ready to torque it on, she said, "And I must tell you, know that Vlad will back you up, and I as well, if you decide there is a problem with a mission. Goodbye, Jimmy Smith."

Chapter 25 - The Wherefore & the Why

"With your spirit settled, accumulate practice day by day, and hour by hour."

Miyamoto Musashi

Wanting sim time on the mockup Rock controls, Jimmy braced his feet in loops on the spaceside hab wall. Running switch sequences was for him like running through *kata* for karate training. It not only solidified his technique, but usually calmed and emptied his mind, which was echoing with recent intense interactions with various Russians.

In the F-14s Jimmy had flown, switchology, the pilot's term for which buttons are to be hit when and to do what, varied with the mission and the weapon loadout. The Rocks had a much less varied loadout, but the timing for maneuvers was tighter and the consequences of misadventure were immediate, spectacular, and final, demanding the twitchiest of reflexes and leaving no opportunity to bounce ideas around the prefrontal cortex. Jimmy believed that mindless repetition wasn't just mindless repetition. It was *mindless* repetition.

At his back, Polya drifted about the module, hovering before each work panel in turn, making his everlasting checks of telltales and propellant levels.

Jimmy switched through three mission sequences, until the worry planted by Katia returned to shatter his calm concentration.

Jimmy asked, "So you're a multi-deployment ISS interceptor platoon veteran, what do you think of the mission profiles you've seen?"

Polya looked up from his panel at the glossy white wall, not at Jimmy. "Why concerns with mission?"

He pushed gently against the panel and spun to face Jimmy. As he hung in free fall he began to lecture, arms waving and legs jerking as though he wanted to pace.

"So what if happens Muammar Ghaddafi is not dead? If dictator lives in spirit? In crew of fanatics three hundred meters down off coast of North America in old Russian boomer?"

Jimmy had not seen Polya so animated. His index finger jabbed at each new threat.

"Saddam is truly dead. But what if long range artillery shows up in Syria, ready to toss nuke?"

"What if Kim Jong Un is stupid as looks indicate? If has missile engineers much too smart?"

"What if Chechens get hold of tactical nuke, fits on truck?"

Polya continued, "If terrorists are ready to launch, none of big three nations can make pre-emptive strike. Lofting ICBM is tossing match at powder keg. But leadership of all three would like to see pre-emptive strike."

Jimmy held up a palm, "We can't hit any of those things. Well maybe a missile fired in our direction, but not a sub, not a launch facility, and not a terrorist truck-missile. We are only two hundred miles up, moving at seventeen thousand miles per hour, and if we are very lucky we can drop a Rock to take out anything inbound more or less directly in our path. ISS protection is the mission I trained for."

Polya waved a hand dismissively, "And it is mission you will fly. But you have not wondered? Why they launch against ISS?"

Jimmy's face pulled back in a snarl, "Or why they would launch against the World Trade Center? The ISS is not a military threat to anyone. It was full of civilian scientists until we snuck aboard. It is a symbol of the best in both our countries, and others. A symbol that a terrorist might target."

Polya raised his palms to his chest, as though restraining himself, "As far as world knows, ISS is not threat."

Jimmy stared. "What?"

Polya stared back under heavy black brows, "What is main problem with preemptive strike by ICBM?"

Jimmy thought about it. The exact location of the launch would be picked up by the satellites of the U.S. Space-Based Infrared System. The missile would be tracked in boost phase and midcourse. Both Russia and the U.S. had enough ABM capability to take out an isolated missile.

He laughed. "A launch would be seen, tracked, maybe intercepted."

"I leave aside test and demonstration failures of American ground-based defense. What if launch site is very close to target, warning is not available?" asked Polya.

"You mean like basing missiles in Cuba ninety miles from the U.S.? An obvious prepositioning for a first strike with minimal warning? Then we offer to start the war early, with a first strike of our own." Jimmy's voice had descended into a growl.

Polya's tone remained flat, "Or basing warhead 320 kilometers above target. Warhead already moving at twenty-seven thousand kilometers per hour."

Jimmy stared again, wide-eyed. A very old and still much-respected treaty forbade just that. The nuke would not be detected until it was already in re-entry.

Polya went on, "Anyone knows of warhead, and hostile to our countries, will try to shoot down. Have been trying to shoot down. Ablated throats did not happen while Rocks were dropped on exercises."

"Let me guess," Jimmy said. "We carry a Long Range Standoff Weapon, the one developed under our peace-prize winning President. So now it has reentry capability?"

Polya nodded, "With W80 nuke, and right thermal barrier coatings, will work. You know LRSO has stealth characteristics. It would be stake through heart of regime with evil designs. Stake they would not see coming."

He continued, "But is not stake. Is dagger. Russian dagger. Kh-47 Kinzhal hypersonic missile. NATO knows as Dagger. Mach 10 over 2000 kilometers, if ground-launched. Untested, as yet, fired from orbit."

Jimmy of a sudden noticed the smell of the canned atmo in which the three of them lived. His nausea was back.

He said, "So we're a first strike weapon."

Chapter 26 - Ways & Means II

"His face has the grave cast of one accustomed to seeing everyone around him accept the inevitable."

Infantry Journal, v. 1, p. 6

In the darkness of his sleep space, Jimmy tried to relax under the bungee net but the ticklish-sharp pain in his ribs promised another week's discomfort. Cracked. Sleep seemed far away. He had a nine hour rest scheduled, and then the men would assume ready status, relieving the Apples, the women's interceptor platoon two habs over. Katia's platoon.

Polya, Vlad, and he had no platoon callsign. He thought it unlikely that he could create a handle with the cachet of 'Apple 1' which the Apples' leader enjoyed. Katia's callsign would be 'Apple 2'. He smiled.

Each interceptor platoon deployed for 90 days, but deployments were staggered and overlapped by 45 days. Polya had explained that the senior of the two chose the callsign for the newbies. The Apples had suffered through extended watch and drop cycles and were all brown-bottom astronauts. The men previously occupying *Columbus* had immediately pounced, and 'Horse Apples' was set in stone. Now it was the Apples' turn to choose for them.

Some cynical, even gallows humor was to be expected. The switches not only endured primitive sanitation, they accepted long odds against surviving the dropping of a nuclear ramjet into reentry, forcing it through atmosphere at wildly hypersonic speeds while guiding onto a directly oncoming target, getting off an aimed shot, and avoiding debris closing at twice orbital velocity.

Rocks dropping at Mach 20 pushed air ahead of them into shocks of such intensity as to ionize atoms of nitrogen and oxygen into incandescent plasma flowing back in a shining envelope from the shock front. It was the stuff of stellar atmospheres, and the sheer intensity of the thermal energy radiated from this shroud of hellfire was the main threat to their thin titanium skins. Rocks were heat-armored in ceramic thermal barrier coatings and ablative layers, lest they melt or ignite.

Jimmy turned so that the sleep net exerted its gentle pressure at his shoulder and hip rather than on his chest, though worry had begun to jab at him more painfully than his rib injuries. He relaxed his facial muscles and began to count his breaths, but his thoughts continued to drift.

The Rocks needed hypersonic speed to meet hypersonic threats, threats boosted to orbital speed by huge rockets. Everyone on the ISS was vigilant for antisatellite attacks, which could be air-launched or ground-launched, co-orbital or kinetic.

Kinetic energy kill vehicles aimed to carry out 'non-cooperative docking', a term of fatalistic Russian humor that Jimmy was just coming to appreciate. Kinetic energy vehicles just hit you at very, very high speed. The collision would convert nearly all that speed to thermal energy, and a hit by a multi-kilogram kill vehicle would leave only a few metal fragments of the ISS. Some of these remnants would be coated with carbon condensed from the plasma cloud. This coating would be the only recoverable human remains.

Co-orbital vehicles took a different approach, spending hours or days to match orbits, to creep up and then detonate or open fire at close range. The Russians, for a while when they were Soviets, had orbited a system of straight-up battle stations with 23 millimeter autocannons which fired a swarm of inch-thick heavy metal slugs.

Such a battle-sat could wreak terrible damage. Autocannons had long been mounted on aircraft to kill other aircraft, or to kill vehicles and troop concentrations when flying ground attacks. Even main battle tanks were vulnerable to the larger autocannons firing depleted uranium or tungsten penetrators. The ISS was not a tank, or an APC, or even a Humvee. The ISS was a collection of aluminum cans optimized for lightness.

Jimmy gave up the count at one hundred breaths. This was as bad as the night before bad-weather carrier flight ops. He would just have to stay sharp and maintain.

The switches would watch the ISS sensors and the sensors distributed in various orbits and the computer in the main module would watch for a ground launch or for a fighter aircraft making a supersonic zoom climb, signature of an air-launched ASAT missile. Ground-based mainframes would crunch detailed orbital mechanics models to predict attack profiles developing from launches, from aircraft, or from other orbital craft.

Polya, Vlad, and Jimmy would by turns take a five hour duty cycle, buttoned up in a Rock waiting for the surveillance algorithms to tell them to drop. Or not. Whatever the weapon, whether launched atop a giant rocket or boosted from a supersonic fighter's pylon or creeping up from a neighboring orbit, they had to get to it and kill it before it unleashed its heavy metal rain or high explosive or simply acquired unstoppable momentum on a collision course

Chapter 27 - At the Office

"At the beginning of the Space Age, it was unanimously considered obvious and inevitable that nuclear power plants and nuclear engines would quickly become the mainstay of space operations."
James Oberg

Jimmy was going to need a session on the bungee treadmill. Floating was undemanding, but restoring bloodflow would be refreshing. He had pulled a five hour shift monitoring his panel for threats while Vlad floated in his blue softsuit in Rock 2. Now Jimmy floated suited up in Number 3. A switch rarely stood more than one watch per day in a Rock, fourteen feet from a minimally shielded reactor.

He keyed his throat mic. "Anything likely this orbit?"

Polya drifted before his work panel, considering the question carefully, though it was routine. A hostile launch might happen all the way around the Earth. But he, and the mainframe, could see farther than that. And Jimmy could get there, fast. Orbital mechanics did not rule his trajectory. The Rock had a NERVA[4] engine but did not carry propellant as would be done in a nuclear rocket. Like the decades-old SLAM[5], it compressed a supersonic airstream into

---

[4] NERVA is Nuclear Engine for Rocket Vehicle Application – a fission reactor for heating gaseous propellant carried by the spacecraft.

[5] Supersonic Low-Altitude Missile – like the NERVA, built around a reactor, but operating in atmosphere as a ramjet, heating an incoming airstream. Check out Google Images for the SLAM Missile or Project Pluto. It's a nuclear-powered, nuclear-tipped Cold War doomsday missile with a ramscoop hanging underneath, and does look like an ICBM with a massive stallion-style erection.

its ramscoop and ejected it even faster at insane levels of superheat. The new wrinkle was, rather than flying supersonic at low altitude, the Rock compressed the tenuous uppermost atmosphere at hypersonic velocities. The stubby delta wing carried control surfaces and the Rock could ascend or descend or change orbital inclination to circumpolar or equatorial as needed, as long as Jimmy's speed and choice of trajectory did not heat the titanium fuselage above its ignition point, making his craft into a very big flashbulb filament.

Polya said, "Checking."

He continued to cycle through the layers on his display. Thousands of airliners clouded the skies, mostly over Europe, the U.S., and East Asia. Of the ten thousand or so aircraft in flight, a hundred or so were military. Aircraft without transponders, such as those engaged in combat or smuggling, showed on the non-transponder layer, identifiable only from the radar and optical tracks obtained from national technical means, spysats. The layer from the U.S. Space Surveillance Network would show twenty thousand or so objects in orbit, anything over 10 centimeters in size. The operational satellite layer showed around a thousand tracks. Perhaps half were in low Earth orbit, neighbors to the ISS. Most of the rest were geostationary, too high to pose an immediate threat. Some in elliptical orbits cycled from high to low altitude, and so merited watching.

He said, "Still checking."

None of the hundred or so known rocket launch sites was active. Not the one in Libya, or Egypt. Pakistan and India had not gone ballistic over Kashmir. North Korea was quiet. No launch flares or ascending tracks appeared in the data from the geostationary eyes high above him or from his neighbors in low Earth orbit. Switching the display to the scheduled ground launch layer showed an Iridium satellite would go up, then a Soyuz, a Chinese Long March, SpaceX, Arianespace from Europe, a Delta from Canaveral, an H-2B from Japan. The H-2B would be inbound for the ISS with an uncrewed cargo vehicle. But nothing was scheduled for the next few days.

Polya would, on detection of a threat, command Jimmy to 'drop his Rock'. Jimmy would initiate an intercept mission by flipping up a clear shield, then palming the large red button labeled 'DETACH', releasing the three taut guy wires which clamped the Rock to the cylindrical ISS module. Whether standing watch in their Rocks or within their habs, the other switches would learn of the sortie by the *thunk* ringing through the station's structure as the wires snapped free.

Separated from the station, only Jimmy would feel the thrust as he retreated from the ISS on attitude thrusters, spun the Rock to orient the nose retrograde, and then fired the main nozzle to drop into re-entry. Much the same as dropping a Soyuz, Jimmy would fall faster and faster into atmo, building a shockwave before him in the thickening air, heating up all the while, a typical flaming re-entry from orbit. Until he cranked up the ramjet. Then things would get energetic.

But the threat layers were empty. None of the aircraft were supersonic. None had bent their courses sharply upward. Nothing orbital was on a collision course. No direct-ascent intercept trajectories appeared because no launch sites were active.

Polya's reply was metronomic, "No probables."

Jimmy returned to his headsup display and his systematic review of arrays of switches, telltales, and screens. All clean and green. Another hour, two thirds of an orbit, and the Apples would take the duty. He could hand-over-hand back along the ratlines and lock back into the hab. He needed a workout and a wipedown before their offduty meal.

Chapter 28 - Woolgathering

"The thing that scares us most, more than combat and dying really, is failing in the eyes of fellow pilots or ourselves."
Lt. Wes Huey, F-14 pilot.

It is difficult to land any fighter on a carrier. And the F-14 Tomcat was one of the more difficult planes to fly slowly. The big fighter was by design rock steady at Mach 2 and more, but it landed at 150 knots, where stability suffered. When it wobbled, its hugely powerful twin engines made it easy to over-correct.

Looking down on a tiny patch of gray nearly lost in the horizon-spanning dull green sea, Cricket was nervous, and it made him stiff as he continually nudged stick and rudder to juggle the amber ball of the carrier's Fresnel lens between lines of green light. The ass end of the carrier suddenly got very big, but he held glide path and let the afterburners roar as the wheels thumped the deck, anxiety stabbing his belly as he hooked the number three wire and the decel bent him forward from the waist. He bounced a few times as the landing gear pogoed.

"Never again to slip the surly bonds of Earth," he muttered.

"Say again, Cricket," said the Landing Signal Officer.

"Uh, no problem. Good to be home again," said Jimmy.

Hundreds of landings at airfields had prepared him for his first carrier trap, which was scary nonetheless. Every following carrier landing had scared him as well. Night landings. Thick gray weather landings. Deck pitching landings. Blue sky calm midday landings. They all made him nervous. His voice got noticeably higher when he turned onto approach.

A good pilot even among carrier pilots, he nearly always caught the three wire. His row on the greenie board stayed green. Jimmy twice attended the Top Gun air combat school at Miramar, and served as an instructor.

He had zero combat engagements. Never been shot at. Zero rounds fired in anger. He wondered how scary combat could be.

They were retiring the Tomcat, and he wasn't about to step into an F/A-18, the slower, cheaper child of compromise midwifed by some congressional committee. The F/A designation, fighter/attack, said it did air superiority as well as ground attack. It "added flexibility to the commander's planning" by ticking both mission boxes for the price of one airframe, by being a multimission mediocrity. A Russian Su-27 would kill it. Air-to-air, the mediocre died.

So that was it. The end of his service to America, in which he had been so fortunate to become an aviator and an officer in the Navy in which his father had served, to have answered to every duty, sometimes commended, yet never to have looked upon the face of battle.

That was the end of it until he met Tom, a man who thought he could imagine the countenance of the low Earth orbit battlespace, who placed his bets on an entirely new spacecraft, and was asking Jimmy to risk his skin in it.

Polya's voice, like gravel pouring into a steel bucket, jolted him back to the present.

"You have systems check due two minutes ago."

Jimmy keyed the mic open. "Checking."

Chapter 29 - When the Stars Threw Down Their Spears

What the hand, dare seize the fire?

William Blake

"Typical American. Warrior who is novice at chess. Not well read. You have not read Pushkin. You have no poetry."

Jimmy and Polya floated above a thin magnetic chessboard clipped to one of the mock armrests. Jimmy had agreed to play at the other man's insistence, and because it was the only set of inflatable chess pieces he had ever seen.

He rolled his eyes. Agreeing to a chess match was as far as his multicultural sensitivity would stretch just now. "Not many literature majors make it into fighter squadrons, or the astronaut corps. I'm sure the journalists and the inclusion-police will want that rectified soon, and we'll have pasty-faced emos swanning about in low Earth orbit."

He paused, remembering, "But I did like Blake when they dragged me through freshman lit. Also Hemingway, but Blake was the poet I liked."

A furrow between heavy black brows told him that Polya was not familiar with Blake, or maybe emos. The Russian turned away, his hand at the earpiece he always wore. Jimmy looked back to the thin steel board and the ruins of his Sicilian opening.

The Horse Apples had the duty. And Rock 5, piloted by Apple 2, that would be Katia, was the hot Rock. He hoped her five hours went by more quickly than his duty had with only Polya to talk to. He tried to recall the poem about the tiger.

Polya was suddenly back at his shoulder, pushing him toward the suit locker. "Softsuit now. Galina drops."

Jimmy drifted toward the inboard end of the module, looking back to say, "Who's Galina?"

"You did not hear name. Apple 2 will drop very soon. You are backup. Is imminent ground launch warning. Multiple sites. Multiple threats incoming."

Oh, that Galina, Jimmy thought. Katia. Perfect fineboned fantastically striated tender greedy Katia.

He braked his drift near the hardsuit storage, and grabbed his dark blue softsuit from the doorless space next to it. Donning the softsuit was not so elaborate as squirming into a hardsuit, taking a few minutes if one took care with the seals. It took additional minutes to slide into the lock and do an emergency blow.

Outside, Jimmy scrambled along the ratlines strung down the length of the hab cylinder. A shock oscillated through the ISS structure and down the lines, momentarily focusing his entire awareness on his grip. So they had detached Rock 5, and Katia.

At his Rock, he hit the external release, the clear crystalline blister hinged up, and he drifted feetfirst into Rock 3. He had not got the blister buttoned up when Polya grated out an order.

"Rock 3 detach. Now, detach."

So they were probably dropping him too and he hit the big red button to cut loose. Just like the briefings said, the *thunk* got into his guts and lungs as the tensioned guy cables let go. He brought down the blister, the massive bubble of artificial sapphire that served as the Rock's canopy, to seal him into the cockpit.

The Rock's attitude thrusters drew on liquefied air from a nearly empty belly tank just forward of the reactor. They hissed in an oft-simulated sequence to nudge him away from the station.

Polya's voice again sounded rough in his earpiece, "Three surface launches confirmed. Designate Vampires 1, 2, and 3."

So the infrared detectors staring through astronomical-grade lenses from geosynchronous orbit high above had spotted the thermal blooms of rocket launches. Jimmy recognized the Vampire designation as U.S. Navy terminology for missiles incoming to a ship.

On the left armrest there was a big red toggle like an oversize light switch the size of his thumb. He snapped it to the detent labeled RAMJET STDBY and the flight control computer – astronauts didn't use autopilots, but Jimmy thought of it as the autopilot – closed down the neutron reflectors on the NERVA just a hair. The high-power-density reactor instantly ramped up to standby temperature, its ceramic core glowing red.

Ahead and to his left, and considerably Earthward, a ruby dot appeared against the huge gray blankness where India lay under a cover of cloud. The tiny ember brightened through orange, into yellow. Soon a long tail of glowing yellow plasma and sparks of superheated ablation debris streamed back from Rock 5 in a long thin teardrop of light.

"Jesus," Jimmy murmured. He had watched a lot of re-entry film. Katia was glowing too bright, diving steep and deep, very fast for atmo that thick.

Polya gritted in his earphone, "You have problem?"

Active radars on the ISS tracked Jimmy and kept an infrared commo laser locked onto Rock 3. The Rock fired a second laser back to create a two-way digital tightbeam datalink. Polya would be in his head until he rounded the limb of the planet.

"No. All nominal with Rock 3. Apple 2 ahead and below shows heavy ablation and ionization trail."

"If Apple 2 ignites or skips, engage incoming."

The encrypted digital laser link had plenty of bandwidth for modulation, but Polya's voice was flat.

Chapter 30 - And Watered Heaven with Their Tears

"... the foolish Phaeton straight did crave
The guyding of Sunne's winged Steedes, and Chariot for to have.
... But Phaeton (fire yet blazing stil among his yellow haire)
Shot headlong downe, and glid along the Region of the Ayre
Like to a starre in wether cleare of Winter night
Which though it doe not fall in deede, yet falleth to our sight."

Ovid, Metamorphoses

Ahead, the leading edge of Katia's yellow plasma track began strobing, quickly oscillating in brightness, and Jimmy thought she's tumbling and then the track went white and a filament of brilliant white stretched out brighter and brighter like a spear of light across the planet's darkening face. The entire monsoon cloud layer over India reflected the glare as the track broke into a rain of meteors, themselves tumbling and breaking apart and all the pieces streaming white fire. Katia's ramjet interceptor, bigger than an F-16, was gone in less than a minute.

Jimmy swallowed. He heard himself say, "Rock 5 ignited fuselage."

Polya rumbled at him, "You are hot Rock, Jimmy."

Dirtside as well informed him. He was to drop. Now.

Shock faded, and it was then that the fear fell upon him heavy and cold and liquid and painful in the belly. He understood the old phrase. His guts had turned to water. It was the worst fear he had known, but of a kind he recognized. He knew if he did not move soon it would paralyze him.

Katia, he couldn't call her Galina, had gotten too deep into atmo going too fast, going for the quickest intercept, trying to take out all of whatever swarm of antisatellite ordnance was incoming. Runaway combustion of her titanium fuselage and continued atmospheric frictional heating had left her Rock and the entire fissile core of its reactor, some 17 kilograms of plutonium, along with her flesh and blood and bones, smeared across the nightside stratosphere in a cloud of incandescing electrons and highly ionized atoms. Dropping into re-entry seemed like a terrible, terrible idea.

Time to stop thinking about it. He needed to get down to atmo where he could feed the ramjet and get to the threat. The committee in his head shut down with the first touch in a well-practiced switch sequence. The small joystick, pressed left and held, opened up a yaw thruster to swing the nose around retrograde. A button valved liquid air from the belly tank into the intake of the warm reactor, which flashed it into superheated vapor shooting from the main nozzle. The acceleration couch pushed him feebly for a few seconds until he closed down the valve. He dropped toward the planet below.

He keyed the mic, "Maneuvering to engage vampires."

It consumed further scarce propellant to swing the Rock's nose back to posigrade, pointed along his trajectory. He then inverted, rolled the craft so that he gazed up at the Earth through the sapphire blister. He listened for the first high scream of atmosphere to vibrate through the fuselage.

Flashing through the highest reaches of the stratosphere, where meteorites are seen to burn, ever-thicker ghosts of atmosphere whispered in the Rock's throat and pressurized the reactor. His harness met his chest in a gentle push. Air resistance was decelerating him.

The whisper built to a thin howl and quickly swelled to a chorus of madmen shrieking in the airstream. Jimmy levered the big red toggle over to the RAM INITIATE detent, closing the neutron reflectors. The core flashed to yellow-white heat, the basso roar of the ramjet drowned all other sound, and a long golden spike of incandescent exhaust sprang forth from the nozzle. The push from his harness disappeared and thrust came on quick, four gees shoving him into the couch harder than the Soyuz which had boosted him to orbit.

Funneling the immense energy of the reactor into the exhaust spike, the Rock's speed was limited only by atmospheric heat generation and by wing loading. His velocity soon went superorbital, and the Earthward lift from his stubby delta winglets had to make up the difference between the centripetal force flinging him spaceward and the inadequate centrifugal pull of Earth.

A shockwave formed ahead of the Rock's rounded nose and in its extreme pressure gradient molecules of tortured air disassociated into atoms, atoms were stripped of electrons, and a shining red tinge appeared. Soon streamers of reddish light whipped about, coruscating just outside the thick sapphire blister of the canopy, brightening until he flew within an incandescent rose-red teardrop.

He liked red. Red was relatively cool, compared to the melting and ignition temperatures for the thermal coatings and alloy of his fuselage. Temperatures established by test and well understood. Pretty well understood. As well understood as the first operational high-stratospheric nuclear ramjet could be.

The ionization envelope screened out any attempt at radio linking. The station's infrared laser could get through as a one-way datalink until things got really hot. But through the hot plasma layer, the digital watchers couldn't read the dimmer emissions of the Rock's return laser. He couldn't say anything and as he dropped below the station's horizon, losing line-of-sight, he could hear nothing.

With the datalink shut down, his onboard computation must predict the trajectories of his Rock and of the vampires by obsessively iterating the simple and therefore fast equations[6] of Newtonian mechanics, extrapolating from last known positions and velocities by integrating accelerations. His headsup displayed the trajectories in arcs of red and blue.

The vampires to a high probability carried kinetic kill vehicles. With luck, the pattern recognition algorithms, all neural nets, would correctly vote among themselves to identify exactly what boosters were now accelerating at him and at the station. Past that, for the remaining forks in the decision tree Jimmy was on his own.

Switchology in the Rocks was simple but not easy. Recharging the belly tank with liquid air required him to trip a thick green toggle to the PROP RECHG detent. He struggled against acceleration to get his left hand forward of the switch, then hooked two fingers over it and let gee force take his arm back.

-----

[6] OK, so $F = m \cdot a$, Newton's force-mass-acceleration relation, and so $a = F/m$, where m is the vehicle's mass (It is helpful in discussing these matters to pronounce this as VEE-hick'l) and F is force acting on it. Update velocity, $v = v + a \cdot \Delta t$ and update position $x = x + v \cdot \Delta t$. Repeat for many many time increments Δt to build a trajectory.

The way the projected trajectories fit with the observed paths allows estimates of C_D, A, and m, which are vehicle drag coefficient, cross-sectional area, and mass. Knowing these characteristics allows guesses as to what vehicle is approaching.

Want more details? Jimmy's force computations would include the estimated thrust of a booster, the gravitational attraction $F = G \cdot M_{Earth} \cdot m/r^2$, as well as drag force from passage through atmosphere, $F = \rho(r) \cdot C_D \cdot A \cdot v^2/2$, where atmospheric density $\rho(r)$ is a function of orbit radius r, M_{Earth} is mass of the Earth, and G is the universal gravitational constant. Add up all these forces, and then calculate acceleration.

Bleed air, a portion of the hypersonic airstream howling through the ramjet throat, gated into a turbo-compressor in series with a thermoelectric chiller to refill his belly tank.

As the telltale for the belly tank pressure cycled from red to green he threw the green toggle switch back to PROP READY, cutting out the auxiliary turbine. He now had a full accumulator of liquid air. He would need most of it to get to the coming intercept, and would need the rest if he survived.

Perhaps later he would think more about survival and recovery to the ISS. Right now Jimmy had a couple important decisions to make about threat interception. All in an instant the console telltales, the bright streams of plasma whipping past, and the tactical situation on the headsup snapped into clear bright focus.

It had always been only anticipation and memory which shook him, and once past an initial tendency to freeze if an engine flamed out or a carrier deck pitched just the wrong way, his attention locked on and every other part of him just watched. He wasn't analyzing and he wasn't worried any more than a hitter facing a ninety-five mile an hour fastball. It pleased him that the familiar clarity came over him when rounds fired in anger were incoming.

The vampires' predicted paths continued to evolve on the headsup until the neural nets agreed to call them Safirs, Iranian missiles with 50 kilogram payload-to-orbit capability. So the exatmospheric kill vehicles were likely to be small, hard to take out once deployed as a third stage. He had to get there during second stage boost.

Setting the next switch would commit him to an automated intercept, and he very deliberately flipped the big yellow toggle on his left armrest to TRACK/INTCPT. A reticle appeared on his headsup. He could not see the first vampire but the Rock's computer knew it was there and more behind it. The autopilot would see to it that he was boosted up into a collision course with the Safirs.

...

Polya watched through netlinked spysat eyes as Jimmy painted his ionization trail across India. Deep red, as safe as it got. The brilliant slash of Rock 5's incineration had faded but still burned in his mind's eye.

The American was diving to the threat, but staying clear of thermal runaway. He was a good switch. It was too bad about his fixation on the degenerate English poet. Such tastes went far toward explaining the destruction of American music by the British in the 1960s.

Things that Jimmy didn't have time to think about worried him. How did an Iranian rocket get established in a westbound trajectory over India, traveling toward Iran? Perhaps an unsuspected Iranian sea-launch capability in the Bay of Bengal, or maybe a site in Bangladesh or even the hinterlands of Myanmar. The optical signature of the launch had been picked up, but he had been given only the alert that a direct-ascent attack was inbound.

The tracks of the three incomers were nearly coincident. The ascending rockets had been launched in series from very close sites, so that the second and third followed in the lead vehicle's wake. He was grateful but puzzled that the Iranians had not distributed the launches, giving different orbital inclinations. That would have made intercept by a single Rock impossible. The post-mission hotwash[7] might satisfy his curiosity, if the ISS survived.

The station had the capability to change orbital inclination and altitude, but only very slowly. If even a single kill vehicle got by Jimmy's Rock it would be impossible to evade.

...

Jimmy's headsup was overwritten by a "COUNTDOWN TO POPUP" announcement, below which red digits decremented once each second from 30. He was the man in the loop here, but he was satisfied that Iranian vehicles were on intercept course with the ISS. The engagement was necessary. He pushed his right arm forward, reaching with thumb and forefinger to grasp the subscale joystick on his right armrest.

On cue, Jimmy rolled the blister to spaceside and brought the nose up and the ramjet added its thrust to the spaceward lift from his stubby delta wings to 'pop up' into the mesosphere. The plasma envelope died in the vanishing airflow and the engine's roar faded until the autopilot gated liquid air from the belly tank into the still white-hot reactor core, switching the Rock from ramjet

---

[7] A mission review conducted immediately upon mission completion

to rocket. Thrust weighed on Jimmy anew until the autopilot satisfied itself that orbital altitude had been achieved.

Its field of view now clear of red-hot plasma, the Rock's forward-looking infrared acquired the lead vampire's second stage exhaust. Acquired it in the predicted position. The neural nets were right, it had to be a Safir.

The autocannon's bright red toggle was double the width of the other switches on his armrest and striped diagonally in white. He snapped it forward to the DEPLOY detent and the weapon bay door opened onto its stops with a *thunk* and the headsup flashed 'GAU DEPLOYED'. He could only trust that the electric actuators had extended the bundled barrels from the weapon bay and oriented it properly.

From there, his part in the gunnery was to get the fire control algorithm set up to shoot. He tripped the autocannon switch forward to ARM with his left thumb. Each of the gun's seven barrels was the length of a man, fat and nasty blue-black like a water moccasin, and the whine of the electric motor spinning up the mass of steel set his teeth on edge. When the targeting radar acquired all three Safirs and painted them as red chevrons on his headsup he drew the heel of his right hand back and down onto a red oval the size of a dill pickle at the base of his right armrest. This "pickle" tripped AUTOFIRE, the Rock's fire control algorithm.

Everything shook. Not just vibrated, but kicked viciously with each banana-sized slug of depleted uranium blown out of a thirty-millimeter barrel. The Avenger spat sixty of these per second, and at each hammerlike pulse of recoil stress waves shot out from the gun mounts beneath the cockpit floor to warp through the fuselage and course harsh and strong through Jimmy's body. The Rock's fire control limited the burst to one hundred rounds and for one and one-half seconds his vision fogged and a ripsaw sounded in his skull and his every particle of flesh pulsated and the autocannon's recoil seized the Rock to slow it as though he had flown into a wall of Jell-O.

He had taken the Safirs nearly in enfilade. The Autofire algorithm toggled the point of aim over to the second and third Safirs and two more bursts rattled Jimmy from teeth to toes and threw him into his harness as the big cannon pushed back on the Rock.

Then Autofire was done with him and his maneuver to avoid debris was to de-orbit and he hit the joystick with mindless precision to flip the nose retrograde. The recoil from the big Gatling had already braked his Rock, but he kicked on the main nozzle to de-orbit more quickly, hoping to duck oncoming fragments. Assuming he had hits. He had no time to wait for his bursts to close the range to the Safirs. He dropped once again toward the planetary sea of air.

Now to retract and stow the Gatling, and quickly. He was headed back to the stratosphere where a weapon extended into the hypersonic airflow would tumble the Rock into a disintegrating fireball just like Katia's. His hands twitched like a video gamer's, running through obsessively practiced switch sequences which ended in a slick airframe, nose flipped back to posigrade, and the blister filled with the unfathomable bulk of Earth.

Chapter 31 - Meanwhile, Back at the ISS

"Everyone knows rockets blow up. Hardly anyone expects they will."

Sarah Scoles, Wired

The orbital neighborhood over southwest Asia had a good number of surveillance assets, optical, infrared, and radar, but it was beyond even the best radars to track the swarms of slugs issuing from Jimmy's autocannon.

Rockets are more obvious. A rocket operating in the lower atmosphere emits a blinding sword of fire. In the near vacuum of the mesosphere a blue-white glow springs out from the nozzle into a near hemisphere unconstrained by air pressure. On Polya's flatscreen there appeared three perfect bells of flame, the optical take from a spysat in a medium orbit.

It more than surprised him when the lead Safir bloomed into a sphere of hot gas, despite his aerospace training which told him that all rockets badly want to blow up and could do so in myriad ways.

Rockets resonate with the sound waves of their own exhaust plume reflected back from the launchpad, like a violin amplifying the stick-slip of a bow drawn across its strings. Their structures also vibrate sympathetically with turbulent pressure fluctuations when boosting through atmosphere. And structure and fuel lines pick up and amplify thrust oscillations in the rocket motors. Such self-reinforcing feedback loops could shake a booster apart in seconds. Or they could blow up from white-hot exhaust leaking through solid rocket seals, or from oxidizer and fuel fumes mixing in interstage spaces. Huge energies, harnessed by the lightest possible structures, awaited the release of a single spark.

Still, the autocannon's depleted uranium[8] penetrators were not explosive rounds, and punching even large holes into a rocket in the all but airless uppermost mesosphere was unlikely to produce such a dramatic blast. A deflagration, maybe, but not a detonation.

When the follow-on pair of Safirs flamed out he imagined that subsequent bursts of heavy metal slugs from Jimmy's Gatling had passed undamaged and undeviated through the lead Safir's expanding gas and debris cloud. Any hit to propellant pumps, tanks, fuel lines, or nozzles would shut down a rocket engine. The dirtside compute cluster projected that none of the Safirs would achieve orbit. It was a clean-sweep win and the close-in weapons of the ISS would not need to engage.

This last point was a particular relief. Even the fragments of a Safir, or of a kill vehicle released from a Safir, would retain enormous kinetic energy and would not be deflected greatly when hit with a short-range missile, of which the ISS carried two, or by 20 millimeter projectiles from the turret of the Vulcan, the smaller CIWS[9] version of the GAU-8 Avenger carried by the Rocks. The Whipple shields and debris protection blankets of Nextel and Kevlar scarcely entered his mind. They would have no significance if a kinetic energy kill vehicle transected the ISS.

Chapter 32 – The Flight of Phaeton

---

[8] DU, Depleted Uranium, is useful because of its high density for the GAU-8 Gatling's original mission of penetrating armor. Also, it is cheap; a by-product of producing enriched reactor fuel from natural uranium.

[9] CIWS, the Close-In Weapons System, for carrier and cruiser defense against cruise missiles, is a robotic turret with an autocannon. Its acquisition radar detects incoming missiles, and targeting radar tracks not only the missile, but also the outgoing projectiles from its autocannon, correcting its aim while firing. The CIWS is sometimes left on, but safetied, so that it pivots to track but not fire on aircraft returning to the carrier, thereby testing its detect/track function. This practice is intensely disliked by Naval aviators.

"As if another Phaeton got
Guidance of the sunnes rich chariot."

Christopher Marlowe
Hero and Leander

As the first insubstantial wisps of the stratosphere shrilled into the ramjet, Jimmy hit RAM INITIATE, but throttled back to a mellow *thrum*, not needing attack gees.

To make up an orbit on the ISS, he let his speed slowly build to nearly 26,000 miles per hour, aiming to complete three orbits in the next three hours while the station completed two.

There was a kind of stillness within the sapphire bubble, bathed in the engine's deep note and gazing into the ever-renewing bright frenzy of every shade of red whipping past with a high thin ululation like the wind across an unimaginably high stony summit. Shrouded in ionized fire, no commo reached his ear.

It was a spring-loaded calm, underlain with watchfulness, alert for any departure from the delicate equilibrium he had achieved with the hypersonic airstream. The watcher within him would not relax, even knowing that an instability would destroy him before either eye or ear could register it.

Recharging the propellant accumulator provided something other than unbearably energetic plasma to look at on the second orbit, watching the belly tank pressure telltale until he could snap the green fuel toggle to PROP READY so the autopilot would consent to his putting the Rock back into TRACK/INTCPT. It occupied him further to enter the station's orbital parameters, but he was still strung tight and beginning to suspect that when people said lonely they meant afraid.

For almost all of the third orbit there was nothing to do. He waited for the autopilot's countdown to begin, wanting to roll his blister spaceside and raise the nose and be done with it. He waited as a soldier waits, motionless and silent, but very busy nonetheless avoiding thinking about whether the autopilot could match the ISS orbit before expending all his propellant.

Chapter 33 - Analysis & Machinations

"Movie stars! Is there anything they don't know?"

Homer Simpson

Dr. Thomas Broadhead leaned on his elbows, head bowed over the latest breakdown of expenditures. Why would it cost that much to lease an office building, a simple frame of steel, glass veneer, air conditioners, and crappers? They were nearly in Reston, halfway to Dulles. Definitely outside the Beltway. Far outside.

Tom Broadhead did not mind working from suburban Virginia rather than in the Pentagon, Crystal City, or any of the multitude of DC area think tanks. He needed to stay out of sight, particularly Congressional oversight, though he thought that term inapt for the imposition of legislators' uninformed opinions onto active executive branch operations. He could not forget the hearing in which that blonde actress from the King Kong movie testified. Not on movies, on U.S. policy. They would break his rice bowl if they knew. If they knew. He kept the office budget dark under a sham securities trading operation.

Of course, the satellite dishes cost nothing. Installed *Supra et Ultra* on the roof and maintained by colleagues at NRO[10], the datalink fed him the output of spaceborne electronic intercepts, as well as optical, infrared, and radar imagery and spectroscopic data.

A Beowulf compute cluster he had put together himself sat atop the datastream, sifting for launches, projecting trajectories, checking national security communiques. He was proud of his low-budget supercomputer hiding in plain sight. His analysts gated the data into the right software, and interpreted the product of the crunching.

His people needed pay, but they were seconded from NSA[11] or DIA[12] or wherever he found the right motivation and skills. The analysts gazed into multiple huge flatscreens in darkened, sound damped chambers. The rooms were electronically shielded lest someone read the tiny radio emissions from

---

[10] NRO is the National Reconnaissance Office. You can Google it. Maybe don't use your own PC.

[11] Again, Google it. You didn't hear it from me.

[12] DIA is Defense Intelligence Agency. Don't Google this one. I don't want you to get in too much trouble.

keyboard switches making contact and were windowless so no one could bounce a laser off the glass to read the vibrations caused by human speech.

Jenny walked in without knocking, brushing a strand of honey-blond hair back into its bell-like curve.

She said, "They got the three Safirs, but the lead one was a defensive counterweapon."

Tom sat up, his back stiffening. "How so?"

"The thing blew up. The flash spectrum shows absorption lines from good old TNT. It probably pushed out shrapnel, maybe ball bearings like an oversized Claymore. It probably would have taken out a missile."

She paused, absently brushing back the stray lock to lodge within the collar of her white cotton blouse.

"A search radar went active shortly after the lead Safir dropped its first stage. There were no radio frequency emissions from the second and third rockets. They were the killers. Safir number one saw the slugs from the Rock and triggered prematurely."

He said, "They expected a counter-ASAT missile."

"Yep. They expected an anti-missile missile. The lead Safir was an anti-anti-missile missile."

Tom dropped his reading glasses to dangle from their cord. Layers of thrust, parry, and riposte typified his conflict with the Iranian theocrats. By this time they knew that he knew that they knew what he had pointed at them from the ISS. He rubbed his eyes. As yet, the mullahs didn't know that his station defense was a manned interceptor capable of shredding multiple ASATs and that it was reusable, assuming it survived the intercept.

He said, "Throwing heavy metal around still has its place. About the other Rock burning up. It was a Russian pilot?"

"Russian," Jenny said. "Probably the former cosmonaut Galina Ivanova. She dropped out of sight about the time the interceptor platoons were staffing up. We still don't know for sure who they have up there."

"Surprising," Tom said. "Most of the pilots are somewhat less, uh, recognizable."

"And more disposable," Jenny said. "It's not like they can eject."

Tom didn't want to linger over it. His measure of effectiveness, cost/benefit in polite terms, more commonly called bang for the buck, would include the expense for the training that had brought the Russian pilot up to readiness, but the pilots were free. They seemed to want to be there.

"So get with Beijing. It's their turn to send a pilot. With either good Russian or good English. The turbans will try to hit us again."

He liked to recruit internationally. He didn't need a cover for lost personnel if the personnel were not his.

He went on. "We should consider getting some younger people into the Rocks. Young guys or young women with high testosterone levels. The older they get, the more they think about losing a valuable aircraft. It makes them overcautious."

She shook her head. "You have two *Spetsnaz* Airborne helicopter pilots, a Navy fighter jock, and two Marine AV-8 Harrier pilots up there now. Testosterone levels are unknown, but all of them have flown multiple high risk missions. Airborne assault, carrier landings, combat air patrol, close air support."

Tom pushed his glasses back onto his nose. "Well, all that can work on your mind, after a while. I don't want any hesitation. And we don't need the chance of publicity. No more cosmonauts. No taikonauts."

Jenny said, "I could probably get ahold of some A-10 pilots. There are hundreds of them on active duty but the Air Force wants the Warthogs decommissioned to help pay for the new F-35, so some of those guys, or gals, will be looking for a ride. We might get the Killer Chick to come on board."

Tom said, "Not her, someone would notice."

That particular USAF Captain had brought home a Warthog that was a flying hunk of battle damage. She had a DFC, and was probably a personal hero to Jenny.

He went on, "But you're right. We're way behind the curve on recruiting Warthog pilots."

He had watched Hog pilots in Afghanistan, flying down the enemy's throat, shooting him in the face on the way in. Warthogs carried the big GAU-8 Gatling, so they knew the Gun.

Tom let his chin drop back into a palm, distracted momentarily by Jenny striding away in her soft beige knee-length skirt.

Chapter 34 - Carrier Landing

"...yet crossing a river in the same boat and caught by a storm, they will come to each other's assistance just as the left hand helps the right.

Sun Tzu

A very tired Jimmy tried to keep his touch light, feathering propellant from his attitude thrusters to nuzzle his piglet back up to Mama.

The Rocks had no Soyuz-style hard docking setup. Vlad was there, hardsuited, to clip on and tension the three lines that attached the interceptor in the same way that guy wires support a radio tower.

Jimmy got the sapphire blister open, but lingered awhile in the cockpit beneath the eternal black of Spaceside. He had escaped incineration, evaded the debris of the ASATs closing on him at twice orbital velocity, and had made a successful rendezvous with the station without exhausting his stored propellant. He would not run out of air in an unreachable near-miss orbit. The drop in his adrenaline level unmasked his deep fatigue.

The interior of Rock 3 had warmed appreciably via conduction from the three thousand degree surface temperature achieved by the leading edges. The titanium fuselage with its thermal barrier coatings had not reached a thousand degrees, but it might char through a glove if he got careless.

Vlad applied slow cautious twists to attach ammonia lines to carry the Rock's accumulated heat load to one of the big gray rectangular radiative panels that leafed out from the main truss. He then went handlining back to the habitat.

Shying from the Rock's exterior surfaces, Jimmy jumped from his acceleration couch directly for the ratlines running along the spine of *Columbus*. The gap he leapt was less than half the length of the Rock's fuselage, not a difficult feat, but a miss would require rescue by a squadmate in a hardsuit.

Vlad offered his hand at the open airlock hatch and guided Jimmy into the docking tunnel. The hatch closed from outside, and Jimmy keyed in the sequence to bleed in air while he lay in the tight docking tunnel. He thumped the wall twice when the hissing faded and the pressure telltale went green.

Polya pulled him through feetfirst into the brightly lit white-walled hab cylinder. Jimmy drifted down its length and grabbed a loop beside the suit locker. Stripped of the lightweight helmet and the blue softsuit, his tee was soaked with sweat and the acrid stink of combat was on him.

Polya seemed not to notice as he laid a hand on Jimmy's shoulder. He said, "You have three hits. Kills. Three vampires destroyed in boost phase."

Polya said, "You want to wipe down? Here is tea, and Ranger cookies." The Russians favored the large sugary chocolate chip cookies from American MREs.

The corners of his somber mouth lifted for just a moment before he pushed off down the hab axis to assist Vlad.

The hot black tea was as good as he remembered. He didn't remember the Ranger cookies being this good, and realized he hadn't eaten for several tense hours.

When Polya returned from locking in Vlad, Jimmy asked, "So they were Safirs for sure? Iranian?"

They were Safirs" said Polya, "Basically, Safirs." That was the Iranian booster designed to loft satellites to LEO, a kill vehicle being just a satellite which carried out diplomacy by other means.

Jimmy toweled away the sweat with cleansing wipes, and then got into a clean set of shorts and tee.

His head light with relief, caffeine, and sugar, he said, "I would hate to take out a vehicle carrying a bunch of fourth graders' experimental terrariums and kill all those cute little frogs."

"Iranians do not launch children's experiments," said Polya.

He had that look he got when he was about to comment on American culture, as though he thought boosting pet frogs to space was a typically American idea.

Jimmy pushed off to drift back down the length of the hab. His sweaty tee and shorts would have to airdry. He hooked his feet and a hand into loops beside his sleeping pad. His platoon mates lingered nearby while he ran down the mission, Polya typing into an iPad strapped to his thigh. Past the bare fact of the fuselage ignition, no one spoke of Katia. The sugar buzz faded and warm viscous exhaustion flowed back into all his limbs. Jimmy pulled the bungee net over himself.

Polya gazed at him for a moment, and then looked to Vlad. Vlad tapped his chest. Polya drifted nearer Jimmy's sleep space. He hoisted his tee above his belly and chest. Four tattoos, each a ragged red hemisphere tapering back into a cone of orange, stretched across his left pectoral. On looking closer, they represented ionization envelopes on a Rock gone hypersonic. Cyrillic script filled small scrolls below.

"*Kreshcheniye Ognem*. Baptism by Fire," said Polya. "If you survive deployment, you wish to be marked?"

"I'm marked enough," said Jimmy, his voice clouded with sleep.

Chapter 35 - Analysis & Machinations II

"My logisticians are a humorless lot ... They know if my campaign fails, they are the first ones I will slay."

, *Alexander of Macedon*

Tom said, "Hey Siri, call Juana Abreu." He spoke slowly. Sometimes Siri was dense about recognizing Hispanic names.

The iPhone said, "Calling Juana Abreu, office."

He fidgeted, sliding the phone back and forth on his glass desktop. The phone did not connect into anything like a cellular network. It sent digital radio packets to his router, and then through SIPRNet.

A young man's voice sounded from the iPhone, "Admiral Abreu's office. All calls are being held."

"Yeah, she's waiting to talk to me," Tom said.

The young man said, "I'm sorry. Hello, Dr. Broadhead. Engaging encryption." Tom brought up the iEncrypt app to add a layer of security atop SIPRNet. The DoD classified network had vulnerabilities elementary enough to be exploited by WikiLeaks. The CIA had its own network, but interconnect with DoD was clumsy.

Then Juana came on, "Tom, finally. So the Navy boy came through?"

"We have got to get that railgun up there. The Navy has to get the rate of fire up. And we need at least a hundred shot durability. Soon."

"You don't want to tell me about the intercept?"

Tom huffed, "Amateurs talk battles, professionals talk logistics. That's why I'm calling you. I need that five thousand mile per hour projectile. I need you to get it for me. Jenny will send over the mission hotwash update as soon as the Rock pilot is debriefed."

Admiral Abreu sounded more reserved. "NAVSEA can supply a prototype railgun, optics, radars, and the aiming mechanism. We can supply a pulsed DC power supply. We can supply a convective/radiative-cooled nuclear reactor. Who is going to put all of that together? Who's going to boost it to orbit? You need to boost additional people, hab modules, life support, and hardsuits. I can't help you with boost. Or staffing."

"Leave that to the High Command. My problem," Tom said. "You know how to work up production and deployment schedules and costs better than anyone else in Washington. You've got more deep black budget lines than anyone in DoD. That's what I want from you. You have the workforce to line up the vendors and the contractors. Sign off on the cost-plus purchase orders. Get that BAE company ready to turn the crank on the railgun and the reactor. I'm tired of incinerating my warriors."

He stabbed the call kill icon. Juana understood urgency and expected he would operate at speed. He needed to talk to Jenny again. He needed techs as well as pilots. Maybe Navy nuclear guys with experience in keeping small reactors happy in confined spaces, far from home. And some additional inter-service transfers if any of the Navy railgun people wanted to come aboard as gunners. Or perhaps some of the BAE engineers had a taste for adventure.

The NASA head administrator happened to be a former Naval aviator. An aviator who had spent a lot of time overflying what once was Mesopotamia. If his people couldn't repurpose some of the big rockets designed at Marshall Space Flight Center, then he could jawbone SpaceX or United Launch Alliance. Getting boost capability would take more time than getting the weapon together.

Best get it moving. Tom launched iEncrypt and texted the head of department ER (big rockets) at Marshall Space Flight Center, "Please call. Need heavy lift."

The Chinese had a railgun program. And Jenny had good Mandarin and good cred with certain of the Party cadres. It wouldn't hurt to have parallel programs for development of what would amount to the High Command's first purpose-built battle station. Programs known to each other. A leading program to goad a lagging program.

Tom leaned back, wanting a cappuccino. For better than a century men had boiled water to drive turbines to drive generators to make electricity. A reactor was just another way to boil water, and a Rock was built around a reactor. The railgun would have all the power it demanded.

Designed to have a two hundred twenty mile range in atmosphere, the gun would work even better exatmospheric. He wanted a sort of canister round to give a dispersed pattern of slugs for orbital intercepts.

But then again, the ISS orbited at only two hundred miles up. He locked his hands behind his head, dreaming of an angry mullah, gesticulating in mid-rant, bullseyed with a hypervelocity slug.

Chapter 36 - Hogwash

"Great power carries with it the means to greater power."

Gen. Clinton Martin, USAF

Vlad and Jimmy flanked Polya at his work panel, awaiting the post-action hotwash. Jimmy had been allowed three hours sleep, awakening yet again to the memory overwhelming stress. Only 87 days, calendar days, to go. Each would bring sixteen sunrises to the ISS and sixteen transits of the shooting gallery that was planet Earth.

Polya's flatpanel flashed up the logo of the new U.S. Air Force Ramjet Command, a stylized white Rock riding a spike of bright yellow exhaust against a space-black background. Then the dirtside datalink switched to the deskcam feed from Air Force Brigadier General Clinton Martin.

Jimmy had seen this one-star only in orientation videos, but recognized him immediately. Not just from the slicked-back black hair and prominent nose and jaw. It was the perpetual squint under the eyes. Caged eyes, they called it. The General sat at attention, chin back. You would need a lever to turn his head. You had to relax to shoot straight. Had this guy ever fired a round?

General Martin peered at his monitor. "You men are to be congratulated. The loss of your comrade is deeply regretted. She will be very much missed."

"Thank you, sir," said Polya.

The General continued, "The loss of the FS-2A is attributed to pilot error. It was Kuznetsova's first drop. She selected a trajectory which attained excessive velocity for local atmospheric density."

Jimmy piped up, a bad habit of his, "Sir, the trajectory was aggressive, the ionization and ablation trail showed that, but she tumbled before fuselage ignition."

"The conclusion of our analysts, on reviewing thermal imaging, is that excessive ablation of the leading throat edge induced aerodynamic instability. Thermal erosion led to tumbling." The General pressed a hand flat on the desktop.

Jimmy wasn't done, Polya's aeronautical lectures fresh in his mind. "The instability could have resulted from an incompletely closed weapon bay door, or from a misaligned blister. Both of those problems induced instability in wind tunnel tests. Ablative throat linings erode uniformly, by design, and have never been observed to induce instability."

General Martin raised his hand, then chopped it down, pointing into the cam. "Lock it down, Commander. Your flight doctrine going forward will adhere to the altitude/velocity tables worked up by our analysts."

The General continued, "Future drops will be authorized from this office, by me. You pilots, including the Russian pilots, operate only under my orders."

Polya said, "This was explained as joint covert operation with CIA. CIA is sole authority over American covert ops."

The one-star raised his right hand again. It stabbed forward, and the Ramjet Command logo reappeared on the flatscreen.

"Jesus," Jimmy said. "I bet that guy calls his memoir *Critical Command Decision*."

"He would have been political officer, if Soviet," said Polya. "I see I have very clear instructions for hotwash write-up. Apple 1 will not like at all. I do not like at all."

Vlad turned his palms up, but said nothing.

Chapter 37 - Old Friends II

Tom said, "Hey Siri, answer call." He launched iEncrypt, and said, "Hello, Jerry."

Jerry was not the head guy, the politically appointed NASA Administrator. Jerry was deep state, and could find the buried bodies, figurative and actual. He had family interred at Arlington. Recently deceased family.

"Tom. I can give you an Atlas, probably two, in a pinch three, if the funding is there," said Jerry.

"An Atlas won't boost a thirty thousand kilogram railgun," Tom said.

"The Navy railgun? Get BAE to go over the structure. It's a prototype, and operating in microgee removes some dead weight loading, so they can get the structural mass down. And they can integrate it with the launch vehicle," Jerry paused, "You still operating Fort Apache up there? Too many arrows incoming?"

Jerry did not wait for an answer. "Lifting that railgun is a Delta IV Heavy mission, or a Falcon Heavy if that's ever available. The Vulcan Heavy from United Launch Alliance will not be ready by 2020. I know that because they promised it by 2020. The Space Launch System in *maaaybeeee...* 2023 could do it."

"But you've got the wrong idea. You're spending eighty percent of your effort sustaining and protecting human assets. The railgun is not necessary for ISS defense because the ISS is not necessary for your primary mission. The ISS is not remotely the best hardware choice for what you have in mind."

Tom cleared his throat, "You know what I have in mind. Cameras whited out by the flash. Buildings tattooed with the silhouettes of true believers."

Jerry did not miss a beat. "OK. What am I? I launch on a standard Atlas. I have multi-year LEO endurance. I am highly maneuverable. I am unmanned. I

96

have re-entry capability. My landing is automated. I have a payload capability of a couple hundred kilograms. Then think about payloads."

Tom ignored Jerry's question. He said, "Payloads? Tiny 200 kilo payloads? Are we gonna talk about Davy Crockett again?"

The Davy Crockett weapons system was a nuke-tipped recoilless rifle deployed to the Fulda Gap. A Cold War tactical nuke. Jerry had talked about the Gap, a lot, and how the terrain had given birth to tactical nukes. The Fulda Gap was actually two terrain corridors where several open passes ran through hills, paths suitable for armored advance, and the shortest feasible route for Soviet invasion across the East German border. For 38 years, a single U.S. armored division stood ready at the Gap for a massive tank battle against three to five Soviet armored divisions. Opposing observation posts stood a few hundred yards apart, point-blank range for armor. The Point Alpha border surveillance camp had been manned by the 11th Armored Cavalry "Blackhorse" Regiment, and Jerry had been with the Blackhorse.

So what had happened at the Fulda Gap? Nothing. Far away from borders, the war was fought in think tanks, defense laboratories, and on proving grounds. A-10 tank killers and AH-64 helicopter gunships came into being, platforms mounting autocannons, high-explosive rockets, and antitank guided missiles. Tanks, antitank rocket launchers, and recoilless rifles fired, at ever-higher muzzle velocities, armor-piercing fin-stabilized discarding-sabot rounds carrying sub-caliber penetrators, giant needles of hyperdense tungsten or depleted uranium. High explosive anti-tank (HEAT) projectiles carried shaped-charge warheads to cut through massive armor with explosively formed liquid metal jets.

Tanks grew ever more ponderous, protected by thick slabs of rolled homogeneous armor, then by advanced composite armor layers of metal and ceramic, then by reactive armor which directed a counter-explosion out at the projectile. The feedback loop between increasingly impregnable tank armor and deadlier armor piercing projectiles wove a tangle of cause and effect that neither side was confident of understanding.

To cut this Gordian Knot, the Soviets planned to blast a path for their armored advance with tactical nuclear weapons. These were low-yield nukes, but orders of magnitude more powerful than any previous battlefield weapon. The U.S. planned to resist the Soviet tanks with their single armored division, and failing that, to nuke the armored advance. The Davy Crockett was born, a recoilless rifle no longer than a man is high, with a bulbous finned head carrying a micro-nuke, a metallic dickoid monstrosity that shot a load of fissile isotopes.

Jerry had commanded a section of Jeep-mounted Davy Crocketts. The recoilless rifle had a maximum range of two miles and doctrine called for him to fire the nuke, saddle up his vehicles, and try to exit the lethal radius before the fallout got thick. He had not felt at all confident of surviving an engagement.

Jerry stood atop the watchtower, which was like a forest service fire tower but made of concrete, when Tom drove up to the museum built at Observation Point Alpha. Jerry remained there unmoving, looking east over flat green fields leading to woodland and scattered low mountains, turning only as Tom emerged from clanging up the metal staircase.

Tom looked into his face and knew what he needed. This man needed to talk. Of his son, shipped direct from Afghanistan to the cemetery at Arlington. Of his own service with the Blackhorse and the Davy Crockett. Of his transition from launching nukes to launching satellites for NASA. Of how those years of staring into the muzzles of a thousand Russian tanks, finger on the trigger of a nuke, had not made the world safe for his son.

Only when he had fallen silent did Tom, who was present on that day and in that place by design, suggest that Jerry could be of help against the Taliban and their sponsors. He said nothing as yet of his own trigger-pulling in Afghanistan, and nothing of the shadowy organization branching out from intelligence networks into the defense and space establishments of nearly every developed nation.

Jerry had picked up Toms' suggestion and in time, knew all. He was not unreflective, having been an officer of armor in those decades when it was the tip of the spear. He understood war on a long timeline and a large scale. He had experience with launch vehicles back when they were the province of the Army, and had risen within NASA. Now if Tom needed a rocket with big throw weight, his first call was to Jerry.

In turn, Tom had picked up the first of many ideas from Jerry. Of a nuke that weighed thirty-six kilos.

Jerry said again, "OK," calling Tom's attention back to their phone call. Then, "I know you understand the payload."

He went on. "The vehicle I'm talking about is the X-37B. The Air Force is calling it an Orbital Test Vehicle, OTV. It's a deployed spacecraft with four or five completed missions, all successful. You could load it up with a W54 or whatever the follow-on micro-warhead is now, and launch it on an Atlas. You don't even need heavy lift. It loiters for years in LEO. You forget it until enough snakes cluster together with enough venom to do immediate grievous harm. Your OTV re-enters, glides along to the reptiles' nest, and sterilizes it."

Tom leaned back, "You're talking about a robot with a nuke, with no man in the loop."

Jerry said, "Think of it as an exatmospheric remotely piloted drone. Carrying a very big Hellfire with a very big boom. Or an ICBM with a long pause between boost and re-entry. Very flexible. Lots of opportunities for mission redirection. No life support, no resupply, no crew rotations. Nothing else has loiter time like that."

"I'm not convinced. That's a lot of automation to string together. And the ionization envelope during re-entry would block any remote commands. Commands like an abort."

Jerry said, yet again, "OK. Will you listen to a short story?"

"Sure," Tom said. "As long as Martin doesn't call."

"A decade or so ago, Yamaha, you know, the motorcycle company, sold a small unmanned helicopter. Called it the RMAX. It was GPS-enabled. You just programmed in waypoints, and set it off. It carried a payload of maybe fifteen or sixteen kilos. They used it for crop dusting, spraying fields in pre-programmed patterns."

"One day the Japanese police showed up at company headquarters. Yamaha had sold half a dozen of the subscale birds to China. The Americans were upset because the bird could fly anywhere you told it to, within range limits, and release whatever you loaded it up with. That's a very good description of a cruise missile. Except this cruise missile could land, fully automated, lie in wait, and take off again to attack whenever the target showed up. Yamaha had their helo sales restricted for years after that."

Tom thought about it. With the midget helicopter, Jerry was giving him an example of weaponizing a remotely piloted vehicle, and expecting that he would extend the idea to the OTV. Tom was having entirely different thoughts. He knew the Air Force would never let go of the OTV. But the subscale Yamaha helo had possibilities of its own.

He said only, "Good to know."

Chapter 38 - Hijinks

I am ready to fly without coming back.

Valentina Tereshkova

Polya asked, "How did you get from carrier deck into orbital mess?"

Jimmy said, "I thought they wanted a Space Shuttle door gunner. I was up for it."

"Fokkin' A," said Vlad. "Gunner."

His habmates had warmed to him since he flew the intercept. He had taught them to say "Fokkin-A Tweety Bird" or just "Fokkin-A" like college kids would to indicate emphatic agreement. It was funny when Polya said it, but unbelievably droll coming from tight-lipped Vlad.

Jimmy continued, "I flew over four hundred sorties from aircraft carriers. That's four hundred all-weather carrier landings in an F-14 that doesn't fly well subsonic. No actual combat sorties. None. I got out of flying for a while, then this spooky guy came up with this gig. Very unexpected. Not at all the same as the astronaut selection process."

Jimmy had followed the Iran-Iraq air combat, including over a hundred victories for Iranian F-14s, with satisfaction nearly equal to his massive frustration. Years later, the CIA guy had showed up. Or he implied he was CIA.

"I thought they wanted a Blackbird pilot when he said hypersonic. The SR-71 defined the term. Well okay, the X-15, but that was a rocket. But he said no the Blackbird will stay retired. So I guessed maybe the SR-72. Maybe Lockheed got the scramjet working and planned to bump it up from Mach 3 to Mach 6 or better. But why put an old pilot, with old reflexes, in a new airplane?"

"Then he said how about Mach 20 and I knew he was spooky. CIA black program spooky. Mach 20 to me meant boosters, big rockets."

Jimmy paused, considering, "You guys know Tom?"

Polya said, calm as ever, "We know Tom."

Vlad said, "Fokkin-A we know Tom."

"He bought me a cup of coffee one time. Told me what a nuclear ramjet was, and about the SLAM, the old Pluto missile, and NERVA and the Russian nuclear cruise missile program. I knew he wanted someone willing to take a risk. More than combat air patrol risk. More than test pilot risk. More than nuclear-powered vehicle risk. And more than astronaut risk. Because the mission would be all of those risks at the same time."

"And you had nothing better to do, yes?" Polya's brushy brows lifted in the center. "Tell me, Tom has ever asked you to pull trigger?"

"That's kind of personal. But no. How about you?" Jimmy asked.

"I pulled triggers on Taliban long before Tom showed up," said Polya. "Vlad I bring along because is useful as pilot and with hands and is deeply aggressive. Is his nature."

He went on. "So you do not have agenda? Is still not clear why you are here. To be sure, your skills are suited, but what reason you have for wanting this?"

"It was a chance to fly a high-performing aircraft. And in all those years as a Naval aviator, no one took a shot at me. It's important to me to know if I can hack it. Not so much whether I'm a killer, but whether I can go in harm's way, and remain master of myself."

Polya spoke briefly in Russian to Vlad, most of which Jimmy understood. It was a translation of what he had just said.

Vlad nodded. He said something, and Jimmy caught it as well, *"Vozmozhno, on voin."*

Jimmy's Russian let him know what Vlad had said. 'Maybe he's a warrior.'

"So this ISS protection mission is not our entire mission?" Jimmy remembered Katia's last words to him, and the talk he had had with Polya.

"Rocks have capabilities which are not revealed to you," said Polya. "We think you are best fixed-wing pilot among us, best able to exercise Rock capabilities. We talk with Tom soon. You will see."

Chapter 39 - Choosing the Bait

"... lure the enemy in depth"

Mao Tse-Tung

"Hey Siri, answer call. Yes, General Martin." Tom punched iEncrypt.

"Tom, I'm worried about the last intercept. No casualties on the ISS, but they threw three birds at us this time. And we lost a Rock to pilot error."

"General, we lost a switch as well. The margin for error in intercepting a direct-ascent kill vehicle is vanishingly thin. In addition, the Rocks are the first of their kind. In fact, the Air Force opposed the program; claimed it wouldn't work. That is, until it did work, at which time the Air Force demanded control of the program. You may recall, that happened as well with the U-2, the SR-71 ... "

The iPhone nearly exploded with the one-star's interruption, "The United States Air Force will control all strategic air assets associated with national security!"

Tom said, "Give me a moment, General?" He thought about it. Martin had come up through Air Force ranks straight out of college AFROTC. His rise had been fast, his career spent entirely within a training command. The command headed by his father, it happened. He had never gotten his ticket punched in a combat command; hence the CIA's interceptors had been embedded into the USAF Ramjet Command. It gave Martin table-of-organization command of Rock drops. It was likely that he wanted yet more authority.

Tom said, "Nearly everything in orbit which lies within U.S. Air Force Space Command authority is a satellite. GPS, communications, meteorological, surveillance. Except for the ramjets. And one other asset in which you might take an interest."

Tom heard Martin draw a deep breath, preparing for a high-volume pissing contest. But then the general said nothing for the better part of a minute. Finally, he said, "Huh?"

Good. He was wondering what additional asset he might arrogate.

Tom said, "Would you like to talk to a friend of mine? He has some interesting stories."

Chapter 40 - Scheming

"If the enemy is in range, so are you."

Infantry Journal

Duty cycles had expanded by an hour for each of them, to make up for losing Katia. Polya, at his work panel, peered at displays, monitoring threat layers. Vlad had locked out to sit a watch in Rock 2.

Jimmy had awakened to a sleep space smelling like dirty socks, but for the first time had no flashback to hand-to-hand combat, zero gee sex, or ramjet combat sorties. He ran through switchology at the mockup Rock armrests, pausing for bites of an ill-understood Russian breakfast. The kind of mission Polya had described had never been executed. Jimmy had never even simulated such a mission, and had to work up switch sequences on the spot.

Polya looked up from the panel. His hand went to his earpiece. Then he punched the dirtside commo onto the hab speaker for Jimmy to hear.

Tom crackled through the radio, "The loudest sonic boom ever recorded was from an F-4 flying at Mach 1 at 100 feet above the sound pressure level sensor. They recorded a pressure of 144 pounds per square foot. That's 170 decibels."

Polya said, "Good morning to you, too, Tom."

Tom went on, "If that F-4 had been flying at Mach 2, it would have produced about four times the sound pressure, about 576 pounds per square foot, or 182 decibels. The lethal range for sound pressure acting on a human begins at about 180 decibels."

"If the altitude doubles to 200 feet, the sound drops by a factor of 4, so you have to double your speed to get that back. You have to fly at Mach 4."

"So if you fly higher, fly faster, and you'll still shock 'em to jelly," said Jimmy. He put aside the pouch of breakfast kibble with its Cyrillic label.

"We can work out flight profile from that," said Polya.

Tom crackled back on, "You are clear on the objective, then? We want to warn these guys off from shooting at us, not incite them to further attacks. So borderline lethal. Pop a few eardrums at 150 decibels."

"We're talking about pressure levels directly beneath the aircraft?" said Jimmy. "It's less intense if someone is off the flight path to right or left?"

"Correct," said Tom.

"We will work something up," said Polya.

Jimmy said, "If the F-4 was just accelerating into supersonic flight, they would have measured a focused sonic boom. That's more intense than the steady boom from constant velocity flight."

Tom said, "I'll get on that. There were other experiments in the mid-90s that indicate about double the sound pressure from a focused boom. We can run some ray-tracing sonic boom models to better predict the footprint."

Jimmy had one more concern. "Let me guess. Polya said earlier you want nap of the Earth hypersonic flight. I'm guessing you want a flight path through downtown Tehran. Basically you want me to drag my tailhook through town and blow things apart with the sonic boom overpressure."

Tom said, "Not Tehran. We won't target civilians, a lot of whom dislike the imams. They have considerable civil unrest just now. There is a launch complex near Shahroud, in the northern Iranian desert. The Imam Khomeni Spaceport. The objective is to demonstrate our capability. I ask that you flatten every structure associated with that launch facility."

The crackle from the hab speaker died, and they heard only the background rumbling and creaking of the ISS. Jimmy rooted through the food cache, hoping for an MRE, while Polya locked Vlad in from his duty cycle in Rock 2. Then they began to talk of the mission.

Chapter 41 - Setting the Trap

"To subdue the enemy without fighting is the acme of skill."

Sun Tzu

Leaned back in the chair, Tom fell into reverie. The lead Safir had most likely taken out the two follow-on vehicles. In late boost phase, second stage still attached and firing, they were big targets, and the lead Safir's debris and the shrapnel field from its warhead were much more likely to have scored a hit than the slugs from Jimmy's Gatling. The storm of slugs had tripped the lead Safir's target acquisition radar. It had exploded early, still within significant atmospheric density.

Iranian mission planners had expected a missile counterattack from the ISS after their birds had achieved orbital insertion. The lead Safir was meant to take out that defensive missile. After second stage separation, small hardened satkillers would have been released from the follow-on birds, and would have had a good probability of passing unharmed through a debris field.

And about the Rocks. He had made some conceptual errors in the design. Twenty millimeter was big enough. He didn't need the armor-killing thirty millimeter GAU-8 Avenger to perforate the minimalistic structure of a missile. Twenty millimeter worked just fine for the Vulcan Gatling used on CIWS. The lighter version of the Vulcan which armed the F-22 and the F/A-18 Super Hornet fighters would work even better. He could throw up a much larger cloud of the smaller slugs, improving hit probability.

The depleted uranium was another mistake. Armor piercing rounds passed through fragile spacecraft leaving a thirty millimeter hole. High explosive would blow out much larger cavities. Changing the caliber and the loadout would take time and effort, but it was needful.

He was limited. The hypersonic flight regime was so damned nonlinear, with shock waves bouncing around between control surfaces. He could hang a missile below a supersonic fighter. A hypersonic Rock so armed would tumble and ignite.

He called Jerry. Tom said, "Get the Delta IV Heavy. I want to boost the railgun."

Jerry sounded tired. "No X-37B cruise missile? The OTV, cheap, unmanned, quick, massively deadly?"

Tom said, "Air Force Global Strike Command can adapt the OTV as a strike weapon. I want to hit enemy birds in boost phase. Without throwing tender human flesh at them. I want the railgun projectile with terminal guidance that the Navy is working on. I also want their shrapnel projectile, the canister round with the thousands of tungsten cubes. It's ideal for the satellite protection mission."

Tom said nothing of his daydream of dropping railgun projectiles from orbit onto surface targets.

He went on. "You can expect a call from Martin. He will want to know how the OTV can work as a first-strike weapon. He will want it for Space Command. Air Force Global Strike Command will chew him up and spit him out. Space Command will put him to surfing Google Maps. We will be rid of him."

Chapter 42 - Getting Down and Dirtside

"If you find yourself in a fair fight – you didn't plan your mission properly."

David Hackworth

Jimmy and Polya had a short discussion of what Jimmy meant by a tailhook, and why he would want to drag it through the sea when returning from a sortie. The explanation was difficult because it involved entirely intangible motivations completely disconnected from carrier-based aircraft mission objectives.

After, Jimmy asked, "Perhaps you will tell me how exactly how I'm to attain such a chickens-flying-in-the-barnyard altitude? In a Rock? There are a couple hundred miles of atmosphere to get through, and about ten thousand miles per hour of atmospheric braking to do."

Polya said, "Soyuz and other capsules re-enter with atmospheric braking. Bleed off all velocity and then deploy parachutes. American Space Shuttle used same braking, but kept velocity to glide to a landing."

Jimmy asked, "And why are you telling me this? I watch the news coverage of space missions."

Polya glanced away, then back, impatient. "Previous vehicles had no fuel for powered flight during and after re-entry. Rock's NERVA has approximately unlimited stored energy. After braking during re-entry, you do not glide. You continue flight under ramjet propulsion."

"And the landing, following the sortie?" asked Jimmy. "There's no landing gear on a Rock."

"You do not land. You close down reactor neutron reflectors. Ascend, back to orbit," said Polya.

Jimmy went absolutely still. Then he said, "Fokkin-A. What could go wrong?"

Chapter 43 - Chalk Talk

Never think that war, no matter how necessary, nor how justified, is not a crime.

Ernest Hemingway

They decided on 150 feet of altitude and a velocity of Mach 5 for the attack pass. Tom had uploaded further overpressure measurements from the Air

Force's boom experiments. A swath approximately 200 feet wide centered beneath the Rock's flight path would experience lethal overpressures. The launch complex would be sparsely manned. And killing a few soldiers was not objectionable to Jimmy. Tom had suggested an attack that would kill buildings but spare people. But once he had been shot at, once the three Safirs had come at him, Jimmy considered that dying was in their job description.

Then they had to correct for terrain. Photos of the Imam Khomeini Spaceport at Shahroud showed three clusters of large buildings, all of which lay on a flat patch of brown desert. The pictures had been taken from the south, and along the left or western edge of the plain ran a range of long, low, but sharp hills, dark gray and jagged. More barren steep hills loomed to the north and east of the plain. The launch complex nestled in a flat cove of desert bounded by hills where only the southern approach lay open.

One set of a dozen buildings, said to be used for rocket body processing, lay near the western hills. A road running southeast connected this processing center to a large assembly building. A second road ran from the assembly building almost due south to the launch pad and its large gantry. They would ignore the gantry, whose open structure would let their pressure wave pass through.

Much discussion followed. Of the turning radii of the FS-2A Smart Rocks, and that it was quite large. The Rock was an interceptor, with speed and range, not a dogfighter. No tight turns, on pain of ripping off the thin hypersonic wings. Of the three ranges of hills jutting up eight hundred feet above the desert. They talked of the alignment of valleys between the hills. The hills were long ridges, but they curved, making an attack flight path along the valleys between them impossible.

Jimmy would make a hypersonic attack pass, coming in from the southeast to hit the assembly building and passing northwest along the road to hit the processing center.

Only a couple miles of plain separated the northern hills from the processing center, requiring too steep a pullout for a hypersonic craft, wing loadings which would snap the wing roots. The attack pass had to be done entirely above the range of hills.

To compensate for the increased height above the desert floor, nearly nine hundred feet, they set the attack speed to Mach 10. Speed was one thing of which they had plenty. Speed and range. Ground level overpressure from the boom was expected to reach 180 pounds per square foot, a 173 decibel sound pulse. They expected to pop eardrums and to shatter buildings.

Chapter 44 - Shock and Awe

"If you wage war, do it energetically and with severity. This is the only way to make it shorter and consequently less inhuman."

Napoléon Bonaparte

Jimmy dropped Rock 3 into the stratosphere over the cold blue-gray North Atlantic, some 4,000 miles from Iran. Such a distance would have allowed even the unpowered Space Shuttle to maneuver in its bricklike descent to a landing strip. To avoid crushing himself with deceleration or cooking himself from heat buildup, he powered up the ramjet and stayed up at 135,000 feet, the upper stratosphere where atmospheric braking and frictional heating were gentler.

Gingerly probing the hypersonic airstream with the Rock's control surfaces, testing the lift of the stubby delta winglets, elevating the nose a few thin degrees to vector some thrust downward against gravity, losing speed to the increasing drag, he crept down into atmosphere, eyes locked on the fuselage skin temperature readouts.

When the ionization envelope faded, Jimmy released his harness and sat up to press his faceplate against the sapphire canopy. Forward through the lowest point of the blister, the nose still glowed cherry red. Ablative layers at the nose and inside the throat of the ramscoop armored the Rock against the heat, lest its titanium fuselage ignite.

More speed bled off above Gibraltar and eastward toward Asia along the center of the Med. The sky, gone from black to blue, reappeared as the familiar domed ceiling, rather than the thin skin seen above the limb of Earth against the black of space. Slowed to Mach 3, the ride was smooth.

Below as well, all was blue until he went feet dry at the Syrian coast. Past the coastal range, there was only the dun of desert. As he entered Iraq, he picked up the Euphrates, contrasting dark blue against desert sand. He nudged the joystick to follow the river southeast toward Baghdad and was still high supersonic at Mach 3 passing over the city. From there a broad tan alluvial plain patched with green took him to Basrah where the Tigris joined in. Then he went feet wet over the coast of the Persian Gulf.

Two hundred miles of blue water lay between Iran and the Arabian Peninsula. Following the Iranian coast, he began a gentle left turn as he passed the last ramparts of the Zagros range close by on the Iranian landmass to his left. Jimmy flew a long hairpin around the end of the mountain range to the east and northeast and then north into flat Iranian desert.

His approach vector lay to the northwest along the road which joined the processing buildings to the assembly complex at Shahroud. The desert plain rose steadily to meet him, and so Jimmy leveled out at 6,000 feet above sea level.

He caressed the slider on his left armrest to crank down the neutron reflectors just a hair, the new energy engorging the exhaust spike so the Rock's roar swelled, and his approach began at Mach 5. Five minutes in, he had halved the six hundred miles from the sea to the launch site.

The Rock's nose blocked the downward view ahead. To each side the desert a thousand feet below was blurred by his speed to apparent uniformity. Farther off there streamed past sharp ridges of very dark brown rock, gone before he could get a good look. Still the Earth rose up beneath him.

Polya, patched through on the orbital commo net, said, "Dust trail is visible from space."

The station had circled the Earth during Jimmy's drop and approach, allowing Polya a direct view through the Celestron as the rooster tail shot across the desert.

Jimmy inched the slider on his left armrest forward until the GPS readout indicated a groundspeed of Mach 8. The dense air of the troposphere howled into the ramscoop, the nozzle roared a yet more crazed note of rage, and the buffeting from slight density gradients in the air vibrated his teeth and eyeballs, blurring his vision.

The vibration was a worry, it seemed the airframe had a structural resonance at around 20 Hz, as two to three gees of acceleration pulsed twenty times each second through his body. He left the speed at Mach 8, not trusting to push the aircraft or himself further. He listened for the tone that would signal his passage over the launch site, hoping the GPS vectoring worked.

He was wishing for a rubber mouthpiece to bite down on, something to damp the vibration in his head, when a bell sounded in his earpiece, and a dark shadow flashed by close below to his right. This was the line of razor-edged hills north of the launch complex, telling him he was headed for the headwall of the much higher mountains west of Shahroud.

Jimmy jerked the slider back to Mach 3 and yanked the nose up, praying dear God don't let me pull the wings off. Peaks flashed past and then he was over the Caspian Sea and climbing out.

...

The Air Force had tasked a Reaper to record the attack pass and the flatscreen at Polya's work panel streamed the uploaded video, taken at a low angle as though the drone were far from the launch complex. The view centered on the cluster of blocky processing buildings. Jagged gray hills plain appeared beyond.

A marginally visible linear smudge ghosted across above the buildings, which immediately flashed into an expanding cloud of wall and roof panels, furniture, and structural debris.

"Zooming and slowing display rate for replay," Tom crackled in Polya's earpiece.

The frame rate of the video was adequate to show in slow motion how the overpressure wave of the boom imploded the windows, and almost immediately the walls and roof exploded as the underpressure wave passed. A single human figure flew among the debris, then ragdolled onto hard dry ground. Dust was suddenly everywhere, opaquing the image, completing the 300 mile long rooster tail Jimmy had ripped across the desert.

"Christ, I think we killed a janitor," Tom said.

"Is in uniform," grated Polya.

He had become dry with the waiting, his voice even hoarser than usual.

He went on, "Satellite launch site is farther east at Semnan. This is launch site for ballistic missile tests. Entirely military."

He pushed off toward the food cache to brew tea.

...

Jimmy in a few minutes went feet dry over the southern Russian coast. It was strange to consider Russia as friendly territory. Staying northbound until he approached the ground track of the station's orbit, he then bent eastward by thirty-four degrees to match its orbital inclination. He pitched the nose up and pushed the slider gradually forward.

The boost to orbit was smooth, not exceeding three gees, less taxing than the Soyuz. No comparison to the jolt from a cat shot, riding an F-14 as a huge steam-powered catapult threw it from a carrier deck. Rock 3 was a good ride, if you didn't ram it too hard through dense atmo down on the deck.

Jimmy got on the networked commo. "Rock 3 on orbital ascent trajectory. Telltales green. Detailed systems check to begin shortly. Will advise when I catch up to you, Polya."

Polya came right back, "Station here. I will see you before you see me. You have left only fragments at processing center. We must wait for images of assembly building."

"The pass was at Mach 8," said Jimmy. "We need to talk to the airframe structures people about their dynamics calcs."

He had also passed over the edge of the small city of Shahroud, over an industrial park, a technological college, and a couple of mosques. None of those institutions had shot at him, and he hoped that his pull-up had been quick enough to spare them.

Tom's connection was still crackly, "I've got more drone images here. The assembly building has been, wow..., widely distributed."

Chapter 45 - The Lunacy Begins

Life is either a great adventure, or it is nothing.

Helen Keller

"Incoming are two birds. Matching station orbit."

Polya spoke from his usual place, looking over his work panel. He looked unconcerned, even pleased. His hand was raised to his ear and he threw the toggle to engage the hab speakers.

"No reason to get excited." Tom Broadhead crackled over the speaker system.

He went on, "Milk run incoming. Delivery as promised. Brief the mission, Polya."

The crackle in the speakers died as the dirtside link cut out.

The new orbital vehicles turned out to be white cylindrical tanks equipped with attitude[13] and translation[14] thrusters. Each tank was the diameter of a Rock's ramscoop intake and about half the spacecraft's length. Polya and Vlad hardsuited and locked out to tie them down.

Jimmy monitored from his workspace display as the Russians affixed three guy wires to each tank to tie it head down to the hab cylinder in the same way their ramjet interceptors were docked. He then helped each man into the hab from the lock tunnel, biting back his curiosity. He was assisting Polya out of his hardsuit torso when the Russian finally spoke.

"You would like to go to Moon?" Polya was grinning at him in a way he had never seen.

Vlad too was grinning. "Is chancy, a little. In softsuit for few days."

---

[13] 'Attitude', as in rotating the vehicle to change where it points – It's a navigational term, not an emotional one.

[14] 'Translation', as in moving in a straight line – nothing to do with languages.

Polya again, "I want to send Vlad. But does not want to go alone."

Jimmy looked at them for several seconds. He said, "OK, you've got my attention."

Polya said, "New tanks contain liquid hydrogen. Propellant. Base of tank carries integrated turbopump, feeds hydrogen to reactor core, makes rocket of ramjet. Nuclear rocket. Kind of rocket can go to planets."

"I know you guys are SpecOps helicopter jocks, but not even Vlad is nuts enough to try to take a Rock to Mars," said Jimmy.

Polya spoke carefully, "Rocks have plenty range for trips within solar system, but not so much life support for manned interplanetary trips."

He suddenly threw his hands up. "But Moon is only hours away."

"It takes days to get to the Moon!" said Jimmy.

Polya looked at him, disappointed. "Nuclear rocket gets twice thrust from same amount of fuel."

A shadowy memory of one of the Star City briefings came to Jimmy.

He said, "It takes days in a chemical rocket. We could accelerate twice as hard in a Rock."

Polya broke out another of his rare smiles. "You are fast study, Jimmy."

Chapter 46 - Sea Change

... into something rich and strange.

Wm. Shakespeare

Brigadier General Clinton Martin slouched in his desk chair, borne down by dark, entirely realistic thoughts.

A most sudden and drastic transition had begun when Clint had sought to consolidate under his own control all the Air Force's maneuverable orbital assets. Those assets included the X-37B. His choices for continued employment with the Air Force were severely constrained by the aftereffects of that debacle.

Clint felt himself broken down into his constituent parts. Worse, some of them needed discarding before he attempted reassembly. And he needed a new framework, beginning with a spine.

His aide poked his head around the edge of the doorway to the anteroom. "Sir, an Admiral Abreu is here. She's asking to see you."

"Admiral Abreu is new to my acquaintance." Still, this was a very highly placed officer. "I suppose I had best see her."

"Shall I turn on the lights, Sir?"

Clint nodded and the aide flipped the switch and ducked quickly out.

The Admiral walked slowly into his office, looking only at him. She was a small woman, dark of hair and eye, in Navy whites.

She was brusque without being unfriendly. "You could wind up your career overseeing early warning radars. On the tundra."

Clint said nothing, unable to correct that statement in any of its particulars.

She went on, "I can offer an alternative."

Clint's mouth had caused him severe difficulty of late, and he again kept it firmly shut. The Admiral's eyes still had not left his. He raised a hand in invitation.

"This alternative would depend upon your meeting my personal standards for conduct becoming an officer of combat troops. That would include support for anyone under your command who meets with less than unqualified success. Plenty of people will point out defects in the conduct of a mission. A commander supports his people. He judges, he disciplines when he must, but he is the last to accuse."

It was true. He had been arrogant, not only in overreaching his authority, but too quick to judge the Rock pilot, especially so for one innocent of combat. He straightened up in his chair.

"He leads from the front wherever possible," the Admiral said.

What could she possibly be talking about? She was Navy. What could she do for him? But she wore more stars than he did. And any way away from where he was now looked like up. He nodded.

"What you have been, since leaving your training command, is an Air Force incursion into what is called the High Command. What is offered is a chance for you to become a High Command incursion into the Air Force."

"You are likely familiar, in a distant way, with the mission and structure, or lack of structure, of the totally deniable CIA Special Activities Division, the paramilitaries. The High Command is an even more loosely structured, even more deniable outgrowth of SAD[15]."

"Would you like to accept this opportunity, a guarantee that you will go in harm's way, to perhaps qualify for further High Command ops?"

They stared, one at the other, until Clint's slow nod broke the gaze. He rested his forehead on the fingertips of his left hand, suddenly tired to death again.

"Good. You will transit to Kuwait in two hours' time where you will reattach to the Air Force Training Command, ostensibly to familiarize with electronic warfare on the EC-130 Compass Call. You will in actuality be the mission cover as you deploy with the Compass Call."

Quite a talking-to, actually. Clint asked nothing, just nodded one more time. It felt like this would be the first honest thing he had done in his career.

Chapter 47 - From the Earth to the Moon

"Mine was a little more sticky than that. Throw that away,"

---

[15] Spoken by spelling it out, "ess ayee dee".

"You will look things over on Moon's backside," said Polya.

Jimmy's core musculature locked up. If he could restrain his laughter, perhaps the Russian would continue speaking of the Moon's backside. Half of the Moon forever faced away from Earth, out of view of telescopes and planetary radars like the huge parabolic dishes at Goldstone in California. This lunar hemisphere was sometimes called the dark side, though it saw as much sunlight as the other. Better to call it Farside.

Their excursion would be limited by the mass of propellant in their bolt-on hydrogen tanks, by the ability of their recyclers to renew their oxygen, by the water and nutrients they could wedge into the very tight blisters of the Rocks, and by the sustained gee forces they were willing to withstand. They would not be limited by their energy supply. The fissile isotopes in their reactor cores would outlast the airframes of the Rocks.

Most difficult would be the close confinement, the continued lack of bathing, and the problem, occupying engineers and medics ever since Alan Shepherd had peed his pants while still on the pad, of waste handling.

Jimmy had a set of isometric exercises that would maintain some muscle tone, and enough persistence in their application to get his heart rate and breathing up. The sweat would just have to dry. After the first couple unwashed days in space, his skin developed its natural population of bacteria, and his stench moderated.

The new Boeing blue softsuits had a circular baseball-sized port at the crotch. It functioned as an airlock, so that, even in vacuum, a rolled-up inflatable bedpan could be introduced into the suit and then extracted along with the nasty stuff. Still, when the time came for the basest necessity, Jimmy intended to peel the softsuit down. If the Rock depressurized he would die with a bag taped to his ass. But he would not have a bag taped to his ass inside his suit.

Injecting the Rocks into lunar orbit could be done in a well understood way. The new wrinkle was the Rocks' ability to do extensive maneuvers, expending energy in a way impossible to earlier lunar surveying craft, which had entered polar orbit to wait twenty-seven days for the Moon's rotation to display the surface below them. The Rocks would enter an equatorial orbit, then thrust normal to their orbital velocity, increasing the inclination of each orbit to bring unseen surface into view.

At an altitude of only thirty kilometers, Jimmy and Vlad would see a strip of lunar surface about six hundred kilometers wide. Their side-looking survey cameras and infrared detectors had adequate resolution out to about one hundred and fifty kilometers, so each orbital pass would image a strip of only three hundred kilometers in width. To survey the entire Moon would take thirty-five orbits, or two and one half days in low lunar orbit. But because the two Rocks could interleave their coverage, they would need just over a day for their survey.

Data acquired in their cameras would feed digital image analysis, edge and pattern detection. Anything with straight edges or right angles would trip an alert. Of even greater interest would be regions of high infrared contrast, anything made of metal.

Chapter 48 - And a Trip Around It

"What enables the wise sovereign and the good general to strike and conquer, and achieve things beyond the reach of ordinary men, is foreknowledge."

Sun Tzu

It took only a handful of orbits before Jimmy had a hit. The quick discovery was a mercy because each orbit required adjustment of both orbital velocity and inclination to maintain the Rock's planned ground track.

The Moon is not nearly as homogeneous as our Earth. Asteroids hit the young Moon at astronomical velocities and embedded themselves beneath its crust. These highly dense bodies are mass concentrations, mascons, which increase the pull of gravity near them. Five of these buried blocks lie beneath Nearside, more on Farside.

Passing over a mascon causes a decay in the trajectory of a body in low lunar orbit, and repeated passes lead to an elliptical crater with the familiar starlike pattern of lighter gray ejecta on the ancient dark regolith. And so conducting a surface survey from low lunar orbit requires constant attention, short thruster burns for orbital adjustment, continual brief expenditures of propellant. It was the abundant energy of their reactors which allowed the Rocks to boost large propellant tanks to the Moon, and so to power the frequent burns.

But now certain hotspots in the infrared survey correlated with white blotches in the optical data and demanded a better look. Jimmy had to break out of the search pattern the two Rocks had been weaving over the craters and rilles as each covered ground not surveyed by the other.

"Heads up Vlad, departing from orbital inclination program."

As soon as Vlad clicked his mic twice Jimmy hissed a timed gout of hydrogen to nudge his orbital plane into the desired inclination. He would have a two hour wait before he returned to this region of Farside, directly above the spot marked out by the survey software.

As his Rock cleared the lunar horizon, giving him line of sight to Earth, Jimmy said, "Dirtside, I have something."

He gated the survey data into the dirtside datalink, which for this mission was routed through the radiotelescopes of the Very Long Baseline Array[16] in the U.S. and a few of the larger specimens of the more than one hundred other radiotelescopes operating over the surface of the Earth, steel ears large enough to extract his faint digital signal from the cosmic background. The dirtside analysts panned, zoomed, and enhanced, and agreed that he had something.

The narrow-field high-magnification camera had resolution better than six inches, and when he was able to again overfly the site its images showed cylinders, white like most spacecraft to help control heat buildup from sunlight, standing upright in an unorganized cluster on a crater floor, each on four legs surrounding a rocket nozzle. They had been soft landed, a thing not hard to do in the Moon's lax gravity.

When Earth rose again above the lunar horizon Jimmy sent the high-res data. Ben, Tom's senior analyst dirtside, had the commo duty.

He said, "It's an oxygen cache. Someone is building up supplies. Probably to establish a base." Ben sounded like he had a comb-over and a spare tire.

---

[16] Astronomy is everywhere, if you care to look.   https://tinyurl.com/yazyab78

Jenny jumped onto the datalink. "Good, we know where it is now. JAXA[17] has been launching far too much into lunar transfer orbits. They don't need that many communications and survey satellites. We knew something was going on, but not where."

Chapter 49 - Preemptive Strike

"Harass and smite the Midianites, for they harass and plan against you."

Bamidbar 25:17-18

Vlad breathed propellant from his Rock's attitude thrusters, gently stopping the slow pitchover which had flipped it into a retrograde orientation in its orbit. With no atmosphere to work with, the Rocks were ballistic and all maneuvers consumed stored propellant for which the nearest resupply lay a quarter million miles Earthward. Moving slowly saved gas.

His current orbit would take him directly above the tank farm, but from thirty kilometers altitude his autocannon rounds would be too widely dispersed to guarantee hits. To confine the burst to the oxygen cache he would have to skim the lunar surface, maintaining a thin five hundred meters of vacuum between the rough regolith and his Mach 5 Rock. In doing so he would risk propellant expenditure, and more.

"You are not hung over today, Ben?" he asked.

"Dirtside is hydrated, caffeinated, and non-crapulous."

"He's saying he's not hung over," said Jimmy.

Ben said, "Make your burn duration ten seconds. Make your decel one quarter gee. Burn on my mark."

Later, when the Rocks had nearly transited Luna's Nearside once more, and behind them the Earth dipped near the lunar horizon, Jimmy called, "You there, Ben?"

---

[17] Japan Aerospace Exploration Agency

"Still conscious," said Ben. "On my mark, Vlad. Say when ready."

Vlad sounded cheerful, "Ready now, Dirtside."

Ben said, "Initiate burn now. Burn."

Vlad pushed the slider on the left armrest to fire the Rock's main nozzle, stopping the motion when the deceleration pushing him into the couch built to a soft one quarter gee.

The nuclear rocket fired, its thrust steady as usual, until the timer ran down and he smoothly brought the slider back to its aft stop.

Ben addressed a reminder to him, "Set your autofire range to two point five kilometers."

Vlad said, "Pitching to posigrade. Gun must to point forward, yes?"

"Proceed with pitch maneuver, hotshot," Ben said.

And then went on instructing, "Jimmy, set max magnification on forward-looking optics. You will have about a minute to designate the target. Vlad can hit it if the targeting laser is steady when the target comes into view. His onboard fire control …."

"Boy, that guy is Captain Obvious," Jimmy said.

Vlad too was relieved that Earth had dropped below the lunar horizon and they heard nothing more of Ben. The captain Jimmy spoke of was unknown to him, but no stranger than the small yellow bird that the American swore by.

…

Jimmy remained in the higher vantage of his circular orbit, the better to relocate the oxygen cache and paint its tank farm with his targeting laser, and to serve as combat camera. The recorded video would allow Ben's analysts to do damage assessment.

Through the sapphire blister of his Rock, he watched Vlad drop down away from him and begin drawing ahead. For half an hour they transited Farside, with

Vlad continuously dropping toward the surface. If Ben had timed the burn right, Vlad would pass just five hundred meters above the tank farm.

A quarter orbit after Vlad's burn, approaching the middle of Farside, his Rock had drawn ahead of Jimmy's by fifteen kilometers and was not easy for Jimmy to pick out against the rough gray surface.

Jimmy switched his attention to the flatscreen display from his targeting optics. The weapons bay door on the ventral side of Vlad's Rock was out of Jimmy's view.

Jimmy called over the datalink, "Is the Gatling deployed?"

"Deployed," Vlad said. "Make sure laser is lit."

Jimmy brought up the pipper in his targeting display, which lit off the infrared laser.

Onscreen, the nearby lunar surface was blurred by his pace, but in the distance silvery gray regolith scrolled toward him. The sun lay low in the dark sky of the late afternoon of this long lunar day here in the middle of Farside. Shining from his back, it cast deep black shadows over the hollows while hills and elevated crater rims glowed bright silver. Crescents of night-dark shadow bit into the flat gray discs of crater floors. Timeless, cold, colorless, desolate, airless, lifeless Moon, right outside the window. Jimmy smiled.

The crater where the tanks huddled rose up over the horizon three minutes before Jimmy would pass over. For nearly half that time the rough lunar hills and the crater wall hid the tanks from him, but he knew at which crater to point his high-res optics and soon the cluster of cylinders shone out as a sunlit white patch on the bright gray circle of the crater floor.

He reported, "Tank farm in view."

Looking across thirty kilometers of rough ground limned in stark silver and black, Jimmy joysticked the pipper onto the center of the tank cluster.

"Target painted."

As he closed the range at nearly two kilometers per second, Jimmy kept the pipper centered with smooth displacements of the small joystick at his right armrest, each movement minutely adjusting the alignment of the IR laser tube. The concentration required locked him into a familiar mission focus, alert yet calm, a near-trance.

...

At Jimmy's announcement, Vlad was fifteen kilometers from the oxygen cache. Now near his lowest approach to the surface, his horizon was closer than Jimmy's, and the hilly terrain hid the tanks from him.

A glance through the blister showed only smooth gray below black sky, all lunar features blurred away by velocity and proximity. The ride was perfectly smooth, the blur the only indication of his speed. Up to this moment, at the crux of the attack run, Vlad was a chunk of living cargo, Spam in a can, his course set by Ben's burn calcs, and the shooting left to fire control algorithms.

He breathed steadily, and rested his left hand atop the thrust slider on the armrest. He would need his quickest reaction. Else the ten thousand pounds of the autocannon's recoil would drop his Rock moonward to plow a furrow into the regolith.

The black cubical enclosure of an infrared seeker adhered to the inner surface of the sapphire blister, obstructing a small portion of Vlad's forward view. At ten kilometers from the tank farm, the seeker picked up the return from Jimmy's IR laser. Flashing its own visible red laser, Vlad's fire control continuously monitored the range to the tanks as well as continuously fiddling with the Gatling's point of aim so as to drop its depleted uranium penetrators on target.

As dead regolith flashed by just below, Vlad drew five quick breaths, his hand clamping ever harder on the slider. He must not ramp up thrust before the Gatling had completed its burst, lest he disturb the fire control's point of aim.

The range closed to two and one half kilometers and the electrical whine of the Gatling spinning up was overwhelmed by its roar as recoil threw Vlad forward into the harness and a shock shot through the Rock's frame as each round departed, shaking the bones within his flesh.

At the Rock's nose, the muzzle flashes from the Gatling's whirling barrels flowed together into a long gout of orange flame.

Throughout the one hundred round burst, even as the decelerating Rock began its plunge toward the regolith, Vlad willed his left hand to remain motionless. All the while the Gatling growled its long note of rage.

He anticipated the end of the burst and slammed the slider full forward just as the autocannon's roar died away at five hundred meters range. Fission rate leapt to near runaway pitch, and a sun-bright spike of exhaust exploded from the Rock's nozzle.

...

An eyeblink later, in the magnified view on Jimmy's display, dark circular holes appeared in the sunlit fronts of the tanks as white-hot incandescence jetted from their backs into deep shadow. Behind and around the tanks, dust plumes sprang up as penetrators impacted the loose lunar soil.

Uranium is a pyrophoric metal. Heated slightly in the presence of oxygen, not even to the boiling point of water, it burns.

Accelerating slugs of uranium to supersonic speed down the long rifled barrel of a Gatling is an excellent way to deposit frictional heat into their surface layers, and as they transited the tanks of pure liquid oxygen the slugs' skins burned explosively in starlike bursts of sparks, each leaving an incandescent trail to further bursts.

Over the one and one half second burst, the pattern of hits tightened from a twenty-five meter patch fired from extreme range to a densely churned five meter circle of gray dust, tank wall fragments, and the stark white bursts of flaming slugs.

"Oh, you got 'em, buddy." Jimmy said.

From Jimmy's perspective, Vlad's Rock appeared to have zero separation from the regolith. He waited for the explosion of dust that would signal its impact, but then the golden exhaust spike leapt into being, and the Rock quickly rose up and away into the black.

124

The Japanese would return to the cache. Perhaps the craters the slugs left would be mistaken for meteor impacts? Sure, a meteor swarm, centered on a secret tank farm. Vlad had just fired the first shots of the next war, one which might take decades to reach full heat, a contest for hegemony of all cislunar space, and a conflict that only the High Command had seen coming.

Far above now, Vlad's exhaust spike died away. His uncalibrated acceleration had cast him off into an orbit that would have to be tracked and analyzed.

Vlad lit up the local commlink, "Is routine lunar ground attack mission, yes?"

Chapter 50 - Getting Back to Business

It will be a dangerous century.

George Friedman, The Next 100 Years

The main nozzle thrummed as a spike of incandescent hydrogen plasma built behind Jimmy's Rock. Thrust pressed him back into the couch for long minutes. It would take another borderline claustrophobic day of living in this tiny can before he saw the ISS again.

They had no water recycling and Jimmy's throat was dry. He knew better than to eat without anything to drink. He was hungry and thirsty, but probably would be continent.

He wanted to beg for a faster return trajectory, but propellant had to be reserved for course correction and for braking as they approached low Earth orbit.

A veteran soldier can fill endless empty hours with talk. Vlad and Jimmy spoke over an extremely high frequency radio band so that their emissions would attenuate in the uppermost layers of the atmosphere, guarding against eavesdroppers. The relay to Ben from a commsat in geosynchronous orbit was encrypted.

He said, "How did that Farside base threaten us? The ISS is like an aircraft carrier, but with spacefighters. And our Rocks, as ramjets, control access to low Earth orbit. As nuclear thermal rockets we can roam all of cislunar space. We can take out any booster, any satellite we please."

125

Ben, an operations research double-dome from way back, replied at once. "So how do you attack a carrier group? The Japanese will build a missile launch complex. One they do not wish to build on Earth, with eyes staring everywhere from low Earth orbit. The Iranians tried that. The Japanese base will be at the extreme range of our strike spacecraft. And a base difficult to surveil, as difficult as maintaining a stable low lunar orbit."

Vlad said, "Missiles we see coming. Missiles we can hit. I would enjoy target practice."

"Here's the difference," said Ben. "It is expected that the Japanese will build railgun launchers to throw rocky chunks of the Moon which will have the same radar signature and optical albedo as meteors. A boulder in an apparently harmless trajectory can be redirected as it nears LEO, by lighting off an attached thruster."

"Our meteor watch has been cursory. It picks up the largest rocks and tracks the ones that are on courses which could cause damage. We need to start looking more closely. We need to start asking ourselves, have we picked up a space rock, or a Japanese kill vehicle? We need to ask, could a small trajectory change make that rock into a kill vehicle?"

"And we can't just keep a watch on Farside, because of the orbital decay problem?" asked Jimmy.

"To maintain continuous lunar surface surveillance, we would need a station like the ISS in a high lunar orbit, and a small fleet of Rocks, both to defend the station and to look closer. The new Japanese base will be subsurface. We would need ground penetrating radar to monitor construction of a subsurface base. Or to detect new construction that is better planned and concealed than what we have seen on this trip. Of the two systems, the subsurface base has the smaller logistical train."

"Same war, new enemies," said Vlad.

"The Japanese are playing the long game," said Ben. "A few decades from now, a stealthy barrage of Lunar boulders could sweep our battle stations from low Earth orbit. They would then launch their own LEO stations and be king of the hill."

"It is doubtful that they will abandon the project. The payoff in global projection of power is just too high, and necessary for an aspiring hegemon. Japan will not want to accept the limitiations of its declining labor force, limited territory, and dependence on imported raw materials and energy. The next Pearl Harbor will happen in low Earth orbit."

"So our next trip to the Moon will be another strike mission?" asked Jimmy.

"It may also be the first time someone shoots a railgun round at a Rock," said Ben.

They each thought about that for a minute, picturing a Rock thirty kilometers up from the surface of the Moon, scanning a strip of surface three hundred kilometers wide, and visible from the surface for one hundred and fifty kilometers ahead. A Rock limited to a Mach 5 orbital velocity, its maneuvers constrained by the Moon's lack of atmosphere, flying toward a railgun firing a Mach 8 projectile.

"Do you want numbers on that engagement?" asked Ben. He continued after a short pause. "The Rock needs ninety seconds after it clears the horizon to close to autocannon range with the railgun. The railgun projectile can close with the Rock in thirty-four seconds."

"That's worst case. Best case, if we allow for a sixty second decision time for the railgun, then the Rock can close the remaining fifty kilometers in thirty seconds. And the railgun projectile can close to the Rock in eleven seconds."

"So do we put our own railgun up into high lunar orbit?" asked Jimmy.

"You then have a ship attacking a shore battery. The shore battery does not have to float. That is to say, the moonbase will have walls and armor perhaps an order of magnitude thicker than the station's. The traditional approach was to land marines and take a shore battery by ground assault. But what obsoleted coastal artillery was the development of guided missiles. We may be able to drop our own boulder on a Japanese moonbase. If we have located the base and not a decoy."

"Twenty-first century is getting interesting," said Vlad.

Vlad and Jimmy got in a full sleep cycle. When Ben awakened them the ISS was in view, looking no larger than an oddly squared-off brown-winged butterfly. Closer, there appeared a white cylinder, a fresh hydrogen propellant tank tied down to *Columbus* alongside the gape-mouthed sharkbody of Rock 1. It was shorter than the tanks which had fueled their expedition to the Moon.

Nearing rendezvous, they received slow waves from a pair of fatlimbed hardsuits. Apple 1 and Apple 3, both former Marine aviators who went by Judy and Alyssa, had turned out for the recovery of Vlad and Jimmy's Rocks.

Chapter 51 - Thick as Thieves

"The Saudis can't fight out of a paper bag.
If it weren't for us they'd be speaking Farsi in a week."
Senator Lindsey Graham

Tom punched the end call icon. Took a few breaths with the iPhone pressed to his chest. "Hey Siri, answer call. Yes, Dr. Dexter."

Dr. James "Point" Dexter was an NRO administrator, like Jerry at NASA, not *the* admin, politically appointed, but a highly placed longterm professional. Deepstate.

Point plunged into his message without greeting or preamble. "Between Baghdad and Tehran lie the Zagros mountains, a formidable barrier to invasion. The mountains lie within Iran, so in their last war the Iraqis had to first invade Iran to cross them. In southern Iran, however, there is a desert plain at the southern end of the mountains, near the border with Iraq. That border ends at the Persian Gulf."

Point continued, "The Iranians are massing nine divisions, all their armor and motorized rifle divisions, on that flat desert plain near the town of Ahvaz in Khuzestan province, where the last war began. That means that no Iranians have yet crossed the border, but the Iranian invasion force has crossed the mountain barrier, and that no geological obstacles lie between it and Baghdad. The Iranians obviously hope to replicate the American and British success in pushing up along Route 1 from Basra to Baghdad. It looks like Iran-Iraq round two is about to begin."

Tom said, "The Iranians haven't responded to the destruction of their launch complex. This may be saber rattling."

Point said, "The logistic train doesn't lie. They have positioned fuel, food, and bullets to the fullest extent possible. This is their response to the flattening of the launch complex. To truncating the minarets on a couple mosques in Shahroud. They are coming for the Iraqis, and the Americans and the other westerners who supported the Iraqis in the last war. A lot of our people and a lot of our friends are between Basra and Baghdad."

"But no Russians. And no Chinese" Tom said.

Point replied, "Iran-Iraq 1980 to 88 killed about a million. Eight years of trench warfare, human wave attacks, and poison gas. Our High Command network, Russian and Chinese contacts included, would be horrified to see that repeated."

He went on, "The Chinese government will stand by Iran, and will perhaps provide logistic support. The Russian government works with Iranians in Syria, and sells them hardware, but dislikes the Iranian support of Taliban in Afghanistan and Houthis in Yemen. They would be very displeased to see Iranians invading a neighbor. The Saudis, like most of the Arab world, would be horrified to see Iranians moving against Baghdad.

Point kept talking, as he habitually did, "The Israelis too would be irate to see Iranians moving westward for any reason. Americans have far too much invested in Iraq to sit idle. An Iranian army attacking across the Iraqi desert would likely be hit by any and all of five nations. Iraq, and just possibly Israel, will counterstrike within Iran. I'm asking you for a less horrific alternative."

Tom said, "What I've got are Rocks, the FS-2A ramjet interceptors, high hypersonic capable, high firing rate Gatling armed, five of 'em. Also, one Dagger, with megabang. The railgun is in planning."

Point said, "Railgun? Never mind. Your Rocks may be able to stop the attack without inflicting megadeaths. I'm conferencing in General Harold Trimble, Chairman of the Military Advisory Board of the Center for Naval Analyses, CNA. Admiral Abreu speaks highly of him."

"Hello Dr. Broadhead, Dr. Dexter" said Harold.

129

"Just Tom" said Tom.

"People call me Point" said Point.

"Point? You go by 'Point Dexter'? Aw, gawd. Oh, sorry, of course, Point," said Harold.

There was a silent seven seconds, then Harry went on, "Please call me Harry. The Military Advisory Board sees your capability as being analogous to an aircraft carrier deploying attack aircraft capable of delivering a new level of power in ground attack. It is anticipated that the Iranian force, after its initial move westward, will deploy in a roughly north-south line along Route 1, and so will be in enfilade for an attack coming from the Persian Gulf lying to the south."

"It is the opinion of a team of senior analysts, assembled at the MAB from leading defense think tanks, IDA, MITRE, SAIC, and CNA, that a flight of several FS-2A Smart Rocks entering Iraq from the Persian Gulf coast could perform a low altitude hypersonic pass along the entire Iranian column, and in so doing inflict crippling damage on a preponderance of the Iranian materiel, stymieing the attack."

Tom said, "Yes, Harry, that might stymie the hell out of them."

Tom went on, more slowly and clearly, "Point, when did CNA, not to speak of all those other Beltway bandits, get read into High Command operations?"

"When you left a three hundred mile long blast track across central Iran, ending at their new military launch complex," Point said. "It looks like a nuclear strike smeared out across half the country."

Harry said, "If we can talk operations? The initial Iranian advance westward into Iraq will be very brief, perhaps an hour to reach Basra. Their mechanized brigades will then turn north along Route 1 and drive toward Baghdad. A repeat of the attack profile you flew against the Shahroud launch complex is expected to be very effective against lightly armored personnel carriers and unarmored troop transport trucks. The unsupported armor will have to turn back."

Point said, "It is highly desirable to deal with the Iranian attack quickly. Route 1 makes a left at Baghdad and becomes the main route westward to Damascus.

The Syrians are already mobilized and are fighting a rebellion as well as remnants of ISIS. They are supported in this fight by the Iranians, and we fear they will launch a separate attack up Route 1 from west to east against Baghdad. At that point, the Russians will withdraw all support for resisting the Iranians, and may well operate with the Syrians."

"So, if I'm counting right, you expect China to stand behind Iran, Russia to stand behind Syria, and the U.S. behind Iraq" said Tom. "A global conflict."

Tom went on. "You've got the wrong war in mind, guys. The Iranians are not invading Iraq. They're linking up with Iraq as they did to fight ISIS. Iran already moves their militia, men and materiel, into and across Iraq. This is their regular army. This is the heavy stuff you see massing near the Persian Gulf."

"The Iranians are not going to Baghdad. They are not going to Syria. If they were they would go through Diyala province, further north, the route they use now for Shia militia units bound to fight ISIS. The Iranians will turn south, perhaps passing through Kuwait to access the roads, then push on, possibly toward Riyadh, but probably along the western shore of the Persian Gulf, then across Oman to Yemen on the southern coast."

"The Saudi oil fields, Kuwait, Qatar, Bahrain, Abu Dhabi, Dubai, and Oman will be their prey during the southward push. Also, the east-west pipeline that crosses the Arabian Peninsula passes just north of Riyadh."

"If the Iranians and their allies win, they will have control of both sides of the Persian Gulf and its oil. They will have enclosed the Saudis. They will have denied the western shore of the Gulf to many large U.S. Army, Navy, and Air Force bases. They also will have unified the Shia Crescent, the region in which most Shia Muslims live."

"Intervention by Americans, Russians, or Chinese would be unthinkably complicated to maintain deconfliction. And as mentioned, if deconfliction fails, the Americans would likely line up opposed to the Russians and Chinese."

Point at first said nothing. His people at NRO gathered intelligence. He only dabbled in analysis, which typically lay further upstream. Then he said, "I will bounce that off some of the history majors around town. Not everybody in a think tank is in operations research or statistics."

Harry said, "With respect to operations, again? The Iranians have the Russian S-300 ABM and antiair system. It's truck mounted, so it can deploy with the invasion force. Each truck carries four SAMs. They are capable of intercepting air vehicles with velocity up to Mach 8."

Tom said, "We have not seen them fire a SAM. They had a ten minute look at Rock 3 during the attack on Shahroud. They have to detect, identify, obtain a firing solution, and get approval to fire within the ten minutes it takes to transit their country at Mach 8. They bought a Russian SAM system. If they follow the old Soviet model of command and control, the alert has to go several levels up the chain of command, then back down. While they are thinking, we have come and gone."

Harry came back quickly, "They have been thinking. We have to assume that they will be ready to take a shot."

"I too will think," said Tom. He swiped the call closed on his iPhone.

Chapter 52 - Dark Meditation

"War, often accompanied by genocide, is not a cultural artifact of just a few societies. Nor has it been an aberration of history, a result of the growing pains of our species' maturation. Wars and genocide have been universal and eternal, respecting no particular time or culture. Archaeological sites are strewn with the evidence of mass conflicts and burials of massacred people."

E. O. Wilson

Tom said, "Siri, call Jenny."

Jenny's "Yes Tom." came almost immediately, probably through the mic on her headset. Jenny spent a lot of time telephoning.

"I'm going to think. Would you like to put things on hold for an hour?" said Tom.

He turned off the iPhone, and the desktop computer. Jenny cast a wider comm net than he and often strode in with new events or analyses. She was not his assistant. She was the analyst best hooked into the People's Republic of China and many of the backoffice functions of the American defense department. She had taken it upon herself to screen out distractions. She knew to burst in with any existential threats, but no less serious development would interrupt him.

In his stateside time, Tom had thought almost exclusively about the various species of nastiness that could suddenly effloresce around the old regions of the Levant, Persia, Mesopotamia, and Afghanistan.

Every effort by the Americans had left an opening for Iranian influence. In Iraq, in Syria, in Afghanistan. The next frontier for the Iranians was Saudi itself, almost contiguous with Iran, holder of much of the other half of the Persian Gulf oil. By doing in the Saudis, the Iranians could expand to the western border of Asia at the Red Sea.

Tom's career had begun with his boots on the stony desert ground of Afghanistan. The Afghans had not fit for long into any of a half dozen or so empires of conquest. Only Sunni Islam had conquered them, and that very late. Each of the ethnic peoples was united by language and tradition, like the Pashtu and Pashtunwali that Tom had studied and practiced in the field.

Tom's wish was for the Afghans to be left aside for a time. Whatever survived among the ruins left by the Taliban and a multitude of warlords, by al-Qaida and the Haqqani network, by Russians and Americans and Pakistanis, and now by Iranians, would be virulent and probably ugly. Perhaps the Taliban itself would regain control.

He knew of no weapon which could address an insurgency, other than the kind that wore boots, an untried 18 year old toting a rifle with a full auto switch. The Afghans, if reluctant to take up and tote that weight themselves, would submit to the Taliban and the Iranians who supplied them. Depending on who was asking, four of every five supported the overthrow of the Taliban. That was hard to believe, held up against the performance of Afghan officers and troops.

Afghanistan was the exception, a countercurrent to the political-theocratic force streaming through Asia. There, alliances between Taliban and Iranian militia units happened. But it seemed to Tom unnatural that the Sunni Afghans would continue to work with Shia Iranians, absent a foreign enemy. Elsewhere, the southwest of Asia came down to Shias *versus* Sunnis of various shades of faith.

Iraq is outgunned by Iran. It is a smaller nation by a factor of two. Iraq's government and military were supported by Western countries and the Saudis in its invasion of the newly theocratic Shia Iran, and then destroyed by the Americans in Gulf War I. Iraq was destroyed again in Gulf War II, along with, to the horror of the Saudis, the Baathist government. Iraq now looks to Iran's leadership, ties its economy to Iran's, favors its Shia citizens, and allows free passage of Iranian militia units.

Iran has its own problems. It can purchase weapons only with difficulty, even from the Russians and Chinese, leaving it with an antiquated air force. The Iranians were now making their own tanks, yet to be proven in battle. Their strategy is twofold, to defend against invasion, bulwarked behind high mountain ranges, and to exert influence in the region.

Of the possible dance partners around the cradle of Western Civ, the Saudis and Iranians regarded one another with most interest. The Saudis had suffered no great attrition to their arms. They wished to project power, to become the regional hegemon, as did the Iranians. Saudis flew F-15s, and expected to have air superiority over any battlefield contested with Iran. Worldwide, F-15s were 104-0 in air-to-air duels. But poor readiness and training would limit their effectiveness. U.S. bases had moved out of Saudi before Gulf War II.

Tom liked the flat desert terrain of the Arabian Peninsula. Low mountains ran along the western side and wrapped around the southern coast of Yemen. The rest of the huge block of desert was a level plain, inviting tanks and mechanized armies. The Iranians would have to come out from behind their mountains. They would have to fight on the flat, where the Iraqi army had died in masses in the Gulf Wars.

Tom hated the thought of putting masses of American boots into another land war in Asia. America was tied down in Iraq, in Afghanistan, in Syria, distracted by Ukraine, distracted by China building islands on which to build bases in the South China Sea. Tom wanted to spare his country another war. A massed attack from the Iranians would require a massive response. He wanted to avoid the risk of drawing in the Russians or the Chinese.

He also wanted to spare the Iranians, and Iraqis, or Syrians or whoever deployed with the Iranians, from the destruction of their air force, from suppression of their ground-based air defenses by planes and missiles they could not see, from anti-armor strikes by Apache helos and Warthogs, and finally from high altitude B-1 and B-52 strikes, leaving, after just hours of war, a few survivors reeling from broken inner ear structures, bleeding from ears and eyes and noses.

If the Americans did not oppose the Iranian invasion, he wanted to avoid the risk of an Israeli nuke. Replied to by an Iranian or Pakistani nuke.

The terrain suited him. It would allow very low altitude hypersonic overpressure assaults by his Rocks, at some hard-to-quantify risk to his few assets. He was relieved to feel the familiar cold within himself. He wondered if all who decided to go to war felt as he did.

Chapter 53 - Cold Comfort

"Great power carries with it great responsibility,
and great responsibility entails a large amount of anxiety"
H.G.R. Robinson

Tom looked up from where he leaned back in his chair, his head feeling heavy. Jenny was dimly visible in the office, now grown dark with nightfall and his neglect of the lights. She ignored the light switch beside the door and padded over to stand beside him. She bent, putting her arm across his shoulders and then pressing the side of his head against hers in a hug. He could not recall their ever having touched.

He said, "Remember what they put Ollie North through? Imagine what they're gonna throw at me." He laughed.

She straightened, releasing the hug.

"Why have they come out?" she asked. "The Iranians, why come out from behind their mountains?"

"Theocracies can be pretty stable, but none has lasted forever," said Tom. "The Iranians have economic unrest. Or perhaps a Martin Luther has appeared, an antiestablishment reformer. An external enemy is needed to retain control of the Artesh and the people."

"Shall I tell them to drop?"

He nodded silently, and then said, "Tell Polya to plan the op, drop at his discretion. Ben's analysts will support from dirtside."

She let her arm slide from his shoulders and walked out faster than she had entered. She softly shut the door and left him in the room's dimness.

Chapter 54 - Meeting Up

*"Gully Foyle is my name, And Terra is my nation.
Deep space is my dwelling place, And death's my destination."*
Gulliver Foyle

Polya raised a hand to his earpiece, as was his habit, telling Jimmy and Vlad that his attention was on the commo rather than on them. He listened for a couple of minutes.

When he dropped his hand he said, "Was dirtside. Is to be ground attack mission. We ratline to Second Platoon. I am senior officer, but Apples are senior to us in service. We must talk."

They softsuited and pressurized their blue suits, taking turns at the umbilical near the lock. Small oxygen bottles were clicked onto a bracket at the left pectoral. The softsuits lacked CO_2 scrubbers, devices like the rebreathers used by Navy Seals, which greatly extended the hardsuit's oxygen supply.

Vlad led and Polya shepherded along behind as they took turns locking out of the hab. One by one they hand-over-handed along the set of lines that led to their Rocks, then along more lines running along the spine of the *Destiny* module, continuing across the station's central truss and along the spaceside spine of the *Zarya* module, and finally along the hab in which the Apples made their home, which was the Russian *Zvezda* module. Nearly half an hour was required for the careful movement. No one wanted to rip a suit or drift away. NASA would have required tethers and hardsuits for an EVA of this length, ratlines or no. But the switches had signed on with the High Command, signed on for risk, and asked no one for permission.

At the free end of the *Zvezda* module they again took it in turn to lock in. Alyssa, a long slender woman with a close-trimmed velvety-looking natural, pulled each of the three men feetfirst from the lock. She wore cotton shorts and a tank top as Katia had. Her arms and legs were muscled, but lacked the crisp definition that had marked Katia as an elite athlete.

The women's module was half again as long as *Columbus* where the men lived. Four sleeping spaces were spaced along the Earthside wall and four work panels lay along the spaceside wall.

The hatch connecting *Zvezda* to its neighbor module had been tack welded shut, like the hatch in the men's hab. Jimmy wondered again about the extreme compartmentalization that required them to make an EVA to meet with the Apples. It wasn't preventing fraternization. Alyssa had pushed off and drifted over to the work panel at the far end of the hab. Judy reached out and encircled her waist to pull her in, and continued to hold her, her abdomen resting against Alyssa's hip and their legs nearly entwined.

Looking on, Jimmy understood that the urgency Katia had shown during her visit with him wasn't about him. There were more pheromones floating about than at a sorority party weekend. He pushed off to float the length of the module to the suit storage area work panel beside the two Marine aviators, who continued to hover near. He asked, "You have room in the locker for our softsuits?"

Judy looked over. Jimmy thought she had been breathing in the scent of Alyssa's tight curls. Judy had a cap of straight black bowl-cut hair that floated away from her skull as if electrified. It was too short for a ponytail, though that too would have floated up like a rooster tail in the microgee. She was snub-nosed in an Irish way above a heavy lower jaw and squarish chin.

She said, "This hab is designed for four." Then she smiled, "You can all fit, if you're good friends."

Soon the men were free of their Boeing blue suits and ready for inside work in soft cotton shorts and tees. Vlad and Polya looped their feet at unoccupied work panels. Jimmy stuck a foot in the loop at the base of a sleeping pad, one which looked unused.

Jimmy sniffed. A peculiar acidic note cut through the effluvium, the ISS pong he had nearly stopped noticing. It was faint, but biting.

137

No sooner than noticed, spoken. "It smells different in here."

"Well that's odd," said Judy. "Ain't nobody here but us unwashed and unshriven gyrenes."

She drifted down the hab toward the men. "You lot smell like a busload of fourth graders."

"No one said you stank," said Jimmy. "I don't mind the scent of Friday afternoon gym clothes."

"You smell like a roadkill possum in August," said Judy.

Vlad chimed in, grinning, "No, it is you who smell like pu…"

Jimmy slapped a palm over Vlad's mouth. As a flush rose on Judy's cheeks, he said, "Vlad misspeaks sometimes, in English. He means to say that you smell like low tide in the Louisiana delta."

Judy's clenched jaw relaxed. "Well tell him thank you very much. And that he smells like a truck stop shower drain."

Polya looked up from scrolling through screens at a work panel. "Is low pressure in one coolant loop. You leak ammonia into hab."

He reached over to flip the toggle that linked the *Zvezda* hab speakers into the dirtside datalink. "Jenny, we are ready. What is mission?"

Jenny came up on the datalink. "Near as we can tell, every single Iranian tank, armored infantry, and mechanized rifle division is sitting on the Iraqi border. Down south, right next to the Persian Gulf and Kuwait. They brought a lot of bullets, beans, and black oil, so they plan to stay wherever it is they're going. We think they will dive south into Saudi or Kuwait. If they do, they will string out along Route 80, a straight road through a flat desert. We want you to part their hair for them."

"Thank you, Jenny. We plan now." Polya cut the datalink.

The switches looked about at one another.

Polya said, "Rock 3 is cooked. Ceramic lining is badly eroded at throat of ramjet. Thermal coatings of fuselage are spotted with faults. Rock 3 is exatmo only. Nuclear rocket, not ramjet. Small hydrogen tank can be rigged in few hours."

Jimmy did not like the sound of that. "I want to drop," he said.

This was becoming a discussion, a thing outside Russian military culture. Polya raised a hand, displaying his palm.

He said, "You have dropped." He shook an index finger. "First complete re-entry by Rock. No one knows how to do this. Data were logged. Altitudes, velocities, thrust levels, angles of attack."

He pointed at Jimmy now, "We use data as control inputs. You are our guide."

"Speaking of Jimmy's experience, I strongly suggest a limit of Mach 8 down on the deck," Alyssa said. "It may be a peculiarity of Rock 3, but that resonant vibration is just the kind of thing that kills aircraft and pilots."

"You operate exatmo, Jimmy, with hydrogen propellant tank. Do not let spacecraft creep up," said Polya.

"The silent six in the ISS main hab have the 20 millimeter Gatling and the short range missiles," said Judy.

Polya's hard dark-eyed stare rested on Jimmy. "We have aluminum can and one Kevlar curtain between our air and kill vehicle. Jimmy, boost Rock to orbital threat. Do not let close. Do not let close at speed and do not let creep up to match orbits."

"I guess that's what I signed on to do," said Jimmy. "Anybody wanna trade Rocks?"

Silence stretched across long moments. Then Judy said, "I've been shot at by these bastards longer than you have. I want to crush some flesh."

For another little while they listened to the grumble of the bearings as the station's solar panels realigned. Jimmy shrugged. He would do it for the unit, such as it was.

Judy said, "Um. The silent six also have the Dagger, if we want to get proactive."

"We have nothing to say about Dagger. No one knows that you know of Dagger. Is between me and Tom Broadhead," said Polya. "Four will drop. Jimmy will keep ISS alive."

Chapter 55 - Booting Up

Be intent solely upon killing the enemy.

Miyamoto Musashi

Polya detailed Judy and Alyssa to affix the hydrogen tank to Jimmy's Rock. The Apples had their hardsuits handy, and both Marines had wrangled propellant tanks while EVA. The men remained in *Zvezda*.

Polya spoke first, "You are prophet, Jimmy. We follow your path through Iraq. Will put us right on to Iranian column."

He continued, "Invasion is war. We seek to kill. Hit with linked booms. Tight formation. Constructive interference of shock waves. Multiply intensity."

Vlad said, "This is armor. Armored column."

Jimmy started when Vlad spoke up. That was rare. Vlad went where you pointed him, no questions and no comments.

Polya replied, "We hit them with wall of air. We do not destroy tanks. Do not knock tanks over. If hatches are closed, crews do not feel much. But APCs and trucks…. APCs go belly up. Trucks tumble. Men are meat pounded with mallet."

Vlad said, "So the tanks?"

Jimmy knew what he was asking. Iranian tanks would still be on the loose, pointed at Kuwait, or Bahrain, or Saudi.

140

Polya said, "Tanks without fuel trucks, without ammunition resupply, without infantry support. Tanks run for home. Do not get far."

"Ben said nothing of their air cover," Jimmy said. "Iran's air force is antique, but I flew F-14s, and they have some, and they fly quite well[18]."

Polya waved a hand. "We fly Mach 8, we do not worry about Mach 2 fighter. If you want worry, worry about missiles. Iran is customer for Russian gear. Russians do not hope for air superiority. Expect air attacks. Build very good SAMs. You can see American U-2s, pieces, in museums of Cuba, Russia, China."

"But you won't see any SR-71s there." Jimmy said. Roughly one hundred missiles had been fired at Blackbirds. No hits, ever.

Then he asked, "So you want to part their hair. What's the minimum altitude? How low are you willing to risk?"

Polya said, "I think fifty, sixty meters. Maybe two hundred of your feet. Autopilot error band probably does not kill us all. I do not trouble Ben to calculate pressure level. Will be strongest we can make. Will be heinous. Will be war."

Chapter 56 - Platoon Business

"This is a shitty war, but it's better than no war at all."
Lewis B. Puller, USMC

The women returned and the switches were gathered for the second time as a full group. By the time the Horse Apples had cranked the hydrogen propellant tank onto Jimmy's Rock 3, Polya had a mission plan.

Assuming the Rocks survived re-entry, they were to coalesce into a loose half chevron bound southward along the valley of the Euphrates, and then near Basrah where Jimmy had continued into the Persian Gulf the flight would gather

---

[18] Above one of the most vicious ground battles of the 20th century, Iranian F-14s handed the Iraqi air force its own bloody buttocks.

into close line abreast. South of Basrah they would bend slightly right along Route 80 toward Kuwait, skimming just above the asphalt.

"Is it too risky?" Jimmy asked. His mission to Shahroud had been bleeding-edge-of-the-envelope all the way. Attacking an armored column would run the same risks and would as well put them in the crosshairs of Iranian antiair batteries.

Alyssa thought a moment, then said, "Ground attack or not, there's not the shadow of a chance that we ever walk on dirt again. The entire world has the ISS on the Mark 1 Eyeball every time the sunset glints off our solar panels[19]."

Judy chimed in, "The Iranians have had us bulls-eyed for months. Our objective is to run them out of Safirs before we run out of Rocks. Rocks are about as sophisticated as crowbars and switches are just meat plus training. Meat and metal are cheap, so it's effective attrition."

"Is glorious. Inspiring. Like trench warfare," said Polya. "We must attack. Break stalemate."

"Survival can't be that rare. We're flying Rocks that have obvious marks of previous missions." Jimmy said.

"We're not," said Judy. "We're flying new Rocks. You're flying our old ones. Except Polya. His Rock is new, but he's an old switch, the only old switch among all of us. That's to say he's the only switch to have survived a full deployment to return dirtside."

"So four Rocks were lost last deployment?"

"Five counting Katia's. The previous platoon in your hab was the Nellies, as in Nervous Nellies, 'cause they were from Nellis AFB and obsessive about mission planning. When they bought it, we were left alone for nearly a month. We'll make it home if we last another thirty-seven days, but I don't expect it."

They proceeded to the vital matter of the men's callsign. Jimmy had flown F-14s as Cricket, as in Jiminy Cricket, as in he had a high voice. The handle was not his choice but was the edict of his fighter wing on his first deployment.

---

[19] For a good time, check out   https://spotthestation.nasa.gov/home.cfm

Polya smiled at the two women. He said, "You can call us *Zhar-Ptitsa*, Firebirds. Ancient Russian legend. Bird from faraway land. Is blessing. And omen of doom. Bird of red and yellow flame, like Rock."

Judy laughed, "Isn't that just poetic as hell?"

Until Katia had painted her incandescent death across south Asia, Jimmy had thought to let these other switches kid around with his unit's name. Katia had changed his mind. She had died pushing the envelope, dropping deep and fast to ramp up the ramjet quick. She had done it for the unit, to get herself between the accelerating rockets and the ISS. He knew what it took to drop a Rock into that fire.

Judy went on, "I was thinking 'Hot Turds'. You drop 'em quick."

Jimmy said, "You're not calling us turds."

"Yeah? Why not?" Judy had a hard glare at him.

"Because I'll break your mouth," he said.

He kicked his feet free of the loops and cocked his leg to push off from the sleeping pad.

Vlad clapped a hand on his shoulder with a grip that made Jimmy wince. He smiled, an amused smile that thinned his closed lips, while those disturbing white-gray eyes were opened up, anticipating battle. He raised and dropped his brows.

By the time Jimmy looked back Polya was halfway down the module, snagging Judy by the arm to arrest her flight toward Jimmy.

Polya told her, quietly, "He will hit you."

"No I will by God hit him."

Judy was still big-eyed with rage. In his free hand, Polya grabbed a helmet and sent it down the hab toward Jimmy and Vlad. A softsuit followed.

"Meeting is adjourned," he announced.

143

Vlad raised his brows at Jimmy, who nodded. The Russian released the clamp from his shoulder, and Jimmy began pulling on his softsuit, wriggling his shoulder to shake off the discomfort.

By the time the men were ready to lock out, Judy had informed him that he was a brown-shoe candy ass with two drops under his belt and no right to question orders. He didn't tell her that he had gone through USMC boot camp at Parris Island before transferring to Naval Aviation.

Polya said, "Unit name is not order, is tradition."

Alyssa drifted over to help them into the lock. Jimmy spoke softly to her.

"Katia was a magnificent combat pilot and no horse apple. And I am no turd."

She asked, "You know anything about the Marines?"

He said, "Mud-movers are carrier-qualified. Not like these Air Force 'flare to land ...' uh, pukes." He had almost said 'flare to land, squat to pee' pukes.

"You wanna know my favorite memory of boot camp?" she asked. "We had just learned to stay in step, single file, bound from the bus to the barracks, and our lovely DI explained the halt command to us."

"Yes?" Jimmy was puzzled.

"She said, well actually she screamed at us, the way they screamed everything, 'Now when I say 'Halt!' you will stop marching, feet together, and I don't wanna hear nothin' but twenty dry cunts suckin' air!'"

Alyssa continued, "Day one. Hour one. That explained it all. The Corps is everything. You are nothing."

Chapter 57 - Sentry Duty

They sicken of the calm, who knew the storm.

Dorothy Parker

After the second hour, the harness straps were beginning to hurt. The harness pushed Jimmy into the acceleration couch so he wouldn't float about inside the blister if the Rock decelerated or if he pushed on controls. It would be easy to forget to tighten the straps if he detached in a hurry to meet a threat. So he remained snugged up into the couch.

What Jimmy could see best through the blister was the white wall of the *Columbus* module on which the nose of Rock 3 rested, surrounded by blackness peppered with unwinking stars. The view to port included only the *Harmony* node. His fuselage blocked the rest of the station. Leaning his helmet on the sapphire allowed a glimpse of the outer curve of the cylindrical hydrogen tank mated beneath Rock 3.

The tank covered the ram scoop, and so the Rock could no longer function in atmosphere, but was now a nuclear rocket capable of extensive exatmospheric orbital maneuvers. Fitting the tank required hours of EVA in hardsuits and Jimmy was glad that Judy and Alyssa were experienced fitters.

Jimmy was good at waiting, as most career soldiers were. He thought over the meeting of the platoons once again. He was not surprised at gallows humor in designating callsigns. They were Marines, after all. One Marine Corps helicopter pilot he had known on carrier duty had answered to Ramp Strike, a term for the brutal and fatal impact of an aircraft on a too-low approach with the sloped aft end of a carrier flight deck.

He drifted into a memory, of Marine Drill Instructor Staff Sergeant D. Tilley. A boot as a matter of routine gets smoked with incentive training, physical training carried to the point of exhaustion. And DIs scream so hard at recruits that they can pass out, give themselves hernias, or do serious and permanent damage to their vocal chords. SSgt Tilley suffered no ill effects from the decibels he generated, and Jimmy got proficient at pushing himself up from the mud, searing hot asphalt, and chilly wet beach sand of which the base seemed to be made.

At the platoon's first encounter with the sheer twelve foot wooden wall of the obstacle course the boots milled about, unable to jump and scrabble high enough to reach the top edge. Jimmy popped out with the first thing that came to mind.

"Sergeant, can we give a leg up?" It was the first time he ever risked himself for the platoon.

The Sergeant placed his very hard nose one precise inch from Jimmy's, and Jimmy braced for the blast. But then he asked, quietly, "You think you know the right thing for this unit? You want to be the guy who decides what to do? Because I will require you to become that guy."

What had followed was not PT. It was extra mental evaluation after hours and Tilley putting him exclusively on the spot for speedy decisions that affected the boot platoon. The very strong recommendation Jimmy had received on graduation had gotten him into OCS.

Jimmy punched his mic to active, "Hey Apple 3." He hated that callsign.

It took a minute for her to reply, "Yeah?"

"So what got you into Marine Aviation?"

"Test scores. And desire. Flying a jump-jet sounded like an adventure. A jump-jet with a Gatling, missiles, and bombs." Alyssa said.

She asked him, "How about you? Why go Navy? You didn't want to fly close air support for the Marines?"

"Naw, they thought I was smarter than that."

"For a sensitive guy, you've got a nasty rap. You might wanna keep your fuckin' mouth off my Corps."

"Yeah, that's been bothering me too. You can call me Cricket, or Twinky, or Donut Diddler. But you don't call my unit anything but warriors."

She didn't reply, so Jimmy checked again that the Rock's new control system software was activated. The upgraded real-time code would balance the hydrogen flow rate against the reactor's fission rate to determine core temperature. To one side of the balance lay loss of thrust, to the other core meltdown.

"You awake, Ben?" Jimmy said into the throat mic.

All the switches had deployed to their Rocks. Ben would monitor how they followed the mission plan. Polya would be making the decisions when their plans became OBE, overtaken by events. Peering into multiple flatscreens in his dimly lit office in Virginia, he was supremely well positioned to track the Rocks through NRO surveillance products and NSA intercepts that pipelined into the Beowulf cluster.

Along with the computational products like additional decryptions and orbital mechanics trajectory predictions, Ben's crew of data fusion analysts interpreted and re-filtered intel. In a never-ending feedback loop, they busily typed queries to guide collection and analysis in real time. Satellites rotated, redirecting optical and infrared sensors. Dirtside, huge parabolic antenna dishes pivoted. Submarines raised ELINT masts. Israeli and American RC-135s, American U-2s, and Global Hawk drones lifted off or altered course.

Teams of SIGINT specialists selected frequencies, and then collected, compressed, and uplinked data to their service or agency. Analysts decrypted, interpreted, summarized, and passed it along. The Beowulf cluster in the Virginia suburb eavesdropped on the entire cycle.

"Dirtside is fully conscious." The voice in Jimmy's earpiece was high-pitched, nasal, nerd-synthesized.

With Polya sitting in his Rock rather than at his control panel, Ben continually scanned summaries and maps of force disposition. And as Polya had, he scanned the air and space threat layers fused together from all the surveillance data flowing through the Beowulf cluster.

Ben continued, "No surface launch activity. One flight of F-16s has gone supersonic, but on the other side of the planet from you. No spacecraft are maneuvering."

Judy broke in, "Dirtside, how about ground force activity? See any massive invasion forces streaming over national borders?" She sounded just as aggressive over the comm as she had in the hab. Jimmy shrugged. Attack pilots. Mud movers.

"Stand by," Ben acknowledged. Then he recited, reading a bulletin, "Live infrared imaging from NRO shows Iranian tank engines still hot. Troops remain in trucks, APCs, and fighting vehicles, also engines hot. Iranian strike aircraft are on the flight lines. Saudis are deploying by road toward their north and east, but are still en route. Saudi combat air patrols are orbiting near Kuwait City. Israeli F-15s are on the flight line, but engines are cold. Two American carrier groups are making flank speed from the Indian Ocean. In other words, no change over the last couple hours. The Air Force EC-130 with General Martin is still not talking to us."

Alyssa spoke up, "Is anyone watching Semnan? We shoulda hit Semnan. The terrain is easier, much flatter than Shahroud."

"Semnan launches civilian satellites" said Polya. "Is true, Safir could go up from Semnan. But previous three Safirs they threw from much farther east."

Ben said, "A stealth drone passes by Semnan at random times, and its side-looking video is continuously displayed on my screen. Semnan shows only sentries and office workers. No rockets being fueled. Nothing on the pad."

"Semnan has a thousand-meter hilly outcrop due east, and the northern mountains are about as high as at Shahroud," said Jimmy, willing to speak up as ever. "The terrain is not that good for nap-of-Earth hypersonics."

Ben went on, "NRO and NSA message intelligence indicates everybody is chattering. There are troops mustering and aircraft moving to flight lines from Pakistan all the way across northern Africa. Russians and Chinese aircrews are at heightened readiness, but no strike packages are on the flight line. High Command focus is Iran-Kuwait-Saudi. Russian and Chinese High Command contacts are providing intel on Iranian air defense radars."

And still no one had any word of or from Brigadier General Clinton Martin, USAF.

Chapter 58 - Ancient My Enemy

"If he come to slay thee, forestall by slaying him."

Sanhedrin 72

"Hey Siri, answer call."

Tom stretched an arm across the gap between the coffee table and the couch where he lay. He turned the iPhone microphone to him and said, "Hello Ben." Strangely, despite the early-hours call he was relaxed, his job done, the tactical operation delegated.

Ben apologized, "Sorry to bother you at home. A new player has emerged."

"You need guidance to deal with this new player? You don't need my permission, whatever you do."

Ben piped on in his high thin desk jockey voice, "The Israelis are offering a gift, a one-time service. They say they can interfere with the S-300 missile systems."

Tom sat up. "I'm not seeing a downside. And it's believable. The Israeli air force operated against S-300s in Syria without much trouble. We could use the help."

"Yeah," Ben said. "The Iranians will have us painted with their Sepehr over-the-horizon radar. Their Ghadir OTHRs are nearly as good. Even if we approach at Mach 8, they'll have fifteen minutes early warning. How well they've networked their air defense is unknown, but even a phone call to an S-300 site would work with that much warning."

"The Sepehr is operating right now?" Tom asked. He pictured the tall spindly fencework of steel antennas, arranged into a huge hollow square, megawatts of radiated power bouncing off the ionosphere.

"Sepehr is switched on and emitting," said Ben.

Chapter 59 - Land War in Asia

"Muster against them all the men and cavalry at your disposal."
Quran 8:60

Sitting in the back of a military truck is hard duty. The bench is hard, the truck crowded and the air stale. It is not restful. Sitting in the back of a motionless truck in the southern Iranian desert is quickly debilitating. The dark green smelly oiled canvas roof blocks the sun, but the heat is vicious, the air burns the throat. Sweat runs down faces before it can evaporate. The soldiers fall silent, enduring the heat and the leaden dread in their bellies.

Near the end of the column the trucks of a motor rifle division idled. The grunts in the next to last truck had sat long, their uniforms stained a darker green by sweat. They were Artesh, regular army, not Revolutionary Guards or Basij, who now handled mostly internal security. The grunts formed a part of one of six infantry divisions of the Artesh. They were not in one of the four armored divisions, riding a BMP-2 infantry fighting vehicle armored against light weapons. They were in a truck with six wheels, a flat bed, two benches. They were grateful for the shade of the canvas roof.

The soldiers were glad when the trucks lurched into motion. Jolting on the hard benches punished them, but the breeze coming over the cab cooled them. It was said that they would spend another hour or two in the truck, then they could climb out. They had not been trained extensively in mechanized assault. They had not been briefed about Iraqi experience in counterattacks against advancing American units. About how the Iraqis approached within rifle shot aboard troop trucks, and sometimes buses. They had not been told of the 25 millimeter gun atop each Bradley Fighting Vehicle, how its three round burst of high explosive could shred the truck and all of them in an instant.

All of them had seen the size of their encampment near the border town of Ahfaz, the thousands on thousands of tarps pitched to shelter men from the sun, and the acres of vehicle parks. It seemed that green canvas covered the earth. They got a sense of their numbers, and drew strength from it. A few of them had fought in Syria, a fight as vicious as any, if on a smaller scale. They did their best to feel nothing.

The trucks ground on. Conversation died away as unanswerable questions occupied the men's minds. Yousouf, platoon top sergeant, sat on the right hand bench at the end nearest the back of the truck. He leaned back against the canvas cover and looked out of the opening through which the men climbed into and out of the rear of the truck. Looking back and out to his left he could watch the desert glide by.

The two squads in Yousouf's truck remained quiet. Some of the men dozed, dark-haired heads bobbing. He began to see buildings, the outlying areas of Khorramshahr, and then they turned sharp right. In the distance he could make out the strip of green along the Shatt-al-Arab waterway. When they turned left he knew they would continue toward the west across the Iraqi border and then cross the waterway at Basrah.

Yousouf remained awake and watched. The truck slowed at the border but did not stop. They entered Iraq, the force of whose arms had killed the better part of a million of their countrymen just thirty years before. No one shot at them today. No artillery landed nearby. The Americans were indeed the great uniters.

The truck turned sharp left and soon Yousouf looked out from a narrow bridge. Then they left the bridge and wound around a long hairpin on an island in the Shatt-al-Arab. A wider bridge took them the rest of the way across into Basrah.

The truck crawled through Basrah, then resumed its faster grind along a desert highway, heading south. Despite himself, Yousouf dozed.

Chapter 60 - Dropping the Rocks

"Only fools fight."

Burton A. Tibbits

Ben lit up the datalink, "Ready for orders?"

Polya, in his best gravelly monotone, clipped off, "What is situation, Dirtside?"

Ben sounded tense, more squeaky than usual. He said, "Four armored and five mechanized infantry divisions have crossed the border into Iraq at Basrah. They are southbound and are presumed to be heading for Kuwait. We want to hit them while they are strung out on the highway which runs south from Basrah to Kuwait City."

Ben's voice pitched up even higher, "Detach and de-orbit now. We do not want to wait another ninety minutes to complete another orbit."

Polya echoed the order. Four switches strapped to acceleration couches in their ramjets hit DETACH buttons. Closely spaced jolts pulsed through the attachment lines that still locked Jimmy's Rock to the station.

Polya grated out, "Acknowledged, Dirtside. Flight is detached."

The four Rocks rose above the station into Jimmy's view through the sapphire canopy of Rock 3. The Rocks slowly fell behind the station as they rose, each of the sharklike fuselages gaining separation from the others like a school of fish breaking up.

"Make noses retrograde, blisters spaceside." Polya said.

The four Rocks spun on attitude thrusters, pointing their main nozzles forward along their orbital velocity vector.

"On my mark, execute stored maneuver sequence 'Jimmy1'." They would replay the sequence of burns and control inputs that Jimmy had used to feel his way down through the atmosphere.

Over the Atlantic, still nearly five thousand miles west of the Arabian Peninsula, Polya said "Drop".

Pale yellow fire glowed at their nozzles, a mere ghost of their full-power exhaust spikes, and the Rocks fell as one toward the broad expanse of cloud-dappled blue ocean.

Chapter 61 - The Topside War Begins

"AIM towards Enemy."

Instruction printed on U.S. Rocket Launcher

"Jimmy, this is Dirtside. A low Earth orbit bird is maneuvering."

Jimmy flinched away from his earpiece. Ben's adenoidal tenor, always annoying, had become piercing. The analyst was excited.

He took a moment to compose himself, and then asked, "What maneuver, Dirtside? Orbital altitude adjustment? Station keeping?"

"They are still fifty kilometers below you, but they just completed an orbital inclination adjustment to match the ISS orbital plane. That is a fuel-intensive maneuver so they must be serious. Designating maneuvering satellite as Vampire 1."

Jimmy had not picked up all the orbital mechanics there was to know. The training at Davis-Monthan had focused on the Gatling. The training at Star City had emphasized the Soyuz and its orbital maneuvers. But he was no Buzz Aldrin, who had written his doctoral thesis at MIT on orbital rendezvous.

He pictured the ISS orbit as a circle, lying in a plane just like it was drawn on a sheet of paper. The craft Ben was calling a vampire orbited in a smaller circle, one lying in another plane which had been tilted at an angle to the ISS orbital plane. Ben was saying that Vampire 1 had spent a lot of propellant by thrusting at ninety degrees to its orbital velocity so that the two orbits were now in the same plane.

Ben squeaked again in Jimmy's ear. "I anticipate a follow-on delta-vee[20] burn to enter a Hohmann transfer to ISS altitude."

A Hohmann transfer was the cheapest way to gain altitude. The right amount of posigrade thrust would put the vampire into an elliptical orbit spiraling up from its current altitude to reach the station's altitude.

Ben wasn't finished. "The timing of the burn is critical. Vampire 1 is in a lower faster orbit, catching up to the station. When it is slightly behind the station, the vampire will burn. One-half orbit later it arrives on ISS orbit near the ISS. Half an orbit takes about forty-five minutes. Clear?"

Jimmy spoke. "Dirtside, so Vampire 1 will approach at low velocity relative to the ISS. Why not just take it out with the 20 millimeter Vulcan Gatling on the ISS?"

"Vampire 1 may carry a missile, a laser, or its own Gatling. It may outgun the weapons on the ISS. It is desired that you intercept as soon as possible."

Jimmy wanted to say that the unknown bird might also outgun his Rock, but he was still puzzling over orbits. He said, "So help me out here, how do I get to the vampire?"

---

[20] He's talking about Δv, change in velocity

"You lurk. You're going to ambush it from behind. That means you slow down. Detach from the station and boost posigrade on my mark. That will put you in a higher, slower orbit above the ISS and falling behind it."

"So that takes me away from the station and further from the vampire."

"When the vampire burns to enter his Hohmann transfer going up, you will thrust retrograde. So you will drop and speed up. In about a quarter orbit, midway through his transfer, you will be near the vampire."

"So it will take me twenty minutes to dive onto this bogey's tail?" said Jimmy. "Not exactly a furball[21]."

"Snark, snark," said Ben. "Detach. Burn posigrade. Lurk up there. Then burn retrograde. Fall upon the sonofabitch and kill him. Clear?"

Jimmy had that twinge in his belly. He was going to war again.

Chapter 62 - Lay of the Land

"If your attack is going well, you have walked into an ambush."
Infantry Journal

There is a broad valley which arcs from the Mediterranean coast all the way across Syria and Iraq to the Persian Gulf. The Tigris and Euphrates rivers run into the valley at Baghdad and flow south along it all the way through Basrah to the Gulf. At no point does the valley floor rise more than seven hundred feet above sea level. It is even lower and flatter in southern Iraq. From south of Baghdad to the Gulf, the alluvial plain of the two great rivers lies at less than sixty feet above sea level.

Jimmy's approach for his attack on the Shahroud launch complex had followed the centerline of the Med, and then followed the valley all the way to its end at the Persian Gulf. He had then continued into Iran. Polya too planned to fly above the Med, then to descend into the great curve of the valley across Syria and Iraq. Near the mouth of the conjoined Tigris and Euphrates at the

---

[21] Jet jockey talk for a dogfight, aircraft turnin' and burnin' to get a shot up each other's tailpipe.

Persian Gulf he would find the Iranians, nine divisions, strung out along an arrow-straight highway.

The rosy ionized glow of re-entry veiled each of the flight of four Rocks as they mimicked Jimmy's flirtations with thermal runaway and crushing deceleration, until they leveled out at Mach 3 high above the North Atlantic. At this great altitude, there was no particular sensation of speed, only the lat-long numbers whirring by in the corner of the headsup.

Polya polled his flight, "Status?"

"Fokkin' A," Vlad came back.

"Straight and level atmospheric flight. All nominal," from Judy.

"Blue sky!" said Alyssa.

Then Polya spat out "Discontinue pre-programmed maneuvers."

And the switches were once again man-in-the-loop, in atmospheric flight, smooth and cool at supersonic velocity.

The Rocks linked to GPS satnav, much like automobile travelers used, but with far greater precision in both location and altitude. A new Air Force wrinkle had them communicating directly with the GPS satellites via their commo lasers. The laser timing pulse packets from the GPS satellites worked just like GPS radio packets had, since they propagated at the same velocity. But no radio frequency jamming would disrupt nav or commo.

The flight set course for Gibraltar and then eastward along the Mediterranean. It was just after they had cleared the island of Malta, in the center of the Med, that the Iranians saw them.

Chapter 63 - Orbital Matchup

"Try to look unimportant; they may be low on ammo."

Infantry Journal

Jimmy had to hustle. He hit 'DETACH' and moved away from the station. Then he had to align posigrade, nose pointing in the direction of his orbital velocity. For once he had plenty of propellant for his attitude thrusters, in the attached hydrogen tank. He left the bubble oriented spaceside so the view was mostly black. To either side, Earth spread to its far horizon giving a nearly palpable sense of planetary bulk.

Jimmy's 'burn', an emission of reactor-heated hydrogen propellant, pushed him gently into the couch for a few seconds. As thrust died he brought the Rock's nose down to watch the ISS move ahead and drop away below as he climbed.

"Burn complete, Dirtside."

Ben came back, sounding a touch hoarse now as well as squeaky, but not so edge-of-hysteria loud.

"Stay sharp. Vampire 1 is approaching their window for transfer to ISS orbit. Don't turn on any lasers or radars. Pretend you're a commsat."

Chapter 64 - Eye of the Ayatollah

"The easy way is always mined."

Infantry Journal

The crows are leaving Tehran, driven out by pollution. But if such a bird did fly there from the southern coast of the Caspian Sea, it would find that Tehran lies about fifty miles inland across the Elburz Mountains, which run along the northern edge of the country. Leaving the city for another hundred and fifty mile flight to the west toward Iraq, the crow would encounter the town of Bijar. And less than twenty miles north of Bijar, near almost nothing else, the bird would look down upon a strange quadrilateral of four tall spindly steel cagework walls, over one hundred and fifty feet on a side. Near each corner of the square would appear a pair of vertical masts, of thin metal framework like radio masts, perhaps one hundred feet high.

This assembly of steel is the visible portion of the Sepehr over-the-horizon radar. The Sepehr flings its low frequency wave up against the ionosphere, bouncing it downward, and reads the faint return bounce. The Sepehr gazes southwest, as far as all of Egypt, and westward, over Iraq and Syria as far as the Mediterranean, and around to the north, as far as Moscow, and upward two thousand miles above Earth.

The great radio eye looks over the Zagros mountains, which offer no shelter from it to any aircraft over southwest Asia. The Sepehr sees ballistic missiles, including hypersonic ICBMs, cruise missiles, stealth aircraft, and even small drones, anywhere within this great volume of space.

Soon after the Rocks flew over Malta, out in the middle of the Med, the Sepehr saw them. The radar of course saw many aircraft, and of itself thought nothing of any of them.

Eastward from Ahfaz, where the Iranians had gathered their armor and troops on the border with Iraq, across the Zagros mountains toward the interior of Iran, lies another small city, Abadeh. Within Abadeh, the Air Defense Force maintains a base for the collection of data from all the Iranian air defense radars and for the fusion of all these radar intercepts into a tactical picture of airborne or spaceborne craft. Into this data fusion system the Sepehr radar sent the packets of information describing what it had seen.

Much upset and confusion had overtaken the data fusion center when Jimmy skimmed the entire length of the central Iranian desert to blow apart the launch complex at Shahroud. After some data reduction on the Sepehr's packets, and review by a few of the analysts at the base, and some time for the analysts to master their shock and horror at the resemblance of the tracking data to the data gleaned from Jimmy's attack a few days before, the time-position data for the four hypersonic vehicles was escalated to the command center bunker. In the bunker, the track came to the attention of the commander of the Air Defense Force. And this man saw the Rocks for what they were.

Chapter 65 - Orbital Matchup II

"No soldier outlives a thousand chances.
But every soldier believes in Chance and trusts his luck."
                                                    Erich Maria Remarque

"Vampire 1 is maneuvering. Prepare to burn retrograde."

157

Ben sounded like he had locked down the nerves, but Jimmy had a case of lonesome. The station had pulled ahead in its orbit far enough to drop below the horizon, out of view. Above, all was black nothing .

He yawed the Rock to bring the nose retrograde, and rolled the blister Earthside[22]. Blue-white Earth filled the sky above his head. The bogey would approach above the far rim of the planet.

"Rock 3 ready to burn," he said.

It would be several minutes before he did his retrograde burn, timed to drop him onto the ascending bird like a falcon on a pigeon. Jimmy brought up the display from the targeting optics and zoomed and panned around above the translucent bluish skin of atmosphere at the horizon.

Space is big, and he hadn't found the new bogey when Ben called for the burn. After, as Jimmy dropped toward the planet, he swung the nose back to posigrade where he expected the maneuvering satellite to come into view ahead of him, out where his autocannon pointed. He hoped the bogey didn't have eyes in the back of its head because with his next move the targeting radar would come on.

He threw himself into the switchology. Flipping the TRACK/INTERCEPT toggle on the left armrest brought the targeting reticle up on his headsup. He pushed the GAU toggle forward to the DEPLOY detent. The *thunk* of the weapon bay door meeting its stops was familiar and reassuring, even more so was the headsup flashing "GAU DEPLOYED".

Jimmy chomped his bite valve and drank some water. He waited for the bogey to climb into his sights.

Chapter 66 - Into the Valley

Anyway, it's what we do.

Marie Colvin

---

[22] Jimmy is still a neophyte space pilot. He could have achieved both maneuvers in one by pitching the nose up and over.

Polya spat a command, "Make speed Mach 8."

He knew the Sepehr must have seen them by now. It was said to be more powerful than the Russian radar at Duga, and that radar would have seen them. But the Sepehr would have read their speed as no more than Mach 3. Cranking the speed up early might steal a march on the Iranians, who would expect a Mach 3 transit over Syria and Iraq, as Jimmy had done. It would also increase their risk.

He eased the slider on his left armrest forward, watching airspeed build in the headsup display. His engineer's training warned him that random vibration came on rapidly with speed, and soon the Rock resounded as if from ever more frequent blows. He resolved to ignore the buffeting, though it made his bones want to jump out of him.

The four Rocks ate up the eastern half of the Mediterranean in just under ten minutes. They could not waste time. Just inland of the Syrian coast a second over-the-horizon radar, the Ghadir near Ahvaz, would acquire them. In an additional two minutes the Rocks would approach the Syrian border with Iraq where yet another two Ghadirs could look down on them with their ionospheric bounce.

Watched by four over-the-horizon radars, the Rocks would need another two and one half minutes to bring them over Baghdad, where they would begin their attack run down the valley of the Euphrates. If the Iranians had an accurate estimate of their speed, would they believe it? The radars would see aircraft down in the densest layer of the atmosphere, skimming sun-heated sand where turbulence convected up like bubbles in a pot left too long on the boil. When the deltas in distance, divided by the deltas in time, came out to Mach 8, would the console jockeys believe?

Impacting at Mach 8, a single rifle bullet would blast a fragment cascade through avionics, reactor, and pilot. If the Iranians saw their track for true, and if they believed their radars, the convoy would meet them with a wall of SAMs, shot, and shell.

Chapter 67 - The Shooting Starts

"The military don't start wars. Politicians start wars."

159

Brigadier General Alireza Sabahi Fard commanded the eighteen thousand troops of the Islamic Republic of Iran Air Defense Force. The General was slightly stout, and in his late forties. He had the black eyes and hair of a Persian. He wore camo fatigues, stars at his shoulders and a four-day stubble, as Shia Islam encourages closely cropped beards. He would have looked unkempt to Western military eyes, more like a noncom in the field.

A patch at his shoulder bore an upraised arm, assault rifle clenched in its fist, the insignia of the Pasdaran, the Revolutionary Guard. The Pasdaran were an oddity, tasked with internal security for the protection of the Islamic revolution, foreign operations including outsourcing assassinations to professional hitmen and drug cartels, but they had as well had responsibility for strategic air and missile defense. The Pasdaran operated their own ground, air, and naval forces in parallel with those of the Artesh, the regular army.

Fard stood behind a row of technicians and analysts who sat before keyboards and screens. Here in the command bunker the General stood atop not only the data fusion network which gathered detections and identifications from his country's radars, but also the communications network which distributed the integrated air and spacecraft intel to antiaircraft guns and to missile batteries.

And now his strongest strategic radar saw attackers coming, the analysts thought four of them. The estimate of their speed from the Sepehr data was at least Mach 3, as fast as the last intruder who had approached through Iraq. Very few aircraft ever flew at Mach 3. The MiG-25 might still be flying, but the American SR-71 was said to be retired. He did not believe it was a Russian approaching. It was some new threat, but surely the same as the craft that had leveled Shahroud.

And the intruders ground track stretched across the same Syrian and northern Iraqi desert. If they too turned south at Baghdad, the expeditionary force lay directly before them.

In addition to the Sepehr, he had hundreds of short-range tactical and battlefield radars, and three newer Ghadir strategic radars, over-the-horizon radars of over six hundred mile range, which he expected to soon detect the attackers.

He had at his disposal nearly two thousand antiaircraft guns, but these threw projectiles at laughably slow velocity compared to the speed of the four attackers, like throwing stones at a goose on the wing. He had various surface-to-air missiles, both antiair and anti-ballistic missiles. More importantly, he had within his command eight S-300 missile batteries, SAM systems obtained from Russia just a couple years back. And most importantly, two of these antiair batteries had joined the column of troops and armor now entering Kuwait.

He had not the luxury of waiting for the Ghadirs to confirm the track. The Supreme Leader had thrust the bulk of the army out beyond the mountain-guarded borderlands, seventy thousand men strung out over sand and low scrub without possibility of cover or concealment. He had to assume that the attackers would turn at Baghdad, would make for the column.

The General turned to a communications aide bent over his console. "Message Jafari and Fadavi: Halt your vehicles, now. Deploy anti-air missile batteries. Link to Air Defense communications network for azimuth and range of flight of four high-speed incomers, at least Mach 3. They will be coming down the river valley from Baghdad. You have twenty-seven minutes. Engage at maximum range."

Chapter 68 - In the Valley

"The truth of the matter is that you always know the right thing to do. The hard part is doing it."

Norman Schwarzkopf, Jr

Integration of mobile assets such as Major Jafari's S-300 battery into the central Air Defense Command was recent, they having previously reported to the unit to which they were attached, whose commander, Brigadier General Kioumars Heydari, was a radio call away. Integration with the Air Defense command bunker offered strategic intel, but required unfamiliar satellite up- and downlinks. Major Farzad Jafari received the command to deploy nearly seven minutes after Air Defense Commander General Fard's instruction to his communications aide.

Jafari began screaming into the radio net which linked his vehicles. Four large missile transport trucks, his command vehicle, and two radar vehicles halted immediately, and a gap in the column opened along the road to the south ahead of him. The trucks and APCs behind jerked to a surprised halt.

To erect his launchers needed a full five minutes. There were four of them, four large trailers each of which carried four missiles encased in fat dull green steel tubes, two stacked on two, all lying lengthwise along the bed of the trailer. He would launch one missile from each trailer in nearly simultaneous firings.

Hydraulic pumps whined, shiny cylindrical legs extended beneath each missile trailer, and the trailers lifted slightly, leveling and stabilizing the launchers. The hydraulics whined louder as all four tubes on each trailer pivoted at the back ends of the trailers. They moved as one, arcing up to point to the sky.

Wider than the span of a man's arms, as tall as a small silo, each steel tube held a solid rocket behind a warhead of two hundred kilograms of high explosive and fragmentation charge. The detonation of the 48N6E2 missile, known to the West as the Gargoyle, killed any aircraft within 300 meters, nearly a third of a kilometer.

At Jafari's orders, digital radio data links were established among his command vehicle, the launchers, the surveillance radar, and the targeting radar. This local Wi-Fi bypassed the optical fiber coupling which could have networked the units, and which was much more secure against digital intrusion. But cabling took time. His battery was crucial, the southernmost battery in the column and so the one with the most warning and the best chance of intercept.

Within the dull green walls of his command vehicle the Major gazed into a flatscreen. Through the satellite uplink antenna, he opened a digital radio connection to the Air Defense data fusion network. Data from the Sepehr and the Ghadirs' long-seeing radio eyes streamed across the network, scrolling in orange text down his flatscreen. General Fard had spoken of Mach 3, but these numbers showed the incomers moving at incredible speed, faster than any aircraft. Only one cruise missile moved that fast, the hypersonic Russian *Kinzhal*, the Dagger, capable of Mach 10.

If Daggers were inbound, he did not have twenty-seven minutes, or even twenty. He punched keys to orient his 96L6E surveillance radar back along the road to the north. It pivoted its planar emitter/antenna to lie across the line of the highway, an olive drab vertical rectangle protruding from the bed of its dedicated truck. If the radar acquired the incomers at maximum range of two hundred kilometers, he would have less than two minutes before they arrived. He would have to launch in less time than that if he wanted an intercept. He waited to acquire.

Chapter 69 - Flight of the Cyberwarriors

"In God we trust: All others we monitor"
5th Reconnaissance Squadron, USAF

USAF Brigadier General Clinton Martin hung from a handstrap in the cargo compartment of the EC-130H Compass Call, one of a dozen such electronic attack aircraft flown by the United States Air Force. The Compass Call was a Herc, a C-130 Hercules to which literally tons of electronic warfare modules, control and monitoring computers, displays, and crew stations had been added.

Nine airmen in olive drab coveralls sat at consoles around the padded walls, also olive drab, of the cargo compartment. They were the electronic warfare mission commander, a weapon system officer, and a mission crew supervisor, who was an experienced cryptologic linguist and oversaw four analysis operators, plus an acquisition operator and a maintenance tech.

A heavy-looking pod hung under each wing of the four-engine turboprop, and sponsons stuck out on each side of the fuselage, low down, midway back from the wing to the tail, making the Herc look like a flying boat. The pods and sponsons each held a half-ton of electronics, power supplies, phased array emitters, infrared and optical detectors, and radar receivers.

Clint was three hours into his TDY to Kuwait. Ali Al Salem Airbase had retained the ruin of the old Kuwaiti officers club, the building where invading Iraqis had shot all the captured Kuwaiti military personnel, except for their General. He had been hanged. It reminded Clint that he was not in Europe, where Geneva was, where the Convention had been drawn up. He was in Asia, far from Geneva.

He had made contact with the 386th Air Expeditionary Wing, USAF, and joined on as supercargo on one of the four EC-130s operating over Iraq and Syria, ostensibly to train him in offensive counter-information and electronic attack. As a one-star he was able to reroute the Herc's flight and move up departure time.

The EC-130H climbed to eight thousand feet, flying due east on a bearing of ninety degrees. They were about fifty miles north of the Iraq-Saudi border, which also ran west-to-east toward the Persian Gulf and Kuwait. At this altitude the aircraft had line-of-sight to a horizon one hundred miles away.

Clint crouched to peer over the shoulder of the nearest cyber warrior, a chubby twentyish airman with straight black hair pushing down to meet his collar.

Simms, his name was Simms, Clint thought. He had just been introduced round, and the airmen sat before electronic consoles along the wall of the fuselage, their backs to him. He could see no nametags.

Airman Simms spoke, "I'm scanning the phased array emitter in the port underwing pod. The beam will sweep along the Iranian column, ranged at twenty miles ahead and bearing from forty degrees to one hundred thirty degrees, about northeast to southeast."

Clint knew that pod emitted digital radio packets, on-off radar pulses coding binary packets. The cyberwarriors intended to inject malware into the encrypted Wi-Fi networks of the Iranian air defense batteries.

Another airman, a young blonde woman, called out, "A surveillance radar just switched on. Freq correlates with S-300 SAM battery. Azimuth bearing sixty-one degrees, range 19 miles."

Clint had forgotten her name. He knew she monitored the radar receiver, searching for hostile radio frequency signatures as well as ultraviolet and infrared emissions.

Chubby Airman Simms, near Clint, replied, "Vectoring emitter array to hostile battery."

Hostile battery. Hostile antiair battery. The next three minutes were uneventful, but for the thudding of Clint's heart. He could feel it pulse in his throat.

Chapter 70 – In the Valley II

"War is the unfolding of miscalculations."

Barbara Tuchman

Major Mohammed Fadavi, commander of the S-300 antiair missile battery near the trailing northern end of the column, received the same order on which Jafari had acted, and at the same time. He too issued hurried orders on the local radio net, voice loud in the command vehicle and tight with urgency. He had been given twenty-seven minutes, time enough to prepare. Still, his torso was tight with nerves. He had been ordered to engage. It was to be a shooting war.

Fadavi ordered his vehicles to pull off the highway to the right, so as not to obstruct the remainder of the column. It was a matter of five minutes to maneuver the huge big-wheeled trucks to a flat area of desert a hundred meters from the road.

In those five minutes, Major Jafari's battery at the leading southern end of the column completed its deployment, elevating its dark green missile tubes to form vertical launch towers, linking up communications, making radars ready for target acquisition.

In those same five minutes, the Rocks transited across half of Syria and all the way east across Iraq to Baghdad.

Having reached suitable ground, Major Fadavi ordered his battery to deploy, which would require an additional five minutes. The Rocks would arrive in three.

Chapter 71 - Hypersonic Attack Run

"If once you make a decision to use military force to solve your problem - then you ought to use it. And use an overwhelming military force. Use too much. And deliberately use too much."

Gen. Curtis Lemay

South of Baghdad, Polya thundered over the alluvial plain of the Euphrates. Flying right down on the deck, his shockwave raised a huge plume of dry desert soil. The remaining Rocks deployed in a half-chevron spaced back and to his right, just ahead of his shock cone.

All knew there would be no hiding from the long-wavelength gaze of the Sepehr. By staying on the western side of Polya's rooster tail of dust, the trailing Rocks sought to hide their numbers from the higher-frequency surveillance radars of Iranian SAM batteries.

Vlad, Alyssa, and Judy craved the cover of the billowing dust, but drifting into the plume could abrade their throat linings and thermal barrier coatings, eating through in a moment to bare metal. The Rocks' leading edges glowed red-orange with the heat of their passage. Stripped of their coatings in the thick oxygen down on the deck, the titanium of their fuselages would ignite.

Polya got on the local link, a terahertz frequency radio whose short wavelengths attenuated rapidly in atmosphere, keeping his message secure. His voice carried another frequency. A structural resonance of the Rock's airframe, excited by the turbulence of their passage, shook him twenty times each second, modulating his words and giving his grating speech an even more robotic tone.

He said, "Tighten up."

Air does not flow around a hypersonic craft; it is bludgeoned aside as its molecules rip apart. Shock waves form at every leading edge and reflect from wings, tail, fuselage, and control surfaces, exerting inherently chaotic aerodynamic forces. The Rocks were at best metastable, their balance no more secure than a pencil resting on its point. The switches, ever mindful of the highly nonlinear response to control inputs in the hypersonic flight regime, relied on the electronic reflexes of their flight avionics. Pilot inputs were suggestions, to be followed when the near-random aerodynamic perturbations allowed departure from straight and level flight.

As they neared Basrah, the three Rocks surfing Polya's shockwave crept forward into line. Four abreast at a scant two hundred feet, an instant away from arrowing into the dull brown sands, they closed up to even smaller intervals, bouncing among ragged updrafts and currents of hot desert air made nearly solid by their pace.

Behind, their intersecting shock cones churned dust and rock into a fury on the desert floor. Stones leapt into the sky at their passage, and were instantly obscured by dust leaping even higher.

Ahead, just south of Basrah, lay the trailing northern end of the Iranian column, long files of slow-moving armor and canvas-topped trucks crammed with men.

Chapter 72 - Desert Witness

"There will be strange signs in the sun, moon, and stars"

Luke 21:25

A lone Bedouin, rocking along on a camel, spotted the convoy of trucks out at the horizon. Tariq was looking east, knowing the road from Basrah to Kuwait ran somewhere nearby. Kilometers of buff sand dotted with gray-green hummocks, relieved only by a few flat gray rock outcrops, stretched to a faraway glimpse of black asphalt ribbon. What drew his eye was motion, not the silvery heat shimmer above the desert, but a steady current of drab greens and browns. As far left and right as he could see, it flowed along the road, moving south.

He withdrew binoculars from a case slung from his saddle. The glasses were quite good, with large objective lenses coated against abrasion and a wide field of view. He pulled the camel's head back and held the reins taut for a moment to still her. He threw a leg across the saddle, balanced his Kalashnikov across his lap, and rested elbow on knee to steady his hand. The black-rimmed field of view was filled with tiny canvas-topped trucks, and then with the turtle-like tracked vehicles that had the small cannon up top and also a number of low slung tanks, with the big guns protruding from flat turrets.

The north polar regions and even the Moon were mapped before Arabia. Uncharted ancient desert tracks had carried the Queen of Sheba to see Solomon in his glory, crossed the desert to join Babylon to Damascus, oldest city in the world, and stretched to the mouth of the Euphrates. Tariq knew the faint tracks in this piece of country not as a map, but as a diagram of the culture and history of his family and tribe, their kinship ties, their customary visits, the movements of their herds, trading expeditions, and raids. He was just south of the Iraqi border. He was west of the Kuwaiti border in the vast emptiness of northeast Saudi Arabia, his country, looking east into Kuwait. And he knew that the flags painted on the tanks and trucks were not Saudi, Iraqi, nor Kuwaiti. They were Iranian flags.

He waited and watched. He stilled the camel again when she shook herself. The camel he rode was a *rub*, a six-year-old. He called her *Rima*, "gazelle". The convoy continued to flow to his right, south toward Kuwait City. Minutes later the vehicles at the rightmost limit of his vision halted. And then a wave spread back up the convoy as each tank or truck stopped short of the vehicle ahead.

A flutter ran through Tariq's belly. Iran was no friend of the Saudis. This was not a safe place for him, within eyeshot of more soldiers and guns than he had ever seen. Iranian soldiers and guns. He stowed the AK to hang heavy in its scabbard. The track he followed would not appear on their maps, and few would suspect that anyone would wander such emptiness without a large vehicle and without companions. Indeed, Tariq was sometimes called "a son of the road", a tramp, for his solitary wandering, which was foolhardiness in Bedouin eyes. His only safety lay in their ignorance.

Yet he wanted to see what the soldiers did. Why had they halted, out here in the great emptiness? He glassed the convoy again, left to right. Again motion drew his attention, toward the right where a group of four large dull green trucks sat head-to-tail along the road. Their flatbed trailers were longer than the large freight haulers he often saw on the road. On each truck four large green cylinders stacked two on two were pivoting up, the front end rising over the course of nearly a minute, until they formed a tower at the trailer's tail.

Tariq lowered the binoculars. He stared for minutes more, turning his head to look across the occasional wind which would have carried the desert fines into his eyes, until there was a flash where something sprang upwards from one of the long trucks and now white fire flashed even brighter. Before he could get the binoculars to his eyes, the fire leapt into the sky, climbing impossibly fast and high and building a solid-looking pillar of puffy white smoke.

The fire shrank to a spark in the distance and winked out far above. Tariq was a nomad, with a liking for traditional ways. But he was a Saudi, and not a poor man, and not an ignorant man. He had seen such things on Al-Jazeera and he understood that a missile had launched.

But now a new thing showed itself in the sky. A thing of which he knew nothing.

A small dust cloud appeared, away in the distance, far to his left just above the horizon. It streaked along the road, overtaking the column of trucks and tanks. It did not tower high and broad like a sandstorm, and it moved faster than any sandstorm he had seen. Tiny bits of white glinted at its head.

He shied back from the preternatural speed of it, and *Rima* shook her head. The dust shot along the convoy from its tail on his left to its head at the far right, leaving a dark brown low cloud like a stretched-out serpent, hiding the whole length of road. Seconds later, a deep bass boom sounded and then a distant roar. The low dark brown cloud remained.

He had seen the Iranians launch a missile, and he had seen a great dark serpent of dust explode along the road from horizon to horizon. The dust serpent had grown as fast as the missile had climbed. Danger forgotten, Tariq continued to watch, but through the dust could see nothing of what the Iranian soldiers did.

A new spot of fire appeared on the horizon, this time from far beyond the roadway. It was as if a piece of sun leapt up from sky rim to zenith in a few moments. The flame grew to a blinding spear of white fire. It flashed overhead, another missile like the one from the truck, but much closer, looming large, riding its white sword of flame and leaving another puffy smoke trail.

As he spun in the saddle to watch the missile speed away, a blow struck him over his whole body, piercing his ears as if he were inside a thunderclap. *Rima* jumped into a gallop, and he had to do quick work with the reins to stop her running away with him.

When he looked back, the low dense cloud still hid the Iranians. He turned to where the missile's trail of smoke led away to the west. His home lay that way. He turned his camel about and flicked the reins. He began following the smoke trail in the sky.

Chapter 73 - Worm's Eye View

"Do we go after these terrorists in their heartlands, from where they are plotting to kill British people? Or do we sit back and wait for them to attack us?"

David Cameron, in the House of Commons

What Tariq saw from afar began without warning for Yousouf and his men. The truck lurched to a stop, waking the men as they were thrown forward against one another. Yousouf climbed down. The whole line of trucks had stopped. He waved the platoon out to let them relieve bladders. The men clambered down and clustered on the asphalt, and some knelt to pray. Others walked alone into the scrub.

Yousouf walked forward, shaking out his limbs, and stepped up onto the front bumper of the truck. As far as he could see, motionless files of tanks, troop trucks, armored personnel carriers, and infantry fighting vehicles stretched to the south, what he knew to be several divisions of motorized infantry and armor. Everywhere men were dismounting their vehicles.

Yousouf stepped down and walked back along the roadside, watching that no one wandered away to lie in a wadi until the war rolled on without him.

Probably they were in Kuwait, still north of Kuwait City. The asphalt led nearly straight south here, as it had since Basrah. The plan was to make a right turn inland leaving Kuwait City behind and heading for the Saudi border, then a turn south again toward King Kahlid Military City. It was a richly symbolic objective, an entire city built by the Americans and serving as their base in the first Gulf War. Taking it would drive a wedge between the oil fields of the Gulf and the main body of the peninsula.

Yousouf stepped up onto the back bumper of the truck. The trailing end of the convoy lay within his vision, otherwise the column of vehicles facing him looked very much like the motionless trucks and armor he had seen to the south. Men in sweat-darkened green stood about at the roadsides. Near the northern end of the column, a battery of air defense vehicles carrying missile canisters like huge green logs had pulled away to the left of the pavement. As he watched, the missile tubes began elevating.

An air attack? A shiver went through him, a flash of cold under the desert sun. As he searched the sky to the north a brown smudge appeared in the heat haze at the northern horizon, just the color of an approaching dust storm but without a storm's towering height and sky-spanning breadth. Little more than a speck at the lower rim of the sky. Yet the dark wisp grew, doubling and redoubling before his gaze.

Clinging to the truck's rough canvas cover, his mind blank with panic, Yousouf caught his breath as the brown stain at the limit of his vision blossomed huge before him. Then the cloud was upon him and the sun was blotted out and he was thrown into the blackness as if slapped by a giant hand.

Chapter 74 - Thunder in the Valley

"Who believes, fights in the cause of Allah.
Who disbelieves, fights in the cause of Satan."

Quran 4:76

Major Jafari gazed unblinking into his flatscreen. The mast of the surveillance/acquisition radar extended seven and one half meters above the desert. At that height it had ten kilometers of direct visibility to the northern horizon. Though the radar could see an aircraft for two hundred kilometers, it would not see a low-flying target until it approached within ten, far too short a distance to engage a high-Mach-number target. The realization seized him in his core, making it an effort to draw breath against his stiffened musculature. He needed missiles in the air now.

Punching in a launch sequence, he set up four of his Gargoyles to go up with one minute between each. He oriented the target engagement radar, the kind called Flap Lid in the West. It was a digitally steered phased array and had no need to mechanically track a target once pointed vaguely to the north along the attack vector. He switched on the high-power beam even though no target had as yet been acquired by the 96L6E surveillance radar.

Jafari initiated the launch sequence and the first Gargoyle leapt from its tube on a gout of compressed gas, seeming to hang in the air just an instant. Then a pillar of flame shot back from the missile and it sprang upward, leaving a rapidly growing column of smoke behind. The missile shot blindly upward, its seeker questing for a target's reflection of the Flap Lid radar's beam.

Chapter 75 - Flight of the Cyberwarriors II

"Never draw fire, it irritates everyone around you."

Infantry Journal

The young blonde cried out, "Targeting radar! It's a Flap Lid! We're picking up a sidelobe. Same azimuth and range as the SAM surveillance radar."

She didn't have to spell it out. An S-300 battery had just gone hot.

"Countermeasures emitter power is still at maximum," Simms spoke in front of Clint.

The pilot spoke over their headsets, "I've got visual on a dust cloud, bearing 45 degrees, transiting southward. Bearing increasing at nearly two degrees per second. What moves that fast?"

"That's the Rocks!" cried Clint.

"I've got UV detection! Launch! Launch! Launch!" The blonde airman was screaming.

Chapter 76 - Targeted

"… a doom so sure, so speedy"

Grace Greenwood

The Rocks, still nap-of-the-earth at two hundred feet and now bringing sonic havoc to the northernmost trucks of the motorized column, were seen by Major Jafari's surveillance radar at a distance of twenty-three miles, much farther than Jafari's pessimistic estimate. Yet at the speed the ramjets were making this afforded only fourteen seconds of warning before the Rocks reached the battery. No matter, missiles were in the air.

The Gargoyle, fearsome killer of killers, could achieve Mach 6 and was rated to engage incoming targets traveling at up to Mach 8, the speed at which the Rocks were screaming over the desert.

As the first-launched Gargoyle neared its maximum altitude of seventeen miles, its white-hot flame shrank back into the nozzle as the last inner-wall crust of solid fuel was consumed, and it flamed out. It continued to sniff for a radar return, but as the Flap Lid targeting radar scanned only empty air no reflection reached the Gargoyle's seeker. Its climb slowed and the missile began to fall.

The host of men scattered along the roadside shied away from the roar and painful incandescence of another Gargoyle launch. Jafari watched the spike of white fire on his flatscreen as the long white missile darted into the sky. Seconds later, the sweet warble of the surveillance radar sounded and his heart leapt. The incomers had been acquired. The Flap Lid would paint them now, and the radar return would guide the Gargoyle home.

The second Gargoyle had shot up nearly eight miles when the Flap Lid's radar beam found the Rocks and reflected to strike the missile's seeker. Still burning its solid core, the missile's digital brain tilted carbonized composite vanes in its exhaust stream, vectoring its thrust to turn it abruptly back down and northward.

In the pair of seconds during which the Gargoyle reversed its course, the Rocks traveled three miles. They would require an additional twelve seconds to reach the S-300 battery's launchers and radars. The missile sped northward, its radar lock solid. It had ample time to meet the Rocks at their two hundred foot altitude, and would intercept them nearly twelve miles north of where Jafari's battery crouched on Route 80.

The relative velocity at which the Gargoyle closed with the oncoming Rocks was nearly Mach 14. The explosion of the fragmentation charge carried in the Gargoyle's warhead would add a trivial amount of energy to the unimaginable kinetic violence of a Mach 14 impact.

It was in those final seconds that the S-300 battery's network glitched.

Chapter 77 - Hacked

"We're rapidly approaching the time when you can tell an SA-10's radar that it's a Maytag washer and put it in rinse cycle instead of firing cycle."

Air Force Chief of Staff John Jumper

The targets on Jafari's radar display suddenly jumped, as though each of the bogeys had instantly leapt backward by several kilometers. Something in his chest dropped. The aging Russian electronics sometimes went dark, but he had never seen this kind of hiccup. A delay in packet switching? But that would cause a jump forward when the packets caught up.

His belly tightened with dread. Could his network have been penetrated, despite the encryption of its radio packets? Such a thing was rumored to have happened in the Syrian civil war when an S-300 battery failed to identify Israeli aircraft. It was said that opcodes for the S-300 had been stolen, allowing a digital radio signal, emitter unknown, to enter the battery's wireless network.

Digital signal packets had not only intruded into Jafari's network but claimed executive level access to reset a multiplier used in range calculations. Believing the packets lie, the surveillance radar continued to calculate and report the Rock's positions, sending azimuth and elevation angles to the Flap Lid targeting radar. The Flap Lid steered its beam to the empty sky at the reported azimuth, the radar returns from the Rocks disappeared from Jafari's screen, and the Gargoyle arrowing toward hypervelocity annihilation with the Rocks went blind.

The missile's closest approach was as it darted by still unseeing within meters of Alyssa's Rock. A *thump* too low-pitched to call sound boomed out over the continual shaking and jolting of hypersonic passage. It was the impact of the Gargoyle's conical shock wave on her fuselage. Sealed behind titanium plate and sapphire, she was startled, but uninjured.

The Gargoyle, seven and one half meters long and fat as a white-painted telephone pole, passed entirely unnoticed by the other switches, so brief was its proximity.

Chapter 78 - Toads beneath the Harrow

"I have killed peasants, men and women, old and young ...
We killed 23,884 Turks, without counting those burned in homes
or the heads cut by our soldiers...
Thus, your Highness, you must know that I have broken the peace."
Vlad Tepes, 'The Impaler'

The Rocks drove their apocalyptic pressure waves along the highway, and the long lines of drab green trucks, antiaircraft guns, antiair missile vehicles, all but the tanks and heavier APCs, were tossed like toys. Many came apart, their crews, cargo, and troops scattered into a dark snowstorm of flying men and tumbling boxes and sheet metal panels driven hellbent before the shockwave. Those peering north, as Yousouf had been, caught a glimpse of madly blossoming darkness before nearly solid waves of the violated atmosphere struck them down.

The many men gathered by the roadside outside their stopped vehicles were thrown bodily, their lungs force-filled and ruptured by the overpressure. Nasal and sinus membranes and inner ear structures tore. An instant later, the underpressure wave lifted every particle of sand, stone, and soil from the roadway and its desert borders, eyes were plucked from sockets and blood streamed from every mouth and nose and ear.

In the wake of it, a brief rain of stones pattered to the pavement. Dust thicker than a sandstorm blocked the sunlight. Within the blackness all was still. Those not killed outright were stunned. Those who lived to awaken were deafened.

Near the northern end of the column, the second of the Gargoyles, cheated of its target, exhausted its fuel and skipped twice in huge splashes of sand, making giant bounds off the desert floor before a fin dug in and it tumbled and flew apart, raising its own long dust cloud.

Major Jafari lay dazed in his overturned command vehicle as the third Gargoyle in his launch sequence thrust horizontally out of a capsized launch vehicle into the belly of an APC lying nearby. The solid rocket motor lit off, its torch burning into the mouths of the fat steel launch tubes of the trailer from which it had sprung. Three missiles remained in the tubes, and their aluminum casings burnt through and their solid propellant ignited in a white-hot sphere that engulfed the trailer and surrounding vehicles, burning hot enough to melt and then ignite their steel, liquefying and igniting the asphalt of the highway, finally melting the sand of the surrounding desert into a rosily glowing circle of liquid glass.

By the time the fourth Gargoyle launched, also from the horizontal tube of an overturned launcher, Jafari began to feel the heat of the nearby hellfire.

Chapter 79 - In the Valley III

"If you're wondering who the sucker is in a poker game, it's you."

Brigadier General Kioumars Heydari himself, commander of ground forces of the Artesh, the Iranian Army, rode with his most senior staff officers within a Rakhsh 4x4 wheeled APC, a vehicle made in Iran. The 16th Armored Division snaked its tanks and BMPs out along the road ahead.

His commo officer, a Sergeant Lofti, said, "The column behind has halted."

The Brigadier had ordered no halt, had been notified of no breakdown which could block both lanes of asphalt on Route 80, knew no reason for halting the column. And this was because the regular army and revolutionary guard maintained separate lines of commo.

He said, "Driver, stop. Lofti, find out what has happened."

The sergeant began radio inquiries. The tanks ahead began pulling away. The Brigadier got a grip on his own mind, maintaining silence in a discipline learned in the hellish years of the last war. He listened to the confused radio reports. Still with no clear idea of what had stopped the column behind, the Brigadier turned to the commo tech, "Lofti, Halt the 16th. Driver, pull up to the rear of the tanks."

The Rakhsh in which they rode was still motionless, facing south, when the Rocks overflew with a sound that was pitched so low that it sounded as a single beat, lower than the detonation of an artillery round, lower than anything the General had ever heard. The air in the vehicle's interior bore down on his skin and then breath gushed from his lungs as the over and underpressure pulses visibly compressed and then expanded the armored hull of his APC. In the next instant the Rakhsh, having a high center of gravity and large flat sail areas making up the armored enclosure, pitched rear over front and landed on its roof.

Chapter 80 - Hell at High Noon

"The sun shall be turned to darkness..."

Acts 2:20

Lit by faint crimson light, men crawled from overturned trucks. In near blackness they choked on air thick with dust, hanging their heads low. Some struggled to rise, heads spinning, staggering and falling back to the asphalt as delicate bones and membranes in their inner ears, broken by sonic shock, failed to balance them. They crawled toward the light.

Yousouf awoke to pain. It was as if a spike had been driven from ear to ear. A duller throb extended over most of the right side of his head. He reached up to feel viscous mud, dust wetted by his own blood. His earlobe was gone. His scalp and face were rough, skin scraped away.

He had been clinging to the canvas cover, looking to the north over a mechanized army in or around their trailers or vehicles. He remembered the oily smell of the green canvas. Faster than thought, a puff of smoke on the horizon had exploded into blackness that struck him a stunning blow. He must have flown along the road, abrading his head as he fell to the asphalt.

He rolled onto his belly and got hands and knees beneath him on the pebbly asphalt. A hint of ruby light bleeding through the dust beckoned him. He crawled, wanting to fall away onto his right side, dizzy. He leaned left to compensate and crawled on. At road's edge, the asphalt gave way to gritty desert soil, hard packed at first and then loose sand. The light grew brighter and less reddish. His hand fell on fabric. It was the lower leg of a man lying in the sand.

Yousouf crawled along the length of the man. His placed his hand below the man's sternum. The belly rose and fell in a strong rhythm. The ribcage vibrated with each exhalation, as if the man were groaning. Yousouf realized he could hear nothing. He hooked his arm beneath the man's armpit. He crawled, dragging the soldier toward the light.

They left the road behind and the dust thinned as Yousouf dug each foot in turn into the sand, thrusting to pull the dead weight along until they emerged into the hot windless noon of a sunstruck desert day. He could see the man now, a soldier like himself in drab green battle dress. Brown streaks of dust were caked into blood running from his ears and nose. A red froth bubbled from one corner of his mouth. He looked wide-eyed at Yousouf, dark Persian eyes beneath black brows, still heaving in air. Something was wrong with his lungs.

He held the soldier's forehead and levered the chin down. The airway looked clear. The breaths were deep and strong. Yet the man was suffocating. Yousouf gripped the soldier's hand with both his hands and waited. For a few minutes the soldier breathed in great gasps, then stopped.

177

He had been a good soldier; his battle rifle was still slung across his back. Yousouf slipped the sling from the man's shoulder and dragged the rifle toward him. He set the butt in the sand, gripped the barrel in both hands and pressed up to his feet, wobbling as if he had spun about in some childish game. He looked along the road where the convoy was still cloaked in dust. A few hundred meters away, a dozen tanks had emerged from the cloud. They idled there, fat muzzles pointing various ways, looking as stunned as he felt.

In the other direction a high pillar of smoke rose up from the cloud. At its root, brilliant white fire flashed through the dust. Something burned terribly hot there, all across the roadway. Yousouf remembered videos of nuclear strikes. But he thought he would not have lived had a ground zero occurred a few kilometers away.

He did not think the Saudis could kill an army in an instant. This was like the apocalypse spoken of in the hadiths. But he thought it had been done by men. It had to be *Al-Shaytan Al-Akbar*, the Americans or possibly the Israelis.

Yousouf was right. It was neither a miracle of *Allah* nor a manifestation of *Shaitan*. It was the work of men.

Yousouf was wrong. It was not the doing of the United States. It was the work of the High Command.

Chapter 81 - The Cyberwarriors Bug Out

"Move along."

Obi-Wan Kenobi

The Compass Call pilot watched as the dust cloud spread far to the south, obscuring nearly half the horizon ahead. He keyed his mic. "Fast movers gone by."

Satisfied that the Rocks had transited the Iranian column, he spoke again into their headsets. "It looks like they completed the attack pass. Going home."

It had been a hectic few minutes. The radar and launch warning analyst had kept screaming out, well, launch warnings. Four of them, though only two had climbed. None had detonated. A large fire near the head of the Iranian armored column had shown up on the IR detectors.

The pilot pulled the Compass Call into a turn. He straightened out on a bearing of 165 degrees, southward toward the airbase at Ali Al Salem.

In the cargo compartment, Simms laughed. "These are not the droids you're lookin' for!"

He bumped fists with the blonde, but almost immediately she sang out, "We're being painted."

"Patterson, do you mean the Sepehr, or the Ghadir?" asked Simms.

She shook her short blond bob. "They are both active, and both see us. But this isn't a low-freq over-the-horizon pulse. It's another S-300 surveillance radar. Fainter, like it's farther away. Bearing 40 degrees, toward Basrah, but probably farther away, in Iran."

Chapter 82 - The Shooting Continues

"To the last I grapple with thee."

Ahab

In the Air Defense command bunker, General Alireza Sabahi Fard had seen the EC-130H Compass Call, or anyway had seen a large plane shining bright in his radars as it come up from the south, from Kuwait or farther along the coast of the Gulf. The Sepehr had picked it up. And then a Ghadir. Then finally an S-300 battery near the border, across the waterway from Basrah, had acquired, range 112 kilometers.

The General had seen the photos of the Shahroud facility, its walls thrown about like playing cards. He stopped himself from imagining the effect of such a weapon on the column of vehicles. He knew he now had no shot at the attackers who had swept through at Mach 8. But this big slow-flyer was well within range. And it was not one of his. So one of theirs.

He spoke to his commo tech, "Message the battery near Basrah. Engage aircraft at bearing 220 degrees, altitude eight thousand, moving away."

Chapter 83 - Orbital Matchup III

"Doubt is not a pleasant state of mind, but certainty is absurd."

Voltaire

A red spiky star appeared on his headsup reticle. Jimmy's targeting radar had acquired the vampire. Hissing attitude thrusters stabilized the Rock as electric actuators trained the Gatling on target. On his tail, so take the shot. He pushed the GAU switch forward to the ARM detent and the whine of the electric motor spinning up the big Gatling fed back through his fingers.

On the point of hitting the AUTOFIRE pickle, a thought occurred to him. It was a damned inconvenient tendency, but doubt was a lifelong habit. As was also his habit, he immediately voiced his concern.

"Dirtside, are we sure that this is a vampire?"

Ben made no reply. After a minute, Jimmy told himself to have patience. Ben had other Rocks to think about. Another minute passed and then he called out his question again.

This time Ben replied immediately, hard to hear over the whine of the still-spinning autocannon. "Do you have an alternative explanation?"

"I've got time before it climbs out of range. I'm going to take a look."

Jimmy brought up the optical imaging window on the headsup. Under magnification, the bogey leapt into view, a white cylinder with a fatter cylindrical portion at its leading end, which tapered to a rounded point. Standard peniform upper stage design, but the fat section was distinctive, a cargo fairing he had seen before.

He said, "Dirtside, that's a Chinese rocket. It's the third stage of a Long March 7, still attached to the cargo fairing."

Ben said, "Checking database."

The Chinese upper stage had been pulling ahead, but Jimmy was now down near its altitude, pacing it from fifteen hundred meters behind.

Ben finally came back. "That Long March went up several months ago. Classified military payload. The third stage is intended for insertion into higher orbit, which it is doing, directly into the ISS orbit. Suggest you perforate bogey."

If he kept dropping, Jimmy would fall below the Chinese rocket and speed ahead, losing his shot.

He said, "Give me burn parameters to track the vampire. I want to enter its Hohmann transfer orbit."

"Shit. Stand by."

As Jimmy waited, the cargo fairing, the bulbous polymer composite housing designed to protect the payload, suddenly flowered into two petals. The halves flew outward, likely under the impetus of explosive bolts. The vehicle which emerged was entirely new to Jimmy.

Jimmy gated the optical feed into the dirtside datalink. He said, "What is that?"

"Huh," said Ben. "Stand by."

Chapter 84 - The Rocks Bug Out

"These things that now sink down in us like a stone, after the war shall awaken, and then shall begin the disentanglement of life and death."

Erich Maria Remarque

Polya grated out, "Ascend to twenty-five kilometers."

The nose came up and the desert dropped away and the buffeting died, and they climbed to the upper stratosphere, a rarefied domain where only the fastest of aircraft thrived, haunt of the legendary Blackbird and the X-15.

Polya's next order was that they make their intervals ten kilometers, and the Rocks spread over thirty kilometers of sky by the time they went feet wet over the Arabian Sea. He took them all the way south to the equator, too far and too fast for pursuit by Iranian antiair missiles.

As they passed over the empty Pacific and charged their belly tanks, Alyssa asked if anyone had heard 'that bang' during the attack run. No one had. Polya could only suggest she wait for the hotwash.

They turned east to follow the imaginary line of zero latitude until they reached the descending node of the ISS orbit, the point at which the orbit crossed the line from north to south. There they turned fifty-six degrees southward to match the ISS orbital inclination.

Now the Rocks opened up to full-throated ramjet thunder, putting on speed until ionization envelopes flickered about them with a gentle rose colored light.

It was a place Polya knew well, and he relaxed just enough to lose his tight combat focus. Within his softsuit he was swimming in sweat, cooling now but still acrid, and the stink was the kind that got up close and cut you, the smell of a man held long in fear, a hint of the deep brown death-rot in a lightless coffin, a stink in which a thousand corpses screamed.

All the switches had been here before. From here, all were familiar with the ascent to orbit.

Chapter 85 - The Shooting Continues II

"From Hell's heart I stab at thee."

Ahab

The communications tech, a tiny, thin Sergeant, turned to General Alireza Sabahi Fard, "The Basrah battery has lost target and surveillance radar tracks."

Fard spoke, a loud order. "Launch! One round, from the Basrah battery."

The tech's keyboard clicked like a cageful of crickets.

Fard voice rose to a shout, "Lieutenant Ila!"

Faces turned to him all along the command bunker.

He added more quietly, still with a snap to his voice, "Prepare to assume guidance."

Lieutenant Majid Ila stared for a moment with the rest of the operators. He was like them young and dark and had a squarish head and a long high-bridged nose but wore his hair with a side part that marked him out from the close-cropped enlisted grades at the other consoles.

His eyes widened as he understood the order, and then he turned and bent to his console. Staccato flurries of keystrokes, each burst ending in a percussive return, designated the coordinates of the S-300 battery near Basrah as the zero point for range measurements and as the viewpoint for graphical display of target and missile tracks.

The flatscreen gave him the radar picture constituted by the data fusion system, which was fed from the Ghadir radar at Ahvaz near the Iraq border and from the Sepehr farther away in the interior[23]. A number of bright yellow circular icons appeared, labeled with range estimates and tentative identifications. As he right-clicked icons they disappeared from the flatscreen until one last return, labeled as a C-130 Hercules and appearing at the correct bearing, he designated with a left button mouse-click.

The icon turned green. The digitally constructed view adjusted to look along the vector from the Basrah battery to the Hercules.

"Guidance ready. Awaiting launch," he said.

He stared into the screen for another four minutes until a yellow arrow rose form the bottom of his screen. It was the Gargoyle, tracked by the Ghadir as it leapt up from the battery. He double-clicked it with the left mouse button, then

---

[23] Data fusion combines multiple sources to improve accuracy. Although the precise nature of the Iranian Fakour data fusion algorithm is not known, an example can be given: Both the Ghadir and Sepehr provide a position estimate as a range and an azimuth. The two azimuths provide a third position estimate by triangulation. The two ranges provide a fourth estimate of position by intersecting circles. The estimates can be weighted according to their expected errors and summed.

clicked once again on the green icon of the Hercules. The arrow turned red and Farsi text scrolled across the bottom of the display, confirming the targeting.

The Gargoyle raged upward at its maximum acceleration until the first guidance packet arrived. Immediately, it dove toward the Hercules.

Looking at the Ghadir's range estimate, the digits scrolling down like a short-circuited gas pump meter, Lieutenant Ila called out, "The Gargoyle is under active radio guidance."

Chapter 86 - Clint Bugs Out

"Consider yourself as a dead body,
Becoming one with the Way of the warrior."

Yamamoto Tsunenori,
in Ha Gakure (Hidden Leaves)

Before the Herc's rear doors had fully opened, Patterson cried out, "Launch detected! Launch! Launch! Launch!"

All waited silently until she continued, "UV signature of launch, bearing twenty degrees, approximately toward Basrah. Ultraviolet signal is brightening rapidly. It's a Gargoyle!"

Simms said, "And that would be the AAR-47 Missile Warning System. Also probably right."

"Gargoyle has climbed to forty thousand feet. Bearing now constant." Patterson said.

"As in, 'Constant bearing means collision'?" Clint asked.

Grady ignored him. After a moment, Simms said, "That's right."

The airman up near the cockpit said, "JSTARS reports launch east of Basrah, probable S-300." The orbital sensors had no trouble detecting a launch whose over-the-horizon glow had lit up Patterson's detectors.

Grady keyed his headset mic open, "Suggest alter course to 220 degrees, max speed."

The Compass Call turned through fifty-five degrees, heading directly away from the missile.

"Bearing is still constant to Gargoyle. Range still closing," said Patterson.

"Guys, we had two minutes thirty seconds ago," said Simms.

Grady turned to Clint, "If you can control the chute, orient yourself to look toward the east. That's away from the sun."

He reached to the sheet steel enclosure suspended at Clint's chest and flipped a few toggles. "You're ready to go on my command."

They waited. And Clint, despite himself, thought. Grady wanted him looking east to keep the decoy facing the approaching SAM so his body did not block its emissions. He was about to call a hypersonic missile to himself. Would he see it coming? And he was also about to jump out of an airplane. He had never piloted an airplane. Even freshman physics came back to haunt him. If the chute malfed, falling a thousand feet would take about – he multiplied 1000 by 2 and divided by 32, hmm, same as dividing 1000 by 16 or 250 by four, to get 62 and the square root of that was – about eight seconds to watch the ground coming up at him faster and faster[24]. Was it true about people dying of heart failure on the way down? Else he would float down over the course of about forty-five seconds, with only the missile to worry about.

He was to free himself of the decoy, letting it fall twenty seconds before he touched down. In a perfect world, the Gargoyle would impact the decoy while Clint was still high enough to survive the blast wave and also high enough that the fragment cloud was less dense, at the extreme outer reaches of the warhead's kill radius.

Time dripped by while he tried to figure how long a Mach 6 missile would take to close in on him from the horizon.

---

[24] Didn't take freshman physics? How will you stave off boredom in a falling elevator?

Grady reached up to Clint's head and punched a button on the timer. "Now, go, go, go."

Clint walked through a gelatinous wall of fear. His head throbbed, and as he neared the end of the aluminum ramp he realized it was his heartbeat. He stepped off into bright light. The airstream roared and shoved him and then the static line tugged and he was jolted by the canopy springing open above. The rushing air slowed and he hung in sunshine and silence.

Clint looked down, wanting to see the ground for orientation and to see how fast it was coming. Bushes of low scattered scrub threw strips of shadow across dun sand. He seemed to hang without motion. He threw the box cutter out horizontally as far as he could. He knew he had a forty-five second ride and he wanted the decoy emitting at altitude for as long as possible.

Above, the canopy had cutouts in several rear panels. He had been given the steerable version of the T-10 and it glided forward as it descended. He reached up to the toggles and pulled on the right one until he had turned his back to the sun. He hung in the air, facing east, from where the Gargoyle would come.

Chapter 87 - The Cyberwarriors Bug Out II

"Another running gun battle today.
We're runnin', they're gunnin'."

Commander, USS Wahoo

Clint asked, "How did you know how to do that? To misdirect that battery's targeting radar?"

Simms was matter-of-fact. "So, the Air Force owns and operates an S-300 battery in Nevada. And we fly exercises against one operated by the Greeks."

"The Flap Lid just turned on!" the blonde cried out. She was Patterson, Clint remembered. Airman Patterson.

Simms turned to Clint, "We are now being painted by the targeting radar from an S-300 battery. If the battery fires a Gargoyle, it will read the reflection from us to home in."

"Are you sure?" Clint asked Patterson.

She turned a frown to him, "The ALR-69A Radar Warning Receiver says so. It was right when we flew exercises against the Greeks. It was right two minutes ago when they shot at the Rocks. It's right, right now."

For the first time since the engagement began, the analysts' supervisor spoke. This was a Master Sergeant named Grady, Clint forgot if that was first or last name, with a gray/black grizzled crewcut above a Middle East tan. He keyed the headset commo. "Recommend reducing altitude to one thousand feet. That will reduce our visibility radius to thirty-nine miles."

Simms turned to Clint, "If they are over the border, in Iran, they must be at least 70 miles from us. We'll duck down behind the horizon."

Everyone's belly got light as the pilot nosed the Herc over.

"Unless they are networking with the Ghadirs," said Grady.

They continued descending, and then briefly got heavier as the pilot leveled out at one thousand feet.

Patterson said, "Not seeing anything from the Flap Lid. No surveillance wavelengths either. We are below the battery's horizon."

Grady spoke to an airman at the forward end of the compartment. "You have a link to JSTARS?" He got an affirmative. Clint had never worked with a JSTARS aircraft, a flying data fusion center and a very high level asset.

Sergeant Grady turned back to Clint and went on, "The S-300 fires the Gargoyle, which can track via missile. If they pick up our location from over the horizon with the Ghadir, they can launch, then send updates to the missile via digital radio packets. They can still target us."

Simms was bent over his keyboard, doing a spreadsheet calc. "Transit time would be under two minutes for a Gargoyle," he said. "What countermeasures…"

Patterson cut him off, "Let's jam them. I don't want a Mach 6 missile coming at us."

Grady didn't object to her interruption. He said, "Simms?"

"Can't jam or deceive the battery like we did last time. This S-300 is below the horizon and at long range anyway. And the Gargoyle datalink antenna is rear-facing. It won't see our packets," said Simms.

"Jam the Ghadir?" Clint asked.

Simms said, "The Ghadir is far away. Emitting on its freq would just give it a bright return at our location."

"OK." Grady said. "The Ghadir has about half a kilometer range discrimination. Azimuth about the same. So their aim will not be that good."

"The Gargoyle has about a quarter kilometer kill radius. They could get lucky," said Simms.

Grady called out, "Hendricks. Deploy the towed decoy. Set freq to match Ghadir. Max emitted power."

A tall airman with close-cropped natural hair, seated further down the cargo compartment from Clint, went to work powering up the little glider and the cable system that would feed it into the airstream behind the Compass Call. If it worked, the Iranian console jockeys would see it as a bright spot, brighter than the reflection from their EC-130.

She looked up the cylindrical compartment at Grady. "ALE-55 towed decoy ready. Confirm deploy?"

"Check that," said Grady. He had been thinking. "That towline is shorter than the Ghadir's discrimination. It will see one spot."

Grady thought for a moment. "Prepare the disposable decoy."

The tall young woman frowned. "As you know, Sergeant, the disposable decoy electronics have been loaded inboard for maintenance. No propulsion available."

"What does that mean?" asked Clint.

Simms said, "She's talking about a MALD, Miniature Air Launched Decoy. That's a radio-frequency-emitting missile that can mimic the radar signature of nearly any aircraft. You drop from the wing and it flies away from your aircraft to draw off enemy missiles. It was being worked on, so the power supply and emitter were brought inside the aircraft, and the missile got left behind."

Clint didn't ask how the hell did that happen. The Rocks were already dropping into re-entry when he had deplaned at Ali El Salem. He had scrambled the Compass Call himself, drop your socks priority.

"Hendricks, prepare disposable decoy for parachute deployment," said Grady. "Request volunteer for ballast."

She shook her head, but arose and went to the back of the plane and bent to loosen the tiedowns on a squarish box on the port side of the compartment.

As Hendricks worked, Grady went to a locker on the starboard side and removed an olive drab canvas bag like a backpack with a smaller chestpack attached to its brown straps. It was a parachute and backup chute.

"I'm ballast," said Clint. And then realized what he had said.

Grady looked at Clint. "That's not necessary sir. One of the airmen can jump with the decoy."

Clint said, "Every airman here has a task vital to your aircraft and people getting home. I can't do any of those tasks."

Grady looked at him for a long moment. "Hendricks, bring the decoy," he ordered.

Grady unbuckled the backup chute and walked forward with the rest of the parachute. He paused at a tool locker and removed a couple tools or meters of some kind, plus a roll of duct tape. He approached Clint.

Clint turned away, and Grady helped him into the chute harness. Clint was awkward stepping through the leg straps. Grady adjusted the harness as best he could over Clint's heavy dress uniform.

Hendricks handed Clint a thin sheetmetal box the size of a stereo component. Her mouth was compressed, grim.

Grady said, "Hold it out from your chest."

He took a turn around the enclosure, then around behind Clint's neck across his shoulders. He repeated this loop until the enclosure hung suspended by a duct tape strap.

Then Grady taped a small black box to the side of Clint's head, right over his ear, taking three turns around. Grady said, "Timer."

Clicks sounded in Clint's ear as Grady set a dial on the front of the box. "And what does it time?" he asked.

"You hear the ding, you use this." Grady handed him a box cutter, blade extended. "Cut the decoy free and let it fall."

Events had taken on a growing sense of unreality. Clint asked, "This is an Air Force procedure?"

Grady said, "This is something we worked up today while the pilots did their preflight, when we realized we didn't have an operational MALD."

They walked to the rear of the Compass Call, Clint moving ducklike as he balanced the weight of the electronics. Grady rigged the static line from Clint's chute to the rail running along the side of the plane. He said, "This is a T-10 chute, rate of descent 22 feet per second. I will start the timer. Then, on my command, you will run out the back, the chute will deploy, and you will descend for twenty-five seconds. Cut the decoy free when the timer chimes."

And thus it was that Clint stood at the back of the compartment, watching the rear of their big bird open like a clamshell onto empty sky. As the lower door leveled out the hydraulics hit their stops with a bang.

Chapter 88 - Orbital Matchup IV

"Friendly Fire Isn't."

Infantry Journal

Ben had the video feed up on his flatscreen. What he noticed first was a long slender white cylinder. He knew the discarded Long March cargo fairing was somewhere near fifteen meters in length, so the tube looked to be twelve or so and about a meter in diameter. It lay atop a boxy white module, sunk halfway down into it all along its length.

He hit a speed dial button on his console and said, "Jenny come in here please, now."

He keyed his mic open, telling Jimmy, "Vehicle not recognized here."

Jenny burst in, letting hallway lighting into the gloom. She leaned on his shoulder to get a look at the screen.

She said, "Xiaofei sent the railgun."

She said, "He must think he's being watched. He didn't reply to my query."

Ben said into his mic, "Jimmy, uh, don't fire on the vehicle. Stand by for burn parameter upload."

Jenny drew her iPhone. "Hey Siri, call Tom, home." She punched iEncrypt.

Ben bent to his console, uploading duration and intensity for Jimmy's burn.

Jenny murmured into her iPhone as Ben worked. In a few moments she straightened and said, "He's coming in. Ten minutes."

Ben had just completed the setup for Jimmy's burn, pasting numbers from a computation window to the digital datalink, when a priority chime from a surveillance analyst interrupted.

"Ben, it's James. *Tiangong* 2 just began maneuvering. And a booster is fueling on the pad at the launch site at Wenchang."

Chapter 89 - Disposable Decoy

"A good scare is worth more to a man than good advice."

191

Hanging in bright light and silence, Clint looked down. As far as he could see, red-tinged brown earth came up at him with increasing speed. He began to worry about his landing, but then recalled that a four thousand mile per hour missile would arrive at about that time.

In the event, he landed before the missile arrived, in a slow drift to his left. The technique was to hit with slightly bent knees and arch the body so as to roll along the left leg and torso, the feet ending up above the head to absorb energy. But the extra forty pounds of electronics taped to his chest buckled his legs, transforming his roll into a crumple. In a flash of panic he extended his straight left arm, which transmitted the shock of impact directly into his left shoulder.

As he recovered sensation and breath, Clint moaned. It annoyed him, that knowing no one could possibly hear he cried out anyway. Then he had to get off his left side and groaned again at the hot fire in his shoulder. With his right hand he cast off the duct tape strap and pushed the electronics module aside. Every tiny move stabbed him as he sat up, clutching his left upper arm and trying to immobilize it. What of the Compass Call? He scuffed his feet to pivot on his butt. The late afternoon sky was still clear and just above the horizon to the southwest the Herc was no larger than a toy, apparently unhit.

The missile. Clint gained his feet by leaning carefully to the right and pushing up with his good arm. He turned around to the northeast just as a blinding white streak passed above him. He spun just in time to see the Gargoyle's warhead explode in silence into a large black puff near the gray C-130. The shockwave of the missile's hypersonic passage reached him a quarter second after that.

The sonic boom was very much like an explosion and it dealt a clublike blow and stabbed icepicks into both of his ears. He hunched in misery, then straightened to look for the Hercules again.

The inky puff at the end of the missile's smoke trail appeared to be above and possibly short of the aircraft. The Herc flew on, with the low sun glinting bright gold on its fuselage. Then the left wing bent up and came off the plane. The right wing rose, rolling the Herc left. Then the nose came up and it fell out of the sky tailfirst. It would take eight seconds, more or less, to reach the ground.

Clint watched the broken plane fall below the horizon. Having been deafened, he did not hear the missile's detonation, the sound of which reached him nearly fourteen seconds after the explosion.

Chapter 90 - The Shooting Concludes

"What would Stalin do?"

Alexander Fokin

The tech next to Majid Ila called out, "New return on bearing 220 from Basrah battery. Identifies as C-130 Hercules."

Lieutenant Ila said, "The software won't accept new targets once guidance has been established."

They waited. On his flatscreen, Majid watched the rapid convergence of the red icon to the green one.

The Gargoyle's red arrow disappeared from the flatscreen. The Hercules icon persisted and he thought it was a miss, until a few seconds later it winked out as well.

"Probable hit on the C-130," Ila said. He slid back from the console and turned to smile at the General, but Fard was grim, his black gaze glittering from a stony face.

Chapter 91 - Desert Thoughts

"When you sleep in a house your thoughts are as high as the ceiling, when you sleep outside they are as high as the stars."

Bedouin Proverb

Clint stood unmoving, looking southwest with the sting of the sun baking his face to where the EC-130 had gone down. Two seconds. He estimated that the missile had been visible for two seconds before the kill. Too little time for a heart attack.

His lower back trembled and the weakness spread and forced him down. He swayed as he knelt, unsteady in his head. He had to replace his upper arm bone into its socket, but he had no strength and no clear idea how to do it. He would not be walking to the crash site, miles away.

A breeze reminded him that he was still attached to the canopy by pulling him over onto his side, luckily to the right. When the canopy collapsed he struggled to his feet again, marveling at the exquisite sensitivity of his injury. With infinite caution, he detached and discarded the parachute harness.

He waddled around the puddle of white fabric, spreading and weighting the edges with stones. Stones were in abundance, and sand, and dust. He had no water. But now he had shade, and some shelter against the coming chill of a desert night.

He scooted painfully under the smooth nylon, and then rolled onto his back.

He lay in his sweat and in the pain from his head and from his shoulder. He would likely die of dehydration and heat the next day or the next after that. It surprised him that he did not dwell on it. But if someone did come to his aid, what would he tell Juana?

As the only survivor, the only soldier who had parachuted to safety from an aircraft under attack, his was the only, unsupported, account. He knew the High Command only from his abrasions with the platoon of switches, his brushes with Tom, and his come-to-Jesus moment with Juana. Would they kill him? Somehow that possibility was not the most frightful. He would tell her what happened. They would decide.

The sky dimmed, tinged with orange from a sunset he could not crane his neck to see. Stars appeared and grew so outlandishly brilliant that he pulled the canopy over his face. His habitual worry remained quiet and Clint slept, made fitful only when an involuntary movement stabbed him with renewed pain.

Chapter 92 - The Rocks Come Home

"You have no time outside to look around and go 'wow.'
It would not have been appropriate."

Tom Akers

The Rocks popped up into their final climb, their magnificent cloaks of light dying with the thinning of the atmosphere. They ascended on a minimum energy trajectory, knowing they must further draw down their belly tanks to get the delta-vee needed to circularize their orbits when they reached ISS altitude. And propellant had to be reserved in case they needed to drop again. This mission promised, as had previous missions, to exhaust the Iranian's arsenal. Yet always there came again the time to drop.

They approached the ISS while it was above the planet's dayside, and everyone looked for Jimmy's Rock, but the station was bare. No Rock ready to drop in station defense. No one to assist them to tie down.

"Alyssa, go EVA for tiedown." Polya sounded tired.

Alyssa sounded tired too, "Let my Rock drift?"

Polya gave his orders. "Let drift. Transit ratlines to hab. Hardsuit. Secure Judy."

Then he shouted, "Stay alert! Stay alert! We are almost up mountain. Do not fall now!"

He resumed his usual even rumble, "Judy also hardsuits. Two hardsuited switches secure Rocks."

Alyssa hinged up the blister, leaving only her softsuit between herself and the void. Katia was gone and now she was the smallest and most slender switch, the one who could most quickly get through a docking tunnel in a hardsuit without assistance.

The ramjet's exterior, especially its leading edges, would char her softsuit. She would have to leap the twenty meter gap to *Zvezda*. Crouching on the acceleration couch, she struggled to focus on the ratlines while the Carpathian Mountains crept by beyond the module. Wishing she had Katia's catlike spatial ability, she leapt.

It was so easy to die up here, and High Command procedures were ad hoc. She had come to believe that she would die unnoticed. Few in the intelligence services or in the military knew about the Rocks, built not so much with a black budget as with funds misappropriated from black budgets, and covertly deployed. Perhaps today's mission would bring attention.

He hand found the lifeline right next to a bracket, stopping her short as she pivoted around the ratline to flop clumsily against *Zvezda's* hull. She breathed awhile, knowing that while the other switches waited they must occasionally spend propellant from their attitude thrusters to keep station near the ISS.

Tom Broadhead's voice buzzed in their earpieces, making her jump, which could have carried her away. She gripped the ratline tighter.

"Polya, a Chinese craft is inbound. The crew request assistance."

"We must tie down Rocks," said Polya.

"Proceed. Just wave to greet the two of them. Their radio freqs are not the same as ours. I will ask them to keep station with the ISS until you have rested. Adequately rested, to avoid mishaps."

Tom continued, "They will arrive in twenty minutes, in the *Tiangong* 2 prototype space station. They will be with another vehicle. It's the railgun, Polya."

Chapter 93 - Hot Washup I

"Just as the Security Council was largely irrelevant to the great struggle against Communism, so too it is largely on the sidelines against international terrorism..."

John Bolton

Admiral Juana Abreu addressed the three others gathered around the table. It was rare that the American contingent of the High Command met in person. And always before they had met in New York, not Washington. Their Russian and Chinese contacts followed two-way text translations via encrypted datalink. A few more Americans and one European were also hooked in.

"We have tens of thousands of Iranians, some badly hurt, lying in desert sun, their vehicles overturned. Many more are walking back along Route 80 toward

Basrah. The armor is dispersed and retreating through the desert, toward the same destination."

Jerry spoke. "The U.S. has offered humanitarian aid. So have the Kuwaitis. Nothing from the Saudis yet."

"And the man in the big turban, he's willing that they die for the cause?" This from Tom.

"No word from Tehran," said Juana. "At least, no word that has percolated through the Joint Chiefs from the White House."

"What is the body count?" asked Tom.

Juana spoke again. "Judging from aerial photos they took roughly forty percent casualties, nearly ten percent killed. The Kuwaitis and the U.S. Air Force have planes and drones over the highway. They have not been fired on."

Tom was unsurprised at this last. Above ten percent losses, units decohered, ceased to fight. Unless they were Gurkhas, or Japanese. He said, "DIA will recommend that a combat air patrol be established. Then the Army units stationed at Arifjan south of Kuwait City will send in water, food, and medical relief. An Iranian F-4 or F-14 would be suicidal to attempt an approach."

Then the fourth person arose. The Secretary General of the United Nations spoke. "We have to disclose now. Soon, anyway."

Chapter 94 - Bedouins I

"When a guest comes he's a prince. When he sits, he's a prisoner. When he leaves he's a poet."

Bedouin Proverb

Clint squinted against brightness. Someone was holding up the silky parachute canopy.

He followed a shadowy arm back to a brightly lit shape. Folds of fabric, a Biblical robe. A headdress. A Bedouin had found him.

He struggled against the imperative of the pain in his shoulder to roll onto his good side and get to his feet, confronting the man who had lifted the canopy.

The silvery morning sky lit a deep brown face split by a high narrow nose, peering from within a white headscarf. Another wrap lay beneath the headscarf, checked red and white.

The Bedouin dropped the parachute. His other arm cradled an AK held casually across his body in the crook of the elbow, the indestructible Kalashnikov battle rifle developed by the Soviets and distributed more widely than any other infantry rifle. The muzzle lay at right angles to his line of sight to Clint.

The man said, "As Salaam Alaikum."

The words were faint. Clint was surprised he could hear at all. He knew enough to say, "Alaikum Salaam."

The man grasped his robe at his chest and recited several words. Clint thought the first was "Tariq". He had known a Turk of that name.

Clint placed his own hand on his chest and said, "Clinton Martin, United States Air Force."

Then Clint pointed at the Bedouin and said, "Tariq."

The man nodded. He pointed at Clint and said "Clean Martin. Air Force. American."

Clint nodded, squinting into the other's gaze in the dimness under the headscarf. He wanted, before shade, before water, before food, to make the pain stop. He unbuttoned his uniform blouse and slid the fabric off his left shoulder.

The Bedouin looked at the lumpy wreck of Clint's shoulder joint. He pointed at it, and then jerked his other hand, miming a tug.

Clint took a breath. Such field adjustments were intensely painful. But perhaps it would help. He nodded.

The man Tariq bent to lay the rifle in the sand, something an American soldier would never do with an M4, but such was the robustness of the AK's action, giving it value far beyond that of its modest accuracy. He stepped to Clint's left side and grasped his wrist, covering the shoulder with his other hand and slowly moving the arm about.

Clint said, "*Uhhn.*"

Tariq took a single deep breath, and released it slowly, lowering Clint's arm. He pointed to the Earth, and swept his right hand out parallel to the sand while stepping back.

Clint went through the complicated and delicate procedure to get down on his right side. He rolled onto his back on sand already too warm in the new day.

Tariq sat straight-legged next to him, placing a foot against his left side. He slowly brought the arm out perpendicular to Clint's body and leaned back, gradually increasing the pull.

Pain spiked through him and Clint cried out and the head of his armbone shifted and then the ball of bone *thunked* back into its nest of cartilage.

Tariq gently laid down Clint's arm and bent his knees to sit cross-legged beside him in the sand.

When the weakness passed, Clint nodded and did his best to smile. He would not use the arm today. But the shoulder was not afire.

Tariq reached a hand forward to just beneath Clint's left ear. He pinched something between his thumb and forefinger from the skin. He held up brownish-red powdery dried blood for Clint to see.

Clint nodded and then shrugged, right side only.

Chapter 95 - Excursion

"Afraid of the dark and suspicious of the light."

Anonymous

Polya floated, it seemed without motion, just above Earth passing slowly by to his left. The sun at his back did nothing to light the blackness to his right. He flexed the joints of his hardsuit's arms. Everything that kept you alive in space was spindly and insubstantial. Everything that could kill you was immensely powerful, or just immense beyond imagining. The pull of a planet. Debris fragments at orbital velocity. An infinity of hard vacuum, eternal and patient as gravity.

"Hello Apple 1, proceeding with EVA." Polya said in his monotone.

He hissed propellant from the self-contained propulsion system. Judy awaited him on *Zvezda* at the tiedown point for Rock 4.

The switches had focused all attention on tying down their spacecraft, including Jimmy's Rock. The Chinese craft had arrived just ahead of Jimmy, under the muzzles of his Gatling.

Alyssa's Rock 4 had drifted a few hundred meters during their rest. Stepping through frames of video to analyze the Rock's motion relative to the ISS had revealed the slightly different ellipticities of their orbits, and how the Rock regularly approached and receded. Polya jetted to where he knew the Rock would arrive and killed his momentum with another hiss of propellant.

When the ramjet drifted within reach he opened the blister and climbed in as far as the bulk of the hardsuit allowed, leaving the blister open. Luckily, he did not have to bring the reactor temperature up, or make any delicate adjustments to the controls. The Rock's attitude thrusters nudged it close enough for Judy to attach a tiedown cable. She reeled the ramjet in with the electric winch and then attached two more cables to form a semi-rigid support like the guy wires on a radio tower.

Polya looked past Judy and the ISS to the two spacecraft keeping station two hundred meters away. He recognized the white cylinder with winglike paired solar cell arrays as *Tiangong* 2. China's temporary space station had been lofted to orbit to test and adjust rendezvous, docking, and automated resupply. It had been designed to give temporary life support to two taikonauts.

Polya looked to the second Chinese vehicle. While the switches rested, the two Chinese spacemen had constructed a spindly three-dimensional truss protruding back from the railgun. Its many triangles resembled the tower of a high-voltage power line. The two hardsuited figures were now deploying a large gray rectangular panel on each side of the truss. These would dissipate waste heat, but from what source?

Polya keyed his throat mic. "Dirtside, what are Chinese intentions?"

Tom came right back, "Ask them. Chien has good Russian and English. And Suh has good English."

Polya climbed out of the Rock sealed the blister. He watched as Judy returned to the shelter of *Zvezda*. He then jetted up and away from the station, clearing his view of Earth.

The farther he drifted, the stronger grew his sense of being small and alone in boundless void and the more palpable was the immensity of the planet. He was at once inconceivably high and a hairsbreadth above it, a single infinitesimal inescapably connected to all of being. He watched Earth pass below.

Chapter 96 - Bedouins II

"He who shares my bread and salt is not my enemy."
Bedouin Proverb

Tariq thought it hard that they could not speak, especially of the camel. The Arabs gave the beast five thousand seven hundred and forty-four different names. He owned dozens, and could identify the track of any of them from a single print in the sand.

Tariq, Clint thought, was a perceptive and deeply knowledgeable man. Of course he was. Intuitive nonverbal communication and emergency medicine would be needful to a people dwelling in emptiness and apartness.

The two of them crept across the desert, hiking beside *Rima*, a camel so tall that Clint would not mount for fear of a fall on his damaged shoulder. Tariq would not ride while Clint walked. *Rima* carried the electronics enclosure slung to the saddle by the duct tape strap. There was a scabbard for the AK, but the Bedouin had carried the battle rifle since they had arisen from the sand.

Water, from a plastic bladder secured to the camel's saddle, tasted wonderful. They walked for an hour at a time, rested and drank, and trekked on. The sun had begun to decline, having burned Clint to a fine scarlet, when a clump of structures came into view.

A summer camp of two circular tents stood beside a shallow declivity sheened with water. The musk of tethered camels and goats, and of sheep within a fabric enclosure rode on the hot air. Two women in long black dresses moved quickly away, hustling several children into the tents. A young man, really a boy but in robe and headdress, ran up to Tariq and they exchanged a storm of Arabic, after which the youth ran to the farther tent.

The shade inside he would remember with deep gratitude. When his vision adjusted the space was a pie slice of the tent walled off by heavy pale golden fabric, perhaps a third of its area. The ceiling sloped up to a central point, and the outer wall and the ceiling glowed a faint gold with the light outside. Dark blue star shapes patterned the fabric, and ornate borders picked out the juncture of wall and ceiling. Intense red and blue figurings writhed on the carpets layering the floor and upon them rested thick round cushions and low tables. Tariq waved him to one of the low ottomans and Clint sank gratefully down.

The boy came back carrying a tray with bowls of yogurt and pieces of cold meat and flatbread. He and Clint spoke their "Salaams", and the boy said a name too exotic to remember.

Clint fell on the food eagerly, grateful that his right arm was functional[25]. The boy again departed, to return some minutes later with a second tray with a beaked brass pot and three small cups of clear glass. Tariq poured café-au-lait for the three of them.

As Clint considered the flavor of cardamom-laced coffee mixed with camel's milk, Tariq reached behind his seat to a low table supporting a small flatscreen TV. A bulky yellow battery pack sat on the rug below. He picked up a satellite phone resting beside the screen and made a call, speaking rapidly and emphatically and then listening by turns as if being questioned for several minutes.

---

[25] In this, Clint was luckier than he knew. To eat with the left hand would have been gravely impolite.

They drank their coffee in silent comradeship until Tariq arose. He made the gesture that Clint remembered from the morning, sweeping his hand out above the tent floor, palm up. Clint lay on the soft rug, feeling much better save for the ache in his ears. He relaxed, letting the fatigue from the long walk seep into him from his legs. Looking up at the glowing tent fabric, he dozed.

Some time later, a helicopter *thwup-thwupped* in the distance. Tariq arose to shake Clint's shoulder, the good one, as his son hurried in through the tent flap. Clint labored to his feet, hearing the helicopter in his right ear as its sound grew. Tariq took a step toward the tent flap, but stopped as Clint held up his hand.

It was terribly important to him to thank this man for his life, but he had no words. And probably none of the American helicopter crew speak Arabic.

Working one-handed and with some trouble Clint plucked the keepers from the silver stars at his shoulders. He lifted the stars from the fabric straps of his uniform blouse, placing each one face down on the table. He replaced the keepers over the sharp spikes on the back of the stars and walked over to Tariq and the boy. He handed each of them a star.

Chapter 97 - Hot Washup II

"A tactician thinks about casualties. A strategist thinks about victory."

The four people gathered around the conference table were known to Clint as High Command contacts, met not long before. Juana explained procedure. An undisclosed number of additional contacts would follow a transcript. Neither video nor audio was outgoing. The text went out on a time delay of three minutes, and names of any High Command contacts would be redacted before transmission.

Clint was unsurprised at the compartmentalization, probably reflexive, within a clandestine underground itself drawn from clandestine services. What surprised him was that he did not have a seat off by himself, facing the other four across the table. All were spread around as if in an assembly of equals. The arrangement eased his mind, but he remained worried about how they would interpret his survival.

He said, "You have some questions for me?"

He tensed as Juana's glittering black gaze locked onto him. "Grady taped it. Recorded it, I should say, by digital camera in the EW crew compartment. He uploaded the feed through satcom."

"He recorded the parachute departure?" Clint asked. He pivoted in his chair to ease his left arm, still supported in a sling. Painkillers and the mercy of a hospital trolley rigged into the back of the military transport had allowed him some rest on the long droning flight back from the airbase at Ali Al Salem. But he had discontinued the pain pills a few hours ago, wanting alertness for this interview, and the shoulder throbbed at irregular intervals. It added to his unease.

"He recorded the entire mission. Everything that went on with his analysts and techs," said Juana.

Jerry, the guy from NASA, spoke. "We learned something. If you fire a MALD, fire it directly down the threat vector, so the decoy's radar return doesn't diverge from the aircraft return. Let the threat missile detonate early on prox to the decoy."

"Master Sergeant Grady did his best," said Clint. "He turned directly away from the threat. But the decoy dropped to a lower altitude."

"Hindsight says he could have anticipated the problem, and descended at the same rate as the decoy," said Juana. "But foresight doesn't happen reliably in a two-minute engagement."

"Hindsight says we could have anticipated the Iranians guiding the Gargoyle with over-the-horizon radar data. But we hung a fat slow Compass Call out there for them to shoot at," said Jerry.

"The Compass Call did its job. The Rocks got home," said Tom.

"And we retained Clint," said Juana. "A badly needed Air Force contact. Let's break for lunch, and then discuss what to do next with the Rocks."

Clint sat silent, thinking of how saving the Rocks could balance the loss of the most sophisticated airborne electronic warfare platform in his air force and in the world. Of how thirteen airmen had died to save the four switches and their craft. Of how the damage to himself was of no importance. Of how much his fear had been and how he had wanted to throw himself into the path of the Gargoyle to save them.

Chapter 98 - New Neighbors

"If you've made a deal with the devil, probably no one else offered you more favorable terms."

M.E. Thomas

Still very alone in space, Polya swung around the Earth. He stilled his thoughts as long as he was able, wanting every moment of unfiltered perception, but soon the mission nagged at him.

It was extraordinary, he and Tom Broadhead, the GRU and the CIA. The arrival of the taikonauts brought in the Ministry for State Security, the MSS. Three countries poised to launch on one another, the biggest circular firing squad in human history, each sending fighters and weaponry to this tiny exposed outpost. And all their muzzles were pointing outward.

It was past time he got back to work, and he chinned his throat mic open.

"Jimmy, you would like to visit new guys? You will need hardsuit and propulsion pack."

"On the way." Jimmy's voice was high in his earpiece.

He looked back to Earth. The thin lens of atmo at the horizon glowed a translucent pale blue he had never seen before. Jimmy would turn up soon enough.

...

As they drifted over to *Tiangong* 2, Jimmy said, "I'm not a big fan of the Red Chinese. I understand why they're here; they don't like Muslim terror attacks. But they've got about a million Uighurs locked up in camps and if I was a Uighur I'd be a terrorist too."

"Is single party rule. One man at top. One man changes, whole country changes." Polya sounded resigned.

"So one guy decides that he'd rather fortify the South China Sea than sell his country's factory output to the West?"

"Deng wanted best for China. Xi wants survival of CCP."

Jimmy shook his head, a futile gesture in a hardsuit. He said, "Well let's see what these guys want."

As the switches drew near to the pair of newly arrived craft, both of the taikonauts transited from the blocky railgun module over to the modest white cylinder of the Chinese station. One entered the lock, while the other awaited them.

The ideogram on the man's helmet told Jimmy nothing of who greeted him, but the fellow helped him arrest his momentum. He then grabbed Polya as he was about to drift by.

A few minutes were needed to lock everyone in, and to get the hatch seals checked. Then they doffed helmets.

The usual east-west collision of greetings included Polya attempting a bow in zero gee while the smaller of the two taikonauts held out a hand for a shake. To avoid rotating about from the angular momentum of bowing, they ended by gripping hands, still wearing hardsuit gauntlets. They had not enough room to stow four hardsuits.

Polya said, still grasping a hand, "Polya."

"Knee how," Jimmy said. Best he could do in Chinese. "Jimmy."

Chien, the other man, was taller and longer in the face. He said only his name.

The one with the round head and short stature of a southerner said, "I am Suh." Then he looked at Jimmy. "You are American? We will speak English."

Being stereotyped as ignorant of languages embarrassed Jimmy, but he said, "That would be easier, thank you." They need not know that it would have been possible for him to follow most of a conversation in Russian.

Polya asked, blunt as always, "You have railgun?"

Suh said, "Most of one."

He explained, smiling. "The gun can perform if the energy to run it is available. We look to one of your FS-2A Smart Rocks for that energy."

Polya frowned, "You want me to give you Rock?"

Suh nodded. "A Rock's reactor will boil water in a heat exchanger placed into its throat. The steam will spin a turbine and so drive a generator. Before it gets pumped back into the reactor to complete the loop the steam will condense in heat dissipation panels."

Polya said, "Gray panels attached to trusswork behind railgun."

Suh nodded.

"We have five Rocks. Five bodies to do EVA rigging. Will help?" asked Polya.

"It has been our hope to benefit from such help."

Suh's perfect stilted textbook English amused Jimmy. He couldn't wait to coach him in a few profanities.

Suh continued, brow furrowed, "We would first like to establish common radio frequencies. This mission has evolved in an unexpected way, and planning has not been done. Also, we are not happy with this hab cylinder, its life support and facilities."

Looking about, Jimmy understood. There were no racks for equipment. A cluster of food packets was netted in one corner. Clothing floated. No toilet was to be seen. The only evidence of technology was a panel paved with the usual glowing buttons and switches and bolted onto the bulkhead farthest from the lock. It looked like a hasty add-on, as did the quad flatscreens just above it. He supposed that it ran the railgun.

Polya said, "You must come, meet U.S. Marines in *Zvezda* module. Two Marines, but have facilities for four. Jimmy and I stay in *Columbus* module. With Vlad, old attack pilot like me."

Suh's brow smoothed. "It will be a pleasure."

Chapter 99 - Hot Washup III

"Consider this simple fact...
The United States Navy controls all the oceans of the world."

George Friedman
The Next 100 Years

Juana stood at the head of the cherrywood conference table, rubbing the satin finish without noticing.

"What they did to the Compass Call they can do to the Rocks," she said.

She went on. "They will have better coordination, better data sharing and data fusion, quicker handoff to track via missile. The next Rock that overflies an S-300 battery will be vaporized."

Tom said, "We could hit their command bunker, but it's a bunker." A few feet of earth stopped the strongest sonic boom.

"Agreed. Trashing the surface structures of the Pasdaran's air defense base won't take out their command and control." Juana said.

"We won't get away with it a third time. We can't commit Rocks to another surface attack. It would be a waste," said Jerry.

We need to blind them," said Clint. "Like a regular air campaign. Suppress radars and air defense batteries, then send in attack craft."

He continued, "The short-range radars are not a problem. The Sepehr is a problem. The Ghadirs are a problem. They see too far."

Tom sipped from his bottle of icewater. He spoke up. "We don't need to hit the Iranians. We just destroyed their capacity for large-scale war. We need to defend orbital assets."

Jerry leaned forward. "We need to defend orbital assets. But more, we need to consolidate control over near-Earth space."

Juana said, "Trade moves on the sea. Cut a country off from the sea and you cripple it. Information moves through space. Cut a country off from space, especially its military, and you blind it."

"The Rocks are the dominant force in the near-Earth battlespace," said Tom. "Nothing up there threatens them. Nothing can escape them."

Jerry held up a hand, as though to restrain him. "The Rocks need resupply and manning. The ISS is a very soft target. And it is the only home they have."

"A home protected by a deployed and fully functional railgun," said Tom.

Chapter 100   A Last Volley

"For hate's sake I spit my last breath at thee."

Ahab

Brigadier General Alireza Sabahi Fard looked up above the line of control consoles arrayed across one side of the long command bunker. His gaze was arrested by a pair of piercing dark eyes staring from the portrait hung above the array of flatscreens. He watched those eyes as he listened to the voice of the man depicted in the portrait.

"General Ismaili will arrive within the hour. You are to hand over command and report to your quarters."

Fard knew his line, "Yes, Supreme Leader. It will be done."

Ismaili had preceded him in this job for seven years. Alireza Fard did not envy him in returning to it. The launch complex at Shahroud was rubble, and the forward elements of the Artesh, the heavy elements of Iran's army, were a shambles. He felt a relief in knowing that he could not make things worse for himself.

General Fard replaced the handset onto the old-fashioned plastic telephone on his desk. He spoke to his commo tech, the man at the nearest control console.

"Connect the command building at Semnan."

When the commo tech turned to him and nodded, he picked up the handset. Farsi had been the language of poets for two thousand years, and so he took a moment to consider his words.

"Set free the birds. Every one."

Chapter 101   Settling In

"A lone man on a battlefield is not a warrior."

Russian Proverb

Jimmy extracted himself from the docking tunnel into *Zvezda*. Alyssa wasn't helping today. The module was crammed with Russians and Chinese clustered near the airlock, and it reminded him of the crowded gray windowless compartments in which he had spent so much of his career.

He said, "You know, living in an aluminum can full of ass-gas is remarkably like operating from an aircraft carrier."

"Carriers have showers," Alyssa called from the other end of the module.

She hunched her shoulders, arms tight to her sides, as though having an attack of 'crawlies', a burning of the sensitive skin on the sides of a torso left too long unbathed.

Near the other end Judy had a foot hooked through a loop at the end of her sleeping pad. She reached an MRE out of a net bag and winged it down the module like a Frisbee.

She growled at him, "Carriers have Navy food, brownshoe."

Jimmy ducked the MRE and went on, "We're the combat air patrol wing. Suh and Chien are the anti-missile wing. And the silent six are the strike wing."

"And look, here is chicken wing!" cried Vlad, flapping his elbow.

This drew laughs, even from the Marine women. The switches had been shot at and missed, and were deeply happy. Suh and Chien looked puzzled.

"You guys aren't pilots, are you?" Jimmy asked them.

As he had in *Tiangong* 2, Suh spoke for the pair, "Mission specialists. Applied physics of high energy electromechanical systems. As to the mission, the *Tianzhou* cargo craft will arrive in a few hours. It will carry the turbine and generator that will allow a Rock to power the railgun."

Suh drew a deep breath. "What happens in the railgun module is simple, but not easy. It all happens in a strong magnetic field."

Then he was almost twittering as there followed a disquisition of the bank of series-connected graphene-enhanced supercapacitors collecting electrical charge, of the massive surge of current discharged down one rail, across a metallic shuttle and back along a second rail, of how the Lorentz force of the huge current in the strong magnetic field shot the shuttle down the rails, pushing a projectile to a speed limited only by the capacity of the rails to endure the friction.

Meanwhile the men remained near the lock, still unsure of their welcome. Judy drew Alyssa to her, holding her about the waist to keep her perched on her thigh.

Jimmy wondered if the women slept cocooned under the same bungee net, which sounded pretty hot until he remembered the polarity issue and the ugly sparks it could strike.

Chien goggled at the two women, continuing to stare.

Alyssa thrust out an arm to display a single-digit instruction. "Ever seen one of these?"

Suh chimed quiet Mandarin at Chien, who looked down.

Alyssa pushed away from Judy and grabbed a nearby loop, letting her legs float across the module as if she lounged at the edge of a swimming pool.

Jimmy confirmed that her legs remained as long and smooth-muscled as he remembered and then thought to check Judy, who was issuing him another glare.

"So what do we do for callsigns?" Judy asked.

Jimmy leapt at that one. "I'm sure our senior gyrene would like to answer to 'Horse Apple'."

Judy was just as quick, "That's fine, so long as the brownshoe answers to 'Cricket Crap'."

Alyssa shot an impatient look at Judy and said, "I think Jimmy's right about the platoon names. I want my unit to have a warrior's name."

Judy snorted, "We're Spam in a can. If we didn't get cooked this mission we will next."

Polya said, "All fly like warriors. Cook or no cook. No matter." He locked glances with Vlad for a moment.

"We're orbital warriors," said Alyssa.

"We don't fight in orbit. We drop from orbit. We're ramjet warriors," said Judy.

Jimmy looked at her in shock. "You said it. We're the Ramjet Warriors. And we're one unit, not two."

"Fokkin-A Tweety Bird!" said Vlad.

Polya sensed the moment, "Show hands. Ramjet Warriors?"

Every switch thrust out an arm, each ending with a fist.

There were cries of "Ramjet Warriors!"

Suh and Chien stared, puzzled at so much emotion. The tumult went on until Polya waved a hand.

The hand then dropped to rest upon his earpiece. He said, "Go ahead, Dirtside."

He drifted there in the same pose, listening. He turned to look at Vlad and Jimmy, floating by the lock, and said, "Launch complex at Semnan is fueling two Safirs."

The switches' quiet was complete. The shooting war was on again.

Chapter 102   Rigging

"You have to be willing to put up with a little discomfort and some risk."

Megan McArthur

"You can't scratch your nose in a space suit."

John Scalzi

Jimmy could not change an inner tube on a mountain bike without risking a fresh puncture from mishandling it. No way could he do it in micro-gee while hardsuited.

Luckily, the conical heat exchanger was segmented into three arcs which slid smoothly into the tapered throat of the Rock to butt up against the reactor. Cranking on a central threaded rod pushed the segments out against the throat. The rod took a lot of cranking, and he wished for a hydraulic tool. But hydraulics were heavy and costly to boost into orbit, and Jimmy was available. So he cranked. Then he snapped on the water line and the steam line. Designed for assembly.

He sweated and his skin itched everywhere the hardsuit touched him. The wipes were not working to keep his skin's bacterial biome in balance and he smelled like chemicals with grace notes of rotted meat. Fatigue weighted his eyeballs, but flashbacks intruded on his sleep, the Rock juddering at hypersonic velocity down on the deck in thick atmo, the bowling ball of fear in his belly as the line of Safirs came at him, the Rock dropping into a howling re-entry with the ionization envelope building. The switches were preparing for yet another combat op, again to defend against unfamiliar threats boosted to orbital velocities. To live would be a win. What was he doing here?

But then the were the four hundred carrier landings. Four hundred sorties, and never been shot at, never fired a shot in anger. He wanted this test. He wanted to see if he could hack it. Not just hack it, but dominate it, focus on the objective while annihilation rained down and life hung on pure chance.

Jimmy gripped the forward edge of the Number 3 Rock's throat. Even through the gauntlet, he felt the roughness of the heavy ablation which had liquefied and torn out much of the lining.

"Ready for coolant flow test," he said into his throat mic.

"Do not rush it," said Polya.

Jimmy looked over at the ISS. He tried to imagine a kill vehicle passing through their hab module, at what closing velocity, Mach 25, Mach 30?

"How long does it take to fuel a Safir, anyway?" he asked.

"Do not rush it." Polya repeated.

A Safir could be pre-fueled and held ready. Fueling just prior to launch meant that Iran had spent all their ready reserves.

"Suh, are you ready to mate the fluid lines to the turbine?"

Suh was ready. Jimmy handovered down the fluid lines, looking for leaks.

...

Polya climbed into the cockpit to install yet another real-time control software update.

As the Rock's microprocessors digested their new algorithms, Polya recalled in more detail than was comfortable a declassified American think tank report that dated back to the 1980s. The pointy-heads said he must destroy the booster before it deployed its kill vehicles if he wanted to survive.

At the ISS altitude of roughly two hundred miles, the horizon lay thirteen hundred miles away. They would have line of sight to any direct-ascent attack, as well as getting warning from the surveillance sats of an over-the-horizon attack. Suh claimed that to score a railgun bullseye on an ASAT missile in boost phase was no great trick.

Polya looked out over the assembled modules. The Rock was guyed to the railgun module in much the same way it tied down to an ISS module, with three taut cables pulling the two craft together, the Rock's nose resting in the trusswork at the railgun's tail.

Tiangong 2 kept station a few hundred meters north of the railgun. Another few hundred meters past that lay the ISS. The distance isolated the controller in *Tiangong* 2 and the people and life support in the ISS from the huge energies to be accumulated and discharged.

He climbed out of the captive Rock and secured the blister. Jimmy and Suh were drifting together toward the ISS, leaving Chien in *Tiangong* 2 to stand first watch on the railgun.

He heard Jimmy ask, "So do you like American TV? Ever watch cartoons? You know Tweety Bird? Little yellow bird with big feet?"

Chapter 103   Into the Trenches

"Never assume that simply having a gun makes you a marksman."
Jeff Cooper

The five switches and Suh gathered in *Zvezda* with the Marines. Chien, unwilling to leave the control console in *Tiangong* 2, listened in. Suh was talking about his electromagnetic hypervelocity slugthrower again.

One nice thing about the railgun was its velocity. Added to the orbital velocity of the railgun module, it exceeded escape velocity. Missing an orbital target, the projectile would be lost to Earth forever. There was no need to change orbits at each firing, no risk of shooting oneself in the back of the head with a projectile in a closed orbit.

Fired down into thick atmosphere, say at an ASAT missile in early first stage boost, the projectile's metallic hull would catastrophically ablate and then ignite from the friction of its passage, just another fiery meteor. So again, no need to worry about loose rounds screaming around at hypersonic velocities.

Targets in the upper stratosphere or mesosphere were preferred. Hitting suborbital targets would not fill near-Earth space with chunks of debris, chunks nearly as lethal as a kill vehicle to thin-skinned spacecraft.

A solid-fueled ICBM burns fast and spends only 3-5 minutes in boost phase. Iran's liquid-fueled Safir first stage burns longer than that, and then the second stage lights up and continues the boost to orbit. Between the time a Safir surmounts the dense air of the troposphere and lower stratosphere and the time when it inserts into low Earth orbit, there is a target window. The projectile can reach the Safir without burning up, and the Safir's velocity is still suborbital, so that after impact the debris falls Earthward.

So hitting the Safir accelerating into space at Mach 10 to Mach 15 was just one part of the problem. Suh had to hit it within the target window.

Polya pushed off to drift to the lock end of the hab. He rapped the plastic knuckles of his gauntlet on the nearest stiffener frame.

"We must stand watch. Railgun may miss. Rocks must be ready to intercept Safirs."

Suh frowned, "Our acceleration-hardened guidance electronics is mature. We can launch munitions with terminal guidance against targets in the upper atmosphere."

Polya nodded, but continued, "If incoming vehicles enter orbit we will be ready. We have four Rocks. We man all. Direct-ascent ASAT killzone is small portion of orbit west of Iran. Outside kill zone we take nap."

"We man Rocks, Jimmy, Vlad, Judy, Alyssa."

Chapter 104   Under Fire Again

"An aspiring ASAT power will think in terms of multiple engagements against a single target, possibly using salvos of ASATs fired from different locations over time."

James Oberg

Suh sang Mandarin into his throat mic and Chien replied in kind from his console in *Tiangong* 2.

Suh continued in English, "On detection of launch, Chien will fire three canister rounds at maximum rate."

Polya said, "Understood."

Jimmy said, "That canister's borrowed from the Americans, yes? Lots of small shot, held in a canister like the grape shot fired from cannons during the American Civil War."

"Similar," said Suh. "It is a shrapnel round with discarding sabot and 20 kilograms of tungsten subprojectiles, ten thousand small cubes of tungsten."

Standing watch in the Rock had not gotten easier. Jimmy called on his soldier's experience with waiting for the beginnings or endings of things ill or benign. After a time you weren't present, off in some recollection or playing through a scenario that was or could have been or might be. The technique was to gently pull attention back to where you were at. Time and again, pictures and words formed in his mind, tension built in his neck and shoulders, anger burned, sadness ached, sometimes laughter bubbled up. Emotions were his alerts. Each time his attention returned, he scanned the armrest panels for switch positions, looked over the headsup, gazed out at the few white cylinders of the ISS visible over the front of the Rock, and looked further, past *Tiangong* 2, to the railgun module.

It was during one of these nearly-absent gazes out into the black that it happened.

The railgun spat white hate. In an instant of extreme frictional heating and a huge gout of electrical current, atoms vaporized from metallic surfaces, electrons tore from the atoms, and a blast of plasma incandescing at white heat erupted from the gun's muzzle. The hypervelocity projectile was too quick for the eye.

217

The railgun module with its attached Rock pitched back and up. Bursts of propellant from attitude thrusters strove to bring it back on station.

"Test firing successful," said Chien. "A meteor will appear over Mexico."

Suh asked, "Has the autoloader cycled properly? What is the recharge rate on the supercapacitor?"

Polya got on the net. "Suh, join Chien in *Tiangong* 2. Iranians will not be idle much longer."

Minutes later Jimmy watched a hardsuited Suh clamber out the lock of *Zvezda*. The bulky white figure puffed propellant and drifted toward *Tiangong* 2.

...

Polya hovered before his console in *Columbus*. As the flotilla of the ISS and its Chinese guardians approached the coast of North Africa he polled the four switches in their Rocks for readiness. The Rocks would have to be deployed conservatively until he knew how many threats were incoming. He did not want to count on help from the railgun.

Tom Broadhead's voice crackled in his earpiece. "The NRO surveillance bird reports auxiliary vehicles and personnel are clearing launch pads at Semnan."

Polya cut out the switches and Suh and Chien from the groundside link, lest one of them be unable to stop screaming into his mic once battle was joined.

Tom spoke again from dirtside. "The last attack began with three sequential launches from ships in the Bay of Bengal. Three birds, boosting in line. A similar direct-ascent multiple-launch attack is possible during this orbit. There is also a high probability of two birds from Semnan."

Polya pictured rockets, powerful three-stage Safirs lighting up the Iranian desert, with more climbing from the dark expanse of sea east of India.

"Understood, Dirtside."

Tom repeated, "Three birds last time. We know now that Iran has a sea-launch capability. The launch ships have been tentatively identified. They are dispersed, but not widely. U.S. Fifth Fleet has declined to send Harpoons or Hornets for pre-emptive strikes."

Polya grunted, disappointed. Either Harpoon antishipping missiles or F/A-18 attack aircraft could rapidly incapacitate the threatening ships. The Americans had once again declined to go to war with Iran. It was more and more puzzling. American hostages taken, ships attacked, ships detained, crewmen forced to kneel. He knew that Americans had not lost their capacity for anger. He had been on the ground when the CIA arrived in Afghanistan, Tom among them. In a few days, the Taliban who had not run had been killed.

He changed his mind. All of his switches had seen the hairy ass of combat. If one of them screamed, it would be for good reason. He keyed the switches into the dirtside datalink, and gated Tom's data into the tactical net.

He warned Tom, "We are live on tacnet, Dirtside."

Not waiting for acknowledgement, he keyed his mic again. "Will overfly Iran this orbit. This is Iranians' best shot for next few days."

In less than fifteen minutes the cluster of spacecraft had transited the Med, flashed over Syria, and were passing into Iraq.

Tom came back, sputtering in his haste, "Satellite infrared detects launch flashes from the Bay of Bengal. Launches are not sequential. Repeat, not sequential. Launches are nearly simultaneous. Three birds on parallel tracks, with significant lateral separation, not in line like the last attack. Birds are probably Safirs. Designating Vampire 1, Vampire 2, and Vampire 3. It's about to get very crowded up there."

Polya took a few beats, and then said, "Prepare to drop Rocks."

His order scrambled the ramjet interceptors to detach from the station, disperse, and orient for retrograde thrust. Closely spaced *thunks* resounded through the walls as their mooring cables let go.

In less than a minute the Rocks hung over the abyss, needing only to hit the big red thruster button to drop. It was terribly hard to leave it to the switches, to remain in this can.

Suh spoke, "Cycling airlock into *Tiangong* 2."

Tom spoke, "Preliminary trajectory analysis of radar tracks indicates that Safirs will insert into ISS orbit, but traveling east-to-west. You have approximately five minutes to catch the Safirs in boost phase. After the Safirs release kill vehicles into orbit, you will have less than four minutes before uncooperative rendezvous."

Polya knew the closing velocity for the "rendezvous" would be double the orbital velocity of the ISS, because the kill vehicles would be moving east-to-west at the same velocity as the ISS orbited west-to-east. He issued the first drop order.

"Rock 2, Rock 3, retrograde thrust, twenty-five percent of maximum for seven seconds. Maneuver to engage Vampires 1, 2, and 3."

Jimmy and Vlad would be dropping their Rocks toward the upper atmosphere while Judy and Alyssa remained in a slightly higher orbit than the ISS, drifting farther back.

Jimmy got on the tacnet, "Hey Vlad, you hit that center vampire. I will hit the better target of the left or right."

"Fokkin' A, I will hit it," said Vlad, still a big Tweety fan.

Polya had the four Rocks in a cam window on his panel for a few seconds. Then he switched to the tactical display constructed from fusing the data from nearby spysats and ground-based radars and telescopes. Two Rocks appeared as blue chevrons moving Earthward and forward of the ISS, which was represented by an 'own ship' blue cross. The two Marines appeared as nearby blue chevrons spaceward and behind the ISS. *Tiangong* 2 and the railgun showed as blue squares. The Iranian vehicles had not yet appeared on the display.

Tom crackled out, "Fire that railgun anytime now, boys."

Chien spoke for the first time. "The Safirs are still too far ahead. We could fire across the orbital arc, but the projectile cannot transit that much atmosphere without burning up."

Tom spoke again, "The silent six are on a separate commo link. Close-in defense systems, the Vulcan Gatling and the missiles, are standing by to fire forward."

Polya took no comfort from this. Even the fragments from a shattered kill vehicle would perforate ISS modules, and himself. Breaking up a projectile helped him not at all if the massive momentum carried by its pieces could not be deflected or evaded.

Chapter 105   The Warriors Drop Rocks

"The Way of the warrior is death. This means choosing death whenever there is a choice between life and death."

Yamamoto Tsunenori,
Ha Gakure (Hidden Leaves)

Three red chevrons appeared on Jimmy's headsup, one right after another, marking the three Safirs ascending from ships in the Bay of Bengal. He released a long breath of relief. The projected radar tracks had downloaded quickly over the datalink, and now the Rocks' onboard computation would have sufficient data to run their own projection algorithms.

A minute passed, a heartbeat at a time, while the Safirs continued their climb and he fell Earthward. He pitched the Rock over to orient the nose prograde and blister Earthside. Soon the high thin atmo swirling into the ramscoop shrilled through the airframe, telling him to ramp up the neutron flux. He hit RAM INITIATE and thrust shoved him back into the couch.

The Rock sped ever faster toward the vampires coming at him. Vlad would be close by, if not ahead of him. The shock front built at the nose, once again compressing molecules of atmosphere beyond their endurance, and he gazed into the rosy light of the bell-shaped ionization envelope, wondering if he would ever see it again.

He started the propellant recharge. On the headsup the projected paths appeared for his Rock, Vlad's Rock, and the three vampires ahead of him. He was to the right of Vlad, and would fire on the vampire furthest right. The fear was in his belly again. If he took the target to the right he did not think he could adjust in time to hit the vampire on the left as well.

Jimmy completed his propellant recharge and waited for a popup countdown to appear on his headsup. He would pop up in less than a minute.

...

Vlad considered his own headsup. He could see that Jimmy was projected to pop up to his right. Course adjustments were borderline suicidal when controls were made metastable by atmospheric flight at orbital velocities, but he nudged the joystick a whisper to the left. He waited, letting his projected path adjust on the display. He gave a still gentler touch to the joystick and smiled, without noticing it, as his Rock's path was projected to intersect Vampire 1, the missile on the left. What hit him would not hit the station. Would not hit Polya, nor the silent six and the thing they tended.

Then Vlad too watched his headsup, waiting for the countdown.

Chapter 106   Under Fire Still and Yet Again

"Before an attack you never feel particularly well. There is a sort of vacuum in your head; your mood deteriorates. It is an oppressive and unpleasant sensation."

Lyudmila Pavlichenko

Polya pulled at the gold chain around his neck to bring out from under his shirt a gold locket the size of a plum. The miniature of the Archangel Michael the Defender, painted on a wafer of gold, dated back a few centuries. His brother had been given an image of St. George in a similar protective case. He held the locket in his left hand, gazing at his flatscreens.

For Earth viewing, the ISS carried a NASA-modified Celestron CPC 925 computerized telescope. A window on Polya's flatpanel held the digital image from the Celestron as it looked ahead above the blue curve of the planet's rim.

He nudged the view slightly down into the lens-like layer of the atmosphere and kicked up the magnification.

The horizon lay some 1300 miles ahead. The Safirs boosting for orbit had climbed high, and could be seen for nearly 1000 miles beyond the horizon, too faint for the eye, but visible to the Celestron.

Just above the planet's rim three elongated stars rose slowly, flames of the Safirs. He knew the slowness for an illusion lent by distance, that in truth they were accelerating hard, straining for an orbital velocity measured in kilometers per second.

As one, the three first stage boosters flamed out and three ephemeral four-petalled flowers of fire appeared as explosive bolts cut the spent stages free. Then the second stage boosters ignited and the three sparks reappeared, resumed acceleration, and bent their courses toward the orbital path that would lead them to him.

Though he knew that Vlad and Jimmy could not hear, and that Suh, Chien, the Marines, and those dirtside would soon have the information on their own displays, Polya got on the net.

"Vampires 1, 2, and 3 have staged. All are approaching orbital insertion under second stage thrust."

Polya synced the tactical display over the datalink network. Suh and Chien had their own tac display linked into Chinese assets, but redundancy in intel never hurt. Judy and Alyssa, the two remaining switches, were still drifting back from the station in their higher orbit. They as well could view the evolving battle on their headsups.

Closure of the blue ISS cross to the three red chevrons of the Safirs was rapid. Closure of the Rocks' two blue chevrons to the Safirs was more rapid still. Polya, transfixed, reminded himself that the separation had started at some four thousand miles. Perhaps time enough remained for an intercept.

...

In Tom's darkened office in Virginia, an alert window strobed on a flatscreen. An infrared detector on a surveillance satellite had picked up strong emissions from northern Iran. The coordinates appeared on the screen in a couple of seconds. Tom knew them by heart.

He cried out over the commo net, "New launch! Double launch from Semnan! Two birds."

There was a moment when no one spoke, and then Tom continued, his voice squeaky through the radio link's crackling.

"Dirtside here. Awaiting trajectory analysis of radar track for two birds from Semnan. Designating Vampire 4 and Vampire 5."

It took a full thirty seconds, seeming much longer, before Tom spoke again.

"Dirtside here, Ben says Vampire 4 and Vampire 5 are simultaneous launches on parallel and very close courses from Semnan on direct-ascent intercept trajectory with the ISS. They will rendezvous with the station in four minutes."

Tom turned an inquiring look to Ben, whose nearly bald head loomed over his shoulder. Ben punched the microphone button on his headset.

He said, "The timing of the launches will put all five birds, the three launched from Bay of Bengal and the two additional from Semnan, arriving at the same time at the ISS. The birds from the Bay of Bengal are just now achieving orbital insertion, but I repeat, Vampires 1, 2, and 3 will intercept the ISS simultaneous with Vampires 4 and 5."

Polya spoke without thinking, his voice animated for the first time Jimmy could remember. "Chien, retarget on Semnan birds! Hit Vampires 4 and 5 in boost."

Chien spoke gently, but fast, his voice a high tenor. "Retargeting. Switching to terminal guidance projectile for upper-atmosphere shot."

Tom spoke just after, "Check that, Chien. Stay on Vampires 1, 2, and 3. They will reach orbital insertion in less than one minute. Vampires 4 and 5 will not reach orbit for five minutes."

"Chien here. Will fire in one minute on Vampires 1, 2, and 3."

Polya was shouting, "No, Chien! Target Semnan birds Vampire 4 and Vampire 5. Hit in boost phase, in upper atmosphere, with terminal guidance projectiles. Is much higher P-K." [26]

There was a silence. It was true; the guided projectiles were much more likely than the canister rounds to score hits.

"He's right," said Tom. "Leave the Bay of Bengal threat to the Rocks."

"Chien here, Firing on Vampires 4 and 5. Designating round as Glide 1. This appears the better path to me as well."

...

Polya shook his head at all this exchange of opinion. Tom and Chien were, of course, not soldiers. He grated out in his usual rough bass, "Vlad, Jimmy, say status of debris from three birds from Bay of Bengal?"

He waited through some few seconds of silence, then spoke again into the throat mic to drop Judy, "Apple 1, thrust fifty percent of maximum for ten seconds. Maneuver to engage Vampire 4 and Vampire 5."

"Apple 1 here. Acknowledged." It was Judy. She said nothing about the long and hard deceleration. She had been ordered to drop into atmo fast and would re-enter hard and hot.

Polya shook his head again. He, like Tom, had made a mistake. A few minutes before, he had sent only two Rocks to intercept the three vampires from the Bay of Bengal launch.

He grated out an order. "Alyssa, thrust twenty-five percent of maximum for seven seconds. Maneuver to engage leakers from engagement with Vampires 1, 2, and 3."

Alyssa acknowledged. "Kicking out the jams."

But Jimmy and Vlad said nothing.

---

[26] "P_k", pronounced "P-K or P sub k", refers to the kill probability for a specific weapon engaging a specific target.

225

Polya ignored the tac display, drawn to the Celestron's view of the ever brighter flames of the Safirs. The high magnification narrowed the field of view, and the Rocks burst in trailing their glories of crimson plasma like tracer bullets painting their trajectories with streaks of flame. Even faraway as he was, the red streaks visibly closed down the distance to the white starlike Safirs, approaching the crux of the intercept.

Chapter 107   Hypersonic Ramjet Engagement

"I gave him the whole nine yards!"
P-51 Mustang pilot,
referring to the plane's 27-foot ammo belt.

Jimmy stared, fascinated and aghast at the violence of the crimson wind just outside, when a chime sounded and his headsup blared "COUNTDOWN TO POPUP". Red digits spooled down from 30, and he pushed his right arm forward to grip the joystick.

On the count of zero, Jimmy rolled 180 to put the blister spaceside and pitched the nose up. Six gees of ramjet thrust and the lift from his wings pressed him into the couch and the Rock leaped upward into the tenuous gas of the mesosphere. The scream of thin atmo in the scoop died away and the rosy light of the ionization envelope faded, but the deep steady roar of the exhaust never hiccupped as the autopilot transitioned from ramjet to rocket.

The datalink chimed as it re-established, and the tac display refreshed. His headsup showed a good fit between the projected paths for the three vampires and the freshly downloaded radar tracks. Safirs again.

He punched the barber-pole-striped toggle on the left keypad, and the weapon bay door *thudded* open as the heavy Avenger Gatling nosed itself out of the belly of the Rock and the headsup flashed "GAU DEPLOYED". It was good to be out of the plasma envelope and its threat of explosive incineration, and then he realized he was not safe even for a moment and excitement thrummed through him as he flashed past the Earth below, priming the gun, speeding to the attack as the big Gatling commenced its whine.

The vampires came at him, traincars of metal and explosive fuel closing at velocities that would gasify him, and there again was that dread tingle in his belly.

This time he knew he could move through it. He lined up on the rightmost Safir and pickled the GAU with a heelstrike of his right hand.

The gun barrels were bundled like the staves of a fasces, the entire mass blurring to give each its turn before the firing pin as the Gatling gave a long growl and blasted forth a hundred depleted uranium penetrators. The Rock had none of the shock absorption built into the A-10, and the shock of the detonations rang in Jimmy's rib cage, his head, his legs. His bones bounced, straining connective tissue, the firing just as harsh as he remembered.

AUTOFIRE monitored the Rock's targeting radar to track not only the vampire, but also the trajectories of the penetrators fired from the Gatling. Observed errors in converging the penetrators to the Safir triggered electronic reflexes to correct the gun's aim, even as the spinning barrels continued to churn out more slugs.

The fire control algorithm cut the burst after a long second and a half. Jimmy did not attempt to de-orbit to duck oncoming debris. He nudged the joystick, puffing propellant to point the Rock toward the leftmost vampire. Still numb from the shaking of the first burst, he designated that Safir as a target and pickled the Gatling again. The Avenger snarled another long *brrrrrrrt*, and a burst of depleted uranium slugs streaked downrange toward Vampire 1.

...

Vlad popped up behind Jimmy by nearly a second. On the headsup the three Safirs glowed in red. He lined up on the center vampire just as a bright red "COLLISION WARNING" flashed across his headsup display. The Safir on the left would hit him, soon.

The collision warning strobed, tinging the cockpit of the Rock deep crimson like a visual heartbeat. He deployed the GAU nestling in the Rock's underbelly and spun up the Gatling's electric motor as soon as the "GAU DEPLOYED" telltale flashed. The whine ascended to fill the cockpit as the motor spun up the seven heavy barrels to 500 RPM.

His instinct to live was a dull ache that moved with his lungs. He had endured fearful things, attack runs through heavy ground fire with his big MI-24 shuddering with hits on its structure, falling like a stone with engines flamed out, struggling to get an autorotation started. But he had not known this dread compulsion, spreading to take his chest and arms and legs, pulling his hand toward the thrust controls that would take him away from the certain annihilation of his awareness.

Everything, the panels of switches, headsup, what he could see of his suited body, pressed in on him as if there were no boundary between his mind and the world. It was a physical effort to refuse to run. He lined up on Vampire 2, the chevron in the center, and pickled the Gatling. But as he shook with its detonations, he made a bargain with himself.

He did not correct his course after its perturbation by the firing of the Gatling. That is, he made no move to ensure his collision with Vampire 1, the Safir on the left. But he made no move to evade collision. The headsup continued to pulsate its crimson warning. He nudged the joystick, orienting his nose on the leftmost Safir. As he reached for the pickle, the red chevron on his headsup split briefly into two, then three chevrons. And then all disappeared as Vampire 1 continued to break up under the heavy metal Jimmy was throwing through it.

He stared dully at the display, finally thinking that he had best divert his course, when a blinding violet-tinted white rod of light as thick as his arm flashed into existence from lower left to upper right across the cockpit just in front of him. The flash was gone quicker than thought, but he was blinded. Even as light seeped back into the darkness over the next few moments, a dark streak remained across his vision.

He cocked his head to the left, and saw in the corner of his right eye a hole the size of his head clean through the hull below the right edge of the sapphire blister. So cockpit pressure was gone. He leaned forward against his harness and looked left. A smaller ragged hole had appeared low down in the hull. The hole was fascinating, the size of a large coin, rimmed by shiny-edged flakes of titanium plate leaning into the cockpit like petals. An entry hole. A little nearer, his left leg was gone from just above the knee.

He clutched the leg just above the wound, circling it with both hands not because he felt any pain but to keep air in the suit. Why were the tears not boiling from his eyeballs? The edges of his vision went gray and he fell into blackness.

Chapter 108   Who Only Stand, and Wait

"All men are afraid in battle."

George S. Patton

As Jimmy and Vlad popped up and fired, closing all the while at suicidal speed with the three Safirs the action on Polya's tactical display was deceptively calm. The rightmost vampire broke up silently into several red chevrons which disappeared as their fragments became too small to track even with huge Earthbound radars. The Safir in the center of the group winked out, and the chevron denoting the leftmost Safir split into two which shortly winked out as the rocket and its payload disintegrated.

The camview window, his view through the Celestron, showed only the dying, one by one, of the fires driving the Safirs, like bright stars suddenly occulted. The heavy metal slugs from the Rocks' autocannons could have struck a fuel tank, fuel or oxidizer line, nozzle, combustion chamber, or principal structural element of the boosters. Under any of these hits, a Safir would collapse like a thoroughbred shot in the leg at full gallop. Future military boosters were expected to include surveillance radars and thrust-vectoring maneuvering nozzles. They would be useless for any purpose other than warfare, killingly expensive, and perfectly sensible.

He called out on the datalink, "Hits on Vampires 1, 2, and 3. Probable kills."

How close to orbital insertion were the vampires when they were hit? Chunks of rocket debris and fragments of kill vehicle payload might be in the ISS orbit, but moving toward him rather than with him. The closing velocity with the ISS would be twice orbital, 35,000 miles per hour.

He said, "Alyssa, debris cloud may achieve orbit. May mask intact kill vehicle. Keep targeting radar on and oriented posigrade. Deploy Gatling. Engage AUTOFIRE on radar detection."

Alyssa acknowledged, "Understood. Will engage any debris in ISS orbit." She could at least attempt to further fragment the fragments.

Polya was at his core a pilot of attack aircraft, huge armored Russian helicopters bringing autocannons and missiles to bear in close-in assaults on ground forces. Missions of concentrated violence and high risk. A pilot at risk has procedures to follow, hard and fast specifications for what he is to do as he runs out of ideas, altitude, and airspeed. If it's a metallic chip detected in the transmission, land soonest, within half a minute. If it's a flameout, try engine restart. Failing that, attempt to autorotate and look for a flat spot. Repeat as needed, or always unspoken, until impact.

He didn't know a procedure for awaiting, motionless, the approaching annihilation. He had four minutes to live, unless everything continued to work perfectly.

Chapter 109   Look Down, Shoot Down

"No battle plan survives contact with the enemy."

Colin Powell

The railgun flashed while only Chien was looking. The glide round that sprang from its rails through the white gout of plasma was a metallic airfoil a meter in length with knifeblade hypersonic wings. It called to mind a manta ray, as wide as long, flat and thin through the thickness. The glide round's speed hid it from the eye. It traveled at seven times the speed of a bullet and its kinetic energy was fifty times the energy of an artillery round.

Judy was just entering atmo, flashing the reactor to ramjet temperature to heat the thin flow of mesosphere keening in its throat. She dropped at a steep angle to meet the liquid-fueled boosters while they yet climbed from Semnan. The Rock was heating up fast, wings and ramscoop lighting up orange from friction. Through the blister, the rosy light of the ionization sheath sprang into being at the leading shock and wrapped itself about her Rock, dousing the fire of the stars.

Chien's high tenor came over the tacnet, "Glide 1 is away."

By the time Chien announced the shot, the glide round had flashed silent and unnoticed past Judy. Its leading edges glowed crimson at the first hint of atmosphere, then brightened to yellow.

Over a few seconds, the railgun's realtime control software loosed bursts of propellant to compensate for the recoil's gross disruption to its attitude and station-keeping. The autoloader chambered another glide round onto the shuttle as adjustments to the rotational velocity of several inertia wheels realigned the gun on the next projected position of the leading vampire. On Chien's panel, the yellow cross hairs of the targeting pipper moved toward one of a pair of red chevrons. Seeing the pipper align, he jammed his thumb onto the lighted button which bore the firing ideogram.

He said, in his best stilted classroom English, "I am firing once again on Vampires 4 and 5. The round is designated Glide 2."

Glide 1, fired at Mach 10 from a spacecraft already moving at orbital velocity, sliced through ever-thickening atmosphere at a velocity greater than Mach 30. At its bright leading edges, thermal barrier coating rapidly ablated away, then underlying metal-matrix-ceramic composite liquefied and flowed. Its shape distorted, the glide vehicle went unstable, tumbled and decohered, the pieces briefly surviving in their own ablation envelopes. Only the spysats and a couple of Russian ground stations recorded the cascade of fire as each fragment broke into clouds of smaller and smaller fragments, a fractal incandescent comet tail depicting the onset of chaos as the airfoil's metastable flight control collapsed.

Chien said, "I am firing again on Vampires 4 and 5. The round is designated Glide 3."

The boosters continued to climb on their pillars of flame, accelerating into thinner atmo. The second glide round closed in at a velocity above Mach 40, the sum of the rockets' speed with its own. At a preprogrammed time, the round switched on its passive infrared seeker. It immediately locked onto the glow of the rocket exhaust to its left as marginally brighter. Stripped down machine code locked into gallium arsenide firmware gave the round's flight control software sub-microsecond reflexes. Near the rear of the airfoil, attitude thrusters shot out high-pressure gas to roll the airfoil about its long axis, and the lift of its wings steered it to and through the rocket.

The Safir was a traditional long white cylinder with a pencil point forward and three fins aft. Its engine did not falter. No pumps, combustion chambers, nozzles, fuel lines, or oxidizer lines were hit. At its midlength a white jet as long as the rocket shot sideways where the explosively combusting glide round exited the second stage oxidizer tank. Under continued upward thrust from the engine and retarding air resistance at the nose, the Safir buckled in compression at the gaping hole around the fading jet. The second stage folded and fell away like a reed breaking in a strong wind, down away from the wildly spiraling lower section with its flaming still-thrusting engine.

On the tactical displays the upward arc of Vampire 4 was arrested, and then the chevron split into two, both of which dropped in irregular paths back toward the Earth.

Polya said, "Hit on Vampire 4. Probable kill."

Chien said, "I am firing again on Vampire 5. The round is designated Glide 4."

On their flatscreens, Vampire 5 bifurcated into two red chevrons. One followed a ballistic trajectory, obviously unpowered, falling away toward Earth. The other climbed, accelerating.

Polya said, "Vampire 5 is staging. First stage has dropped away. Second stage ignition."

The surviving rocket continued implacably upward. Then it swerved, a diversion of a few degrees to its left, correcting in less than a second back to its original heading. Seconds later Vampire 5 swerved again briefly left. Then right.

"It is using yaw steering," Suh murmured into the mic, meaning that the second stage engine was mounted on a gimbal, pivoting to vector its thrust and so displace the course of the rocket laterally.

"Then it's not a Safir," said Tom. "Likely a Simorgh. Chien, recommendations? Try canister, or shift fire to Vampires 1, 2, and 3?"

None of the remaining glide rounds fired by Chien hit Vampire 5 as it juked left and right at random. The glide rounds had control reflexes that bordered on instantaneous, but their razor-thin hypersonic wings snapped under the aerodynamic loading required to maneuver into the erratic path of the Simorgh upper stage. The airfoils tumbled and ended as Glide 1 had in orange-red cometary plumes of plasma, fiercely burning in destructive re-entry.

Polya's belly filled with ice. The Simorgh next-gen Iranian rocket could loft 350 kilograms to low Earth orbit. A suitcase nuke massed less than that. And a 350 kilo kill vehicle would likely have active homing, autonomous maneuvering, a myriad of submunitions, or all of the above. He said nothing over the datalink.

Chien got on the commo net. "Canister will disperse and will likely hit a Rock."

Polya replied, "Cease firing, Chien. We must get Rocks clear."

Then he spoke again, even more deliberately than usual. "Tom, station needs boost. We discuss on closed channel."

Chapter 110   Aftermath of the Vampire

"Your attention to everything around will diminish and a sort of unpleasant feeling of indecisiveness suddenly overpower you."
Leo Tolstoy

"Godammit!"

Jimmy's cry resounded in the dim-lit cockpit as the debris of battle swept by and over him. There was a sizzle as tiny particles of paint and metal from one of the Safirs micro-cratered his Rock's titanium skin and sapphire blister. And then he was out of the fight, nearly unscathed.

But while the debris field closed on him, his targeting radar tracked a sizeable body flashing past. A body that could well be a functioning kill vehicle. In any case, they had met the threat too late and massy pieces of Vampire 1 had achieved orbit and could very well hit the ISS. There was no point in pivoting and opening fire to send Mach 3 autocannon rounds after bogeys receding at twice orbital velocity.

And another thing. Even linked through comsats into the chatter on the commo net he had no response from Vlad. He began puffing irreplaceable propellant. Each move brought the blue chevrons representing his Rock and Vlad's closer together on his headsup display.

He paused the rendezvous to call out to Polya.

"Polya, this is Jimmy. Attempting rendezvous with Vlad, who is unresponsive to radio calls."

Only then did he think to warn. "The debris cloud from one of the Safirs has achieved orbit. And the Safir may have deployed a kill vehicle."

"Understood. Proceed with rendezvous." Polya did not sound happy, but then he never did.

It was then that the external radiation alarm rang out its high *bong* and flashed crimson across the headsup. He almost said 'Godammit' again, but it was just one more threat atop the lethal vacuum, hypervelocity debris collisions, and the need to very soon drop back into reentry.

He said, "I've got rads showing here. The micro-debris from the Safir is hot."

"You are sure is external?" asked Polya. "Not reactor leak?"

"Cockpit rad counter reads nominal. External counter operation checks good. The rads are outside, on the skin."

After a pause, Polya repeated himself, "Understood. Proceed with rendezvous."

Chapter 111   Dagger

"Adherents agree not to place nuclear weapons or other weapons of mass destruction in Earth orbit, elsewhere in space or on celestial bodies."

Outer Space Treaty
signed 1967 by 90 countries

Tom answered a chime from his workstation. Polya had opened a subchannel on the dirtside datalink and now spoke to Tom alone.

"I want more than boost. What you should have done after last attack. My pilot reports radioactive debris on airframe. They threw nuke at us."

What was meant and what was wanted were clear. If the station suffered debris strikes they would lose the Dagger, their only deterrent to a rogue-state nuke launch.

Tom said, "Clear this channel. I'm linking to the silent six now."

The ISS did major boosts once or twice a month, increasing its mean height by about two miles. The *Zvezda* module, home to the Horse Apples, had a pair of thrusters. Also, two supply craft, one an Automated Transfer Vehicle and the other a Russian Progress, were docked to ISS modules. Their thrusters doubled the available power. So the station had thrusters, but it had all the stiffness and strength of the Tinkertoy assembly which it resembled. It had to move slowly.

He had a brief conversation with two of the six crewmen in *Destiny*, the main habitat module of the ISS. He spoke of two things. Tom asked for a boost to be initiated as of right now.

The second thing he asked of them was to step outside their hab for a brief EVA, and in doing so to take a step outside the laws of their nations.

Chapter 112   Aftermath of the Vampire II

"... come up and dance with death!
Eye to eye and head to head,
This shall end when one is dead."

Rudyard Kipling
Rikki-Tikki-Tavi

Rock 6 thundered along hypersonic in the upper stratosphere, the ramjet and its golden exhaust spike cocooned in frenzied whipping streams of pale orange plasma. Alyssa's dive had been steep; she had pushed the nose Earthward as soon as the wings bit the first wisps of mesosphere, and the ionization sheath shone too bright and hot for the health of her airframe. But by accelerating to the limits of the hardware she quickly closed the distance to the Vampire 1 debris cloud and built up sufficient velocity to pop up all the way back to ISS orbit.

Jimmy's exchange with Polya had gone unheard. As soon as the ionization envelope thinned she deployed and armed her Gatling. She spoke as soon as a clear high *ding* signaled that her commo was again uplinked.

"Apple 3 here, popping up for goalkeeper drill." She spoke loudly over the Gatling's high keening.

Polya's voice was harsh in her earpiece, as if impatient with the flippancy from the gung-ho Marine. "Apple 1, Apple 3, engage vampires at maximum range. Then clear field of fire for railgun canister shot."

Jimmy broke in again, "Vlad is downrange. So am I. Still attempting rendezvous."

Polya said, "Understood. We use 'big sky, small airplane' theory."

He could not wait for Jimmy and Vlad to get clear if the railgun canister rounds were to take out the vampire kill vehicles now closing on the ISS.

The Big Sky Theory held that it was relatively safe to fly close air support missions through an ongoing artillery barrage. Relatively meaning that the probability of a random hit from an artillery round was after all much less than that of being hit by aimed enemy air defense fire.

Alyssa now had the tactical picture from her target acquisition radar. Blue chevrons denoting Jimmy and Vlad were nearly obscured behind a rapidly growing return from an approaching bogey. Vampire 1 had been killed, but this chunk of it had achieved orbit, and could very well hit the ISS, especially if it was a kill vehicle and released a swarm of submunitions. It was coming on fast, at full orbital velocity.

Ordered to engage, she put Jimmy and Vlad from her mind and lined up on the bogey. The electric motor continued to whine as it spun the Gatling's seven barrels at full operating speed. She took the precaution of ramping up the reactor to max temperature, and hit the AUTOFIRE pickle.

The burst erupted for the next two seconds, the airframe transmitting the big Gatling's muzzle energy into her body. As soon as she recovered from that earthquake, she flushed the belly tank through the reactor and main nozzle to accelerate to a higher orbit. The approaching debris left her no time to spin the

Rock retrograde for a burn to return to atmo down below, and so the last of her propellant was spent to climb, to try to get above the oncoming debris field.

Chapter 113   Head to Head with the Vampire

"Thy Fates open their hands.
Let thy blood and spirit embrace them."

Wm. Shakespeare

Judy concluded that she was on a fool's errand. She had a good shot at Vampire 5, the Simorgh. But the ionization envelope glowed ever brighter about her Rock. She was in thickening atmo, approaching the mid stratosphere. At this altitude, to deploy the big Avenger Gatling was to risk aerodynamic instability, to tumble, to suffer thermal runaway from atmospheric frictional heating of the portions of her fuselage unprotected by ablative layers, to break up, to die a meteor in a streak of hellfire.

She grumbled, "Fuck it," the soldier's shortest prayer, consigning herself to chance. The aching in her chest eased. She pushed the GAU toggle over to the DEPLOY detent with her gloved left index finger and reached to grab the joystick in her right hand.

The ride got wild even as she lifted her left hand from the switch. The increased drag from opening the ventral weapons bay door pitched the Rock down as though it had hit the turbulence beneath a storm cloud. Four deployments flying to the attack in Marine Corps Harriers had given her solid core musculature, and she kept her limbs steady as she slammed into the harness that maintained her orientation in the accel couch. Straining, she edged the joystick back and the nose up, mindful of the Rock's nonlinear response.

On the headsup two square parentheses zoomed in on a red chevron, the targeting reticle locking onto the Simorgh.

She cried "Hah! Gotcha."

Still twitching the joystick, she popped the GAU switch over to the ARM detent. The whine of the electric motor spinning up the big Gatling's barrels blended with the shriek of stratosphere forced into the Rock's throat and the roar of the plasma flung from its nozzle. She had now to trust the autopilot to

237

maintain stable flight and to keep the Gatling locked on target, though neither thing was likely. She felt hot rage flush her chest and face, and cried out again as she let go the stick to pickle AUTOFIRE with a blow of her right hand.

The airframe juddered as heavy metal penetrators as long as her hand thundered from the seven-barreled Avenger. Before the burst was complete her limbs ragdolled out and her vision went red with negative gees as the Rock tumbled and the ferocious spin ruptured the blood vessels in her retinas. On a trajectory for intercept with the Simorgh, her arms flung out stiff as iron bars and unable to reach the controls, she remembered an old joke, the one about the last thought of a bug hitting the windshield as its ass passed through its mind.

Chapter 114   Attrition

"The route you have traveled is marked by the graves of former comrades."

Dwight Eisenhower

On Polya's screen a marker winked out. It was Judy's Rock. It did not surprise him. He had watched twenty-four such engagements during the four deployments he had survived and of the switches who had flown those engagements he knew of five survivors, including himself. Four now. Or three, if Vlad was gone.

When the red chevron of the Simorgh broke up, it did surprise him. He got on the tactical commo net.

"Probable hit on Vampire 5." He said nothing of the breakup of Rock 4. The other switches didn't need the distraction.

A moment later he said, "Dirtside, I am switching to command datalink."

Tom's voice crackled to life. "Dirtside here. Command datalink is open."

Polya asked, "Request battle damage evaluation of Rock 4 and Vampire 5, probable Simorgh. What can big eyes see?"

Tom said, "Stand by."

...

In his office in the Virginia suburbs, Tom turned a look to Ben, brows raised. Ben jumped up and ran from the office, heading for his dark analyst's cave down the hall.

Chapter 115   A Visit with Vlad

"The shared commitment to safeguard one another's lives is unnegotiable."

Sebastian Junger

Jimmy's rendezvous was halting and frustrating. For the pilot, space begins at the altitude where the principles of orbital mechanics replace the principles of aerodynamics. For a lifelong pilot of atmospheric aircraft, orbital mechanics was strongly counter-intuitive. He had neither aerodynamic drag, lift, nor weight against which to balance thrust.

Pointing the nose at the rendezvous target and thrusting didn't work. It was the Soyuz simulator training given at Baikonur that he applied. He was ahead of Vlad in their common orbit and so did a v-bar approach, thrusting retrograde and up.

He called it close enough when his Rock lay ten meters from Vlad's. The relative drift was still enough to be worrisome, but he had best hurry across to give what aid he could. He grabbed the emergency O_2 cylinder and clipped it to his waist and then punched a backlit white button to hinge up the blister and popped his harness loose.

He had neither tether nor portable thruster unit. He gripped the edge of the raised blister and crouched on the rim of the cockpit. If he missed Vlad's Rock, he would drift away with no means to alter his trajectory. He jumped, a push as gentle as he could make it.

Drifting across the gap, his stomach fell as he pictured himself sliding off the fuselage and spinning slowly away into the black. He didn't know where he could grab onto a Rock, a craft slick enough for hypersonic flight.

His jump was true, right to the blister. A cool rush of relief ran all through him when the outer blister release appeared. It could have been on the opposite side of the Rock. Jimmy hit the blister release and the sapphire dome popped loose and began hinging slowly open. Still drifting past, he snagged a fingerhold under the canopy and arrested. He waited as the thick chunk of sapphire hinged up, carrying him along.

Vlad was strapped into his acceleration couch, eyes closed behind the faceplate. His left leg was sliced cleanly away, leaving the upper thigh a remnant. Around the wound, dried blood had stuck down the edges of the softsuit leg, slowing the massive air leak. Jimmy pulled at his handhold on the blister to drift himself down to the cockpit.

The holes on each side of the cockpit told the story. He looked back to Vlad's leg. The liquid metal jet from the Safir fragment had perfectly cauterized his wound, leaving a thin layer of cooked flesh over the stump. Jimmy grunted, never having seen a fresh war wound. There was little blood floating about. Broiled flesh didn't bleed.

He found Vlad's umbilical, uncoiled it, and plugged it into the emergency oxygen tank. It would largely escape through the truncated leg of the suit. But he had a plan.

Reaching to his right thigh, he pulled a zipper across to open a cargo pocket labeled "SUIT REPAIR". He pulled out a roll of duct tape and a sheet of what looked like slightly cloudy kitchen clingwrap. The wrap was graphene-reinforced and not at all flimsy. It took the whole sheet gathered over the end of the stump to overlap the remnant of suit leg. Three turns of duct tape tight around the thigh secured the wrap, along with a couple strips of tape down the thigh, over the end, and back up.

Jimmy opened the O_2 valve on the umbilical and waited. He needed to be conscious, so as not to die in deep shock. Vlad twitched his arms out from his body, but his eyes remained closed. Jimmy gripped Vlad's shoulder and pressed his faceplate to Vlad's helmet, near his ear, not knowing if Vlad's commo had survived the hit.

He shouted a loud command, "*Borotsya!*"

It was the Russian for 'Fight!', the command to start a *sambo* match and guaranteed to spike adrenaline. He said it twice more, as sharp and loud as he could.

Without warning, Vlad grabbed Jimmy's arm and spun him. The other hand snaked under his chin. This was very bad; they would both suffocate if Vlad choked him. But the hold went weak and Jimmy broke free.

Polya rumbled over the tactical net, "Who is fighting?"

Jimmy spoke into the mic, "I'm going a third round with Vlad. He's lost a leg. Will recover and return as soon as possible."

"Understood." Polya said nothing more, assuming correctly that Jimmy had his hands full.

A scan of the cockpit showed the Rock's systems were functional, but it would not hold atmo and given the two holes in the hull it would be a very bad idea to drop it into a hypersonic reentry.

Chapter 116   The Cloud

"SCO - Space System Console Operator. Space Fence Operations Center Huntsville, Alabama. $52-73,00 per year. Knowledge of the space surveillance network and satellite catalog is desirable. Degree in tech field. DoD or commercial experience operating space radar sensors is desirable."

Lockheed-Martin Corp, 2018

Ben hunched forward, intent on the matrix of displays tiling the wall across from his desk. There was no light source in his office other than his electronics, nothing to distract from the data trolling he so loved. 'Das blinkenlights', the LED power status lights and the flashing network traffic indicators on his routers, gleamed in highly saturated red and green and blue, pure vivid stars in the darkness.

It was his job to know what everyone else knew as soon as they knew it. He tapped into feeds from agencies whose business it was to eavesdrop and surveil, and despite all their peeping and listening in, he did it discretely. He had just decided that the picture he had of current orbital events was as good as could be got when he jumped at the sound of Tom Broadhead's voice coming from the speakers hooked into his workstation.

Tom said, "Vampire 5, Ben?"

A window popped up on Ben's central screen; Tom had conferenced Ben in on the command datalink. Jenny and the satellite ground station link to Polya were also listed. How did he do that? Ben at times forgot that his babies, the compute cluster and its networking into national command and intelligence assets, were of Tom's design.

Tensed up, Ben sounded like a tenor saxophone. "Uh, NRO space-based radars are mostly directed to Earth observation. And Air Force Space Command ground-based radars are mostly U.S.-sited. But the Russian over-the-horizon early warning radars have a view of both engagements."

"And?" said Tom.

Ben drew a breath. The Russians operated several huge antennas similar to the Iranians' Sepehr, but with more recent technology. The picture was clear, but not pretty.

He responded, "They show two merging radar returns followed by the appearance of a large diffuse return, a probable debris cloud. The cloud is not now widely dispersed, but multiple internal collisions are expanding it in a classic Kessler Effect[27]. The good news is that the Simorgh is now a collection of fragments, and that nothing sizeable is achieving orbit."

He breathed a couple more times, trying to ease the pressure of the blood in his head. "The bad news is that the Rock is also now a collection of fragments. It may have broken up and functioned like a canister round, taking out the Simorgh."

The Rock would make a very good fragmentation round, its reactor and titanium airframe breaking up into lethal, dense, fiery chunks. Any fragments of Judy would have made poor shrapnel. They would have vaporized at once.

---

[27] Collisions create fragments which have additional collisions…

Polya grated through the speakers, "What of other engagement? Dirtside, what happens with Vampire 1 debris cloud?"

Ben said, "The Russians are still getting returns from three spacecraft, plus an expanding debris cloud in ISS orbit. The spacecraft are moving posigrade with respect to the ISS. Those are Rocks. The debris cloud is moving retrograde with full orbital velocity toward the ISS, and is probably remnants of the Vampire 1 Safir".

"Time to intercept ISS?" asked Polya. Thus far the information from Ben matched his tactical display, except for the additional descriptions of debris.

"Two minutes to uncooperative rendezvous between debris and ISS," said Ben.

Polya spoke into the mic, rapid and loud. "Suh, Chien, get into softsuits now. No time to hardsuit. Boost to higher orbit."

Chien spoke. "We have been operating in hardsuits. Only the gauntlets are lacking, to keep hands free for controls. Suggest firing of canister rounds before initiating procedures to increase altitude."

...

Heat grew in Polya's belly, serious anger at himself. He was still in his tee shirt and shorts.

He looked around *Columbus*. In the time since he had asked Tom for a boost, the station had accelerated under thrust more gentle than he could feel, but had now built up enough velocity that a pencil[28] drifted away from the control console along with several food fragments in seemingly animated flight toward the suit locker.

He drew a couple of breaths, "Chien, fire canister at will. Engage incoming debris cloud. Be advised it is closing at Mach 40 relative."

"I am firing canister. The round is designated Can 1."

---

[28] Americans spent millions to develop the Space Pen to write in zero gee. Russians use pencils.

Polya's observations of drifting objects in the hab and his knowledge of the ISS mass and thruster force told him that the ISS had achieved a delta vee of nearly eight meters per second over the past three and a half minutes. He ran quick calculations on his control panel[29], and learned that this would raise the ISS by twenty-seven kilometers over the next half orbit.

The knowledge was cold comfort because the next half orbit would occur over the next forty-five minutes. He could expect an average climb of about six hundred meters per minute. Finally, he pushed off toward the suit locker.

Chien again spoke his evenly spaced words, chiming like a clock. "I am firing canister. The round is designated Can 2."

Chapter 117   Unsheathing the Dagger

"The weaponization of space is inevitable."

James Oberg
Space Power Theory

One after the other, a pair of hardsuited crew slid feet first from the *Quest* module, the stubby cylindrical airlock serving the *Destiny* habitat module. Each snapped a carabiner to a cable running up the endface of *Quest*, as though they dangled from some Everest hundreds of miles high, and they crawled like fat white beetles along the line to the spaceside surface of the cylinder, both the module and the crewmen glowing white in bright sun against the empty black of Spaceside.

Along the spaceside of *Destiny* a thinner cylinder stretched along the entire length of the hab. At the trailing end of this tube, the end facing opposite the orbital velocity, a crewman hinged up a round cover. The two then placed their feet on the rim of the open tube and squatted to grasp something inside.

The fat white figures straightened slowly, moving four thousand kilos with nothing but muscle power. A sleek white shark inched out of the tube and continued to drift away when the crewmen released their grip on the handling

---

[29] Having studied aerospace engineering, Polya is solving the *vis viva* equation, $v^2 = GM_{Earth}(2/r - 1/a)$. It gives the velocity v in an elliptical orbit of semi-major axis a at distance r from Earth's center.

cables. When it cleared the tube they closed the cover and clambered back along the line toward the airlock, their movements still stiff and curbed by the suits but looking even more insectile because quicker, hurried.

In a slow retrograde drift away from the station, a slender cone tapering back over half its length, the rest a cylinder with three fins radiating out near the base, all in white, the Dagger hung above the Earth.

Chapter 118   Hauling for Home

"The body holds five liters of blood. With three gone, there's not enough circulating oxygen to keep vital organs up and running. Hemorrhagic shock, bleeding out, is the most common combat death."
Mary Roach, Grunt

Vlad was looking at him now, slitted Tartar eyes behind the blue softsuit's faceplate. He hit the mic switch with his chin. "Had you choked. Again."

Jimmy couldn't believe it. Vlad looked like he was grinning. Or grimacing anyway, mouth drawn back to show clenched teeth. He must be hurting like hell.

Vlad was indeed working hard to mold a grin from the thin-stretched rictus of his lips. His stump was now a very large ball of pain at the too-abrupt end of his leg. At the same time, Jimmy was here, he was not dead, and he might not become dead at all if they could recover to the station. He held the grin.

Jimmy wrested the emergency O_2 cylinder from its clamp on the cockpit wall and snapped it onto Vlad's suit. The oxygen umbilical wedged in neatly between the cylinder and the suit. He guided Vlad's hand to the metal D-ring on the right chest pocket of his own softsuit. The D-ring was a tie-down, a sturdy attachment point.

He said, "I don't have to tell you not to let go."

Fumbling around the cramped cockpit, he grabbed the booted toe of Vlad's severed lower leg. Everything else in the cockpit was clamped or installed, so as not to smash about under high gee maneuvers. He drew the severed limb close, and released it to float briefly as he shifted his grip to the ankle, where the leg was thinnest. Then he had to use his free left hand to hit Vlad's harness release.

Jimmy poised himself on the lip of the Rock's cockpit, as he had crouched on his own Rock before jumping. He pulled Vlad up to float in front of him, and then grabbed Vlad's upper arm and swung him slowly to the right. As Vlad drifted around behind him, he was alert enough to duck under Jimmy's arm to maintain his grasp on the D-ring on Jimmy's chest. He ended behind Jimmy in a loose piggyback.

Jimmy's Rock had drifted, opening a gap of more than ten, less than twenty meters. It didn't bear thinking about. They had not the leisure to await rescue, lest Vlad weaken to the point of dying.

Jimmy jumped, pushing against a backwards tug as he took up the slack in Vlad's arm. Drifting toward Jimmy's Rock, the Rock appeared to move from left to right and Jimmy knew he had leapt offline. He cocked his right arm, hand behind his ear, and heaved Vlad's leg off to the left.

It was Vlad who pushed off Jimmy's back to grab the leading edge of the Rock's throat as they drifted by. His one-handed grip held, and he arrested Jimmy with his hold on the D-ring.

Chapter 119   Orbital Railgun Engagement

"I've... seen things you people wouldn't believe...
Attack ships on fire off the shoulder of Orion.
I watched C-Beams glitter in the dark
Near the Tannhäuser Gates."

Rutger Hauer

Alyssa drifted in an elliptical orbit miles above the ISS altitude. The station would catch up to her, but would pass by below, and no propellant remained to her for further maneuver. It was no worry. Judy would come for her. If she was in a prison camp on the Tibetan plateau, Judy would come.

Twin bright points ahead were the Rocks of Jimmy and Vlad. Cranking her torso and neck around to look back toward the ISS, she settled in to wait.

Within the first canister round, ten thousand cubes of tungsten like one-quarter scale dice were held to a central tapered spike by the triad of white sabots which formed the canister. When the round neared the predicted location of the debris cloud, a light explosive charge detonated, discarding the sabots like falling petals and driving the tapered spike into the assembly of cubes. Dense bits of shrapnel spread like a cloud of pollen.

The railgun round, fired at Mach 8 from a module orbiting at Mach 20, acquired orbital velocity of Mach 28. The closing velocity to the debris cloud, orbiting retrograde at near Mach 20, approached Mach 50, a speed of 17 kilometers each second. The collisions between cubes of tungsten and aluminum fragments puffed matter into bursts of plasma, star-stuff.

Alyssa flinched at a cloud of sparkles, sudden, huge and bright as fireworks. Frozen for only a moment, she broke into a grin and opened her mic to the tacnet.

"I see hits on the Vampire 1 debris cloud. The canister round is right on. Oorah, slugthrowa!"

No one replied. Were all the switches, Polya, the railgunners, and the relay to dirtside destroyed? It was hard to believe that everyone was too busy to cheer the good news.

She worried and watched, rapt, until a minute later there burst into being another brief flurry of brilliant pinpoints of white light. More hits meant that some debris had survived the first canister round. And that some smaller number of fragments would survive the second.

She spoke again. "Hello! More hits on Vampire 1 debris cloud. Can 2 is right on."

Finally Polya spoke, "Someone will rendezvous to pick you up."

She knew that the pick-up was not likely to be done by him.

Chapter 120   The Cloud Approaches

247

"Under hypervelocity impact the strength of materials is very small compared to inertial stresses. Metals behave like fluids. Beyond 4 km/s vaporization of the impactor and target generates plasma discharges. Typical impact velocities are 14 km/s for space debris. Impact of a 10 cm object on a spacecraft or orbital stage will entail catastrophic disintegration."

NASA Orbital Debris Quarterly Feb 2017

Suh's soft English chimed in Polya's earpiece, "*Tiangong* 2 is boosting for higher orbit."

Suh and Chien were abandoning their combat spacecraft, the railgun module yoked to the Rock, as they turned on the *Tiangong* 2 main thruster. Suh spoke again, "We will rendezvous with the ISS when practical."

Tiangong 2 had a lot more thrust per mass than the ISS, could boost to a higher altitude in far less time than it would take the space station to leave their present unhealthy neighborhood. So the railgunners were egressing the area posthaste, bugging out. Polya could ask to transfer over in a hardsuit, but he hardly had the time. And he could maintain battle awareness and comms better where he was, at his post.

The inbound debris cloud was well understood. The High Command relied on Tom's contacts in NRO, and connections to the American Space Surveillance Network of radar and optical observatories. The SSN monitored objects ten centimeters and larger, the satellite and station-killers.

A Russian Briz-M booster stage exploded in orbit in '07, creating over a thousand debris fragments. Polya expected at least a thousand fragments from the breakup of the Safir upper stage shot up by Jimmy's Gatling, fragments of aluminum or steel up to the size of an American baseball or better.

A far worse storm, perhaps 4,000 sizeable fragments, had arisen from the test of a Chinese ASAT weapon, a ground-launched missile like the Safir. The missile had released a kinetic kill vehicle into a head-to-head 'uncooperative rendezvous' with a weather satellite. The oncoming cloud from the Safir could be that bad.

Smaller specks of aluminum, bits of steel, even paint chips would arrive in their tens of thousands to sandblast the station. Whipple shields, layers of aluminum honeycomb panel and Kevlar fabric, would stop perhaps a bean-sized chunk of aluminum. Not a baseball.

The two canister rounds from the railgun must have thinned the cloud. Not all of the twenty thousand cubes of tungsten had taken out debris fragments, but each hit had imparted a drastic trajectory change if on a larger fragment, and if on a smaller fragment had vaporized it.

He was still under boost, accelerating the ISS to gain altitude, and was no longer dead-centered by the cloud. He could hope.

In space, next to no air exists to provide resistance to the expansion of an explosion. Debris continues to fly apart with a wide range of velocities imparted by the blast. The cloud of fragments would thin with its expansion. But it would also gain size like the spreading pattern of pellets from a shotgun. He would be hit. The only uncertainty was how many times he would be hit and the sizes of the fragments which would hit him.

The smaller ones would be many, and would be stopped by the shields. The larger fragments would be fewer, and would puncture module walls, solar panels, and cooling panels. A very large piece, a metallic baseball closing at Mach 40, would produce a plasma bloom visible from the surface of the Earth.

Polya kicked off to the suit locker to grab a softsuit and slipped it on over his shorts and tee. The emergency O_2 bottles were at the lock end of the hab, and so he kicked off again and there secured a bottle to the clip on the left side of his chest. The lock end of the hab faced the ISS orbital direction, the direction from which the debris would very soon arrive. He drifted over to get behind a bank of three dark gray batteries, each the size of a tombstone, whose mass he hoped would give additional shielding. He floated, waiting and thinking.

The switches, like himself, were like the men who flew the U-2 and SR-71 during the early years of those aircraft. They were the covert air arm of the CIA.

The crew of six in *Destiny* surveilled threats both dirtside and orbital. They maintained the short-range missiles, the Vulcan 20 mm Gatling, and the long-range, hypersonic, nuclear-tipped Dagger. They were the new strategic arm of the CIA, and of its connections in Polya's own GRU, and its more recent connections to the Ministry of State Security in Beijing, that is, of the High Command. They stood ready to loose a weapon thought too fearsome to unleash over the course of the last seven decades.

Chapter 121   Loosing the Dagger

"I know not with what weapons World War III will be fought, but World War IV will be fought with sticks and stones."

Albert Einstein

As the ISS transited above northern India, two things happened in close sequence. First, the Dagger's nozzle flared white, its sword of flame exploding without sound into the airlessness. The missile leapt away from the station, achieving Mach 10 within a few seconds.

Despite their hurry toward shelter, the pair of crewmen pivoted their hardsuits to look and quickly ducked away from the glare. Their interest was understandable, as they were just outside the exhaust cone. By the time they looked back the missile was a distant star.

As they resumed handlining along the *Destiny* hab toward *Quest*, the second thing happened.

There was a sound like static and the faceplates of their hardsuits clouded over. The sound died away as they climbed into the lee behind the airlock cylinder. Their roughened faceplates dimmed the jets of incandescent metal vapor appearing and disappearing in a brilliant instant as they shot from the module's outer wall.

One of the crewmen let go his hold and drifted away. Splashes of bright aluminum surrounded holes in his suit at belly and shoulder.

Chapter 122   The Cloud Arrives

"A place with no shelter, and no possibility of retreat, is called 'desperate ground'."

Sun Tzu

Polya had chosen a poor sanctuary. An aluminum fragment perhaps a couple centimeters across *thocked* through the aluminum and fabric Whipple shield at the hab wall. The fragment cascade from this impact ruptured several cell walls within a lithium-ion battery directly in front of him.

Polya was dazzled by the flash and he strove to look past the deep purple blotch on his vision. Flame jetted from the entrance hole in the battery's cell wall. In seconds the hole grew to the size of a man's palm as the entire contents of the cell erupted and hundreds of red-glowing droplets spewed into the hab, bouncing from metal surfaces, sticking and melting into plastic.

The storm of red-hot metal filled the hab. There was no avoiding it and molten gobbets stuck to his softsuit. Most were like a pea but many were grape-sized and a few were truly frightening and he spent the next minutes dodging them.

A stink of caustic wrinkled his nose. Then the metal bits burned through to his flesh and he grunted a long low protest. He released his hold and floated, beating at his chest and belly in unthinking agony.

When he came back to himself he blinked at the blue cloth of his suit peppered with black-rimmed holes through which peeked bright pink inflamed flesh. In the center of each wound lay a dark gray sphere. They were too many to count.

More minutes passed before he remembered the mission. He opened his mic to the datalink, "Debris hit on *Columbus*. Assessing damage."

Tom crackled back, "*Destiny* reports multiple hits, two crew lost. Assess and advise *Columbus* status."

The red LEDs of the pressure drop alarm were strobing above Polya's workstation. He reached for the suit patch kit, a roll of duct tape in his thigh pocket. Looking at the penetration in the hull, just forward of the ruptured lithium cells, he knew he had an hour before the pressure drop would knock him out. He used three layers of duct tape, each patch larger than the last.

He keyed his mic, "Hole in module needs KERMIt[30], Dirtside. Suiting up."

---

[30] **K**it for **E**xternal **R**epair of **M**odule **I**mpacts, NASA Marshall Space Flight Center

The Rocks. They had limited oxygen endurance, and Alyssa was out of propellant, and Vlad and perhaps Jimmy needed assistance.

He said, "Tell crew in *Destiny* stop thrust. Don't forget Rocks are out there."

He pushed off for the suit locker end of the hab and pulled out a hardsuit. Shedding the blue Boeing softsuit with its lattice of holes, he stopped. The ISS patch kit was intended for repairs made outside the station. But that was primarily because the punctures were more accessible from there. This penetration was visible right here in the interior wall. He fitted the hardsuit torso back into the locker. He pushed off to float up above the suit locker and opened the utility storage cabinet to pull out a KERMIt, the patch kit for module walls penetrated by debris or space rocks.

Still in his skivvies, he drifted back down the hab. He would have to work around the battery bank, but space was available. The KERMIt case provided a clear Lexan disk and an O-ring slightly larger than the hole. He stripped away the duct tape he had applied earlier. Through the hole, the shredded Kevlar of the Whipple shield trembled in the escaping airstream. He centered the O-ring on the hole and pushed the disk down against it.

Through a central hole in the disk he passed a toggle bolt, a threaded rod with a toggle at one end and a knob at the other. The toggle was a nut with two spring loaded wings which collapsed to pass through the hole, and then flipped back out to catch on the edges of the hole outside the module. Polya turned the knob to screw it all down to clamp the disk against the O-ring and the O-ring against the module wall to seal the leak. The last thing was to pull out the MIXPAC, an injector like a double barrel caulking gun, which forced epoxy resin and catalyst through a port in the disk to fill the void between the Lexan and the module wall.

He keyed his mic, "Dirtside, *Columbus* is pressure tight. One battery is destroyed."

Tom's voice crackled to life in his ear. "Get to *Destiny*. Assist the wounded and patch the walls if possible."

Polya pushed off down the hab to check the tactical display. His next stop would be the suit locker, to remedy his stupid, stupid, stupid neglect of hardsuiting before the action. He would keep the KERMIt kit handy.

Chapter 123   Driving Home the Dagger

"For behold, the day is come, burning like a furnace;
and all the arrogant and every evildoer will be chaff."

Malachi 4:1

Launched retrograde at Mach 10 from the ISS moving at Mach 20, the Dagger's posigrade velocity became Mach 10. The missile fell, and its steering vanes bit the thickening atmosphere to turn it through 180 degrees to put its nose into the airstream.

A simpler beast than the Rocks, the Dagger maintained Mach 10 in atmosphere without complaint. It was an easy reach to transit India and within seven minutes of launch the missile went feet wet over the Bay of Bengal. Its inertial and satnav brains led it to preprogrammed GPS coordinates, recently noted as the center of a cluster of three Iranian cruisers.

A new sun appeared in the night sky high above the Bay of Bengal. Lookouts were dazzled by the mere glint of its flash off the waters of the bay. Its glow was seen over the horizon over much of the south Asian night, across India, Bangladesh, and Burma.

The bomb's burst of high-energy gamma rays struck air molecules and ripped away a shower of electrons. These highly energetic electrons mostly died on the waters, but a fraction of them struck ships. There the particles acted as an EMP, an electromagnetic pulse, driving currents strong enough to melt power and data cables as well as the thin conductors on circuit boards.

The nuke detonated at forty thousand feet, about seven miles above the water. Viewed from that altitude, the horizon lay just over two hundred miles away. It happened that the nearest shoreline lay nearly three hundred miles away, and so the EMP darkened the ships and boats on the Bay within that radius, except the small ones lit with kerosene.

Chapter 124   Cleaning Up

"They've got us surrounded again, the poor bastards."

Polya had gotten the outer hatch of the lock sealed when Tom's voice crackled into his earpiece.

"Change of plan. Suggest you make an external survey of the station, then head for *Zvezda* and patch as needed."

The interruption irritated him. He had fought through considerable pain to squirm into the hardsuit and his belly and chest still complained at each movement. He tried not to think about the chemical effects of the pebbles of lithium embedded beneath his skin.

He asked, "What of wounded in *Destiny*? What of damage?"

"The silent six have turned shy. They just pulled the trigger on a kilobanger of a nuke. People will not understand that the EMP from a high airburst kills electronics, not people. They don't want company. They don't want their faces remembered, even if it means not getting help."

Polya said, "As you like." The six were now four, and yet more silent.

He opened up a backpack thruster to move him spaceside, above the station. As he rose, more modules came into view. The habs were peppered with black holes all along the white cylinders, as were the gray heat dissipation panels. The brown planes of the solar panels were cracked like broken saltines. Half of one panel had been carried away, the remnant clinging to the truss by its electrical cabling.

He checked his spaceward velocity with another thrust, then pulsed toward the closer of the two docked Soyuz spacecraft. These were their only rides to dirtside.

Polya drifted about the station for the better part of an hour. As he approached to inspect each visible hole he spotted tens of smaller holes, and hundreds of depressions still smaller. Up close to any of the exterior surfaces which faced posigrade, roughened aluminum peeked through tiny faults in the paint. The larger holes had penetrated the exterior aluminum layer of the Whipple shields. The largest holes, into which he could probe with his pencil, passed through the exterior aluminum, Kevlar fabric and internal walls.

He reported the full penetration hits on modules, panels, and truss members to Tom. The Soyuz craft were unhit. *Zvezda* had not been holed. Best of all, the ISS hadn't been hit by a kill vehicle. They were still gaining altitude, climbing away from the orbit of the debris cloud, having burned posigrade to lift the ISS into an elliptical orbit. Soon they would need to burn again to circularize the orbit at apogee, its highest altitude, and would find out if the station would hold together under thrust.

Chapter 125   Hauling for Home II

"Our situation here is extraordinarily French. Until someone dies, then it's Russian."

Martin Cruz Smith
Stalin's Ghost

Vlad was crammed into the convex hollow of the blister, his helmet touching the top of Jimmy's. Neither could move his head more than a centimeter. Jimmy was free to reach the armrests and the banks of switches there, but could barely see his headsup.

Working from Ben's feedback on his radar track, and his exact memory of every switch on both armrests, Jimmy boosted his Rock into a phasing orbit. This was a higher altitude orbit and therefore had lower orbital velocity. It would allow the ISS to catch up beneath the Rock. It would allow Jimmy to catch some rest.

Twenty minutes later, hanging there above the Earth, Vlad awoke. Their helmets, touching, transmitted his words directly.

"Did you feel the weight in your belly? Could you feel the missile coming at you?"

Jimmy knew of what he spoke, though he had felt a belly full of acid. He said, "I felt it, yes."

"I am so happy," said Vlad. "Happy for you as well."

When the station caught up to them, Jimmy used the last of his propellant to thrust retrograde and bring them back down to ISS altitude.

Polya greeted them in his hardsuit, but did not move to tie the Rock down.

He waved them out of the blister and said, "Get him inside *Zvezda*. Then hardsuit and come help me. We will rig hydrogen propellant tank to this Rock. You will get Alyssa."

Chapter 126   Alyssa Returns

"Only the dead have seen the end of war."

David Poyer

Behind her softsuit visor Alyssa kept her dark brown eyes on him as Jimmy pulled her by her boots from the lock and into the *Zvezda* module. She pushed off of the edge of the hatch to float with her head spaceside, looking over each of them, Polya and himself, in turn. She searched the hab. Then her eyes widened. She looked again. Her face went slack, lips open.

Polya helped her out of the softsuit helmet. Jimmy stowed it with his helmet and began removing his softsuit. Polya was already in shorts and tee shirt. Reddish spots of disinfectant bled through the white tee and blotched his bare legs, marking his burns.

Alyssa hung by the lock, making no move to shed her suit. As Polya reached for her upper arm she threw it around his neck and the other about his chest. Her grip on his neck dug forearm bone into muscle as she pressed her face to his chest. Her body heaved and her face grew hot and wet. Then she bit his right pectoral through the tee.

Polya grunted, but closed his arms around her and clasped her to him. She said something, then again, muffled but clearly the same words. She repeated them again as Jimmy leaned his head in.

Polya looked at him and Jimmy said, "Not enough left to bury. She's saying 'Not enough left to bury.'"

Polya straightened an arm, beckoned him forward, and Jimmy put an arm around Alyssa's shoulders. Polya released his other arm and gently pushed her toward Jimmy, his palm at the juncture of her neck and shoulder. She clutched her rib cage with both her arms, curling around her belly. Jimmy pushed off, and they drifted toward a sleep space, not the one she had shared with Judy.

Jimmy got the bungee net stretched across her. She reached through and grasped his hand in both hers and held it to her belly, still curled up. Her belly was hard. Her grip hurt.

He bent his head close to hers and murmured, "I don't know where you've been. And this is only my second combat engagement. But I know that right now you gotta get Devil Dog tough. We need you."

It was true. They had a Rock and a railgun to recover, holes to patch, watches to stand. She released his hand and crossed her arms tight across her chest. She nodded. She said, "Gimme a minute," then turned her head away to gaze along the white wall, catatonic with loss.

Jimmy drifted back to Polya, who looked at him and said, "Is why we don't mix platoons. Is why we don't fuck squadmates."

Polya turned to Vlad, who was netted onto another sleeping pad, eyes slitted with pain. "You go in Soyuz capsule with Jimmy," he said.

"What do I need legs for, here?" Vlad asked.

Stripped of the suit repair, the browned end of his stump had darkened and withered, pulling open deep pink cracks in the flesh. It passed all belief that he was crunching a Ranger cookie, waving away the halo of crumbs floating about his head.

"I don't want to smell gangrene as you take six days to die," replied Polya.

Vlad laughed, but he knew the truth of it. They had both seen lower body wounds after encounters with IEDs, and how rapidly men deteriorated without care.

Polya pushed off for the suit locker near the end of the hab. In the medical supplies stored nearby he found bandages, and antibiotic salve, and morphine.

"Jimmy, you will fly Soyuz, when Vlad is feeling better."

He bent over the medical box, and then pulled up his tee, pretending to inspect the bite on his chest. It was getting harder to let go of them, the young men and women who dropped the Rocks. They boosted to orbit crazy to fly hypersonic and to fight. They left like lost sons and daughters, burned, shredded, vaporized. Tears stuck fast to his eyes, unable to fall in micro gee. He closed his eyes and blotted lashes and lids with the tee, floating near the locker for long moments, pressing the thin fabric to his eyes.

Chapter 127   Overwatch

"In the void is virtue, and no evil."

Miyamoto Musashi

Suh and Chien had gathered in *Zvezda* with them.

Polya looked at Alyssa. "You and I have duty now. We must go twelve and twelve. Suh and Chien must retrieve railgun."

He paused. Men, women too, had their limits. Their strength varied, but was always a consumable resource. Even those who weren't hit, who suffered the close misses, who witnessed the blasts and the splatter and the wounds and the corpses, were in the end depleted. He knew the signs, but he could not say that he knew when it would happen, even for himself.

There would be new switches. Hot stick-and-rudder jockeys drunk with skill and eager for the test. Jimmy would bring them. But for him there would be no rotation out of the lines. He would give Alyssa the chance, when the Chinese pair had gone. They had one more Soyuz capsule. She could descend, as he had descended to train and to fetch Jimmy and Vlad. He thought she would not. Some died before they broke.

At the far end of the hab, near the suit locker, Jimmy stuffed Vlad, loose-limbed with opiates, into a fresh softsuit. He taped back the left leg so it didn't float around. He pulled on his own softsuit, still damp with sweat.

258

Suh and Chien, both hardsuited, pushed off for the lock end of the hab cylinder. They would need a method to send wireless commands from *Tiangong 2* to the railgun module thrusters. A control loop that would have to be coded as they went along, like so much of what they did.

Jimmy got on the local link. "Nice shooting, Chien." He almost said 'Sayonara' but remembered in time.

Chien, formal as always, said, "It was the dream I have carried through many years, to intercept a boost-phase missile with an orbital railgun."

Suh said, "Fokkin-A Tweety Bird".

Jimmy raised his visor to smile at Suh. He turned to look at Alyssa. "See you next deployment. With reinforcements."

"Bring us some mean ones," she said.

Jimmy said, "Will do. Will requisition one pair of said items. And you smell like the bright green water in an abandoned quarry." He smiled again. He'd been saving that one.

She smiled back, but her eyes grew bright. "You smell like a capsized garbage barge."

Jimmy pushed off for the lock, towing Vlad with a grip on the D-ring on his chest. He looked over his shoulder, locking gazes with Polya. Then he turned back to open the hatch to the lock module.

Tom broke in from dirtside. "A Dagger is en route to the Baikonur launch site. The silent six are now the silent four, but their mission will continue. As will yours. The replacement Dagger carries a high-power microwave warhead. It will fry electronics, like the EMP from a nuke. But it is not, repeat, not a nuke."

"Perhaps we will be hated less," said Polya. "But also feared less."

The microwave EMP warhead was a conventional weapon, not banned from space by any treaty. Not that it mattered. The High Command had entered into no treaties with anyone.

Tom said, "You will need propellant for the ISS thrusters. That will arrive with the Dagger on a Progress cargo vessel."

"Sitting in a Rock for twelve hours will not help readiness much." Alyssa said.

"Suh and Chien can get railgun back up," Polya said. "We softsuit, but remain in hab. If railgun misses, and Safir arrives faster than we can drop, we die."

Chapter 128   Dropping the Soyuz

"Of every hundred, ten should not be there, eighty are but targets, nine are fighters, and lucky we are to have them, for they make the battle. Ah, but the one, one is a warrior, and he will bring the others back."

attributed to Heraclitus

Jimmy turned to Vlad, "Ready?"

Vlad's grin was morphine-loopy. "Fokkin' A Tweety Bird."

Jimmy initiated the automated procedure to decouple from the ISS. The hooks, semicircular arms that clamped the Soyuz docking collar to the station, would creep open over the next two minutes. There was a hollow in him, like something was missing inside.

Vlad slurred, "Hell of trip. Is what you Americans say? We fought good fights."

Thinking he was talking about their personal history, Jimmy said, "What am I gonna say? I went oh-and-three against a *Spetsnaz*."

"No, you are not good fighter. No training. No matter. You are ... warrior. *Istinnyy voin.*"

Jimmy knew what the hollow feeling was. The doubt was gone. His not knowing. He had known before Vlad said it.

"It was a helluva trip," said Jimmy. The mechanically compressed pushers gave them a shove so gentle he felt nothing. Only the camview told him they were drifting away from the ISS.

Vlad slept through the re-entry burn, waking only when the explosive bolts sounded all around them like sledgehammers hitting the hull to separate their re-entry capsule from the orbital and power modules.

Vlad looked out at the crimson light as the protective outer window blackened in the heat. "Never see plasma again. They will give me blade to walk on."

As the deceleration began to bite, Jimmy pushed Vlad down into the couch. He tightened the straps against the oncoming oscillations of their capsule when the drogue chute deployed, and against the eventual 'soft landing' on the dry soil of Kazakhstan. He would not feel safe until the main chute deployed.

Chapter 129   Overwatch II

"In North Korea, grass is a vegetable eaten by the people, and they've got nuclear weapons and ICBMs. So, something more stringent than what's been done to North Korea is going to have to work; otherwise, a military strike is the only option."

Oliver North

As it played out, their adrenaline faded and neither Polya nor Alyssa could stay sharp. They slept in their softsuits while Tom, Jenny, and Ben took it in turn to monitor threats from dirtside.

Chien, a physicist, had good orbital mechanics knowledge and good orbital rendezvous chops. In three orbits, he brought *Tiangong* 2 up to the railgun and its attached Rock. Still hardsuited, Suh locked out of *Tiangong* 2, and flew a ballet around the railgun module.

The long cylinder of the gun appeared intact, but beneath the muzzle, on the leading surface of the module, the sun glinted from a bright rim around the blackness of a pea-sized hole. The railgun module had suffered a single hit from a Safir debris fragment.

No exit hole appeared on the module, but he could imagine how the fragment had caused a debris cascade, breaking up as it shattered circuit boards and brackets, scattering capacitors, chips, and resistors, all becoming shards which in turn flew out into other components in a cone of destruction.

Suh knew better than to make contact with the module, even if he was two hundred miles from standing on a good electrical ground. A huge electric potential existed across the terminals of the supercapacitor within. If shorted to the hull, they could discharge through his body if he touched regions of differing potential.

He muttered, *"Mei yu fatzu."* No help for it.

He lit up the datalink, and gated into it the feed from the camera that rode on his shoulder. He said, "Dirtside, we have lost the railgun."

Jenny was on shift. "Dirtside understands." She switched to Mandarin. "Suggest you and Chien de-orbit. Unless Xiaofei can send another railgun."

"This was our prototype. It has proven its worth, but it is too fragile."

Chapter 130   Summit

"Great men are almost always bad men."

John Emerich Edward Dalberg Acton
first Baron Acton

It is a principle of first-year physics classes that three-body collisions are exceedingly rare. In the sampling space of political leaders of nuclear-capable countries, the odds are long against gathering three such bodies into a single room. Yet three such men sat around a samovar in the old capital of St. Petersburg, drinking black tea from the traditional glasses fitted to delicate ornate metal holders, and looking out at the snow through large windows. The Twelve Colleges building dated to the time of Peter the Great, and had housed much of his government.

The Russian spoke first. "The boundary of the Soviet Union lay some twelve hundred miles to the west of this room. That western border ran through a great flat expanse, ideal ground for movement of an army. Russia's security lay in requiring the invader to cross vast spaces."

He paused, looking to the American, then the Chinese leader, "Today the boundary of Russia lies two hundred miles to the west of St. Petersburg. The defensibility of the western border, and of the southwestern border, is in doubt."

"Russians are aging. Our numbers are slowly decreasing, and will continue to decrease. Our ability to influence events will more and more rely on the export of minerals, especially natural gas, not on the projection of the power of our military."

The Chinese premier rose to speak. "China opened itself to trade in the nineteenth century. It did so under heavy persuasion, threats. But many Chinese profited, and wanted continued trade with the outside world, even when the Boxers became strong. The coastal regions of China were greatly enriched by the exchange of goods, while the interior remained poor."

"The pattern of an impoverished western China at odds with a newly rich coastal China has arisen once again. Any slackening of prosperity arouses labor unrest, social unrest, ethnic unrest in Xinjiang and Tibet. Any stumbles along the path of growth will expose the structure of loans, easily granted to Party cadres, which finance the capital improvements driving Chinese manufacturing. Many of these loans are not well collateralized, and many of the companies operate only to service debt payments."

The American president pointed to a fourth man, suited like them, who stood before the great old windows. It seemed he had brought a briefer to speak for him. This man was known to the company, and they turned to him as he spoke.

"Together we have evolved the first space battle group. The analog of the carrier battle groups which today control the seas. It is a technological coup, but it is a more remarkable political coup."

"Russia recognizes, and accepts, that its military influence will wane. China recognizes and accepts its internal fault lines. The United States anticipates neither a decrease in population, nor any difficulty in maintaining economic output. But America does not wish to see new regional powers arise in Asia.

These principles drive us to common effort in defense of our common high ground."

"To do nothing will allow the resurgence of the Japanese, defeated in 1945, and the resurgence of the Turks, defeated in 1918, to make incursions into Chinese and Russian spheres of influence, to establish regional hegemony, and to aspire to become global hegemons. The Japanese have attempted to build a secret Farside base. The Turks now control a province of Syria. These nations, probably in coalition, will eventually attempt domination of world trade routes on the seas, and to do that it is needful to control global information, which flows through low Earth and geosynchronous orbit."

"It is wisdom to know one's limitations. It is wiser to forestall their consequences. Working together to control the orbital battlespace ensures our control of the seas and thereby guarantees our continued domination of our own spheres of influence. The ferocity of the Iranian attacks clearly shows the importance of what has been accomplished."

"Japan and Turkey are both better positioned than Iran in geography, technology, and economy to become aggressive maritime and orbital powers. Today they operate in space only at our pleasure. In two to four decades they will dare to attack the constellation of battle satellites that will be in place by then."

Tom stepped away from the window and over to the group, shook each man's hand, and took the fourth chair around the delicate marble-topped table.

The Russian, it was still Vladimir Vladimirovich in charge, resumed speaking first. "There was a saying among the Romanians, in the time of the Eastern Bloc. 'The trouble with the Russians is not that they are Communists. It is that they are Russians.'"

He looked about the magnificent room. "Not since Peter has Russia looked at herself clearly. It was the first time that Russia looked to the west. The first redirection of our culture."

The American spoke. "We will, of course, get the inevitable question, 'Why isn't this money spent down here on Earth, so that people can live better lives?'"

The Chinese premier smiled. "What are the chances of that happening? People will continue to produce turds, wars, and children."

The company was silent. He went on. "You may say that people produce as well many works of art. This art consist of documents, images, narratives of all sorts that tell people that they are capable of producing more than turds, wars, and children."

The leaders of three of the five permanent member nations of the UN Security Council had a long laugh at that.

The American asked, "That's from the Analects?" reigniting the laughter.

Then the Russian passed round a tray of biscuits.

Chapter 131   Missa Solemnis

"Come off it, Sheriff. You know we're all fuck-ups or we wouldn't be here."

Sonny Barger

Seen through plate glass, the white cargo van had a yellowish cast in the streetlights as it pulled up outside McDonald's. It would be full dark soon. Tom rested his elbows on a table cluttered with wrappers and uneaten sandwich buns. He could use the protein on offer, but had discarded all the simple carbohydrates. Their coffee was decent, the recently brewed stuff, not the mix of industrial chemicals they called cappuccino.

The ten-block Illinois town felt like a desert, like being in the field. He wondered how far he would have to drive to find fresh vegetables on a menu.

William raised a hand as Tom walked quickly out toward the van. Tom waved back and passed around the front of the van to open the passenger side door.

He climbed in, then craned his head around the seat to look into the back. There was the Fazer, a mechanical dragonfly the size of a pony, its two rotor blades aligned front to back so it fit. The rifle was gone from between the skids, and William had affixed blocky chemical tanks at the sides and a spray bar across the front.

A couple of quadrotors, all in black, hung from hooks above the workshelf on the passenger side wall. The quads were the length of Tom's forearm and about half that in width. A sheet metal undercarriage like a triangular pizza box hung underneath each boxy fuselage. A lens peered out from beneath one of the boxes.

William pulled away from the curb and turned across the street and away in the opposite direction. They drove away from town, headed for an abandoned gas station where they would launch the Fazer.

Tom said, "You think we'll have some luck tonight?"

"I'm sure of it," said William. Eyes on the road, he handed an iPhone across the cab to Tom, and said, "Launch the iSpy app."

Tom swiped over to the icon and poked it. A grayscale infrared image showed the front of the crappy clubhouse the Dawgz used for parties and meetings. At least twenty Harleys squatted in rough lines in front of the rickety wooden steps. The roof shingles were cedar. The walls were bare wood. The Dawgz hadn't added any paint since his last visit.

William said, "They're getting skittish. They watch the driveway. And they let a pack of pit bulls roam the woods."

"How did you get a cam in there?"

William said, "An off-the-shelf quadrotor camera drone has limited loiter time, and they are pretty noticeable. The small quads you see in the back of the van deploy a camera and leave. The camera is much less noticeable than the drone."

As William drove on, Tom unbelted and walked unsteadily back to where the drones hung. He unhooked the quad with the lens beneath and returned to his seat.

On the underside of the quad a softball-sized clear plastic sphere covered a large lens of perhaps forty millimeters diameter. At the sphere's bottom, four articulated steel fingers extended like the talons of an eagle's claw, three forward and one back. Tom tilted the quad. Another set of talons anchored on the undercarriage curled around the top of the sphere, gripping it firmly.

Tom looked at William for a few moments, a smile spreading over his face.

He shook his head slowly. "Avian-mimetic grippers. The camera perches."

William continued to watch the road. "You got to have ducted rotors so the quad can fly within the canopy. Its night vision is good enough to set down on a branch. A pressure switch actuates the bottom claw and a solenoid releases the camera from the top claw and you get your drone out of Dodge."

Tom sat gently shaking his head a while, and then said, "College is going to be a cover story for you. Tell me what you need and I'll get it. Or tell Juana. You know Juana at the Navy. Or Jenny at my office, in case I'm not around."

In the infrared image on the iSpy app, Tom found the guard for the bikes, no longer slouching in the middle of the yard but hiding in deep shadow beside the shack, not knowing how his heat signature stood out.

It was not important which Dawgz were in the clubhouse, but it was of interest whether the evening's entertainment had arrived. It was a Thursday night, no special occasion, but the bikers didn't need a reason for blow, beer and a gangbang, a modern version of the Black Mass.

Tom monitored the clubhouse until the van pulled off the county road onto an empty slab of cracked concrete, the corpse of a Shell station. William set the brake and they pulled the Fazer from the back.

Modern napalm consists of gasoline, benzene, and a polystyrene thickener. A sack of Napalm Mix fuel thickener had cost one hundred and fifty dollars on the open market from the ThrowFlame company. Tom lugged a couple of five-gallon plastic buckets out of the van. Working by the light from the open van doors, he filled the tanks with incendiary fluid until a palm's width of thickened gasoline remained in the last bucket. This he poured into a red plastic one-gallon gasoline can.

The Fazer was marketed as an agricultural robot, programmable to take off, fly a spray pattern across a field, and return to make a landing. Their cover was a pseudo-company in the grand CIA tradition, crop dusters preparing for the morrow's flights.

William walked by with a quad, the one without a camera, gripped in one hand. His other hand held a bright pink cylinder. Atop the cylinder was a shiny steel ring and a steel lever ran down tight along the side.

Tom smiled, "A pink hand grenade? What does it do, spray perfume?"

William looked at him for a moment, still solemn, but Tom felt his exasperation. He said, "The AN-M14 TH3 Incendiary Hand Grenade contains a pound and a half of thermate. That's like thermite but hotter. Four thousand degrees Fahrenheit. I agree. It's cute. Special delivery from Aberdeen."

So his protégé was hooked into the supply line. Thanks, Juana. William walked to the far corner of the concrete and set the quad upside down on its rotor ducts, belly up. He gripped the incendiary at midlength to compress the lever, pulled the ring with his left hand, and pressed the grenade onto the pressure switch in the center of the quad's claw. With a *snick* the talons snapped on.

As William let go, Tom shook his head. Men in combat rigged booby traps with just that kind of deliberation, driven by desperate need yet calm because long inured to the worst that could happen. William was eighteen and a civilian, if such could be considered to live in south Houston.

The claw held, the lever remained closed, and William gently lifted the black quad in both hands. He righted it and set it on the concrete as though it were made of glass. The quad rested at a tilt on the grenade and its boxy undercarriage. He turned and walked back toward the van.

Tom hopped up through the rear doors and opened up a folding chair at the control console behind the passenger seat while William sat at the console near the back. They donned light headsets with boom mics and earpieces. After a few minutes of preflight checks and a look out the back of the van to ensure all the running lights were out, the Fazer and the quad lifted off together.

William said, "Been watching these *animales* for a couple months. They take a while to get the party going, but the goods will arrive in the next half hour."

He hit a switch to activate an infrared beacon on the rear of the quad fuselage and pushed the joystick full forward.

He said, "Follow me."

On the van wall above Tom's console a bright dot appeared on the flatscreen showing the IR feed from the Fazer's camera, and Tom cruised the Fazer along in the wake of the quad. Ghostlike gray trees in full foliage flowed back below. Then the clearing appeared dead ahead, also in monochrome as if intensely moonlit, with two brighter strips from the windows of the Dawgz hangout.

As the weathered clubhouse loomed larger, Tom swung out to the left to orbit the building clockwise so that the wood shingle roof showed down and to the right. He switched on the spray nozzles and continued circling, shifting each orbit inward.

The Fazer's rotor noise brought the probie out of the shadows with a big blocky auto pistol in his hand. He held the gun casually down by his side, the best position for shooting himself in the foot, walking around the shack while peering up into darkness. He couldn't have caught more than a glimpse of the blacked out little helicopter, but when a spray pass splattered him with gasoline jelly he dashed for the clubhouse door.

The nozzles went dry after a few more orbits and by then the entire building and the surrounding yard glistened under a coat of jellied gasoline. Tom veered off sharply, climbed, and told the Fazer to return to its takeoff coordinates.

"Switching to visible spectrum," said William. "This is gonna be bright."

William sideslipped the quadrotor over the center of the building as a half dozen Dawgz stalked belligerently down the shaky wooden steps at the front of the clubhouse. The bikers looked up, seeing nothing but night sky. Motörhead booming through the open door behind them covered the rotor noise.

William punched a button, and the claw released the thermate grenade. The quadrotor bobbed up into the air, the image jumping on William's flatscreen. He dipped the nose of the quad and the pink cylinder came into view near the bottom of the screen, falling away.

The grenade bounced once, then a white glare momentarily blanked the camera. As the intense light of the thermate died away, an orange flame front flashed out from the grenade over the entire expanse of the clubhouse roof and a sea of bright flame lit the clearing and the surrounding trees.

The few Dawgz outside had a hairsbreadth of time to save themselves as tendrils of blue fire ran down the walls from the huge mass of flame on the roof. But Dawgz did not operate on hair trigger reflexes, preferring superior numbers, weak targets, and high living to any sort of training. Fire flashed over the bare shimmering dirt and over the motorcycles. Bikers breathed in the head-high flames as their beards and hair burned away.

Tom and William did not speak as flame-shrouded Harleys exploded, screaming bikers burst out of the burning shack into the inferno of the yard and ran about trailing fire, falling to writhe about, unable to quench the sticky napalm.

William said, "I thought about using white phosphorus, but the napalm has a wider area effect."

Tom nodded, only momentarily surprised that his partner had white phosphorus at the ready.

William nosed the quad around the clearing, following the action in their little corner of Hell, until outside the van the Fazer landed itself on the concrete slab.

William said, "Would you like to go wave them down?"

Tom tapped his microphone to ensure that his headset worked, climbed out of the back of the van, and hustled out to the two lane blacktop. He waited.

William sent the quad north up the county road toward Chicago. He flew for a quarter of an hour until an all-black Harley came speeding toward him, a black vest flapping out away from the rider's hairy belly, a smaller figure clinging on behind.

William said into the comm, "Inbound in about fifteen." He got up and picked up a long black plastic case, closing the doors as he left the back of the van.

Tom replied, "Checking with local overwatch." He said, "Hey Siri, call Chicago PD."

The number in Tom's iPhone was not the PD main number. The call rang once, then without preamble, a woman said, "No cruisers in your area. No reports of unusual activity."

Tom killed the call. The raucous exhaust note cut through the air before the Harley's light came into view. He stepped out into the lane and waved as the noise grew to an obscene flatulent roar. The Dawg lifted a hand from the ape-hanger bars, middle digit erect. The bike did not change speed or direction, making directly for Tom. Tom replied with his own gesture and stepped aside as the bike shot past. The Harley braked hard, skidding the rear wheel out into the road thirty yards past.

The kickstand got kicked down hard. A short, thick Dawg leaned the bike and swaggered stiff-legged back toward Tom. He reached to his side and came up with a couple feet of wooden dowel. The tip was clad in thick steel. It was a tire buddy, the club that truckers thump tires with to check inflation.

As the Dawg drew nearer Tom got a look over the biker's shoulder. A frightened pale face peered at him from the back of the Harley, plump and chipmunk-cheeked and young under brown curls, with a tiny nose. Pretty breasts pushed up above a shiny purple halter of vinyl or patent leather, a muffin top poked out over hotpants, also purple vinyl, and a plump soft tummy bared itself in between. The goods for the party. Excellent with meth and a few pitchers of beer.

The Dawg looped a leather thong to bind the club to his wrist and silently stalked nearer. Then there was a roar and his entire torso bulged as a round from William's .300 Winchester Magnum transited from left to right clear through at the level of his navel. Blood and flesh jetted onto the gravel of the road's shoulder. The Dawg was short and it was a quick drop to his knees, where he clutched his arms across his belly and toppled onto his face. Tom sighed, a breath in, then out. Gut-shot biker.

William walked up in a few moments. Tom took the nine millimeter off his hip, reversed it to grip it by the barrel, and handed it to the young man. Then he reached out to take the rifle. William looked down at the biker. His night-dark hair fell forward, covering the side of his face as he raised the pistol in a two-handed hold lined up on the Dawg's head, finger straight above the trigger guard.

Tom walked over to the frightened young woman on the bike. She slipped off the seat and shrank back from him. He said, "They told you it was a party. It was. They were going to turn you out, all of them."

She said nothing, wide-eyed in the gloom of the ditch beside the road.

Tom walked back to where William stood over the biker. He said, "William."

William turned his black-eyed gaze on Tom and said, "Yes?"

Tom said, "Are you cold right now? Inside, are you cold?"

William nodded. Tom nodded. William looked back to the biker. He fitted his finger inside the guard and took the slack out of the trigger.

Chapter 132   After the Sacrament

"Be not afraid of greatness."

Wm. Shakespeare

They walked back to the van. William handed the nine back and ducked into the rear to stow the rifle. Tom went to empty out the unused napalm. In pure serendipity, he dumped it onto the biker.

Tom thumbed his Zippo and ducked back. A screech drew his gaze away from the flames to where the entertainment had run down the road. The orange glow of napalm reflected from her bare tummy and thighs and the bluish light of a phone shone from her face. Tom tossed the plastic gas can onto the blazing heap of Dawg.

They heaved the Fazer into the van. Tom tied it down and hung the quad beside its twin, while William saddled up and pulled the van back onto the county road.

Tom dropped into the shotgun seat. "Bikers are kind of weak on their anti-air systems."

William remained silent, but the right corner of his mouth pushed up.

Tom gazed ahead into the headlights spread across the road. "So that's the final exam. You passed and it's your program. Choose your targets, staff up, gear up, train, deploy." Tom waited a beat, "Execute."

"I guess I was just waiting for permission. I have wanted this very much," said William.

"We don't ask for permission. Ask for help when you need it. Never permission," Tom said.

"So I guess I'll head back to Houston" said William, "Maybe look up some people, hunt down some *cholos*. Then buy some books for the fall semester."

"*Cholos*?" asked Tom.

"These *Almas Muertas*, Dead Souls. I don't think they're truly dead. I want them to understand what dead is."

Tom pulled out his iPhone. His BMW was at the McDonald's and William could drop him off there. He could feel it coming on, a road trip in the M2. First a cappuccino, then he would go west. And not a McDonald's cappuccino. He said, "Hey Siri, find a Dunn Brothers coffee shop."

Maybe William would let him take the rifle.

Chapter 133   Overwatch III

"... every rocket fired is a theft.
This world in arms spends its sweat, genius, and hopes.
Under the clouds of war, humanity hangs on a cross of iron."

Dwight D. Eisenhower
(paraphrased for brevity)

"Still no word from Tom?"

Polya was always glad to hear from Jenny, but Tom's absence continued to worry him. He had luxuriated through his first peaceful deployment. He drifted at the end of a tether, not counting the hours, Earthgazing. They had fought the nation of Iran to a standstill. The mullahs had no more missiles to throw at them, and spent their days clinging to power like flood survivors clinging to driftwood in the backlash against the debacle of the invasion.

Crews of switches began to cycle through without seeing action. Losses were minimal, by High Command standards. But training missions had to be done, new designs needed proof testing, and dropping experimental craft into hypersonic re-entry trajectories would never be safe. Then they had gone to war again, briefly, with North Korea.

The United Nations now considered them peacekeepers. Very reassuring, but he had always had Tom at his back, from the very first days when they had traded intelligence on ritual mutilation among extremist clergy. Despite the steady stream of new switches, and the constantly upgraded hardware, he felt unguarded, even after so many months.

Jenny said, "He doesn't want to be found. Else they would find him. If they could not, Juana would." 'They' included numbers of formidable folk, and the formidable agencies from which the High Command recruited contacts.

Separated by thousands of miles, the two shared a silence. Then it was urgent to turn away from what had been and they talked of how things had gotten better in orbit. He had been amazed at the hardware they boosted to him.

The was a free-flying debris shield, just a slab of depleted uranium layered with ceramic, carrying its own thrusters and control electronics. It looked like a huge fat gray playing card with a thimble-shaped thruster at each corner. It was needful to interpose armor between orbital debris and orbital assets. But you could not armor an entire station. Luckily the armor had no need to be attached to the habitat modules. Flying a panel out ahead of the station provided a debris shadow, a pyramidal volume of space sheltered from harm.

The new Rocks, FS-2Bs, carried a lighter twenty-millimeter Gatling. Instead of punching entry/exit holes with depleted uranium penetrators, they fired high explosive incendiary rounds, rounds which would detonate into shrapnel inside the minimalist structures of hostile boosters. The Rocks still looked like Cold War doomsday missiles, nothing but killers, ICBMs with ramscoops slung beneath like hard-ons.

A new assembly of habitation and service cylinders, joined end-to-end, took shape at the Russian end of the ISS. Soon to break off from the fragile, barely maneuverable butterfly of the station, it would be an orbital gunship, triple-hulled to guard against beam strikes from the new massive ground-based lasers. A reactor would power a high thrust-to-weight nuclear thermal rocket to make rapid orbital adjustments. Threatened, the gunship would dart about like a minnow in a stream.

Jenny still mourned the Chinese railgun. Her contacts within the Ministry of State Security had become subdued, no doubt terrified, after the prototype was slagged. The American railgun program had been neglected, but what the BAE corporation had done for the American Navy was to cherry-pick the railgun's hypervelocity projectile and propel it from a modified Mark 45 gun, a five-inch deck gun four decades old.

Plans were afoot to mount such a rifle at the nose of the new gunship. The Mach 6 projectile would be fired into the vicinity of a boosting ballistic missile, shed its fairing to expose a glide round, and switch on terminal guidance to home in on the missile's infrared signature.

Developments on a much more massive scale proceeded in geosynchronous orbit, looming like technological thunderheads far, far above. It all spelled hegemony, control of cislunar space, the incomprehensible volume between the cloud tops and the orbit of the Moon.

Then Jenny said, "You're gonna have to come down and stay down. Soon."

He could say nothing. He knew only this life. They would not send him to space again. Or to fight again, anywhere. He could not imagine what would come next. But then he could offer no argument. His bones and muscles and cardiac tissues were nearing critical depletion.

Chapter 134   Requiem

"For those in peril in the air!"

Adapted from John Newton

A cube had been added to the National Air and Space Museum. The lights of the new annex shone against the twilight through clear glass walls, and incredibly, a clear glass roof. Inside, every huge expanse of glass, polished stone floor, and mirrored column gave back clear brilliance from random lengths of slender light-emitting rods hung throughout the upper spaces in patterns like rivers of meteors.

Jimmy wandered and gaped. A big crowd, all in cruelly expensive clothes, spread itself in clumps throughout the huge foyer to await the formal opening dinner.

Toward the rightmost fringe of the crowd Polya slumped in his wheelchair, looking dour. His ever-brooding brows rode even lower than usual as he watched Vlad demonstrate how he could dunk a basketball one-legged by pogoing on the composite blade extending from his left thigh. Vlad was looking vigorous.

Jimmy wandered on. He did not look around for more switches. Alyssa had deployed once more, and had made it back home, but he didn't expect to see her either. The switches coming after his time had not seen combat, and he didn't look for them. And Tom was still AWOL.

In the first gallery huge pictorial panels concisely differentiated between nuclear explosives, nuclear power generation, and nuclear propulsion. A second set of wall panels included early misunderstandings and incidents of deliberate neglect of the health effects of radiation. There were women painting radium onto watch dials, soldiers hunkered down and backlit by harsh iconic hellfire mushrooming in the distance, and portraits of Apollo astronauts who had died of aortal damage years after travelling through deep space, beyond Earth's protective atmosphere and cosmic ray shadow.

For those who had not fled with cries of 'Nukes! Witchcraft!', the next gallery exhibited fission-powered air and space craft, huge shapes suspended in mock flight in the vast bright space. A full-scale model of the Pluto missile, the first nuclear ramjet design and also one of the first doomsday devices, loomed above a floor model of the NERVA nuclear rocket test engine which had been fired on the Nevada test range at Jackass Flats. Around the perimeter of the upper reaches hung quarter-scale models of nuclear rockets conceived at NASA for interplanetary exploration, delicate insectile things quite unlike a Rock.

Jimmy stepped through the portal to the final gallery, moving slowly. His lower back was settling like an old building showing cracks. It was more than simple aging; three deployments to the ISS had leached away a lot of bone mass. NASA astronauts exercised for a couple hours each wake cycle. Switches sat watches, immobile.

The ceiling here was unlit, the glass letting in the night sky above a solitary FS-2A Rock suspended in the glow of a spotlight. Just inside the entry on the left a blackboard-sized placard explained that the Rocks were weapons of mass destruction, nuclear weapons that converted fission energy into atmospheric shockwaves that destroyed structures and equipment more easily than people.

On the right, the text spoke of how lesser powers had too much to lose, and lose they would, before they began to fight, if they went to war. The great powers had even more to lose if they fought one another, and it paid, in economic and humanitarian terms, to enforce a lack of overt conflict among the lesser. As the total destruction threatened by thermonuclear war deterred conflict between the great powers, the threatened destruction of the entire military materiel of an invasion force was intended to deter conflict among the lesser. The hot white lightning of the Dagger, deterrent to rogue nuclear states, was not mentioned.

Jimmy thought that the absence of conflict was not peace, which he understood to mean a lack of fear. That was likely not a possibility on a planet crowded with humans and their instincts and impulses. Their countercurrents provided opportunity for one such as himself, seeking in conflict the one true trial.

Jimmy turned to look back at photos clustered on the wall around the gallery entry. On the right they showed the Secretary of Defense, the commander of the Space and Naval Warfare Systems Command, General Clinton Martin of Air Force Space Command, the NASA Administrator, and the Director of National Intelligence. On the other side more photos acknowledged high-ranking Russian and Chinese officials. In the center space above the entry the Secretary General of the United Nations was acknowledged as the nominal authority over the United Nations High Command of planetary peacekeepers.

Past the placards, the lower gallery walls held mural-sized photos of hypersonic Rocks bathed in ionized gas, bludgeoning through the uppermost reaches of the atmosphere. Higher up were orbital shots of the bright slash of Katia's incineration above India and Jimmy's rooster tail of dust stretching halfway across Iran, a drone image of the fragmenting missile processing center, Jimmy's view of Vlad skimming the Lunar surface, and the largest image showed a distant view of the Iranian invasion column seemingly being consumed by an advancing dust storm as Polya's flight of Rocks passed in a blur above.

In the center of the gallery floor, a hollow rectangle of long tables draped in white and sparkling with glassware and silver for the reception dinner surrounded a deep black obelisk, a highly polished pyramidal spike of onyx tapering upward toward the Rock looming far above. Flecks of brightness from embedded crystals of quartz recalled the pinlights of stars. Jimmy moved through a gap at one corner of the tables to approach it.

Close up, the face of the stone pyramid was wider than the span of his arms. It bore a metallic *bas relief*, a stylized Rock in silver veiled behind a translucent rose quartz teardrop symbolizing an ionization envelope. A gilded exhaust spike was a pallid imitation of plasma's unbearably bright incandescence.

Jimmy stepped around to see the next facet, which bore a bronze plaque. He sounded out the inscription as best he could.

"Non est ad astra mollis e terris via."

He would have to look that one up. Around the next corner the final stone facet bore names cut directly into the stone. The deeply incised black stone reminded him of the wall where America's southeast Asian war dead were remembered. Beginning at head level, leaving plenty of room against future need, more than twenty names ascended the column, one above another. Third from the bottom was the name Ekaterina Kuznetsova.

The stone within the incision was harsh to the fingertips, left grayish and rough, surrounded by cool and absolutely smooth polished blackness.

Jimmy's chest was tight as he walked away back into the crowd, feeling alone even as he breathed the exhalations of aerospace executives, space agency functionaries from Roscosmos and NASA, military officers from Russia, and China, and from America's Army, Navy, Air Force, and Space Command.

There were no Iranian uniforms. And no North Koreans. During Jimmy's second deployment the NoKs had brought a nuke-tipped ICBM to the pad as an incentive to reunification. Alyssa had dropped, flying nap of the Earth to drag her shockwave across their launch complex, blowing it apart as Jimmy had done at Shahroud. The latest Kim hardly knew who to shoot back at. The ISS was crewed by High Command renegades, nonstate actors supported by a network stretching across every advanced society on the planet, recognized by but indifferent to the UN, claimed by no one nation. The High Command tended to shoot first and Kim wanted no part of a Kinzhal, a hypersonic Russian Dagger tipped with an EMP.

Alyssa had nearly cratered, clearing by a gnat's ass the spine of famously frigid mountains that ran down the peninsula, nearly dying where so many fellow Marines fell near the Chosin Reservoir. After the mission, Jimmy could see it around her eyes. She had flirted with incineration one time too many. She was done, would not deploy again.

Finally, he recognized a face. So familiar, surely a squadron mate from back in his Navy days. The fellow was well over six feet, with a broad-shouldered, hard-bellied build despite the gray at his temples. Jimmy could not quite place him. He walked over. Yes, he had the same combed-back mane of chestnut hair, hard cheekbones and jaw that Jimmy remembered.

"Hey" Jimmy said. "Been a while."

The big guy turned. He stood between two elegantly draped, lanky women. Jimmy stood in a cluster of people fanned out as if they were an audience before the three of them. The fellow nodded politely. "You doin' alright? Totally gorgeous gallery, right?"

Jimmy said, "So glad to see such a great turnout. Good to see you again." He bid the surrounding group goodnight and walked away. He had the name now. Jock Stimmer. QB for the Ravens, or was it Washington? Shit, he had recognized him from newscasts. He didn't know the guy after all.

Jock turned to his date, the one on the left. He said, "Who was that guy?"

Chapter 135   Lone Gunman

*"... fools and fanatics are always so certain of themselves,
and wiser people so full of doubts."*

Bertrand Russell

A couple years on the other side of the war, and on the other side of the country, a man stood on a tiny flat of stone, the summit of a mountain. He wanted a high place from where he could see.

He lived now in the Dixie National Forest, the southwest corner of this southwest state. He liked Utah. It had about as much vertical surface as horizontal. Rough country. Squarish red-brown blocks sticking up as buttes and mesas and towers and sometimes just chunks piled together. Though the climate was a sneaky cur, creeping up to bite with hypothermia at the end of a long day of borderline heatstroke.

It reminded him of living the life of a strong young man when he could love as simply as he loved his Gore-Tex jacket for keeping him warm, dry, and alive. How he would keep the jacket near even after returning from a deployment in the mountains. How he loved his rifle. It too kept death at a distance. He held it close like a child in his care, but also as an extension of himself. He had lived unleashed, trekking huge Central Asian mountains, in dogged pursuits along cliffside trails between tiny villages of stone huts, making the world a better place, one shattered brainpan at a time.

It was complicated now. His affection for the gear that sustained him and aided him in his purpose was not simple, because he no longer saw his goals in the same way. He thought that a barbarian was defined not by speaking an uncouth tongue, as defined by ancient Greeks, but by the certainty that his belief was the complete and only truth. He thought a civilized mind was one which could hold opposing views, suspending judgment pending inquiry, perhaps following one, but mindful of another. He understood a decadent mind as one which held that no belief was superior to any other, rendering all belief irrelevant. A barbarian acts with complete conviction, always justified. Anything is possible to him. A decadent acts not at all, even when confronted with barbarism.

He had acted. He had fought for civilization, had hunted down barbarians of a particular single-minded bent. He had not sought to change their minds, but to destroy them. He had pursued the most capable, the most virulent, and rendered them harmless. He saw now that he had pursued that purpose with barbaric intensity. The calm focus he had carried into the hunt was spotty now, interrupted by nagging memory. He felt unsteady.

Beneath his jacket he wore fleece against the morning cold. Over the jacket rested a light rucksack. It contained a tarp, dried food, filtration, and a .300 Win Mag taken down into barrel group and stock, neither piece long enough to stick up out of the ruck. He had packed twenty-five rounds of match-grade ammo. Twenty-three now. The rifle's optics lay packed in foam beneath the top flap of the ruck. He had maps and a lightweight GPS. He studied the patterns of the trails, the better to avoid them. He studied contour lines to go brushbusting along. He told himself never downclimb anything you can't upclimb. He had a rope. He told himself never rappel a drop higher than your rope is long. You are alone. Don't get cliffed out.

He could no longer carry a fifty-pound ruck all day, and so he cut his toothbrush handle, and bought tarp, clothes, and pack of gossamer fabrics. Asked to lighten the rifle, William had programmed a laser to deep-cut the Mandelbrot set into each side of the black nylon stock. Smaller replicas of the image served as checkering on the fore-end and the grip. Then he had run a pocketing routine to hollow out an ammo storage cavity within the base. Protected by the buttplate, individual rounds nested in the nylon, protecting them from knocks and scrapes. He missed that friend. He missed hunting with him and the surprises he worked with the gear. He missed them all, his cheerful murderous Pashtun agents, his quietly determined and deadly friends in the intelligence agencies and the military, and he missed careening through the deadly chaos that was the High Command.

He walked to the edge of Lone Tree Mountain. Across the reddish flats around Cedar City gravel roads snaked up into the foothills, bringing along houses scattered into the low scrub and cedars. The National Forest did not extend to this summit, but neither did the workings and houses of people, and so he liked it here.

The big house was half way up into the foothills, the house he had watched for nearly two months. Where he had seen the hitting and the fear. The women scurrying about in old-fashioned bonnets and long sack dresses. He had ended the hitting, but he had probably made the fear worse. A heavy supersonic bullet striking head-high on the person next to you is nothing but shocking, even if the person has been hitting you.

Hidden from him, a helicopter had been following the valley across the summit from where he stood. He heard nothing until it popped up, perhaps for a dramatic reveal for its load of tourists. He spun, and a stratum of sandstone broke loose and shot out from under his heel.

The sightseers goggled as he dropped out of view. Later that day another helo came and they carried him off a rock shelf and laid him away in a private room. The rifle was of interest to the police. He carried no licenses or cards, but in a few days the woman arrived. She wore a head cloth that covered her hair, neck and shoulders. A lovely dark-eyed woman, slender in middle age. But of course sad, mouth narrowed and tense. "Yes, he's mine," she said.

She walked a way down an echoing polished stone hallway, passing carts and nurses. Standing in sun by the window of an alcove, she felt the stare of a man seated on a nearby couch behind a low wooden table. Exactly such stares had fallen on her in her youth, hard gazes of bearded men half a world away. She turned away, got out her phone. "He has fallen," she said.

When he awoke, she was there. By that time, the rifle had disappeared from the police evidence locker.

"You have to come home now," she said.

END

Acknowledgements

It is a privilege to have Dr. Frank Claudy, an award-winning writer and grandson of the very early sci-fi author Carl H. Claudy, as this work's first reader.

James Tidwell, a lifelong professional illustrator in digital media and a watercolor artist, contributed the cover illustration, suffering through many naïve notions occurring to the author.

Steven K. Allen wanted to know "What was the camel's name?" In the worldview of one embedded with the Bedouin for months, and still maintaining active contacts, this is a sensible question. Steven is highly recommended as a consultant on Bedouins, Pashtuns, and military armaments and operations.

Lindsey Boncore was the most persistent of the early reviewers. Her willingness to read outside her customary genre gave insight into the tempering of gee-whiz geekspeak.

Support from family and friends was unwavering. Stephanie Buchanan, a highly competent and energetic girlfriend by whom I am guided in all things, was relentless in her encouragement, along with our dear friend Mona Kahney.

Made in the USA
Middletown, DE
13 June 2022